FIREWATER

FIREWATER

A TEXAS MOONSHINERS NOVEL

WILLIAM W. JOHNSTONE

AND J. A. JOHNSTONE

P

PINNACLE BOOKS

Kensington Publishing Corp.

www.kensingtonbooks.com

PINNACLE BOOKS are published by

Kensington Publishing Corp.
119 West 40th Street
New York, NY 10018

Copyright © 2021 J. A. Johnstone

PUBLISHER'S NOTE
Following the death of William W. Johnstone, the Johnstone family is working with a carefully selected writer to organize and complete Mr. Johnstone's outlines and many unfinished manuscripts to create additional novels in all of his series like The Last Gunfighter, Mountain Man, and Eagles, among others. This novel was inspired by Mr. Johnstone's superb storytelling.

ISBN-13: 978-0-7860-4727-7
ISBN-10: 0-7860-4727-5

First Pinnacle paperback printing: February 2021

10 9 8 7 6 5 4 3 2 1

Printed in the United States of America

CHAPTER 1

Pike Shannon stiffened as what felt like a gun barrel poked him in the back. This wasn't the first time some hombre had gotten the drop on him, but it didn't happen very often, and Pike was disgusted with himself that it had happened now.

"All right, Shannon," a voice growled near his ear. "Your past has caught up with you at last, you lowdown—"

The voice was vaguely familiar, but Pike didn't waste time trying to place it. Instead, he took advantage of the would-be killer making a big mistake by getting too close to him.

Pike whirled and twisted to the side at the same time. His left forearm knocked the man's gun arm away, while Pike's right fist shot out and smashed into the man's jaw with enough force to knock him off his feet and send him sprawling from the boardwalk into the dust of Warbonnet's main street.

Pike's Colt seemed to leap from its holster into his fist. His thumb curled around the hammer, and his finger was taut on the trigger.

"Don't shoot!" the man said. He pushed himself up a

little on his left elbow and used his right hand to take hold of his chin. He wiggled his jaw back and forth, obviously testing it to see if it was broken, and then, satisfied that it wasn't, said, "Blast it, Pike, is that any way to say hello to an old friend?"

Pike had just stepped out of Sophie Truesdale's café. It was early evening, which meant shadows had started to gather already in the street, but enough light spilled through the café's big front window to give Pike a pretty good look at the man he had just walloped.

"Patrick?" he said. "Patrick Delano, is that you?"

"Who else would be loco enough to think it was funny to pretend to stick a gun in the back of a famous gunfighter like Pike Shannon?"

Pike shook his head slowly and holstered his Colt as he said, "Yeah, you always were pretty loco. Haven't changed much, have you?"

"I hope not." Patrick Delano lifted the hand he had used to check his jaw. "Give me a hand up, why don't you? It's only fair since you're the one who knocked me down."

"Yeah, yeah." Pike stepped forward and reached down. He and Delano clasped wrists. Pike hauled the other man to his feet without much effort. They stood facing each other in the light from the café.

Pike was taller and brawnier, dark-haired and sun-bronzed from a life lived mostly outdoors. Patrick Delano was medium height but also built well, with a shock of curly, light-brown hair above a face that was quick to smile. His blue eyes had a twinkle to them that often made him irresistible to women. Pike's usual expression was more solemn.

The two men dressed differently, too, Pike in well-worn

boots, denim trousers, a butternut bib-front shirt, and a dark brown hat, while Delano was garbed in a brown tweed suit, matching vest, and snow-white shirt with a string tie cinched around his neck. He stooped to pick up the cream-colored hat Pike had knocked off his head and brushed dust off it carefully before settling it back on his curls.

"What are you doing in Warbonnet?" Pike asked. "Last I heard you were in Denver dealing blackjack in some club up there."

Delano nodded and said, "I did that for a while, then moved on to Santa Fe and then El Paso after that. Here lately I've been in a place called Prescott, southwest of here. Have you heard of it?"

"Sure," Pike replied. "Down in Pecan County, isn't it?"

"The county seat, in fact."

Warbonnet was a county seat, too, the center of government in Warbonnet County in north central Texas, a couple of days' ride south of Fort Worth. Pecan County was a hundred miles southwest, a good journey but not really that far considering the vast size of the Lone Star State. Pike had been there once, many years ago when he was a boy.

Before he had left home to live as a hired gun and a rider of lonely trails . . .

But that part of his life was behind him now, he reminded himself. He had come home a year ago, following his father's death.

However, if he had expected a more peaceful existence in these parts, he would have been sorely disappointed, because in the months since his homecoming he had been involved in not one but *two* deadly moonshine wars. Pike and his family had emerged from those bloody conflicts, though not without some losses, and recently things had grown quiet

Quiet enough to make Pike's restless nature start fidgeting around. He didn't like the feeling, or at least he told himself he didn't like it. He was content to help his brother and grandfather raise fine horses on their ranch, to enjoy spending his days with them and with his mother and sister. Pike Shannon was a family man again, and the Shannon family's business was horseflesh, not moonshine whiskey.

If he kept trying hard enough, he might convince himself of that. One of these days.

For now, he was just glad to see an old friend. He and Patrick Delano had crossed trails several times over the years and sided each other in a few fights. Delano worked from time to time as a hired gun, although his true profession, his calling, if you will, was as a gambler. He preferred saloons that smelled of beer and whiskey and smoke to being out on the trail. He was a slick enough gun-handler and could hold his own in a bare-knuckles brawl, but his hands were made for the pasteboards.

"Like I said," Pike went on, "what brings you to Warbonnet?" Something occurred to him. "You weren't looking for me, were you?"

"As a matter of fact, you're a big part of the reason I'm here," Delano said. "Why don't we go somewhere and have a drink and talk about it?"

Pike made a face and shook his head.

"Easier said than done around here," he replied. "Warbonnet County is dry."

Delano frowned at him for a second, then said, "You know, I heard something about that, but I couldn't hardly believe it. I mean, I remember you telling me about your family and how they . . . well, how they cooked up the best moonshine anybody ever tasted. So it was hard for me to believe that they'd ever settle in a place that was dry."

"It wasn't our choice, believe me. The state came up with what they call local-option elections a few years ago, and that made it legal for a county to have a vote on whether or not to allow liquor. Warbonnet County voted not to."

"You don't have to tell me about local-option elections." Delano looked like he had bitten into something sour. "They had one of the blasted things in Pecan County a few months back. And wouldn't you know it, folks voted, actually *voted*, to outlaw liquor! I wouldn't have believed it if I hadn't seen it with my own eyes." A shrewd look appeared on his face. "But I'll bet there are still places where a man can get a drink, aren't there? There's always a place like that."

Pike shook his head.

"Not here in town. The sheriff is a friend of mine, and he keeps a pretty tight lid on things."

"Wait a minute," Delano said. "Did I just hear you right? You've made friends with a lawman?"

Pike didn't like the way Delano's tone made him feel defensive. He said, "Andy Burnett's an old friend of the family. Fact is, he used to cook 'shine, too, in the old days. But that's illegal now, and he's trying to be a law-abiding man." Pike added heavily, "We all are."

Actually, it was worse than he was letting on to Delano, Pike mused. He had worked with Sheriff Andy Burnett to curb the liquor traffic in Warbonnet County, and Andy had tried to convince him to wear a deputy's badge. Not only *that*, but he had even helped out a Texas Ranger by the name of Walt Scott, and Scott had told him he ought to consider joining the Rangers. For a man with Pike's history, having two different lawmen trying to turn him into a badge-toter was downright humiliating.

But he didn't say anything about that to Delano, and to change the subject, he jerked a thumb over his shoulder toward the neat frame building from which he had emerged just before Delano showed up, and said, "But I know where you can get a piece of the best pie in Texas, or for that matter, a bowl of stew or a steak if you haven't had supper yet. And it's my treat."

"You make that sound too tempting to pass up," Delano said with one of his customary grins. He sobered and went on, "I wanted to talk business with you, though, and I'm not sure this is the right place."

"The owner's a friend of mine," Pike explained. "She's got a small private room I'm sure she'd let us use." His forehead creased a little as he went on, "I'm not sure what kind of business we'd have, though, Patrick."

Delano clapped a hand on his shoulder and said, "All in due time, Pike. Right now, you've got me intrigued, and I want to find out more about that pie you were talking about."

CHAPTER 2

Sophie Truesdale looked up from behind the café's counter with a surprised expression on her pretty face. A smile quickly replaced it as she said to Pike, "Well, I didn't expect to see you again so soon."

"Hope you're not disappointed," he said.

"No, not at all." She looked past him and asked, "Who's your friend?"

Pike didn't answer immediately. Even though he had just left the café a few minutes earlier, he couldn't help but be struck by just how downright *pretty* Sophie was, the same way he felt every time he laid eyes on her.

Wavy blond hair fell to her shoulders and framed attractive features. The blue dress and white apron she wore were both snug enough to accentuate the smooth, rounded curves of her body. She managed the difficult feat of projecting a wholesome, good-hearted innocence while at the same time possessing the sort of alluring beauty that made a man want to pull her into his arms and give her a good, hard, passionate kiss.

He couldn't just stand there staring at her, though, even if part of him wanted to, especially when she had asked him a question. With his natural politeness, he stepped aside, motioned his companion closer to the counter, and said, "Sophie, this is an old friend of mine, Patrick Delano. Patrick, this is Miss Sophie Truesdale."

Delano had taken his hat off already. He held it in front of him as he said, "Miss Truesdale, this is indeed an honor. Pike's told me a great deal about you—"

"He has, has he?" Sophie said as she quirked an eyebrow in Pike's direction.

"He sure has, and all of it good. In fact, he said something about how you made the best pie to be found anywhere in Texas and offered to buy a piece for me."

"My, how generous. Both the compliment and the offer. We have peach and apple cobbler—"

Delano interrupted her with a little moan.

"Ma'am, if you knew just how bad I've been hankering for a bowl of peach cobbler . . . well, you'd know what a happy man you've just made me."

"I'll go dish it up," Sophie offered. "And I suppose you'd like a cup of coffee to go with it?"

"Am I in Warbonnet," Delano said, "or have I died and gone to heaven?"

"Oh, don't joke about something as serious as heaven," Sophie told him.

"Yes, but if they don't have peach cobbler in heaven, I'm not sure it's worth going."

Sophie started to look horrified at that sentiment but then said, "You're just having some sport with me, aren't you?"

"Maybe. You can't blame me for thinking I might be there already, though, since I'm looking at somebody who could pass for an angel."

"Go on with your flattery," Sophie said tartly, but Pike

could tell she enjoyed it. "I'll fetch the pie and coffee. Pike . . . ?"

"Yeah, I'll have some, too," he told her. "And Sophie, is it all right if we have it in the other room? Patrick and I have some things to talk about."

"Of course. There's no one in there right now."

The café's smaller second room wasn't completely private—there was no door in the arched entrance between the rooms—but the café wasn't crowded this evening to start with, and none of the other customers were sitting at tables close to the open doorway. If Pike and Delano took one of the tables in a back corner and kept their voices down, they wouldn't be overheard.

Pike had to admit, he was curious about what Delano might want.

They went into the other room, sat down, and Sophie brought their coffee a moment later. She went back to get the bowls of peach cobbler, which she carried out on a tray and placed on the table along with a small pitcher of cream.

"Is there anything else I can get for you gentlemen?" she asked.

"No, I think this is all we need," Pike said.

"Speak for yourself," Delano said. "But I'll wait for another time for the rest of my requests, when we don't have this big galoot intruding on us, Miss Truesdale."

"I know you're just joking, so I won't take offense at you being so forward, Mr. Delano," she said.

"That's right. I'm just joking."

The sparkle in Delano's eyes gave the lie to that statement, though.

Smiling, Sophie left the room with a swish of her skirts. As Pike took a sip of his coffee, he watched Delano follow her with his gaze. He set the cup back on its saucer and said, "You're wasting your time."

"Oh? Is she spoken for?" Delano cocked his head to the side and gave him a shrewd look. "Have you got your loop dabbed on that one, Pike?"

"Nope." Pike wasn't going to admit it, but he *was* attracted to Sophie. There was a big obstacle to any relationship that might develop between them, though, and it could be summed up one word. "She's temperance."

Delano's eyebrows rose. "Really?"

"Full-bore. She was one of the leaders of the bunch that got behind that local-option election, the one that made buying and selling and even drinking liquor illegal in this county."

"Good grief! You let women *vote* here in Warbonnet County? Have you all lost your minds?"

"No, they don't vote," Pike said with a wave of his hand. "But you know good and well how much influence women have on elections whether they cast ballots or not."

"Yes, I suppose that's true," Delano admitted. "And I can see why a temperance gal wouldn't want to get mixed up with a dirty old moonshiner like you."

Pike gestured again, as if telling Delano to let that go, and said, "Those days are over. The Shannons raise horses now, that's all. Some of the finest horses in Texas, too."

"Well, I'm sorry to hear that. Not about the horses, mind you, I'm sure your family does a fine job of that. But are you *sure* you're not in the moonshine business anymore?"

Pike shook his head and said, "Not a drop."

"Well, I'll admit I'm disappointed," Delano said with a

sigh, "because the real reason I came up here was to find you and see if I could buy a big load of 'shine from you."

Pike frowned at him across the table for a long moment, then said, "Why in the world would you need to buy a big load of moonshine?"

"I told you I'd been in Prescott for a while. A little more than eight months, in fact. I got in a poker game in a saloon there, and before the game was over, I wound up winning the place."

"You own a saloon?"

"Yep, free and clear. The Big Boss Saloon, it's called, and I didn't see any reason to change the name. After all those years of drifting around and working for other folks, I was finally the big boss." Delano sighed. "And then, two months later, they had that blasted local-option election."

"Which put you out of business," Pike said, nodding in understanding.

"Well . . . not completely. I've tried to keep it going as a place for fellas to come and gamble and have something to eat. The blasted busybodies haven't made *those* two things illegal . . . yet." Delano shrugged. "But I don't mind admitting, it's been a hard row, Pike. I won't say I'm getting desperate, but the taxes on the place will be coming due in a couple of months, and I don't see how I'm going to pay them. The sheriff's liable to wind up auctioning the place off on the courthouse steps. It may not be worth anything as a saloon anymore, but it's still a good property."

"Then maybe you should sell it now," Pike suggested. "Get what you can out of it and move on."

Delano took a bite of the peach cobbler and chewed with obvious appreciation, then after he had swallowed, he went on, "You know, I considered that. But it would mean giving up. Admitting I was beat." His voice hardened. "I don't cotton to that, Pike. I never did."

Pike nodded slowly. He remembered how determined Delano could be. Once he got his back up about something, he could be downright ruthless. Pike said, "So you decided to start selling liquor again, law or no law."

"That's right. And when I did, I thought about you and your family right away. I figured once word got around that I was selling Shannon moonshine, fellas would come from miles around for a drink of it."

There was a chance Delano might be right about that, Pike thought. Among men who enjoyed homebrewed corn liquor, Shannon 'shine had quite a reputation, even though it had been a while since the family had been active in the business.

Unfortunately, what Delano was asking was impossible. There had been a time, back when Pike's pa was alive, that the family might have made a deal such as the one Delano proposed, but now—

"How much are we talking about?" Pike heard himself asking.

Delano leaned forward, suddenly eager.

"Maybe . . . twenty barrels. To start."

Pike let out a low whistle.

"It'd take five wagons to haul that much. That's a lot of moonshine."

Delano laughed and said, "There are a lot of thirsty folks in Pecan County."

That was true of Warbonnet County, too. Pike knew he and his family could have sold every drop they cared to cook if they went back in the business. They had resisted the temptation to do so, however, and Pike hadn't objected because he didn't want to cause any trouble for . . .

His thoughts ground to a halt of realization. He hadn't pushed for the Shannon family to start moonshining again because Andy Burnett was the sheriff, and Pike didn't want to cause any trouble for his friend.

But Pike didn't know the sheriff of Pecan County from a hole in the ground.

Delano grinned and said, "You're thinking about it. I can tell."

Pike was thinking about a lot of things, including how restless he'd been getting lately. He thought, as well, about the look on Patrick Delano's face when he'd said he was friends with a lawman. That was kind of a special case, but still . . . this wasn't the first time Pike had felt a little ashamed about how downright *respectable* he was getting.

Cooking up a bunch of 'shine and selling it to Delano for a saloon in a county a hundred miles away would be a chance to do something interesting and exciting again, and it wouldn't cause any problems here at home. It was something to consider, all right.

The irony of discussing the matter here in Sophie Truesdale's café didn't escape Pike, either.

He would have pondered it longer, but at that moment, he heard the café door open, followed by a surprised gasp from Sophie as boot heels thudded heavily on the floor and spur rowels clinked. Then a harsh voice demanded, "Where in blazes is Pike Shannon? I know good an' well he's in here, and I got a score to settle with him!"

CHAPTER 3

Something about the voice was familiar, and it was angry enough to make Pike start to his feet in alarm. He'd been able to tell from her gasp that Sophie was spooked, and he wasn't going to let that stand.

Delano started to stand up, too, but Pike waved him back into his seat. Whatever was going on here, it was Pike's problem to deal with. Delano sank back down in the chair but didn't appear happy about it.

Pike stepped through the arched opening between the rooms and asked in a loud, clear voice, "You looking for me, mister?"

It wasn't just one man who had entered the café. Three strangers stood a few feet inside the door, peering around with dusty, unshaven faces.

Strangers to Warbonnet, that is. Pike recognized all three of them now that he had seen them.

The one who had spoken in gravelly tones was Ed Keyhoe. Some called him "Keyhole" because of his last name. He was standing slightly in front of the other two, who had spread out to the sides behind him so they would have clear shots in case they needed to slap leather. The one to Keyhoe's right was VanHook; Pike had never heard his first name. To Keyhoe's left was a man called Purgatory Peters.

All of them were hired guns, killers. They had fought in some of the same range wars where Pike had been employed, usually on the other side of the conflict. Whenever Pike had found himself on the same side as these three, he hadn't liked it, because he suspected that most of their kills came from ambushing unsuspecting victims.

That didn't mean they weren't dangerous, though. They were, and Pike knew it.

"Shannon!" Keyhoe said. "You know why we're here."

"Why don't you refresh my memory?" Pike drawled.

Without taking his concentration off the three gunmen, he was aware that the café's other customers had gotten up from their tables and started edging toward the door. Purgatory Peters turned a baleful stare toward them, causing them to freeze.

"I don't like people scurryin' around behind me," Peters snarled.

From her place behind the counter, Sophie asked, "Pike, what's going on here? Should . . . should I send for the sheriff?"

Before Pike could say anything, Keyhoe snapped, "You just hush your mouth, girlie. We don't need no lawman around here. I got business with Shannon, and I'm gonna finish it after all this time."

He licked his lips and dragged the back of his left hand across his mouth. It was so quiet in the café now that the rasp of beard stubble against his skin could be heard.

"You sent us into a trap, up there in Montana. Got the Hammerhead Kid killed."

"You rode into that ambush on your own, Keyhoe," Pike

said. "I didn't have anything to do with it. And they called the Hammerhead Kid by that name because he was as dumb as a box of nails. Even if he'd made it through that dustup with the Circle C alive, he'd have gotten himself killed before another six months were gone."

Keyhoe shook his head stubbornly and insisted, "No, sir, it was your fault. You double-crossed us, sent us ridin' right into those guns."

Pike's annoyance got the best of him.

"You blasted fool," he snapped. "I told you *not* to ride through Ruby Canyon that day. But you thought you were so much smarter than me, you had to do it anyway."

Keyhoe sneered and said, "Yeah, well, who's the smart one now? There's three of us and only one o' you. Now take what you got comin'!"

His hand dipped toward the gun on his hip. The other two clawed at their weapons at the same time.

Pike had been in this situation so many times in the past that he didn't have to think about anything. His actions were instinctive and automatic. Tucked away in the back of his mind was the memory that VanHook was actually the fastest of the trio, so as Pike's Colt came smoothly out of the holster, he angled it to the left and tripped the hammer.

VanHook's gun had just cleared leather when Pike's slug smashed into his chest and drove him backward so he fell over an empty table. Pike had already swung his Colt to the right and fired again by the time VanHook crashed to the floor.

That second shot punched into Keyhoe's midsection and doubled him over. He had gotten his gun out but hadn't had time to pull the trigger. It slipped from nerveless fingers and thudded on the planks at Keyhoe's feet.

That left Purgatory Peters. His gun was out, but Pike's

third shot hit him in the chest and knocked him backward. Peters's muscles spasmed, and he jerked the trigger, but the bullet went harmlessly into the floor.

VanHook and Peters were down. Keyhoe was the only one still on his feet, and he had dropped his gun as he stumbled back and forth clutching at his bullet-torn guts. Pike was looking at him when movement in the corner of his eye caught his attention and he looked over to see that Van-Hook had somehow hung on to his gun and lifted himself to try again. The weapon was swinging up toward Pike.

More than likely, Pike would have had plenty of time to finish off VanHook himself, but another gun went off with a spiteful crack before he could do that. VanHook's head jerked back with a dark hole now appearing in the center of his forehead. He balanced there like that for a second before pitching forward.

Patrick Delano stepped up beside Pike. Smoke still curled from the muzzle of the Smith & Wesson .32 Delano held. He said, "Are you all right, Pike?"

"Yeah. I'm obliged to you, Patrick." He nodded toward VanHook's sprawled body.

"You would have gotten him if I hadn't," Delano said.

"Maybe, but we'll never know, will we?"

A strangled gasp came from Keyhoe. Pike and Delano both looked at the wounded man, guns held ready in their hands. Keyhoe's eyes were wide from pain, shock, and the knowledge that death was barreling down on him. With blood leaking from both corners of his mouth, he struggled to say, "D-Delano . . . you . . . here—"

"That's right," Delano said. "You weren't expecting Pike to have anybody backing his play, were you?"

Keyhoe tried to say something else, but before he could,

his eyes rolled up in their sockets, his knees buckled, and he went down hard. His final breath rattled in his throat.

Pike looked over at Sophie, who still stood behind the counter with her hands pressed to her cheeks in horror at the bloodshed that had taken place right in front of her.

The other people who had been eating in the café stampeded out of the place now that the way was clear.

Pike pouched his iron and hurried over to the counter. He reached over it and put his hands on Sophie's shoulders.

"Are you all right?" he asked. He was confident that she was, since he knew where all the bullets that were fired had gone.

On the other hand, even though she wasn't wounded, that didn't exactly mean that she was *all right* . . .

"P-Pike . . ." she said in a half-whisper. "Those men . . . those men came here . . . to kill you."

He nodded and said solemnly, "I know, and I'm mighty sorry they caught up to me here in your place. I'd give a lot for this not to have happened here."

"What difference does it make where it happened? Those men are still dead! You killed them!"

"Wasn't time not to," Pike said, "and that was the best way to make sure they didn't hurt any innocent folks."

"I know. I . . ." He felt the shudder that ran through her. Then she tried to straighten up and said, "Pike, you need to let go of me. I'm fine. I—"

He saw her eyes glaze over and knew that despite her protests, she was about to faint. He was in an awkward position to hold her up, reaching across the counter like this, but he didn't want to let go of her and let her fall and maybe hurt herself.

As Sophie sagged forward, Pike called, "Patrick, get around there and give me a hand."

Delano hurried to the end of the counter and through the swinging gate there. He slid his Smith & Wesson back into the shoulder holster under his coat and reached Sophie's side in time to get his arms around her shoulders and knees as she tried to fold up.

Delano lifted her and placed her on the counter, which Pike had cleaned off quickly. Pike untied her apron, took it off her, folded it up as best he could, and slipped it under her head as a makeshift pillow. He wished his mother Mary and his sister Nessa were in town, instead of out at the ranch. They would know how to take care of Sophie.

Hurried footsteps sounded outside, then Sheriff Andy Burnett appeared in the open door, carrying a double-barreled shotgun at an angle in front of his chest. He stopped short and peered around through the haze of powder smoke that still hung in the room.

"I was down the street and it sounded like a war had broken out," said the lanky, affable lawman. Andy's eyes narrowed as he looked at Pike. "Somehow, I'm not surprised to see you here." Then Andy sucked in a breath sharply as he caught sight of Sophie lying motionless on the counter. "Lord have mercy! Is Miss Truesdale—"

"She's not hurt, Andy," Pike broke in. "She just fainted, that's all." He nodded toward the three dead gunmen. "Those hombres are the only ones hurt, and they're in need of an undertaker, not a sawbones."

"I'd better make sure of that," Andy said. He checked the bodies, then nodded grimly in agreement with Pike's assessment. "Dead, all right. Who are they?"

"Fellas with a grudge against me. Or at least they *believed* they had a grudge against me. I tried to tell them they had it wrong, but they weren't in any mood to listen."

"That's right, Sheriff," Delano said. "I can back up what

Pike's telling you. In fact, although he hasn't mentioned it, I killed that one." He pointed to VanHook.

"And who might you be?" Andy wanted to know.

"An old friend of mine named Patrick Delano. Patrick, you've probably guessed by now, this is our sheriff, Andy Burnett."

"Pleased to meet you, Sheriff," Delano said. "I just wish it was under better circumstances."

Andy sighed and nodded.

"So do I." Since there wasn't a threat anymore, he let the shotgun hang at his side. "I reckon I'd better let Cyrus Malone know to bring his wagon down here and collect these . . . customers."

"Yeah, and send somebody to fetch Doc Faulkner for Sophie, too."

"I thought you said she just fainted."

"Yeah, but I reckon he still needs to check her over. Besides, she's been helping him out sometimes as his nurse, so I'm sure he'll want to know for himself that she's all right."

Andy nodded and said, "Yeah, you're right. You'll stay here for now?"

Pike glanced at Sophie's still, pale face and said, "I'm not going anywhere."

CHAPTER 4

The nearest telegraph office to Warbonnet was in Clarkston, the county seat of Chaparral County just to the north. That was because the railroad spur from Fort Worth ended at Clarkston. There had been talk of extending the rails on down to Warbonnet, but nobody knew when or even if that would ever happen.

The Cross Timbers Stagecoach Line, which operated stage routes all over north central Texas, once had run from Warbonnet all the way up to Fort Worth, but the railroad had made the Fort Worth-Clarkston leg obsolete. The stage still ran between Warbonnet and Clarkston every other day, though, and if any telegrams for folks in Warbonnet came in at the Western Union office in Clarkston, the stagecoach delivered them on its next run.

That was what had brought Pike to Warbonnet this evening. Jim Bob Tooley was a hostler for the stage line and also worked on the side as a messenger, delivering any telegrams that came in for somebody in the county. That morning he had ridden out to the Shannon ranch northwest of town and gave Pike an envelope containing a telegraph flimsy that had arrived with the stagecoach the previous afternoon.

Pike thanked Jim Bob, tossed a silver dollar to him, and sat down in one of the rocking chairs on the porch to see who had gone to the trouble of getting in touch with him this way.

His sister Nessa came out onto the porch a few minutes later, looked at him, and then said, "I thought I heard a horse."

"Yeah, Jim Bob Tooley was here," Pike replied distractedly.

"What did he want? And what are you frowning about? You look like you're fixing to cloud up and rain."

Pike tapped the yellow flimsy with the message printed on it in capital letters.

"Jim Bob brought this out from town. Some fella's offering me a job."

"Well, that's usually a good thing, isn't it? No, wait." Nessa was frowning now, too. "When you say a job, you mean . . .?"

"Yeah. A gun job. The kind I used to do."

"But you've given up all that. Haven't you?"

"Yeah, sure," Pike said.

But although he didn't want to admit it to his pretty, redheaded sister, when he had first read the telegram there was a part of him that had seriously considered the offer. A rancher over in Utah was having trouble with another spread, and adding to the conflict was the fact that the man who had wired Pike was a Gentile surrounded by Mormons. This had the makings of an even bloodier range war than usual.

And Pike, Lord help him, wanted in on it.

Not really, though, he told himself. It was just that old

habits died hard. Deep down, he didn't want any part of whatever tragedy was developing in Utah. He didn't know which side was right or wrong, didn't even know if there *was* a right or wrong in this particular clash. He had been mixed up in too many fracases where *both* sides were pretty sorry bunches, as far as he was concerned. That hadn't stopped him from taking money to support one or the other, but those times never left him with a very good taste in his mouth, either.

So he folded the telegram, slipped it into his pocket, and told Nessa, "Don't worry. I'm not just about to get mixed up in it. And there's no reason to say anything about this to Ma, either. She'd just worry that sooner or later I'll drift back into my old ways."

"We all worry about that, Pike," Nessa said quietly.

"Not Torrance." Pike knew that if he were to ride out, bound for some range war, his older brother would take great pleasure in saying *I told you so. I told you Pike couldn't stay away from killing.*

That was a good enough reason right there to turn down this job—just to spite Torrance.

Nessa insisted, "Yes, even Torrance worries about you," but Pike waved that away.

"I'll ride into Warbonnet this afternoon and send the fella a message saying I'm not interested. So Ma and Torrance don't need to know, and neither do Dougal or Fiddler," he added, referring to his grandfather and the family friend who lived on the ranch now.

Actually, Fiddler was more than a friend to Pike's widowed mother Mary, but Pike wasn't going to let himself think about that.

"All right, I'll keep it between us," Nessa agreed, then

paused for a second before asking, "How long before people stop trying to hire you to kill somebody?"

"I don't know," Pike replied, feeling a little prickle of irritation. What other people did or didn't do wasn't his fault. He couldn't control that. "But I'm a changed man."

Nessa nodded, but she didn't look completely convinced.

Now, as Pike stood in the café and watched Dr. Preston Faulkner checking Sophie over, he wondered if turning down that gun job earlier in the day was another reason he was considering the proposal Patrick Delano had made to him.

Over at the stage line office right now, awaiting delivery at the Western Union office in Clarkston on the next day's stage, was the message he had printed out telling the man in Utah that he wouldn't be coming. That refusal was another step away from his old life, and even though he had told himself that was what he wanted, maybe he wasn't sure.

Cooking and selling a big load of moonshine to Delano would be a way of keeping his hand in, so to speak. Keeping that wild streak from vanishing entirely . . .

"She'll be fine," Dr. Faulkner said as he stepped back from the counter where Sophie still lay. "Her pulse is strong, and there's nothing wrong with her breathing. Having such bloodshed erupt right in front of her was just too much of a shock. She should be waking up any time now."

"Maybe we'd better go, then," Pike suggested. "Seeing

Patrick and me might be too much of a reminder of what happened."

"I don't think she will have forgotten it," Faulkner said dryly. "I can still smell the powder smoke in the air, not to mention the blood that's visible on the floor."

Pike grimaced.

"Yeah, we ought to clean that up."

Andy Burnett was still there, too. He said, "I'll see that that's taken care of, Pike. Doc, let me give you a hand putting Miss Truesdale in your buggy, and you can take her back to her house and make sure she's settled in. I reckon that'd be the best way to handle things."

"I don't mind—" Pike began.

"No, you and Mr. Delano can go on," Andy said. "No need for you fellas to hang around."

Pike realized then what Andy was trying to do. The sheriff wasn't happy about how the violence of Pike's past life had caught up to him here in Warbonnet. It was highly unlikely that any other trouble would break out tonight, at least not any that Pike was connected to, but getting him out of town was one sure way of preventing that. Andy was too much of a friend to order him to rattle his hocks out of Warbonnet, though.

So it was up to Pike to be a good friend, as well, and take the hint. He nodded and said to Delano, "Patrick, you're coming with me. We'll put you up out at the ranch."

"I don't want to be any bother," Delano said.

"No bother," Pike assured him. "Besides, we haven't finished talking business yet."

Delano's grin reappeared.

"I'm glad to hear that we haven't. Sure, I'll ride out to

the ranch with you. Besides, I want to see if that redheaded sister of yours is as pretty as you always said she was."

Pike frowned, and Delano held up his hands defensively.

"Don't worry," he went on. "I'm always a perfect gentleman, you know that."

"Yeah," Pike said, sounding like he didn't buy that story for a second. He started to leave the café with Delano but then stopped in the doorway and said to Faulkner, "Doc, will you tell Sophie how sorry I am that everything happened this way?"

"Of course," Faulkner agreed.

Feeling a little better about things, Pike walked away from the place with Delano, who commented, "You know, you shouldn't be sorry about how *everything* turned out."

"What do you mean?"

"As unlikely as it sounds, Ed Keyhoe and his friends could have gotten lucky and killed you. Miss Truesdale would have been devastated if anything had happened to you."

Pike snorted and said, "You couldn't be much more wrong about that."

"I don't think so. From what I saw, that young lady is very fond of you."

"Sure," Pike said, again sounding unconvinced.

Delano stuck his hands in his pockets and said, "You just wait and see."

Pike changed the subject by asking, "Where's your horse?"

A few minutes later they were riding out of Warbonnet, following the Brazos River road as it ran northwest from town. The moon had risen, and that silvery orb seemed to float on the broad, placid surface of the gently flowing stream.

As they rode, Delano said, "You know, I can understand why you'd want to give up the kind of life we used to live, Pike. Ugliness wears a man down after a while, and there's no denying that a lot of what we were mixed up in was pretty ugly."

"Ain't that the truth."

"I reckon that's why I wasn't really upset when I laid down my cards in that poker game and realized I had won the Big Boss. Lady Luck was telling me that it was time to settle down and stop breathing the stink of gunsmoke all the time." Delano paused for a few seconds, then went on, "And for a while there, I was enjoying my life in Prescott. I really was. Until that blasted election."

He made a disgusted noise.

"You know, I'll bet that's why the fella I won the saloon from didn't seem all that upset. He probably had an idea that change was coming, and he was able to get out before it got there."

"But if he lost the place to you at cards, he didn't get anything out of it," Pike said.

"Well, no, I reckon he didn't. But at least he got rid of the place on his own terms, doing something he loved, rather than having the rug yanked out from under him and being forced to sit there and watch what he'd worked for die a slow, painful death."

"I suppose you could look at it that way," Pike said.

"Anyway, I'm not gonna just roll over and play dead for those temperance varmints. I plan on fighting back."

"That's liable to land you in jail."

"They'll have to catch me first." Delano's grin made his

teeth shine in the moonlight. "If something's worth doing, it's worth running a little risk, don't you think?"

"I can't deny that," Pike responded. He had run too many risks in his life to argue with what Delano had just said.

It was late by the time they reached the ranch, but a light still showed faintly in the parlor window. His ma had left a lamp burning for him, Pike knew. They rode to the barn, where Pike snapped a lucifer to life with his thumbnail and lit a lantern so they could see as they unsaddled their mounts and put them in stalls. Pike blew out the lantern because there was plenty of moonlight to see by as they walked to the house.

As they approached, Pike spotted an orange glow on the porch and smelled pipe tobacco. He wasn't surprised when his grandfather called out, "That you, Pike?"

"Yeah, Dougal," Pike replied. "I'm a little later getting back from town than I expected."

"Who's that with you?"

Pike and Delano went up the steps. Pike could see his grandfather sitting in one of the rocking chairs now, a large, bulky shape in overalls. Pike wasn't sure he had ever seen Dougal when he *wasn't* wearing overalls.

"This is an old friend of mine," Pike said. "Patrick Delano."

"Old friend, as in the same line of work?" Dougal wasn't, by nature, as disapproving of the life Pike had led as his daughter-in-law Mary or his other grandson Torrance was, but he didn't rate being a hired gun very highly, either.

"Used to be," Delano answered. "I'm an honest businessman now. It's good to meet you, Mr. Shannon. I recall Pike talking about you on a number of occasions."

"Yeah, Grandpappy, I said you were a wild Irishman," Pike added.

Dougal snorted. "I can think of a lot worse things to be." Without getting up, he extended a hand to Delano. "Good to meet you, son. You and my grandson haven't been up to no good, have you?"

"Well . . ." Pike said.

"Saints alive!" Dougal said. "I suppose you boys might as well sit down and tell me about it." He puffed on the pipe, sending a cloud of gray smoke billowing around him. "The law ain't after you, is it?"

"Not yet," Pike said.

CHAPTER 5

"Five wagonloads," Dougal mused after Pike and Delano had finished telling him about Delano's idea. "That's a whole heap of moonshine. Even if a man had several stills set up, it'd take a while to run that much."

"It could be done, though," Delano said. "Couldn't it?"

Dougal waved the big hand that cradled his pipe and said, "Well, sure, if you had the supplies and the men to operate the stills. It's just a matter of time."

"I'd be willing to wait, as long as I knew I'd be getting that prime Shannon moonshine. The Big Boss Saloon can hold out a while longer."

Pike leaned forward in the rocking chair in which he sat and clasped his hands together between his knees as he asked, "How would you get the 'shine down to Pecan County?"

"Well . . . I was hoping I could pay you enough that you'd deliver it," Delano said. "You could send word to me when it was ready so I could come get it, but then I'd have to line up some wagons and drivers and that would take more time . . . It just seems like it would be more efficient if you were to bring it to Prescott. And as I said, we'll take that into account when we're settling on a price."

Pike looked over at his grandfather and said, "What do you think, Dougal? Could we come up with enough wagons and drivers?"

"We'd have to have some fellas helpin' us just to get the stuff cooked to start with," Dougal said. "I reckon most of the ones who'd be willin' to do that would be agreeable to helpin' deliver the load, too." The old-timer scratched at his bristly white beard. "I'm thinkin' Sam Crow and Will Fisher might be interested. Tom McGreevey's a good man, too."

"Don't reckon I know McGreevey," Pike said.

"Sure you do. He's Forrest Haddon's stepson."

"I barely know that Forrest Haddon's some distant relation of ours."

"Distant relation, my hind foot. Forrest is my third cousin. You young folks these days don't put near enough stock in family."

"All right, that's three men we could ask."

"I can drive a wagon, and so can Torrance," Dougal said. "That makes five. With you goin' along as outrider and relievin' one of us on the wagons from time to time, I reckon we could do it."

"You figure on Torrance going along with all this?" Pike asked with a frown.

"I know you and him don't always see eye to eye, but he ain't never turned his back on family. He worked the stills and helped with deliveries when your pa and your brother Tyree were still alive."

"Yeah, but he's gone all law-abiding lately."

Dougal chuckled and said, "So have you, from what anybody could tell by lookin'. But you're thinkin' about takin' this chance, and I'd bet a hat ol' Torrance will be, too."

Pike sat back, cocked his right ankle on his left knee, and pondered. For now, he would have to take his grandfather's word that this distant cousin-by-marriage of his was a good man, but he knew for a fact that Sam Crow and Will Fisher were. Both of them had worked and fought at Pike's side in the past. Both had wives and kids, though, and might be reluctant to risk their stable lives on a wild scheme such as the one Pike, Dougal, and Delano were talking about.

"If we got a still running here on our place, and Sam and Will each set one up and did some cooking, too, we could get the load done in a couple of weeks," Pike said. He looked at Delano. "It would take close to a week to get down to Prescott with the wagons, after that. Would that be soon enough to save your saloon?"

Delano nodded and said, "I'm confident the Big Boss can hang on for another month, if necessary. Of course, the sooner that 'shine gets there, the better." He leaned forward eagerly. "Do we have a deal, Pike?"

"I can't make any promises until after I've talked to the other fellas whose help we'll need."

"I understand. But assuming they're willing to go along with you . . .?"

Pike turned back to Dougal and asked, "What do you think?"

"It's your decision, boy. You're ramroddin' this deal, if there is one."

Pike thought for a second longer, and in that instant, visions of a life ahead as an honest horse rancher flashed through his mind. He wouldn't be constantly flirting with danger, trouble would be a lot less likely to come calling on his family, and it was possible that maybe someday, he and Sophie Truesdale might be able to overcome their differences and get together. Maybe it was a loco dream, but he could almost see the two of them with a couple of young'uns—or more—running around the ranch . . .

Problem was, although Pike could imagine all that, he seemed to view the images in his head as if through a haze, some barrier that prevented him from reaching out and touching them, making them real. And when he tried to visualize himself in those scenes, he couldn't do it. His body was there, but the face was blank, featureless. Just a phantom, that's all.

All that passed through his thoughts in the blink of an eye, and in that moment, he knew the truth. Some men were cut out for normal, peaceful lives, and more power to 'em, he told himself. But he wasn't one of them, and secure in that knowledge, he said to Patrick Delano, "If I can round up the fellas I need to pitch in . . . then yeah, we've got a deal."

Delano stuck out his hand and said, "Shake on it." He wasn't grinning now. Instead, he was solemn, taking this seriously.

So was Pike. He clasped Delano's hand, and that was it. He had given his word and would never go back on it.

From the other rocking chair, Dougal said, "Now you got the hard part to figure out."

"What's that?" Pike asked.

"Tellin' your ma about it without havin' things end up with her tannin' your hide."

Delano said, "You're probably twice her size, aren't you, Pike?"

"Yeah," Pike said, "but you don't know my ma."

* * *

"Absolutely not," Mary Shannon said. "I forbid it."

"I agree with your mother," Fiddler said.

"You would," Pike said from the other end of the kitchen table, "considering that the two of you—"

"Choose your words *very* carefully," Mary said with a steely glint in her eyes.

It was the next morning. Pike had gotten up earlier than usual and found Mary in the kitchen, where she was preparing breakfast as usual. The smell of coffee brewing filled the house. She had batter ready for flapjacks but hadn't started cooking them yet. The sun wasn't up, but the sky visible through the kitchen window had begun to turn gray with the approach of another day.

Fiddler had come into the kitchen right behind Pike, who had asked the two of them to sit down so he could talk to them. Mary took the chair at the other end of the table from Pike, and Fiddler sat at her right hand.

Fiddler had gotten that nickname because he was known throughout Warbonnet County as an accomplished fiddle player who had sawed out sprightly tunes at countless dances and socials.

He had also spent years mostly drunk, until Pike had befriended him and circumstances had forced him to sober up. In the months since, he had become a staunch ally of the Shannon clan, and Mary had come to rely on his companionship. So it was no surprise that he would back her up in her response to Pike's proposal.

"I meant no offense," Pike went on. "I'm just saying that it's already a done deal, assuming I can recruit Sam and Will and Tom McGreevey."

"You won't have any trouble with the McGreevey boy," Mary said. "He's always been wild and shiftless."

"Does *everybody* know this fella except me?"

"You just never did pay enough attention to family."

Pike swallowed the frustration that tried to well up his throat.

"This is a good deal, Ma. Patrick's willing to pay a top price for the 'shine, and since it'll be sold a hundred miles away in Pecan County, it won't cause any trouble around here."

"But it'll cause trouble for those people in Pecan County who voted not to have it there," Mary argued. "Anyway, you'll have to cook it here, and *that's* illegal in Warbonnet County, too. Do you really want to put Andy Burnett in the position of having to arrest you?"

"Andy won't have to know about it," Pike said. "It'll just be for a couple of weeks."

Fiddler said, "Didn't you say this fellow Delano, this old compadre of yours, was interested in having you supply him with moonshine on an ongoing basis, after this first load?"

"He talked about it," Pike admitted. "But we'd have to see how it goes."

"In other words, you might be breaking the law from now on," Mary said.

"I don't recall you complaining when Pa and Dougal and Tyree were doing the same thing, only they were selling the 'shine they cooked around here," Pike snapped.

He saw the hurt look in his mother's eyes and instantly regretted the sharpness with which he had spoken. He would stand behind the truth of the words, though.

After a moment, Mary said, "I never tried to keep your father from doing what he believed was right. It was . . . in the blood, I guess you'd say. But things change."

"Blood doesn't."

They looked at each other steadily along the length of

the table as seconds ticked past, and then Mary said, "No, I suppose it doesn't. I see Elijah in you, Pike. Honestly, more than I ever saw him in Torrance or even Tyree. Tyree had a wild streak, but that's all it was. Wild. Cruel, even. The wildness that's in you . . . it's the kind that dreams. Dreams big."

Talk like that made Pike uncomfortable, although he had to admit to himself that he liked being compared to his father. He'd always looked up to Elijah Shannon, even if they hadn't gotten along.

"You're bound and determined to do this, aren't you?" Mary went on.

"I think it's a good deal. And it's a way to . . . to not . . ."

"Settle down," Mary finished for him. "That seems like the most awful prospect in the world to you, doesn't it?"

"I wouldn't say that. It's just that I'm not really ready for it yet."

He might not ever be ready for that, Pike thought, but he didn't see any point in saying so to his mother right now.

She nodded slowly. "All right, then."

"You're giving me your blessing for this deal?"

"I didn't say that. But I'm not forbidding it anymore." Mary shrugged. "Anyway, it may not matter. Sam Crow and Will Fisher may have too much good sense to go along with your loco ideas."

"What about Torrance?"

"Oh, I don't doubt for a second that he'll go along with you. He's got that wild Shannon streak, too."

"Torrance?" Pike said. "Wild?" He couldn't imagine how anybody could think his dour, stolid older brother could ever be wild.

"You just can't see it because the two of you are too much alike, but trust me, it's there."

"Maybe so."

Mary put her hands flat on the table and said, "Now, where's that friend of yours? You extended the family's hospitality to Mr. Delano, I hope."

"He's in the spare room. Tyree's old room."

"He's welcome to stay as long as he likes."

Fiddler said, "Once he gets a taste of your cooking, Mary, he may not ever want to leave."

"No, he's got to get back down to Prescott," Pike said. "He's got a business to run, at least for the time being."

"And he'll wait for you there, until you deliver the moonshine?"

"That's the plan."

"There's one thing you haven't considered, Pike," Fiddler said. "If Mary doesn't object, I believe I'd like to go along with you."

Mary stared at him and said, "You would? I thought you didn't like being around moonshine anymore."

"It's true that I prefer to avoid temptation, but a journey such as the one Pike proposes sounds like quite an adventure. And I've become rather good at handling a team of mules, if I do say so myself."

"That's true," Pike put in. "I'm sure having you along would come in handy, Fiddler, if you really want to go."

"You're still getting ahead of yourself," Mary said. "You don't know if you'll even be able to recruit enough help."

"I reckon I'd better get at it, then," Pike said. "*After* I have breakfast."

"You'd better not let anything happen to Fiddler," Mary warned, "or you might never have breakfast in this house again."

CHAPTER 6

The plan came together with surprising speed.

Pike approached Torrance first, later that same day, and introduced him to Patrick Delano, whom Mary had welcomed graciously to the Shannon family home despite her reservations about the deal Pike and Delano had agreed to.

The first thing Torrance said after they had explained matters to him was, "Have you settled on a price?"

"Yeah, we have," Pike said.

"You should have talked to me first before committing the family to anything. I'm older than you, remember."

"Yeah, but Patrick's my friend, and he came to *me*. And if you want to talk old, Dougal's a heap older than both of us. He's still the patriarch of this family, if there is one."

"Dougal turned that role over to Pa a long time ago, and with him and Tyree both gone, it falls to me."

As usual, Torrance's stubborn arrogance put a burr under Pike's saddle. With an effort, he reined in the irritation, named the price he and Delano had agreed to, and said, "All right, what do you think of that?"

Torrance considered for a long moment and then nodded.

"That's agreeable, I suppose. But you still should have asked me first."

Delano spoke up, saying, "You know, I think you're right, Torrance."

"He is?" Pike asked with a surprised frown.

"Yes, what with him being the older brother and all." Delano smiled at Torrance. "Why don't I raise the price, say, two percent, just to be fair to you, Torrance?"

"Make it four?"

"Three," Delano countered.

Torrance extended his hand. "Deal."

They shook on it. Pike said, "What was that about?"

"You're brothers," Delano said. "Torrance should have had his chance to dicker, too."

Torrance nodded and said, "I appreciate that."

"So you'll help with the stills and drive one of the wagons?" Pike asked.

"Yes, I will. And I'll go with you to talk to Sam Crow and Will Fisher, so they'll know this isn't just some crazy idea that you came up with."

"What about Tom McGreevey?"

"Tom?" Torrance laughed. "You should know he'll go along with anything."

Pike just shook his head.

Within a couple of days, Pike and Delano had visited Sam Crow and Will Fisher, and both men had agreed to take part. Tom McGreevey, who lived in the eastern part of the county, showed up ready to work, in response to a message sent to him. He was a stocky, redheaded man in his mid-thirties who hugged Pike and pounded him on the back like he was a long-lost brother, exclaiming, "By the Lord Harry, 'tis fine to see you again, Cousin Pike!"

Pike still had no memory of ever meeting the man

before, but at this point, that didn't really matter. Tom was an enthusiastic partner in the scheme right away.

Dougal and Torrance had gotten to work building a still in a remote corner of the Shannon ranch. Sam and Will would be doing the same in isolated areas of their properties. It was difficult to hide a still for very long. Smoke from the fires and the distinctive smell of the mash were hard-to-miss clues for anyone with any experience looking for an illegal moonshining operation. Andy Burnett, having done a considerable amount of moonshining himself, would sniff out these new stills without much trouble, if he went looking for them.

But Andy had no reason to suspect that anybody was cooking 'shine in Warbonnet County right now, so Pike's hope was that by the time folks might notice anything unusual and report it to the sheriff, the first part of the deal would be done and the caravan of moonshine wagons would be on its way to Pecan County. The stills could be broken down for potential use again in the future, and nobody in these parts would be any the wiser.

That was the way the plan was supposed to go, anyway. Only time would tell whether or not it did.

With everything proceeding smoothly, Patrick Delano told Pike it was time for him to head back to Prescott. It would take him three days, maybe three and a half, to make that ride. Mary and Nessa packed plenty of supplies for him.

As he'd promised Pike, Delano had been a gentleman where Nessa was concerned, acting friendly enough toward her but stopping short of flirting. However, Pike could tell that his sister was pretty taken with the gambler anyway, due to Delano's natural charm. She was the only one in the family who *didn't* know Delano's real reason for being there. Pike told her that his old friend had just come for a visit.

"I'll expect you in about three weeks," Delano told Pike as he saddled his horse on the morning of his departure. Pecan County will be ready, and very glad to see you, that much I can promise."

"We'll be there," Pike said, "as long as we don't run into any trouble."

Delano finished tightening one of the cinches on his saddle and then said with a frown, "I'm a little worried about that."

"The chance of running into trouble?"

"That's right. Pike, if word gets out that you're taking a big load of prime moonshine that far, it's liable to be a tempting target for outlaws. That 'shine will be worth a considerable amount of money."

"I reckon you know as well as anybody that I can take care of myself," Pike said.

Delano waved that away.

"I have no doubts about you, my friend. That's one reason I came to you in the first place. But what about the others? Can they handle themselves in case somebody tries to raid that caravan?"

"Sam Crow and Will Fisher are both tough as nails. Dougal's been a fighter all his life. And Torrance . . . well, Torrance and I usually rub each other the wrong way, but I know he's got plenty of sand, and if anybody threatens his family, he's going to fight to his last breath. You don't have to worry about any of them."

"What about Fiddler? You told me he used to drink too much."

"That was before he sobered up and then threw in with the Shannons," Pike said. "It's true that he handles a fiddle a lot better than he does a gun, but he won't panic and can be counted on to do what he's told. I'm comfortable having him along."

"That's plenty good enough for me, I suppose," Delano said. He put out his hand. "Thanks, Pike. I can't tell you how much this means to me." He grinned as they shook hands. "Here's to a profitable venture for both of us."

"We ought to be drinking to that."

"We will," Delano said, "when you get that moonshine to Pecan County."

Pike spent the next few days mostly on horseback, riding from the Shannon ranch to Sam Crow's farm to Will Fisher's place, checking on all three stills once they were up and running, making sure that Dougal, Torrance, Sam, and Will had all the supplies they needed, and, once the 'shine started dripping, sampling it to make sure the quality was good enough for it to be considered prime Shannon moonshine.

He was satisfied with the way things were going, but that didn't mean he was going to relax. In fact, one morning as he rode toward the still tucked away in some rugged hills north of the Shannon ranch house, the skin on the back of his neck prickled, a sure sign that someone was following him. The instinct warning him now had developed over a lot of long, dangerous years, and he wasn't just about to ignore what it was trying to tell him.

Up ahead, the trail ran through a narrow, brushy gap between two ridges, then took an abrupt turn to the right. Pike knew that just around that bend, a post oak had grown at an angle out of the bluff on one side, and when the tree was bushed out and covered with leaves, as it was at this time of year, one of the branches hung down low enough for a man to reach up and grab it—if he was standing on his saddle.

Pike didn't rein in or glance back or anything else that might reveal he had tumbled to being followed. Instead, he maintained the same pace, rode through the narrow passage, then turned to follow the trail that ran along the base of the bluff.

As soon as he was out of sight, though, he kicked his feet out of the stirrups, looped the reins around the saddle horn, and in a lithe maneuver, stood up on the saddle as his horse kept moving. It was a show-off trick, but sometimes the ability came in handy, like now. He reached up, grabbed that low-hanging branch, and let the horse move out from under him, leaving him dangling.

With only a slight grunt of effort, Pike chinned himself and threw a leg up, hooking it over the branch. Once he'd done that, it took him only a couple of seconds to scramble higher. The growth was thick enough that he wouldn't be seen easily unless somebody was looking directly up into the tree, and whoever was following him wouldn't have any reason to do that. Pike's horse was still moving along the trail up ahead, its hoofbeats clearly audible in the warm, still air.

A moment later, as Pike crouched on a thick branch and hung on to a higher bough to steady himself, the sound of another horse approaching came to his ears. It was moving along at a good clip, not galloping but not wasting any time, either, as if the rider wanted to reach the bend in time to make sure that he wouldn't lose his quarry's trail.

Pike was utterly motionless, not doing anything to stir the foliage even slightly as the other horsebacker came through the gap and then reined around the tight turn. That brought him directly under the slanted tree where Pike waited.

Through the leaves, Pike caught a glimpse of a slender rider in jeans, a checked shirt, and a flat-crowned hat held on with a taut chin strap. Then he launched himself off the branch and plummeted toward the person riding below him.

Pike hit the hombre hard, wrapping an arm around his shoulders and wrenching him out of the saddle and off the horse. The sudden attack spooked the mount, causing it to leap forward as Pike and its former rider tumbled to the ground and rolled over. The horseman was lucky his foot hadn't caught in a stirrup, or else he'd have been dragged along the trail.

As it was, his luck wasn't all that good, because Pike used the roll's momentum to surge up and throw himself on top of the man. His left hand closed around the hombre's throat to pin him to the ground, while his right fist rose, poised to sledge down into the follower's face if need be.

Pike froze in that position, suddenly feeling hollow and sick inside. The rider's hat had come off, and long, red hair spilled out around a face that stared up at Pike with huge, shocked green eyes.

"Nessa!" Pike ripped out.

Then he realized he was straddling and half-choking his own sister and had a fist lifted to pound the stuffing out of her. He let go of her as if he'd found himself holding a rattlesnake and jerked back, getting his feet under him so he could rise off of her.

Vanessa Shannon struggled to push herself into a sitting position. She coughed several times and massaged her throat. Then she said in a hoarse voice, "Blast it, Pike, what's wrong with you?"

"Wrong with me?" he said. "What's wrong with *you*?

You ought to have more sense than to follow somebody
like me!"

"A gun-wolf, you mean?" she snapped.

Pike's jaw tightened with anger. He had been surprised
at first, when he realized it was Nessa he'd knocked off
her horse, and then scared that he had hurt her. Now that
he could tell she seemed to be all right, just shaken up a
little, he was offended that she would talk to him that way.

Although, a little voice in the back of his head reminded
him, for a lot of years a hired gun-wolf was exactly what
he'd been . . .

He forced himself to ignore what she'd just said and
asked her, "What are you doing out here?"

"This is Shannon range," she shot back at him. "I have
every right to be here. So I could ask you the same thing.
What are *you* doing here?"

"I rode out to check on some of the stock—"

"That's bullfeathers, Pike, and you know it. You're on
the way to that still where you've got Torrance and Grandpappy cooking moonshine!"

Chapter 7

Pike stared at her for a second before he found his voice. Then he said, "You don't know what you're talking about."

Nessa scoffed disgustedly and said, "The heck I don't. Did you think you could keep something like that from me, Pike? What would even give you the right to? I'm a member of this family, too!"

"You're a kid—"

"I am not! I'm a grown woman, and you know it."

Whether he knew it and whether he wanted to admit it were two different things, Pike thought. He supposed that, technically, Nessa was mostly grown. A year earlier, she had been thinking about getting married. Tragedy had cut that particular romance short, but she was old enough that getting hitched wasn't out of the question.

Even so, some of the time Pike still thought of her as the gangly, scabby-kneed colt she had been when he left home. He had to remind himself otherwise, and often he didn't want to.

Right now, he didn't have any choice. He said, "All right, you're a grown woman—sort of—but you're still sticking your nose in things that don't concern you."

"Didn't you hear me? I just said that I'm a member of this family, too. If it concerns the Shannons, it concerns me." She extended a hand. "Now, the least you can do is help me up, blast it."

With a sigh, Pike took her hand and helped her to her feet. She brushed off the seat of her jeans and picked up her hat. As she slapped the dust off it against her thigh, she went on, "Are you going to admit that you and Torrance and Grandpappy are cooking 'shine again, or are you going to lie to my face?"

"All right," he said grudgingly. "We've got a still going, up in the hills, but that doesn't make it your business."

"I know you're going to sell the moonshine to Mr. Delano, too," Nessa said with a smug smile on her face.

"Again, none of your . . ." Pike's voice trailed off, then he said angrily, "You little sneak! You've been lurking around, eavesdropping on people. You didn't just figure it out."

"I knew something important was happening, and when your own family won't tell you what's going on, you have a right to find out however you can."

"You might as well tell me what you know."

"I know you three and Sam Crow and Will Fisher are going to cook up a big load of moonshine, take it down to Pecan County, and sell it to Mr. Delano. I heard you and Torrance and Grandpappy talking about it more than once. The two of them have been away from home a lot the past few days, and that's what got me curious enough to try to find out. You never should have figured you could put something like that over on me, Pike. Does Ma know?"

"She does," Pike said.

"And Fiddler?"

Pike just shrugged.

Nessa glared at him.

"So you told everybody, literally *everybody*, about it but me. Darn you, Pike Shannon, I feel like snatching your ears right off your head."

"I wouldn't try it if I were you," Pike said grimly. "You're not too old to put over my knee if I have to."

She sneered at him and said, "You wouldn't dare."

Pike just regarded her coolly, as if daring her to put him to the test.

"All right," Nessa said after a moment, "now that it's all out in the open, you might as well take me on up to the still with you. I'd like to see where it is and how it's set up. You know, I've worked a few runs myself."

"And you've come near to getting in bad trouble because of it," Pike reminded her. But nobody had any reason to bushwhack them now, he supposed, so he shrugged again and said, "Come on, if you're that determined."

They walked after their horses. The animals had stopped about a hundred yards along the trail and were cropping grass contently together. After mounting up, brother and sister rode side by side, deeper into the hills.

A few minutes later, Nessa announced without any warning, "I'm going with you down to Prescott."

Pike looked over at her and burst out, "The hell you are!"

"Unless you want me to tell Andy Burnett what you're doing," she returned coolly.

Pike stared at her in disbelief for a moment before he was able to form a response. When he was able to find the words, he said, "You'd blackmail your own brother like that?"

Nessa's voice took on an earnest tone as she said, "Do you know how far from Warbonnet I've been, Pike? I've been to Fort Worth three times in my life, and that's it! I want to see somewhere new and different and exciting."

"From what I remember of Pecan County, it's not exactly what I'd call exciting. The eastern half of the county is a mix of farms and ranches, and the western half is almost all cattle country. And Prescott, the county seat, is about like Warbonnet."

"I don't care. It's *not* Warbonnet, and that's all I care about."

"Well, you're not going," he said. "It's too far and too dangerous."

"You mean somebody might try to steal those wagon-loads of moonshine."

"I wouldn't be surprised."

"But you're taking Fiddler with you," Nessa argued. "Do you really believe that he can sit a saddle and handle a rifle as well as I can?"

She had a point there. Nessa was an excellent rider and a better shot than many of the men he knew. Certainly better than Fiddler. But she was still Pike's baby sister.

"There's no point in having this argument," he said. "Ma's never gonna let you go, no matter what I say."

"You're wrong. She'll let me go if you ask her. You're her favorite, and you always have been."

Pike stared at her. "What in the world make you think that?"

"It's obvious to anybody who's got eyes in their head. Why do you reckon it hurt her so bad when you up and left home all those years ago?"

"I didn't figure it did, the way I was always getting in trouble."

Nessa blew out an exasperated breath and said, "That just shows how much you know. Trust me, Pike, if you ask

Ma to let me come along with you, she'll say yes. She may not like it much, but she'll agree."

"But I don't *want* you going," he reminded her. "It's too—"

"Dangerous. Yeah, yeah, I know. But if that's true, couldn't you use another good hand with a rifle along?"

Pike scowled. Looking at it strictly from a logical standpoint and not letting emotions get in the way, she was probably right about that. The problem was, it was impossible to consider the question without emotion creeping in.

"There's something else you have to remember," Nessa said after a moment when he didn't respond. "If you don't let me come along, I'll just wait until you're gone, slip away from home, and come after you anyway."

"You'd do that?"

"If you force me to, sure."

Pike shook his head slowly and said, "You really should've been bent over somebody's knee more often when you were growing up. Maybe then you wouldn't have been so headstrong."

"Well, you weren't here to do it, were you? So I'm not sure you have any right to give such an opinion."

Pike rode on, not saying anything more for a couple of minutes, then he told Nessa, "We're almost there. We'll see what Torrance and Dougal think about this."

"If you believe they're more of a match for me than you are, you're wrong."

"We'll see," Pike said, but he wasn't as convinced as he sounded.

They came to a creek and turned to follow it. Post oaks and live oaks grew thickly almost all the way to the edge of the bank. Pike and Nessa had to ride single file. Pike nodded for her to go first. He could already smell the smoke from the fire Torrance and Dougal had going under the boiler.

After half a mile, they reached a clearing in the woods that sloped up slightly to level ground where the still was set up. Dougal and Torrance had erected a makeshift shelter out of branches, too. The trees that hung over the clearing broke up the smoke from the fire and made it harder to see. With the creek so close by for water, it was a good location. The Shannons had used it before.

Torrance had heard them coming. Pike's burly, sandy-haired brother stood next to a log that he and his grandfather used for sitting. The cold remains of the campfire over which they had cooked breakfast were beside the log, as well. Torrance held a Winchester in his right hand, the barrel canted back over his right shoulder.

He brought the rifle down and cradled it in his left arm as he glared at Nessa.

"What are you doing here?" he demanded. He turned his gaze toward Pike and added, "I thought you said you weren't going to tell her about this."

"She found out," Pike said curtly. "Evidently she likes to lurk around like a spy."

Nessa said, "You're just mad because you got out-smarted by a girl."

"It doesn't take smarts, just sneakiness."

Dougal emerged from the trees, hitching up his overalls as he entered the camp.

"Thought I heard a gal's voice," he said. "Pike, you said you wasn't gonna tell her—"

"Yeah, we've been through that," Pike broke in. "But she's here now, and that's not the worst of it. She's got the wild idea in her head that she's coming with us to Pecan County."

"Absolutely not," Torrance said flatly.

Nessa narrowed her eyes at him and said, "I'll tell you the same thing I told Pike: you take me along, or I'll let Andy Burnett know what you're doing here."

Dougal stared at her and sounded scandalized as he said, "Girl! You'd turn against your own flesh and blood like that?"

"Only if you make me."

"She said pretty much the same thing to me," Pike told his brother and grandfather disgustedly. "She made a few decent points, though. She can ride and shoot, and we know she can keep her head when there's trouble breaking out around her."

"Yeah," Torrance said, rubbing his jaw. "That doesn't make me feel any better about being forced into a corner, though."

"Then just admit that me going along is a good idea," Nessa said.

"One thing we got to consider," Dougal said. "If we all go along, then who's gonna stay at the ranch with Mary?"

Pike swung down from the saddle and said, "That's one thing I rode out here to tell you this morning. Since Sam and Will are going with us, I told them their wives and kids could come and stay at the ranch while they're gone. They've got hired men who can take care of their places. Hebner Dawson said he'd come, too, to help keep an eye on things, since he's not really up to traveling much anymore after getting shot a while back. Those kids can take care of the chores, and Lita Crow's old enough to ride out and check on the horses, especially if Hebner goes along with her. They ought to be able to handle things just fine during the two weeks we're gone."

Torrance grunted and said, "Two weeks if we don't run into any trouble. When did Shannons ever do much of anything without some sort of ruckus breaking out?"

Dougal said, "You forget, boy, things went along pretty peaceful-like around here until the past year or so."

"Yeah," Torrance said as he squinted at his brother. "Until Pike came home."

Pike swallowed the annoyance he felt at Torrance's attitude and said, "That still leaves us with the question of what we're going to do about Nessa."

"I'm still sitting right here, you know," she said from the saddle. "And it's obvious what the smart thing to do is. Tell me I can come along . . . and be grateful for my company."

"She also said that if we didn't agree, she'd just run off and follow us anyway," Pike added.

"I believe that," Torrance said. He glared at Nessa for a moment longer, then sighed. "All right. But you're a brat, you know that?"

"A brat who gets to go someplace different for once in her life," Nessa replied, smiling.

"Just don't forget, if the bullets start to fly, you're the one who insisted on this."

Nessa looked a little less certain of herself as she asked with a slight frown, "Do you really think there'll be trouble?"

Torrance said again, "With this family? I reckon you can count on it."

Chapter 8

The settlement was located about halfway between Warbonnet and Clarkston, not far over the line in Chaparral County, making it the second-largest town in that county. But that didn't mean it was very big, although its business section ran for several blocks along the main street.

Since Chaparral County was dry because of a local-option election, just like Warbonnet County, once the sun went down they rolled up the boardwalks in Boliver, as the old saying went. Not literally, of course, but most of the businesses were closed and dark, and not many people moved around the street.

One place where lights still burned was the pool hall. If it had a name other than that, nobody seemed to know it. Everybody in Bolivar just called it the pool hall. It sat on a corner, a long, narrow shack with a tin roof and a dingy aspect. Red paint had been slapped on its walls when it was built, but most of that paint had peeled off over the years.

Four horses were tied at the hitch rack in front of the building tonight.

A heavyset figure in a derby hat and tweed suit that had seen better days waddled toward the place. A screen door helped keep flies and mosquitoes out of the building but let the sounds of men's voices and pool balls clicking together float out into the humid darkness. A man laughed and said, "Good shot," as the heavyset newcomer reached the door and opened it.

Inside were four pool tables, and beyond them half a dozen smaller round tables where men could play cards or dominoes. To the right was a short bar where a craggy-faced, white-haired man in a dirty apron stood wiping circles on the stained hardwood with an equally grimy rag. Officially, the pool hall served near-beer these days, but most folks knew it was actually the real thing and the authorities turned a blind eye to it.

The four men who had tied those horses outside stood around one of the pool tables. Two of them held cue sticks while the other two watched the game going on. A man bent over the table, using the long, tapering stick to line up a shot.

He stroked the cue ball just as the fat man let the screen door bang shut behind him. The ball rolled swiftly across the table at a sharp angle, completely missed the ball at which the player had been aiming, and caromed off the edge of the table a couple of times before slowing down, clicking softly against another ball, and coming to rest.

The shooter straightened up with an angry, disgusted look on his hard-planed face and said to the newcomer, "Look what you made me do!" He switched the cue from his right hand to his left and used the right to draw a black-butted Colt from the holster on his hip. "I oughta plug you, you fat—"

The other man holding a cue reached over and tapped the stick against the gunman's shoulder.

"Take it easy, Henry," he said. "A game of eight ball's not worth killin' a fella over." The words were spoken in a mild voice that had an undercurrent of steel in it. The man smiled slightly and added, "Especially when the judge here's got a business proposition that might make us some good money."

"I'm not a judge any longer," the fat man said. "That ended when I had to light a shuck out of Warbonnet County in a hurry."

"Yeah, I heard about that." Malachi Bouchard handed his cue stick to one of the other men. "Here, you can finish the game with Henry for me. Henry, put that gun away."

With a surly look on his long, horse-faced countenance, Henry complied with the order.

Over behind the bar, the man in the apron didn't appear to have paid any attention to what had just happened. He kept wiping the bar.

Bouchard angled his head toward one of the tables that had dominoes scattered on it, facedown.

"Let's sit down, Judge," he suggested, using the title even though the fat man said it didn't belong to him anymore. "Yates, bring us a couple of beers."

The bartender nodded, picked up a pair of mugs from a shelf, and wiped them out.

The two men sat down at the domino table as the game resumed. Bouchard put a hand on the dominoes and moved them around idly, as if he were shuffling them before a hand but not getting too enthusiastic about it. He was a tall, lean man with a shock of dark hair under his thumbed-back hat, a prominent nose, and a skinny neck.

His resemblance to a carrion bird, plus his last name,

had prompted some wag to dub him "Buzzard" Bouchard. The nickname had stuck. Bouchard didn't mind. In his line of work, an ominous name like that wasn't necessarily a bad thing.

"So," he said. "Phineas Conway. I heard about you. You're related to the Ramsey clan that took over Warbonnet County for a while, aren't you?"

"Doak Ramsey was legally elected sheriff down there," Conway said, "just as I was legally elected judge." A bitter note came into his voice. "It was those damned Shannons who took the law into their own hands and somehow convinced the Texas Rangers to go along with it. Especially Pike Shannon."

Conway's round, fleshy face was pretty florid to start with, under his graying red hair. It flushed even darker with suppressed anger as he mentioned Pike Shannon.

Everything had been set up just the way they wanted it in Warbonnet County, and then Shannon had come home and ruined everything. Practically overnight, Conway had gone from occupying a position of power to being forced to flee in order to avoid winding up behind bars—or decorating a tree limb at the end of a rope.

The bartender brought the two mugs of beer over to the table and set them in front of Bouchard and Conway. Bouchard flipped him a half-dollar. The man shuffled back to the bar. Bouchard sipped the warm, bitter brew and shoved the dominoes around some more.

"Why did you send word to me that you wanted to talk?" he asked bluntly.

Conway guzzled some of his beer, then wiped the back of a pudgy hand across his mouth as he leaned forward.

"Pike Shannon's working on a new deal, and I figure he needs to get what's coming to him."

"Revenge, you mean."

"That . . ." Conway chuckled. "And a big payday for us at the same time. He's gone back into the moonshining business, and he plans to deliver one of the biggest loads ever cooked in Texas to a fellow down in Pecan County."

For the next couple of minutes, Conway filled Bouchard in on all the details of Pike Shannon's deal with Patrick Delano. Bouchard listened with interest, knowing that if the crooked former judge's information was correct, that much moonshine could be worth a fortune.

When Conway paused, Bouchard asked, "How do you know all this?"

Conway looked mighty satisfied with himself as he said, "I have a man on the inside."

"A spy, you mean."

"Call it whatever you like. But I know what I've just told you is true. In less than two weeks, those wagons full of moonshine are going to be on their way to Pecan County . . . and they'll be ripe for the taking."

"Why cut me and my boys in on the deal?"

"Look at me." Conway gestured at his corpulent body. "I'm not cut out for riding and shooting. I'm not an out—"

He stopped short, but instead of being offended, Bouchard let a smile steal across his face.

"Not an outlaw, is that what you were going to say? From what I've seen of life, men who sit behind desks steal more money in the long run than all the men who ride the dark trails and listen to the owl hoot." Bouchard shrugged skinny shoulders. "But we all have our parts to play, and I've long since accepted mine. What percentages do you propose?"

"Equal shares for me and my man on the inside,"

Conway answered without hesitation. "He'll be running quite a risk."

"You won't be. To be blunt, you'll be sitting back like a fat spider in the middle of your web."

Conway flushed again and said, "You wouldn't even know about this deal if it weren't for me."

"But now I *do* know about it. Which means that . . . I don't really need you anymore, do I?"

Bouchard slipped his gun from its holster and rested the barrel on the table edge so it pointed at Conway.

Conway's face turned pale this time. He was the sort of man who liked to talk, but he struggled for words now.

"I . . . I was told that you were an honorable man . . ."

"I *am* an honorable man," Bouchard said. "Once I give my word, I keep it." He waggled the gun barrel a little. "But you, my friend, I've promised nothing to you so far. I tell you what I'll do, though. We don't have any cards to cut, so these dominoes will have to do."

He reached out with his free hand, rested the tip of his index finger against one of the facedown dominoes, and went on, "The highest number of spots wins. All you have to do is beat me, and equal shares will belong to you and your inside man. I swear. Lose, and . . ." Bouchard shrugged. "Is that agreeable to you, Judge?"

Conway swallowed hard. Beads of sweat had popped out on his face. He had to know that he was trapped. If he tried to bolt away from the table and run out of the pool hall, Bouchard could empty that Colt in him before he made it halfway to the door.

The outlaw would get away with the killing, too. Boliver had a town marshal, but by now he was likely sound asleep in his bed—and even if the shots woke him, that was probably where he would stay.

"You . . . you give me your word?"

"I just said so, didn't I?" Bouchard sounded a little ir-ritated that Conway had questioned him.

Conway jerked his head in a nod. "All right, go ahead."

Bouchard started to turn over the domino he was tap-ping lightly, but he stopped and moved his hand over to another one, as if giving in to a whim. He flipped it over, revealing double-five.

"Well, I got some count there," Bouchard said with a satisfied smile. "You reckon you can beat that, Judge?"

Conway's hand shook as he extended it toward the scattered dominoes. He started to take hold of one, then pulled away. He made two more false starts, getting paler and sweatier with each one, until finally he practically lunged across the table, grabbed one of the dominoes clos-est to Bouchard, and turned it over. It rattled on the table.

Conway sagged back in his chair, gulped, and wheezed, "Double-six. Double-six."

"Indeed it is." Bouchard lowered the gun and slid it back into its holster. "And as I said, I'm a man of my word. Part-ners, Judge." He picked up his beer. "Let's drink to it."

Conway's hand still trembled from the strain as he picked up the mug of beer and clinked it clumsily against the outlaw's mug.

"We'll have to do this again," he said, summoning up a weak smile, "once all that moonshine belongs to us."

CHAPTER 9

The next ten days were busy ones for Pike. With Nessa now knowing what was going on, he didn't have to go to the trouble of trying to keep things secret from her. Instead he enlisted her to take over the ranch work for the time being, sending her out every day to check on the horses and make sure they weren't wandering, had plenty of graze, and weren't threatened by any predators. Mountain lions could be found almost anywhere in Texas, although they weren't as common in this region as they were farther west.

That freed Pike up to check even more frequently on the stills, not that he really had to worry about them. Torrance, Dougal, Sam Crow, and Will Fisher were all experienced moonshiners. Tom McGreevey helped out where he was needed, sometimes helping Sam, other times Will. All of them were working diligently, Pike knew, and they were producing top-notch 'shine, too.

The Shannons owned two wagons. Sam and Will had one each. That left Pike with the chore of coming up with another wagon and team of mules. Hebner Dawson solved that problem by volunteering the use of his wagon and team. Hebner and his late brother Cloyd were a pair of bachelors who owned a small farm that produced enough to suit their frugal needs.

Cloyd had been killed in the most recent spate of violence that had torn through Warbonnet County, and Hebner had been wounded. Hebner already sported a scarred face from a still explosion, and now he had a game leg from that bullet hole, too. He had been talking about maybe selling the farm and renting a room in town to live out the rest of his life, but for now he had the wagon and he proclaimed that Pike might as well use it as part of the moonshine caravan, especially since he planned to stay at the Shannon ranch while the rest of the menfolks were gone.

With that settled, as the day of the caravan's departure approached, Pike took one of his family's wagons and headed for Warbonnet, figuring to stock up on supplies for the trip at John Strickland's general store.

He parked the wagon in front of the store at the high porch that also served as a loading dock and went inside to give his list to Strickland.

"My clerks'll gather this up and get it loaded for you, Pike," the burly proprietor said. "Ought to be ready to go in an hour or so."

"Thanks, John," Pike said. He had known it would take a while to gather and load the flour, sugar, salt, beans, coffee, airtights of peaches and tomatoes, and other staples, and he had a pretty good idea how he wanted to spend the time while he was waiting.

He had seen Sophie Truesdale several times since that shoot-out in the café with Ed Keyhoe and his partners. Fainting like that hadn't done Sophie any real damage, but she'd been cool to Pike afterward, anyway. He hoped he could mend those fences a little before he left for Pecan County.

It was early afternoon, late enough for the lunch crowd

to be gone for the most part, but a few customers still lingered at tables. Sophie was behind the counter, so that was where Pike headed.

Through the window in the wall behind her that opened into the kitchen, Pike saw elderly but still spry Johnny Quinlan moving around. Quinlan did some of the cooking and closed up the café most nights. He gave Pike a grin and a wave and then went back to stirring a pot of something on the stove. Son-of-a-gun stew, more than likely, that would be one of the café's offerings for supper.

Sophie didn't have a smile for Pike. Her expression was carefully neutral as she said, "If you're here for lunch, we're out of steak, but there are still potatoes and greens and biscuits. I can carve off some ham for you—"

"That's not really why I'm here, Sophie," he said. "I was hoping maybe we could take a walk together."

She shook her head. "I can't. I'm too busy."

Pike looked pointedly at the few people still in the place and said, "Johnny's already working on supper, and if anybody needs a refill on their coffee, he can handle that, too. I don't see any reason why you can't get a breath of fresh air."

"It's called being a responsible business owner. I suppose I can understand why you wouldn't know much about that."

Pike was determined that he wasn't going to let her get under his skin—but he could tell she wasn't going to make that easy. He said, "Just walk down to the courthouse and back with me, that's all. Won't take more than fifteen minutes."

She hesitated. He thought she was as pretty as he had ever seen her, a little flushed from the heat of the day gathering inside the café. The fresh air really would do her some good, he told himself—and him, too, he hoped.

"All right," she said as she reached behind her waist to untie the apron she wore. "I suppose fifteen minutes wouldn't hurt anything. But it better not be any more than that."

"Word of honor," Pike said, holding up his right hand as if he were swearing to tell the truth, the whole truth, and nothing but the truth.

"Honor," Sophie repeated, then drew in a breath. "Actually, I've been wanting to talk to you, too, Pike." She came out from behind the counter.

He didn't know whether to take her arm or not, and after a second he decided he'd better not, even though the idea appealed to him. Instead he opened the café's front door and politely ushered her out. They turned toward the courthouse, where Pike hoped to linger in the cool shade of the trees on the lawn.

The big, three-story stone building had been set on fire during the troubles a while back and suffered quite a bit of damage, but most of it had been set to rights by this time. A few parts of it were still closed, but the rest was open for county business. Horses, buggies, and wagons were tied up around the square, and folks were going in and out, bound on whatever errands had brought them there.

Pike lightly put a hand on Sophie's arm to steer her toward a corner of the lawn that was shady and not crowded.

"What was it you wanted to talk to me about?" he asked.

They stopped next to a towering pecan tree. Sophie looked around. No one was close by, but she kept her voice down anyway as she said, "I know what you're planning to do, Pike. You're brewing moonshine again, and you're going to sell it to that man who was with you in the café that night. Your old friend, Mr. Delano."

Pike stared at her, unable to keep the surprise off his face. How in blazes had she found out about his deal with Patrick Delano?

He started to deny her accusation but then realized it wouldn't do any good. He didn't want to lie right to her face, and she probably wouldn't believe him, anyway.

She went on, "I'm asking you not to do that. Put a stop to it right now before it's too late."

As she said that, she pressed her fingertips to his forearm, a gesture that he normally found quite appealing. Under the circumstances, though, Pike knew he couldn't let that have any effect on him.

"Sophie, how do you know about that?"

"Does it matter how I found out? I know what you're doing, and that's enough. Just . . . just brewing the stuff here in Warbonnet County is against the law. Don't make it worse by taking it and selling it in another county where it's also illegal."

"What do you want me to do?" Pike asked. This conversation sure wasn't going the way he had hoped, or intended, but now that it was out in the open, he didn't see any option other than to forge ahead.

"Stop it right now. Pour out all the moonshine you're already made, and destroy those unholy contraptions you use to make it."

Slowly, Pike shook his head.

"I can't do that," he said. "I made a deal. Gave my word. You wouldn't want me to go back on my word, would you?"

"If keeping it meant you'd be breaking the law and . . . and doing something evil and immoral, I would."

"You reckon drinking is evil and immoral?"

Her chin lifted and jutted toward him defiantly as she said, "I most certainly do!"

Pike scraped a thumbnail along his jawline and sighed.

"Whether or not something is illegal is a matter for men," he said. "You start talking about evil and immorality, that goes to a different level. It takes a higher power to decide that."

"Indeed it does," she responded tightly.

"So I reckon . . ." He felt a little hollow inside as he forced himself to go on. "I reckon if that's what you believe about me, then I'm not worthy to be around the likes of you."

Regret sprang to life in her eyes as she exclaimed, "Pike! I didn't mean that you . . . well, just because you're doing something that I don't agree with . . . something that makes me feel uncomfortable . . . it doesn't mean I think any less of . . . that doesn't really make *you* evil—"

He held up a hand to stop the flood of disjointed words tumbling out of her mouth.

"No, that's all right, Sophie. I know you. You say what you mean and mean what you say. And you've made it pretty doggone clear that you and I can never see things the same way." His voice hardened as he went on, "It'd be mighty foolish to think that as mismatched a pair as us could ever pull in double harness, wouldn't it?"

She was breathing harder now, her lips open a little as she stared at him. She said, "You thought . . . you hoped . . ." She stopped and swallowed. "What did you want to say, Pike? Why did you bring me down here?"

"Just figured I'd say so long, since I won't be seeing you for a while," he drawled, forcing himself to sound a lot more nonchalant about it than he felt. "In another day or two, I'll be gone for a couple of weeks, at least." He brought his hand up and ticked a finger against his hat brim. "You take care of yourself, Sophie. I'll be seeing you."

As he turned away, she said, "You won't even walk me back to the café?"

"Didn't figure you'd want to be seen anymore with the likes of me."

Her jaw tightened again as she said, "You are an infuriating man, Pike Shannon."

"Yep, I imagine so." His ingrained chivalry got the best of him. "But I won't make you walk by yourself."

"Never mind! Just go on about your . . . your moonshining way!"

She strode past him with her back stiff and stalked off toward the café. Pike watched her go and after a moment shook his head in regret. That hadn't gone well at all.

Maybe it was time for him to stop expecting it to, he told himself.

He let Sophie get a good lead on him before he headed back to the general store. He halfway figured she might stop, turn around, and come back to give him another piece of her mind. But she didn't. She reached the café and went inside without even glancing in his direction again.

When Pike got to Strickland's store, he spotted a familiar saddle horse tied outside, not far from the wagon he had left there. As he climbed the steps to the porch, the horse's owner came through the front door and then stopped short at the sight of him.

"Hello, Pike," Belle Ramsey said. She held a paper sack in one hand, containing whatever she had bought in the store, Pike supposed.

Pike pinched the brim of his hat, nodded, and said, "Afternoon, Belle."

Despite what had just happened with Sophie, he

couldn't help but notice how good Belle looked today. Never one to care much about convention, she wore jeans instead of a riding skirt, the trouser legs outside her boots rather than tucked in. Her shirt was bottle-green and went well with her tanned face, green eyes, dark red hair, and brown hat.

She had been known to carry a belt gun, but today she wasn't. That didn't mean she was unarmed. The butt of a Winchester carbine stuck up from a sheath strapped to the saddle on her horse.

The first thing some folks noticed about Belle Ramsey was the knife scar on her left cheek, which extended from just slightly below eye level down to her jawline. The scar was narrow and white but hard to miss. As far as Pike was concerned, though, it was just about the last thing he noticed about Belle.

The Shannons and the Ramseys were mortal enemies and had been for generations, going all the way back to the Ozarks from which both families had sprung. Belle had already had a falling-out with the rest of her bunch, though, even before her vicious cousin Doak had taken a knife to her face and given her that scar.

These days, she was the last of the Ramseys in War-bonnet County, and Pike figured the feud was over. For months, he had struggled to balance the attraction he felt to Belle against his growing affection for Sophie Truesdale.

He and Belle had a lot more in common, that was for sure. She could ride and shoot and had a lusty streak that she didn't believe in keeping repressed, as Sophie did. She and Pike had had some good times together, although he had a difficult time imagining any real future with Belle.

She was still a Ramsey, after all.

On the other hand, after the conversation he'd just had

with Sophie, it was pretty obvious that he didn't have any future with *her,* either. So he didn't feel quite as bad about noticing how easy on the eyes Belle was today—and every day.

John Strickland's clerks had loaded a pile of crates and bags in the back of the wagon while Pike was gone. Belle nodded toward the vehicle and said, "I see you're stocking up for your big trip to Pecan County."

Pike stared at her for a second, then muttered, "Good grief! Does everybody in Warbonnet know about that?"

"I don't know about everybody," Belle replied, "but I do, and I'm glad I ran into you today, Pike. I want to go with you."

CHAPTER 10

Pike's reaction turned from surprise to anger. Not directed at Belle, necessarily, but at whoever had told her about the deal with Patrick Delano.

Right now, he could think of only one person that might have been.

"Sophie said something to you, didn't she?"

"I'm not in the habit of spending a lot of time talking to Sophie Truesdale," Belle said.

Pike knew that. Sophie and Belle weren't enemies—exactly—but nobody would ever consider them close friends, either. More like they tolerated each other.

Some men might have been vain enough to believe that the coolness between the girls existed because they were rivals for the fella's affection. Not Pike. He knew better. Both Belle and Sophie were much too proud and confident for that.

It had more to do with the fact that Sophie knew Belle's family had been moonshiners for a long time, and Belle knew that Sophie was a staunch backer of the temperance movement.

Despite all that, Pike's hunch that Sophie was responsible for this was strong. He said, "Nobody else would have told you about it. What did she do, try to enlist you as an ally in talking me out of it?"

"If she did, that would have been a pretty foolish mistake on her part, wouldn't it?" Belle replied coolly.

"Yeah. She should've known that you'd be more likely to want to get in on it."

A smile started lurking around the corners of Belle's mouth. It broke out all the way as she said, "That's right. She should have known better. She tried to be friendly about it, though, talking about how she and I are both fond of you and don't want to see you doing anything that might get you in trouble." She laughed. "Darned right I don't, unless I'm going along and getting in trouble, too."

Pike shook his head and said, "Well, that's not going to happen."

"The getting in trouble part?"

"The you going along part."

"Why not?" Belle asked, and she wasn't smiling now. She looked completely serious. "You know good and well I can handle myself when things go sideways. I've saved your rear end more than once, remember."

"I remember," Pike said, "but that doesn't change anything." He looked around, saw that no one was close by, and lowered his voice as he went on, "Those wagons full of moonshine will be worth enough money that they're liable to draw the attention of every outlaw in Texas. That's why I tried to keep the whole thing as quiet as possible." His mouth quirked in a grimace. "Clearly I did a pretty poor job of that, otherwise *Sophie Truesdale* wouldn't know about it."

Belle cocked her head to the side and said, "The way you said her name just now, it sounded almost like the two of you have had a falling-out. She tried to talk you out of it, didn't she?"

"She did," Pike said grimly.

"Did she threaten to tell Andy Burnett what you're doing?"

"No." Pike didn't say anything about his own sister resorting to blackmail by doing that.

"I'm surprised. Seems like the kind of thing she'd do."

"The last time I saw her, I think she was thinking I could just go to Pecan County and straight on to hell while I was at it. Although she'd never say something like that, of course."

"Of course," Belle agreed mockingly. "Well, if you're sorry about what happened, Pike, I guess I am, too, for your sake. But it doesn't change anything. I still believe it would be a good idea for me to come with you. I'll pull my weight, don't worry about that."

"I never would worry on that account," Pike told her honestly. "Doesn't mean I'm going to agree with you, though."

"Just think about it and be fair. Don't be quick to make up your mind. That's all I ask. Can you do that?"

Pike shrugged and said, "I suppose I can."

His mind was already made up, though. He didn't tell her that.

She nodded, went briskly down the steps, and moved to the hitch rail. Pike admired the lithe ease with which she swung into the saddle. As she turned the horse, she lifted a hand in farewell and said, "I'll be seeing you, Pike. Maybe sooner than you think."

He watched her ride away and didn't notice that John Strickland had come out onto the porch until the store-keeper said, "You want me to put those supplies on your tab, Pike?"

Pike turned to him and nodded.

"Sure, that would be fine, Mr. Strickland," he said. He nodded toward Belle, who was still visible down the street. "What did Belle buy, if you don't mind me asking?"

"I don't reckon she'd think it was any secret. She bought a couple of boxes of .44-40 rounds for that carbine of hers. I guess she plans on doing some hunting."

Pike nodded but didn't say anything. If Belle got her way and rode along with the moonshine caravan to Pecan County, she probably wouldn't be doing any hunting.

But she darned sure might be among the hunted.

"Honey, if you keep rubbin' on that counter like that, you're liable to rub a hole in it."

Sophie stopped what she was doing and looked over to see Johnny Quinlan standing there with a worried frown on his face. The old-timer, with his slight stature and thinning gray hair, looked about as mild and harmless as a man could be, but Sophie knew that as a young man he had ridden with one of the ranging companies and fought Comanches when Texas was still an independent republic, and later he had fought in the Mexican War. Age had taken some of the spring out of his step, but he was still plenty tough.

He was also a good cook, which made him an excellent choice to be her helper here at the café.

It was the middle of the afternoon now, and the two of them were the only ones in the place. Some folks liked an early supper, and they would start showing up in another hour or so.

Sophie was glad she didn't have to deal with anybody right now. She was so upset with Pike Shannon that she could barely see straight. When she had gotten back to the café after their argument, she had grabbed a rag and started cleaning. That allowed her to keep moving and accomplishing something without really having to think about what she was doing.

Now, prompted by Johnny's comment, she looked down at the counter in front of her and saw that it was clean, all right. There was no reason for her to keep wiping it—except that she was so mad she might scream if she didn't keep herself distracted.

He was just so *stubborn*. Didn't he see that she was just trying to help him, that every time she pointed out to him what he was doing wrong, it was for his own good? Why would anybody get upset about that?

But maybe what she needed to do was stop thinking about it, she told herself. Maybe if she concentrated on something else . . .

"How's the stew coming along?" she forced herself to ask.

"Oh, it's fine," he assured her. "It's hard to mess up son-of-a-bi—I mean, son-of-a-gun stew."

Sophie smiled indulgently at him. Cleaning up Johnny's language was another of the projects she had taken on, and she thought she was making good progress at it, at least most of the time. She said, "We're probably going to need to cook some more biscuits—"

The sound of the little bell over the door dinging as someone came in interrupted. She turned in that direction and caught her breath.

The man who had just walked into the café certainly wasn't what she was expecting.

He was a stranger to Warbonnet, she was sure about that. Tall and broad-shouldered, he had hair as dark as a raven's wing, worn a little longer than most men preferred.

His clean-shaven face was lean and handsome, and he had the most piercing eyes Sophie had ever seen.

He wore a sober black suit, a white shirt, a string tie, and no hat. It was the sort of getup you'd expect to see on a preacher or an undertaker, but the rakish features made Sophie think he couldn't be either of those.

She might be wrong about that, though, she realized as he approached the counter, leaving the door open behind him. He carried a black, leather-bound book in his left hand. Sophie recognized it as a Bible.

Smiling, he said, "Good day to you, Sister. Would you be Miss Sophie Truesdale?"

"Yes, that . . . that's who I am," she said.

He placed the Bible on the counter. His smile widened as he said, "I'm Brother Lavon Branson."

"Oh! Brother Branson! I . . . I didn't expect you to come see me . . ."

"Why wouldn't I?" he asked. "You're the one who wrote to me and informed me of the sin festering here in Warbonnet County."

"I wouldn't call it—" she began, then stopped abruptly as she recalled the argument with Pike earlier that afternoon. Maybe sin *was* festering here in the county.

"My letter reached you in Fort Worth?" she asked.

"Indeed it did, and I'm glad it didn't arrive later. I was on the verge of leaving and moving on west. But I can't leave these parts if there's something happening here that requires my attention."

"I thought that maybe you'd just write back and say that you were praying for us—"

"Prayer works wonders," Branson said, "but it's even more effective when it's backed up by courage, resolve, and action."

"Yes, of course. I just never thought that I would even meet you, let alone have you here in my café. I mean, you're one of the most notable leaders of the temperance movement."

"I'm just a simple preacher, Sister Sophie," he said.

"And I'm Johnny Quinlan," the old-timer said as he stuck his hand across the counter.

"I'm sorry," Sophie said. "I should have introduced you."

Branson shook Johnny's hand and said, "A great pleasure to meet you, Brother Quinlan."

Johnny just grunted. He didn't seem too impressed that a great man was honoring them with his presence, Sophie thought.

Lavon Branson was known across the country for two things: his hellfire-and-brimstone preaching and his crusade against the evils of liquor. Sophie had read quite a bit about him, knew that he had started out as a minister, but as the temperance movement has spread and grown stronger in the past decade, Branson had devoted more of his time and energy to that cause. He traveled around the country with a small group of followers, conducting meetings that were part religious service, part temperance lecture. Local leaders in the movement always joined in.

A few days earlier, Sophie had read in a recent issue of the Fort Worth *Star*, the newspaper that was delivered on the stagecoach twice a week, that the famous Lavon Branson was in Dallas and would soon be traveling to Fort Worth. The paper named the hall at which Branson would be conducting his meetings, so Sophie had written to him in care of the place.

Already aware of what Pike was planning—and very upset about it, because she had harbored hopes that eventually Pike might reform enough for them to have a future together—she had poured out her feelings in the letter. Obviously, it had found a receptive audience in Brother Branson, because he was here now, as difficult as that was for Sophie to believe.

"Have you come to Warbonnet to conduct a meeting, Brother?" she asked.

"Perhaps, but I'm more interested in this so-called moonshine caravan you mentioned in your letter. I want to know more about it."

Johnny said, "What?" Sophie hadn't said anything to him about what Pike was planning, so he was surprised and confused by Branson's comment.

"It's nothing you need to concern yourself with, Johnny," Sophie told him quickly. "And since everything's ready for supper, there's no reason for you to stay. You can go on home and come back this evening to close up, as usual."

Johnny cast a narrow-eyed glance at Branson, then frowned at Sophie and said, "You want me to leave?"

"You always do about this time of day."

"Well, yeah, but . . ." Johnny glanced at Branson again. "I don't mind hangin' around . . ."

"That's not necessary."

Branson sat on one of the stools in front of the counter and said, "But don't leave on my account, Brother Quinlan. I have no objection to you being here while I visit with Sister Sophie."

It didn't escape Sophie's notice that he used Johnny's last name but her first name. It was a bit of familiarity that might have seemed forward in another man—but not one as devout as Lavon Branson.

Johnny started untying his apron and said, "No, I reckon if Sophie don't mind, I don't, neither. And it *is* gettin' on toward my *siesta* time. When you're as old as I am, you have kind of a fadin' spell in the middle of the afternoon."

Sophie patted him on the shoulder.

"You go ahead, Johnny," she told him. "I'll see you later."

He hung his apron on a hook, nodded to both of them, and left the café.

"He seems like quite a good man," Branson said.

"He is. He . . . looks out for me. I'm sure he meant no offense by his hesitation."

"And I took none. Now, why don't we move over to one of those tables where we can both sit down and be comfortable, and you can tell me about everything that has you so concerned."

"All right. Would you like some coffee? You drink coffee, don't you?"

Branson laughed and said, "I certainly do. And from what I can smell, what you've brewed in that pot will be delicious!"

Chapter 11

Branson sat at one of the tables with its neat checkered cloth. Sophie brought saucers with cups of coffee on them and set them down, then went to the door and turned around the sign so it read CLOSED.

"Do you normally close the café in the afternoon?" Branson asked.

"No, but I might as well," she said as she sat down in the chair across from him. "Nobody will be coming in for a while. After we talk, I'll turn the sign around again."

"All right." He took a sip of the coffee and smiled. "Just as I predicted. Delicious."

"Thank you." Sophie left her cup on the saucer. She was too nervous to pick up the cup and drink right now. She was afraid she might spill it. "I still can't believe you're really here."

"I think you're putting me on too high a pedestal, Sister. I'm just a man, a human being like anyone else."

"That's not true. With your sermons and lectures, you've helped hundreds—no, thousands, I'm sure—escape from the demons of alcohol."

He made a slight gesture and said, "It's what I've been called to do."

"Well, you've been quite a success. Why, I read in the paper that in many of the places where you've taken your crusade, the local criminals behind the brewing of illegal liquor haven't just stopped their loathsome activities, they've gone on the run and dropped completely out of sight! You've put them out of business and scared them off, Brother Branson."

"Call me Brother Lavon," he said. "And I can't claim too much credit for sinners seeing the error of their ways and hiding in abject shame. I'm just the messenger."

"You make sure they get that message!"

Branson sipped the coffee again and said, "I certainly try." He set the cup on the saucer. "Now, tell me more about this man Pike Shannon."

"He's the most *infuriating* man. I used to believe he had a good heart, despite the life he's led. There are times when it seems like he really wants to do the right thing, and I can't deny that he's helped some people around here. The man who used to run things in Warbonnet County was much, much worse, and then there was another terrible man from Chaparral County, just north of here, who tried to take over . . ."

For the next few minutes, Sophie told her visitor about all the trouble with the Ramsey clan and then Solomon Henshaw and his hired guns, and how Pike Shannon and his family and friends had stood up to those ruthless killers.

When she was finished, Branson commented, "Your friend Mr. Shannon sounds quite impressive."

"He's not really my friend."

"*More* than a friend?" Branson asked as he cocked an eyebrow.

"No," Sophie said. "Definitely not. For a while, I thought maybe that . . . No. Let's just leave it at that."

"Of course. It's Mr. Shannon's current plans that have you upset?"

"Exactly. He's gone back to brewing moonshine. Barrels and barrels of the horrible stuff."

"What's he going to do with it?"

"He's loading it onto a caravan of wagons and taking it down to Pecan County to sell to a friend of his. It's illegal there, too, so he'll be breaking the law in two counties. Not to mention, it may well be illegal in some of the counties between here and there, I don't know about that." Sophie shook her head. "If he gets caught, he may wind up in prison."

"You wouldn't like that?"

"Well . . . no. Pike and I may not see eye to eye on everything . . . or on much of anything, really . . . but I don't want him behind bars. That would be awful."

"When is he leaving with this . . . moonshine caravan?"

"Tomorrow or the next day, he said. Whenever they get the last of their vile brew ready, I suppose."

"Who does he have helping him? I'm sure one man couldn't tackle such a big project by himself?"

"Oh, no," Sophie said. "His whole family has been involved with moonshining for years, and he has a lot of friends." She ran down the list of people involved in the scheme. "It was from one of them, a man named Tom McGreevey, that I learned about it. He was in here one day talking to another man and I happened to overhear what he was saying." Her face warmed a little in embarrassment. "I wasn't eavesdropping on purpose, I swear."

Branson chuckled and said, "Staying alert for signs of wrongdoing is no sin, Sister. In fact, it's our duty."

"I'm glad you see it that way, Brother Lavon." Sophie clasped her hands together in front of her. "Now that I've told you what's weighing so heavily on my heart, what do you think I should do about it?"

He reached out and rested one hand on both of hers, his touch light but comforting.

"Let me take some of that burden from you, Sister. I'm going to have a talk with this man Pike Shannon."

"You will? Before he leaves for Pecan County?"

Branson sighed and said, "I'm afraid that may not be the wisest course of action. You see, I rode down here ahead of my friends and fellow warriors in the temperance movement. You know that I have a group of associates who travel with me and help me put on my meetings?"

"Of course. I read about that, too."

"They're on their way here, but they won't arrive for at least a couple of days. As soon as they get here, we'll follow Mr. Shannon and his wagons. When we catch up, I'll try to talk some sense into him and convince him to destroy all that devil's brew and return home to those who care about him."

"But what if he won't listen to reason?"

Branson squeezed her hands and said, "I'm confident that he will. I can be very persuasive."

Sophie nodded.

"I can believe that," she said. "You've almost convinced me that things will be all right after all."

"Of course, they will be." He leaned back and got a look on his face as if an intriguing thought had just occurred to him. "You know what might make it even more likely that I can get Mr. Shannon to see the light of good? If you were to come with me."

"What? Me?" Sophie pressed her hand to her bosom, then shook her head. "No, I don't think Pike wants to have anything to do with me right now. You see, he and I . . . well, we had an argument earlier today . . ."

"But it's always easier to get people to see heaven when you have an angel on your side."

Sophie's face warmed again. Branson was the second man to refer to her as an angel in the past few weeks. The other one, she recalled, was Patrick Delano, who, like Lavon Branson, possessed a considerable amount of charm.

But Delano was a gambler, a gunman, and a saloon owner, while this man sitting across the table from her now was a champion of everything that was good and moral in the world. Such a compliment from him actually meant something.

Even so, Sophie shook her head and said, "I couldn't do that. It wouldn't be proper for the two of us to travel together—"

"It most certainly would be," Branson insisted. "As I told you, I have a group of associates, and there are a number of unmarried women among them. You could travel in a wagon with one of them. Then when we catch up to Mr. Shannon's caravan, you'd be on hand to help me convince him to abandon his scheme."

Sophie wanted to agree, but she forced herself to shake her head again.

"I can't. I have to run the café."

"Mr. Quinlan struck me as a very capable individual. I'm sure he could handle things here for a few days. A week, at the most."

It was true that Johnny could take care of the café. He had done so in the past, when Sophie was busy with her volunteer nursing duties, assisting Dr. Faulkner. He had filled in for her a couple of times when she was sick, too. And he was certainly trustworthy . . .

"I can see that you're thinking about it," Branson said, "but you don't have to make up your mind right now. As I said, it'll be a couple of days before my associates arrive. Think it over today and tomorrow, and then you can tell me what you're decided." He squeezed her hand again. "I'm sorry if I was pressuring you."

"Oh, not at all," she hurried to assure him. "The idea was just unexpected, that's all."

"I'm sure it was. Sometimes, though, we're called upon to take up the struggle, and it's up to each person how they want to respond to that call."

Sophie wanted to respond to it. She really did. But what he was asking seemed a lot more daring than anything she had ever done.

On the other hand, if she accompanied him and they succeeded in bringing Pike around to the right way of thinking, Branson might be impressed enough with her to ask her to go with him as he continued his crusade. Sophie had assumed she would live the rest of her life here in War-bonnet. She had a reasonably successful business, her friends . . .

But to be part of something bigger, something as glorious and worthwhile as Brother Lavon Branson's crusade, the very idea of that all but took Sophie's breath away.

"I'll think about it," she said. "I really will. I promise."

"I know you will," he told her. "And I'm looking forward to your answer."

How could anyone, Sophie wondered as he smiled across the table, ever say no to this man?

The wagons were drawn into a circle alongside a creek five miles north of Warbonnet. There were ten of them, and inside the circle were the mules and draft horses that made up the teams. During the era when immigrants moved west along the Oregon and Santa Fe Trails, it wouldn't have been a very big wagon train, but these days it was unusual to see this many vehicles traveling together.

There was a good-sized campfire outside the circle, with women tending to cooking pots. Men moved around, checking over the wagons, mending harness, graining and watering the livestock, all the daily chores that had to be performed to keep everything in good operating order.

A young man was waiting when Lavon Branson rode up after his visit to Warbonnet. He said, "Let me take your horse, Brother Lavon," and reached for the reins after Branson had swung down from the saddle.

"Thank you, Curtis," Branson said as he handed over the reins. "Have you seen Brother Titus?"

The young man pointed along the creek to the west.

"He and Brother Carter walked off that way a few minutes ago," he said. "I think they said they were going to get in some target practice."

Branson nodded and walked in the direction Curtis had indicated. The creek twisted enough that within minutes the camp had fallen out of sight behind him.

Shots began to boom up ahead. Branson knew it was a pistol going off, in the hand of either Titus Ferrell or Carter Hoyt. They were Branson's right-hand men, and both were expert shots. He knew that at one time in their lives, they had been on the wrong side of the law, before they had seen the light and joined him in his crusade to wipe out liquor and the men responsible for it.

Branson walked around another bend and saw the two men standing on the bank. Ferrell was lowering his right hand, which held a still-smoking pistol.

"Beat that," he sneered at Carter Hoyt.

The other man was lean, with a gray face pitted by childhood smallpox. He looked across the creek at the fallen log that served as their target.

Branson stopped and studied the log, too. He saw a large knot on the trunk with a bullet hole near the center of it. There were several other ragged places, close around the knothole, where bullets had struck and chewed away bark and splinters.

"Pretty good shooting," Hoyt said.

Then his hand dipped to the holstered Colt on his hip and came up with the gun, which spouted flame when its barrel had barely come level. Hoyt fired six times. He'd had a full wheel when he started shooting.

As soon as Hoyt began squeezing the trigger, Branson watched the target instead of the gunman. He saw the splinters flying, and when Hoyt's Colt fell silent, Branson peered intently at the knot. The hole in the center of it was larger now where Hoyt had hit it, but he didn't see any fresh marks around the knot.

That meant either Hoyt had missed completely with his other five rounds—inconceivable!—or else had put all six bullets into that same small area on the knot. That would be incredible shooting. Almost impossible to believe.

But Branson knew what he had seen.

"A miracle, Brother Carter," he called as he started toward the two men again.

Hoyt had already opened the Colt's loading gate. Without looking up from what he was doing as he thumbed fresh cartridges into it, he said, "Practice and natural talent."

"You're not lacking for either of those things," Branson agreed.

"What about me?" Ferrell asked. He was a rugged-looking man with a lumpy nose hanging over a thick black mustache. "That was some pretty decent shooting I did just now."

"Indeed it was." Branson knew Titus Ferrell would never be the shootist that Carter Hoyt was, but he didn't see any point in saying so.

Besides, Ferrell had his own strong suits. He was doggedly determined whenever he went after a goal and could be downright ruthless in accomplishing it.

"You find that girl in Warbonnet you were looking for?" Ferrell asked.

"Yes, I did, and she gave me considerably more information than was contained in her letter. Pike Shannon and those other sinners are taking twenty barrels of moonshine to Pecan County. Think of it. *Twenty* barrels." Branson shook his head. "Enough to cause an untold amount of human misery. And that's only the beginning. If Shannon succeeds, it will be the beginning of a steady liquor traffic between here and there. We have to put a stop to it . . . and we will."

Carter Hoyt slid his gun back in its holster and looked up at Branson with a humorless smile plucking at his thin lips.

"By any means necessary?" he asked.

"As always," Branson replied. "By any means necessary. It's what we've been called to do." He started to turn away, then paused and added, "By the way, I've asked Miss Truesdale to accompany us when we go after that caravan."

Ferrell and Hoyt both looked surprised by that. Ferrell said, "Is that a good idea?"

"I think so," Branson replied, his voice hardening a little as if to make it clear that in such matters, his decision was final. "I believe she might make a good addition to our little congregation. She seems to be very staunch in her commitment to our movement."

"Did she agree to come along?"

"She's considering it. I told her it would be a couple of days before the rest of you got here, so she didn't have to make up her mind right away. I'm confident she'll see the light."

"She's gonna wonder why you lied to her about the rest of us like that."

"Shading the truth in the service of our good works is not a lie," Branson snapped. "I told her what she needs to know . . . for now."

Titus Ferrell and Carter Hoyt watched Branson walk back toward the camp. They had told Branson they were going to practice with their guns for a while longer, although neither man really needed much practice. Both were excellent shots, a skill honed by years of riding on the wrong side of the law, and they had been able to put it to good use since throwing in with Brother Lavon Branson.

When Branson was out of earshot, Ferrell said, "You know he's got his eye on that girl in Warbonnet, don't you?"

"Of course, he does," Hoyt agreed. "He's getting tired

of Elizabeth Meadows. She's been his special *disciple* for, what, six months now?"

"Yeah. Longer than most. That's why he wants the Truesdale girl to come along. It don't have anything to do with persuading Shannon to dump that moonshine and turn back."

Hoyt made a contemptuous sound and shook his head.

"He just wants her in his wagon, in his bunk," the gaunt gunman said harshly. "Then they can agonize over their sins, pray for forgiveness . . . and do it all over again." His narrow shoulders rose and fell. "But that keeps him busy, I suppose, so he doesn't pay much attention to what we're doing. And when the spirit moves him . . . when he starts practically foaming at the mouth like he does . . . it's easy to get him to do what we want."

"How much do you reckon that caravan of moonshine will be worth once we've gotten rid of Shannon and his bunch?"

"The biggest payday yet," Hoyt said as he swiveled back toward the log on the other side of the creek and his gun whispered out of its holster. The Colt bucked and roared as Hoyt emptied it again, sending splinters flying as bullets slammed into the fallen tree.

CHAPTER 12

Pike spent the next day helping load the barrels of moonshine onto the wagons. The runs were complete, and when Sam Crow and Will Fisher brought their wagons to the Shannon ranch late that afternoon, Pike stood on the porch, looked at the five sturdy vehicles lined up with their beds full of barrels, and said to Torrance and Dougal who stood there with him, "That's the biggest doggone bunch of moonshine I ever saw in my life."

"I reckon somebody must've put together a bigger load somewhere, sometime," Dougal said, "but if they did, I never heard tell of it!"

"I shouldn't say it, but I'm kind of proud of what we've done, myself," Torrance added.

Pike nodded toward the wagons and said, "We're breaking the law, you know."

"I know. And I've tried to be a law-abiding man. I never did completely support what Pa and Tyree were doing, when they were cooking 'shine regularly . . . but that right there in front of us represents a lot of hard work."

"Good-quality work, too," Dougal added. "Legal or not,

that 'shine's just as smooth as can be and packs a kick like an Ozark Mountain mule." He licked his lips in appreciation. "I ought to know. I sampled it regular-like, whilst we was cookin' it."

Pike grinned and said, "I made sure that Sam and Will were doing good jobs, too. Yes, sir, Patrick shouldn't have any trouble selling that stuff and getting a good price for it. We're all going to make a nice profit from this deal."

A lot of boisterous voices were coming from inside the house. Sam and Will had brought their families with them when they arrived with the wagons. Mary and Nessa had welcomed the wives and children, and Tom McGreevey and Hebner Dawson were on hand, too. Tonight there would be a big supper with more than a dozen people crowded into the Shannon dining room. Mary probably still had reservations about the plan, but she had put them aside in the excitement of having so much company.

Fiddler confirmed that when he joined Pike, Torrance, and Dougal on the porch and said, "I haven't seen Mary quite this happy in a while. She really does love having guests."

"Are you sure you wouldn't rather stay here with her, Fiddler?" Pike asked.

"No, I'll miss her, of course, but this family has been very good to me, and I'd like to pay back some of that kindness. I'll go along and help out in any way I can, whether it's driving a wagon, tending to stock—"

"Or fighting off outlaws?" Torrance said.

Fiddler frowned and asked, "Do you really believe we'll be attacked?"

"Can happen," Pike replied. "But it's impossible to say

what *will* happen. Only way to find out is to set off for Pecan County and stay alert for trouble."

Torrance rubbed his chin and said, "We're going to need to post guards tonight, aren't we? It's not likely anybody would try to steal those wagons right out from under us before we've even started, but we can't rule it out."

"I thought the same thing," Pike said with a nod. "Hebner already volunteered to take the first shift, since he's not leaving with us tomorrow."

"Let me take the second one," Fiddler said. "I won't be driving right away, so if I'm a little tired, it won't matter. I could always climb in the back with the barrels and get a nap!"

"All right, Fiddler. We're obliged to you." Pike had known the little man long enough now to trust him. Fiddler was no longer the amiable but hopeless drunk he'd been when Pike first met him.

"It's the least I can do," Fiddler said, "considering the way you've all welcomed me."

Torrance suddenly leaned forward and rested his hands on the porch railing as he peered along the lane leading to the ranch headquarters.

"Somebody's coming," he announced.

Pike had already heard the hoofbeats and picked up the movement of the rider approaching the house. He went down the steps and waited as the horsebacker came closer. His thumbs were hooked in his gunbelt, and he had a casual but watchful air about him.

That eased as he recognized the rider. He turned his head a little and said over his shoulder to the others on the porch, "It's Belle Ramsey."

"You told us she wanted to come along," Torrance said. "It doesn't look like she's changed her mind."

That came as no surprise to Pike. Once Belle reached a decision, she wasn't just about to go back on it. She was as stubborn as anyone he had ever run across.

Except maybe Sophie Truesdale. Pike wasn't sure *anybody* could be as mule-headed as Sophie.

Belle reined to a stop in front of the house and rested her hands on the saddle horn.

"Hello," she said as she nodded to them. "I see all the Shannon men are in one place."

"I'm pleased that you include me in that number, Miss Belle," Fiddler said. "If indeed you do."

She smiled at him and said, "I reckon you ought to be considered an honorary Shannon by now, Fiddler."

"And an honor it is," the little man said.

Pike asked, "What are you doing here, Belle?"

He figured he knew the answer to that question already. Belle wore jeans and a brown shirt. The chin strap of her hat was tight. Her carbine was in the saddle boot, and she had a gunbelt with a holstered revolver attached to it strapped around her trimly curved hips.

"I told you I was going to join your little caravan, Pike," she said. "I figured you were probably about ready to leave, and I didn't want you slipping out of this part of the country without me."

"I never said you could come along."

"You promised you'd consider it."

"I did," Pike said. "I considered it. And I still don't agree with it."

The front door opened behind him. Nessa said, "Belle, you made it! Get down from your horse and come on inside."

Pike turned to look at his sister and asked, "You knew she was coming out here this afternoon?"

Defiance appeared on Nessa's face as she said, "I might have gotten word to Belle that we'd be leaving in the morning."

Pike glanced back and forth between the two redheads. "So you're ganging up on me?"

Dougal said, "I reckon you're outnumbered, Pike."

"But she's a *Ramsey*!"

"That feud is in the past," Torrance said. "If the rest of us can put it behind us, you should be able to, as well, Pike."

"Then forget about the fact that she's a Ramsey. She's a woman—"

Nessa said, "I'm coming along, so that argument doesn't hold water anymore."

Dougal scratched at his beard and said, "I believe in protectin' the womenfolks just as much as you do, Pike, but you got to admit, Nessa and Belle are both mighty good at ridin' and shootin', and they don't lose their heads when Hades is breakin' loose like some females do. I ain't sayin' I *like* the idea of them comin' along with us, but I know that if we don't let 'em do what they want, we'll just have them taggin' along behind us anyway. They're liable to run into even more trouble that way."

That was one of the arguments Nessa had used, and Pike still didn't see a way around it. He felt like scrubbing a hand over his face in exasperation, but instead he said, "Do both of you girls swear that you'll do as you're told?"

"Of course," Nessa said.

"As long as you're reasonable about it," Belle said.

"Fine. Then I guess we can give it a try."

Nessa said, "Belle, get down off of that horse and come

on inside. I don't know if you've met everyone we have visiting right now. Pike, put Belle's horse in the barn."

"Sure," Pike said, then added sarcastically, "Anything else I can do for you ladies?"

"We'll let you know if there is," Nessa told him with a smug smile. She linked arms with Belle and took her on into the house.

Torrance grinned at Pike and said, "So, you got a couple of headstrong girls to swear that they'll behave themselves. You know that promise isn't worth a plugged nickel, don't you?"

"Yeah," Pike said over his shoulder with a sigh as he led Belle's horse toward the barn. "Not even that much."

The house was crowded that night, but Mary found places for everyone to sleep. Pike and Torrance gave up their rooms and slept in the barn, along with Tom Mc-Greevey. They were up before dawn, tending to chores and leading the teams out of the barn to hitch them to the wagons.

The tantalizing smells of hot coffee, freshly baked biscuits, and sizzling bacon drifted out from the house into the predawn air. Mary and most likely Millie Crow and Angela Fisher had been up even before the menfolks, making sure the caravanners would have a hearty breakfast before they departed for Pecan County.

The eastern sky was awash with reddish-gold light by the time the men went in to eat. The dining room was packed full, as it had been the night before. Even the Crow and Fisher young'uns were up so they could say good-bye to their fathers. Everyone dug in, attacking with gusto the platters piled high with bacon, biscuits, flapjacks, and eggs. The room was full of talk and laughter, and an air of excited anticipation—and a little nervousness—hung over the meal.

When the last bit of egg yolk had been sopped up with a last bite of biscuit, and the last swigs of coffee had been drained from the cups, the men went to tend to the final details before leaving. For Pike, that meant saddling his horse.

He was doing that when Belle came into the barn to put her saddle on her mount. Pike finished tightening the cinches and lowered the stirrups, then said to her across the partition between stalls, "I can do that for you."

"You ought to know better than that, Pike," she said. "I'll be damned if I'm going to start this trip off by relying on you to do anything for me."

"That proud, independent streak is going to get you in trouble one of these days."

"I'd say it already has." She lifted a hand and lightly touched the scar on her cheek. "But I fought my way through that, didn't I?"

"And saved some lives while you were at it," he admitted. "Anyway, I didn't mean any offense by offering to saddle your horse for you."

"I know you didn't. Just don't think I'm looking for any favors from you, that's all."

"What about a share of the profits from this deal?" he suggested.

"Not that, either. Sam, Will, and Tom, they've all worked for their cuts and earned them." She smiled. "I'm just going along for the ride."

Pike nodded and said, "All right, if that's the way you want it." He led his horse out of the stall. "See you outside."

"I'll be there," Belle said.

She emerged from the barn a few minutes later, holding the reins of her saddle mount. They would be taking along a small remuda of extra draft horses and a few spare saddle horses in case any of the animals were needed, and Pike had already decided that Belle and Nessa would be the wranglers in charge of that group. If the girls didn't like it, that was too bad. They had agreed to follow any reasonable orders, and giving them that job seemed eminently reasonable to Pike.

Of course, what was reasonable to a woman often made no sense at all to a man, Pike reminded himself, but there was nothing he could do about that . . .

Nessa came out of the house and hurried toward the barn. She called to Pike, "I'll get my horse!"

"Be quick about it," he told her. "We'll be ready to go soon."

Indeed, it wouldn't be long now. Dougal and Torrance hugged Mary and climbed onto the driver's seats on the first two wagons. Sam Crow and Will Fisher were saying their farewells to their wives and kids, and as Pike swung up into the saddle, they boarded their wagons and took up the reins. Tom McGreevey was already on the seat of the fifth wagon.

Fiddler kissed Mary good-bye and took his place next to Dougal on the lead wagon. Hebner Dawson leaned on the cane he used to get around these days and watched from nearby. Belle moved her horse alongside the extra livestock behind Tom McGreevey's wagon, and when Nessa rode out of the barn, she joined the other redheaded girl at the remuda.

Pike moved his horse over closer to his mother and held out a hand. Mary grasped it in both of hers and looked up at him as she said, "You take care of all these people, Pike, you hear me? You bring them back safe . . . including yourself."

"That's the plan, Ma," he assured her. "We shouldn't be gone more than a couple of weeks, but if it's a little longer than that and you haven't seen us yet, don't worry. Things always happen that you don't expect, and that can slow you down."

"Oh, I expect things to happen," Mary said. "You think I don't know by now that things always happen where the Shannons are concerned? But I stand by what I said." She squeezed his hand. "Come home safe."

Pike smiled and nodded, then kneed his horse into motion again and took up the lead position in front of the first wagon. He lifted his arm and waved it forward as he called to the others, "Let's move this moonshine!"

CHAPTER 13

Sophie Truesdale lived in a small, frame, whitewashed house on a side street a couple of blocks from the café in Warbonnet. Her parents had bought the house when they moved here from Austin eight years earlier, while Sophie was still in her teens. Her father had started the café and her mother had helped out there, as had Sophie.

Both of her folks had been opposed to drinking, although Sophie's mother was probably more vehement about it than her father, who, she was convinced, liked to sneak a little nip now and then. Since he was her father, she couldn't bring herself to hold that against him.

Then, after a few years in Warbonnet, illness had taken both of them, six months apart, and Sophie had inherited the café and the house.

Shaken by the quick, unexpected loss of her parents, she had considered selling the business, but if she did that, she'd have to find something else to do, maybe even go somewhere else to live. She liked it in Warbonnet and had friends here. Since she had no brothers and sisters, the decision was entirely up to her.

She had stayed to see if she could make a go of the café

on her own, and it had been successful enough for her needs.

Then the temperance movement that was sweeping the country had gained strength in Warbonnet County, and remembering the things her mother had told her about strong drink, she had thrown herself into it. It had come as something of a surprise when the local-option election actually was successful, but Sophie was thrilled. She was convinced of the rightness of the cause.

No one, to her way of thinking, embodied that cause more than Brother Lavon Branson.

Which was why, when he knocked on her door a couple of days after his conversation with her in the café, she was dressed in a neat, dark blue traveling outfit and had a small bag packed.

"Good morning, Sister Sophie," Branson said with a smile when she opened the door. He looked her up and down and went on, "I hope what I'm seeing means that you've decided to accept my invitation."

The feeling of having his gaze travel over her made Sophie warm again, even though she knew he was referring to her outfit, not her body. Instead of answering his implied question, she said, "How did you know to find me here?"

"I stopped by the café, of course, and Brother Quinlan told me where you lived. I hope it's all right that he gave me that information."

"Of course." She had her wits more about her now. He was a disconcerting man in some ways. "And yes, if I'm still welcome, I've decided to accompany you. I really want to do everything in my power to help lead Pike Shannon away from the wicked path he's chosen to follow."

"And I'm sure you will. Do you know if he and his friends have departed yet?"

Sophie shook her head. "No, but Pike said they were leaving either yesterday or today, so I'm sure they have."

"You're dressed for traveling," Branson said with a smile. "How did you know *I* would be here today?"

"I just had a feeling in my bones," Sophie replied. "As if . . . as if someone were telling me to be ready."

"And so you are. I brought one of our wagons into town in hopes that you'd join us. Are you ready to go? Is there anything else you need to do?"

She shook her head and said, "No, I'm ready," as she reached down to pick up her carpetbag.

"Let me get that for you," he said, moving quickly to get the bag. As he did so, his hand brushed against hers. It was a brief contact, but enough to send sparks through Sophie.

She ought to be ashamed of herself, she thought as she straightened up. She had been attracted to Pike Shannon and had grown fond of him, but she had never experienced this sort of strong physical reaction around him.

"You're not going to regret this, I promise you," Branson said as they stepped out onto the porch and Sophie closed the front door behind them.

"I know I'm not," she told him. "I know I'm doing the right thing."

He had left the wagon with its attached team of sturdy draft horses in front of the house. He carried her bag to the back of the vehicle and set it over the tailgate, then moved to help her climb onto the seat. Sophie enjoyed the way he held her hand and put his other hand on her arm to steady her. It would have been all right with her if he hadn't let go right away, but of course he did, so he could walk around and pull himself up onto the driver's seat beside her.

As he picked up the reins, she said, "You didn't bring any of your associates with you?"

"No, we'll meet up with them outside of town. But I assure you, you'll be safe in my company until then."

"Oh, I never thought otherwise," Sophie exclaimed. "I'm sorry, Brother Lavon, I didn't mean to imply—"

"No, no, that's quite all right," he cut in smoothly. "You see, I can understand how a young woman as attractive as you are would become accustomed to dealing with unwanted male attention."

Sophie started to protest that she wasn't all that attractive, but she knew she would be guilty of false modesty if she did that, so she didn't say anything.

"At the same time, such a fine, upstanding lady as yourself wouldn't want even a whisper of scandal to sully her reputation," Branson went on. "If anyone ever says anything that bothers you, let me know, and I'll set them straight."

"I appreciate that," she murmured. The protective feelings she obviously roused in him made her even more certain that she had reached the right decision.

They passed Andy Burnett on the way out of town. The sheriff paused on the boardwalk where he was ambling along and lifted a hand to wave at Sophie. She returned the wave, and as she did so, she saw the curious frown on the sheriff's face. He probably wondered who Branson was and why Sophie appeared to be leaving town with him, but he didn't come after the wagon to ask any questions.

The main east-west road through Warbonnet actually turned to the southwest not far out of town, and it was at that bend where the rest of the wagons from Branson's party waited for them. As Sophie and Branson approached, a couple of men on horseback rode out to meet them.

Sophie felt unease stir inside her as she watched this pair approach. One had dark, coarse features and a heavy black mustache. The other was clean-shaven but had a gaunt, unhealthy look about him despite sitting his saddle with an easy grace. Neither looked like the sort of man who would be associated with a preacher and crusader such as Brother Lavon Branson.

Evidently, he wasn't surprised to see them, though, and had a friendly smile of greeting for them.

"Brother Titus, Brother Carter," he called to them, "I trust all is well?"

"Fine as frog hair, Brother Lavon," the mustached one replied as he reined his horse to a stop. "This is the lady you went to fetch from Warbonnet, the new recruit to our cause?"

"Indeed she is," Branson said. "Sister Sophie, allow me to present Brother Titus Ferrell and Brother Carter Hoyt, two of my staunchest allies in the fight against the evils of alcohol. Brothers, this is Sister Sophie Truesdale."

"An appropriate name for a seeker of truth," the gaunt man said as he reached up and pinched the brim of his hat. "I'm Carter Hoyt, ma'am."

"That'd make me Titus Ferrell," the mustached man said with a grin. "Welcome to our little group."

"Hello, gentlemen," Sophie said. "I'm very happy to be here."

"It's a good thing you wrote to Brother Lavon, Sister," Hoyt said. "Otherwise we never would've known about that caravan full of moonshine."

"And that would've been a real shame," Ferrell added.

"I mean, if it had gone on through without anybody tryin' to stop it."

Branson said, "Yes, we owe a great deal to Sister Sophie, and we'll owe her even more if our efforts are successful."

Sophie caught the glance that Ferrell and Hoyt gave each other, as well as the little chuckle that came from Ferrell's lips, but Branson didn't seem to notice.

"Let me move this wagon back into its proper place, and then I'll introduce you to Sister Elizabeth," he said.

Branson drove the wagon toward the front of the line, which gave Sophie the opportunity to study the other vehicles and the people on the ground as they went past them.

The wagons were all sturdy vehicles and appeared to be fairly new, expensive, and well cared for. The teams of horses were made up of strong and beautiful animals. Sophie knew from her reading that Branson's crusade was funded by offerings and donations at his meetings, and clearly he did well enough to make sure that his friends and associates were well equipped.

The people on and around the wagons were a mixture of men and women, probably two-thirds or three-fourths of them men. Most appeared to be in their twenties and thirties, with a few in their forties. All were well-dressed and clean-cut.

There were no children in the group, at least not that Sophie could see.

However, there were a dozen men on horseback who looked more like Ferrell and Hoyt. Sophie had seen some hardcases and gun-wolves in her time, especially since Pike Shannon had returned to Warbonnet County. Pike seemed to attract trouble from types like that—probably because he had lived such a life himself. The sight of these men

traveling with Branson's group made a familiar sense of
unease spring up inside her again.

She reminded herself sternly she'd been hoping for a
year now that Pike Shannon would change, would reform
and leave his violent past behind him. It was entirely possible that was what these men had done, and she needed
to give them the benefit of the doubt.

Ferrell and Hoyt were still wearing their guns, though,
she noted, and so were the other men on horseback.

But they might need those guns for protection, not only
for themselves but also for the rest of the group. Traveling
across rugged, sometimes only partially civilized country
the way they did, there was no telling what trouble they
might encounter from time to time.

A small knot of women were standing and talking next
to one of the wagons. As Branson maneuvered his wagon
into position at the head of the line, one of those women
separated herself from the group and walked toward what
was now the lead wagon.

Branson set the brake and hopped lithely down from
the seat, then turned to help Sophie. He gripped her carefully under the arms, set her on the ground, and then turned
to smile at the other woman.

"Sister Elizabeth," he said, "this is Sister Sophie."

Elizabeth was older than Sophie, in her late twenties,
and was also a blonde, although her hair was several shades
darker than Sophie's, more like the color of honey. She
smiled and said, "Hello, Sophie. I'm Elizabeth Meadows.
I hope we'll be friends."

"I'm sure we will be," Sophie said. She held out her
hand. "Sophie Truesdale."

Elizabeth took her hand in a firm but quick clasp. She

said, "I know. Lavon shared your letter with me, among others."

Sophie noticed right away that Elizabeth didn't use the "brother" and "sister" so common in Branson's speech. That wasn't a requirement among these people, she supposed. More like a habit. Their crusade against liquor was based partially on the Scriptures but also on the harm strong drink did in this world, not just its danger to a person's immortal soul. There might be members of several different denominations among the group.

"Elizabeth will look after you," Branson said. "Any questions you have, anything you need, just ask her and she'll do her best to help you."

"Thank you," Sophie said to the other woman. "I appreciate you looking after a newcomer . . . a stranger . . . like this."

"Of course. You'll soon see that once you join with us, there are no strangers among us. We are all fellow strugglers against the sins of the flesh."

Well, that was one way to put it, Sophie thought. Guzzling liquor and getting drunk was certainly *one* of the sins of the flesh. There were others.

One thing at a time. She said, "My bag is in the back of this wagon. I can get it and take it to whichever wagon I'll be riding in—"

"No need for that," Elizabeth said. "You'll be riding in this one with me."

"Oh." Sophie glanced at Branson. "I thought . . ."

He laughed and said, "No, mine is the last wagon. I've never believed in putting myself first. Although I *do* like to ride out ahead with Brother Titus and Brother Carter. That's what I'll be doing today."

He reached out to take the reins of a saddle horse that a curly-haired young man had just led up.

"Thank you, Brother Curtis."

Branson put his foot in the stirrup and swung up with athletic ease. He looked back along the line of wagons. The people who had gotten down while they waited now climbed back up onto the seats or into the backs of the vehicles. Ferrell and Hoyt rode up beside him.

"Do you need a hand getting back up on the seat?" Elizabeth asked Sophie.

"Oh, no, I can do it," she replied without hesitation. She didn't want to be a burden to anyone.

She watched how Elizabeth climbed on the wheel and then pulled herself up onto the seat, and she copied that. It was a little awkward in the traveling outfit. Elizabeth, who wore a white shirt and long brown skirt, had an easier time of it, and Sophie made a note to herself to dress more appropriately in the future. She wasn't riding on a train or even a stagecoach, after all.

"Everyone ready?" Branson called in a loud, clear voice. Shouts of assent came from several members of the group.

Branson, Ferrell, and Hoyt turned their horses, and Branson lifted an arm to wave everyone forward.

On the lead wagon's seat, Elizabeth Meadows picked up the reins and said, "Here we go."

"Yes, here we go," Sophie agreed, and she hoped that her voice didn't sound quite as hollow as she suddenly felt at setting out on this adventure.

CHAPTER 14

Pike had enjoyed his time at home since returning to Warbonnet County a year earlier, but even so, it felt mighty good to be back out on the trail again, jogging along with a warm breeze blowing across the landscape and puffy white clouds floating overhead in the vast blue vault of the Texas sky.

He rode about a quarter of a mile ahead of the moonshine caravan, which made deliberate but steady progress along the hard-packed dirt road leading southwest.

Of course, there was more to what Pike was doing than just enjoying a jaunt on a nice day. His eyes never stopped moving as he carefully scanned the surrounding countryside, alert for any signs of trouble. They were traveling through gentle, rolling hills that were heavily wooded in places. Plenty of cover for bushwhackers to lurk.

Pike didn't know exactly when they were going to run into an ambush—but he would be shocked if they made it all the way to Pecan County without that happening.

From time to time he called a halt to rest the teams. That much moonshine weighed a lot. The mules and draft horses had to put quite a bit of effort into pulling the wagons, and even though they had brought the remuda along in case they needed to switch out some of the animals, Pike didn't want to wear out any of the stock.

That also gave the humans a chance to get down from the wagons and move around. A hard wooden bench seat could get mighty uncomfortable after a while.

After one such stop, Belle rode up alongside Pike as he moved out in front again. He glanced over at her and asked, "You want something?"

"I'm just tired of eating dust back there," she said.

"Wrangling those extra animals is your job, remember?"

"I haven't forgotten," Belle responded. "But it's not that difficult. One rider can handle it. Don't worry, Nessa's back there taking care of things."

Pike said, "That doesn't really strike me as fair."

"Well, it is. We talked about it and decided to take turns. I'll ride up here with you for a while, and then I'll take over the remuda and she'll come up here. Does that meet with your approval?"

The sarcastic edge to her voice made Pike want to say that no, it didn't, and then he'd order her to go back to the remuda with Nessa and do her job.

Actually, though, in one respect Belle was right. One person *could* handle the remuda without much trouble. Those draft horses were very placid, and while mules could be balky, they weren't known for starting trouble. None of the animals were likely to try to bolt.

Pike didn't like the idea of Nessa being back there by herself, though, so he said, "A lone rider is easier to pick off if anybody is looking to jump us. Somebody might try to stampede that stock to put us at a disadvantage. There's no telling what else they might attempt. I know Nessa can handle trouble . . . but I'll feel better if you're back there with her."

"You're not just trying to get rid of me?" Belle asked with a frown.

"Nope, not at all. Fact of the matter is, I'd like it if we were out riding together just for pleasure."

Belle looked at him for a moment, then nodded and said, "I'd like that, too. Maybe when we get back."

"Sounds good to me," Pike told her, and meant it.

For a while, it had looked as if something serious might develop between him and Belle—even if she *was* a Ramsey—but over time they had sort of drifted apart. Then his interest in Sophie Truesdale had grown, but anything that might have come from that had ended badly.

And to be honest, Pike thought, Sophie being such a staunch supporter of the temperance movement was more of an obstacle to overcome than Belle being a Ramsey. You couldn't choose your family, but Sophie *had* chosen to hate something that had been an important part of the Shannon family for generations.

"All right," Belle said with a sigh. "So I'll go back to the remuda and tell Nessa that she has to stay there, too. Because we have our orders."

"The two of you wanted to pull your weight," Pike reminded her.

"Yeah, but I don't make any promises as to how she's going to feel about that."

Belle turned her horse and trotted back toward the wagons, as she rejoined Nessa, trailing behind the vehicles. Pike hipped around in his saddle to watch her go.

She was right about one thing—Nessa might not be happy about him laying down the law like this. And if his sister wasn't happy, Pike knew he could count on hearing about it later.

In a stand of post oaks on top of a hill half a mile away, Malachi "Buzzard" Bouchard watched through a pair of field glasses as the redheaded girl turned her horse and rode toward the back of the caravan. Bouchard focused on Pike Shannon for a moment longer, then lowered the glasses and turned to the man who stood beside him.

"Looks like the information the judge gave us was right," Bouchard said to Henry Coyle. "Seven men and two women. We should be able to handle that without any trouble."

Back down the hill's far slope waited eight more men, along with the group's horses. They outnumbered the people with the caravan, all right, and all ten were hardened, experienced owlhoots.

Coyle turned his head and spat on the ground. The horse-faced outlaw said, "One of those hombres is a little fella who can't be much of a fighter, and another is an old pelican long past his best days. And I ain't worried about no females. Take away the judge's spy, and that just leaves four men we need to worry about." He grunted. "Won't be any problem to kill those four."

"Oh, it'll be a problem," Bouchard said. "Don't forget, one of those men is Pike Shannon. We never crossed trails, but I've heard plenty about him. He's supposed to be pure hell with a gun."

Coyle sneered. "I never put much stock in talk, only in what I've seen with my own eyes. When are we gonna hit those wagons? They'll be well out of town by tonight. No point in waitin', as far as I can see. Strike while the iron's hot, as the old saying goes."

"Maybe," Bouchard said, nodding slowly. "I'd kind of like to get a better feel for how well their camp's going to be guarded before we make our move, though. You feel up to doing a little scouting?"

"Sure," Coyle said. "Want me to slit a throat or two while I'm at it?"

"Only if you have to," Bouchard said.

Sophie got along well enough with Elizabeth Meadows, although the woman seemed to act a little cool toward her as they headed southwest from Warbonnet with the rest of the wagons carrying Brother Lavon Branson's followers.

That first day on the trail, Sophie rode beside Elizabeth on the lead wagon, and they made the sort of casual conversation that was natural between two people thrown together like this. Sophie told Elizabeth about her life growing up in Austin, where her father had worked for the state government until he had decided to move to Warbonnet and open the café.

Elizabeth didn't volunteer much except that she was originally from Ohio and had joined Branson's crusade a year earlier after he'd held a series of lectures and meetings in Columbus, Elizabeth's hometown. She didn't say anything about her home life, but Sophie would have been willing to bet that someone in her family either had opposed alcohol vehemently—or else had fallen victim to it. Those seemed to be the most common paths for followers of the temperance movement.

Branson rode out ahead of the wagons with Ferrell and

Hoyt most of the day, but he galloped back from time to time to check on the rest of the group, and on each occasion, he stopped at the lead wagon to ask Sophie how she was doing.

"I'm fine," she assured him.

"Good. We have to stop now and then to let the horses rest, anyway, so if you need to get down and stretch your limbs, let Elizabeth know."

"I know how long to go between stops, Lavon," Elizabeth said.

"Yes, but if Sophie needs a little extra time, that's all right."

Branson turned his horse and rode ahead to rejoin Ferrell and Hoyt. Sophie saw the little frown on Elizabeth's face as she watched Branson ride away. Elizabeth didn't care for how solicitous Branson was being about her, Sophie thought.

If Sophie hadn't known better, she might have said that Elizabeth was jealous . . .

Later, in a grudging voice, Elizabeth asked her how she was feeling.

"I'm all right," Sophie told her, even though in all honesty, she was tired, and sitting on this hard bench seat was getting more uncomfortable with every mile they traveled. She didn't want to give the other woman any more reason to dislike her than she already had.

Eventually the day came to an end. Sophie had no idea of how many miles the wagons had covered—she was no judge of such things—but it didn't seem to her that Branson was making much of an effort to catch up with the Shannon moonshine caravan. That surprised her a little, but she supposed that he knew what he was doing.

They made camp at the top of a long, gentle slope down which they would descend the next morning. In the sunset, Sophie saw the trail winding its way down to a broad valley. She saw a line of trees and heavy vegetation in the middle of the valley and pointed it out to Elizabeth.

"I think that's the Brazos River. It goes through War-bonnet, but it twists and turns so much we may have to cross it more than once before it's completely behind us."

"I'm sure Lavon knows where he's going," Elizabeth said. "He's good at scouting out a path we can follow."

"Of course," Sophie murmured. She hadn't meant anything by what she'd said, but Elizabeth had taken it defensively anyway.

Every other time they had stopped, either Branson or one of the other men had helped her climb down from the wagon. Sophie didn't want to seem dependent, so she figured she could disembark by herself this time. She stood up and gripped the tall wheel, then swung her leg over and felt with her foot for one of the spokes.

She thought she had everything under control, but then as she tried to climb down, her foot slipped. She tried to hold on with her hands, but her grip slid off the wheel and she toppled backward toward the ground.

A solid figure was there to catch her. She thudded against the man's chest. His arms went around her and tightened so she couldn't fall as he braced himself with a little grunt of effort.

"Oh!" Sophie exclaimed.

"Are you all right, ma'am?" the man asked.

Sophie turned her head to look at her rescuer. She saw that it was the sandy-haired young man who'd brought Branson his horse earlier who had caught her. Curtis, that was his name, she recalled.

Her feet were on the ground now, so she was in no danger, but his arms were still around her anyway and they were standing a lot closer together than was proper. Pressed together rather intimately, in fact.

"I'm fine," she told him. "You can let go of me now."

"Oh, yeah, sure. Sorry." He looked and sounded embarrassed as he released her and stepped back.

Sophie turned, smiled, and told him, "There's nothing to be sorry about. Thank you for catching me. That could have been a bad fall."

Curtis tugged his hat off his curly hair and looked like he was about to say something else, but before he could, Branson rode up with a swift rataplan of hoofbeats and swung down from the saddle almost before his horse stopped moving.

"Sister Sophie!" he said. "I was riding toward the wagons when I saw you fall. Are you injured?"

She shook her head. "No, I'm all right."

From the seat, Elizabeth said, "For goodness' sake, Lavon, she just slipped a little. It didn't amount to anything."

"It could have," Branson snapped back at her. "Anyway, all the members of our little flock are valuable. I don't want to see harm befalling any of them."

Elizabeth said, "Mm-hmm," and nodded, but she didn't seem convinced of Branson's sincerity.

Branson jerked his head and said, "Brother Curtis, you'd better go see about the livestock."

"Sure, Brother Lavon." The young man smiled and nodded to Sophie, then hurried off.

Elizabeth climbed down from the wagon with ease and said, "The other women and I will get started on supper. Come along, Sophie, we'll gather some firewood."

Branson began, "Since Sister Sophie has just joined us,

I'm not sure it's necessary that she—" He stopped and held up a hand as Elizabeth turned toward him. "But of course, we all work together to accomplish our righteous goals."

"I don't mind helping," Sophie said. "Just tell me what to do." As she followed Elizabeth toward some nearby trees, she added, "I can help with the cooking, too. I run a café back in Warbonnet."

"I know," the other woman said. "Believe me, I know."

Sophie wasn't sure what she meant by that.

She wasn't sure she wanted to know.

CHAPTER 15

Finding a good place to camp with five wagons represented more of a challenge than if Pike had been traveling alone on horseback, so when he spotted a large open area next to a creek late that afternoon, he waved the wagons off the trail onto it. He wasn't going to pass up a spot with fresh water and plenty of grass for the stock.

The site wasn't perfect, however. Thick woods came up close on one side, providing an opportunity for enemies to lurk in the trees and underbrush. He planned to take one of the guard shifts himself that night, and he'd make sure that whoever had the job on the other shifts understood to be very alert and careful.

The men unhitched the teams, with the exception of Fiddler, who was a pretty good cook. With help from Nessa, he got started building a fire and preparing for supper. Their dinner in the middle of the day had been food left over from breakfast that Mary had packed for them.

Everything went well. Belle stayed in her saddle to keep an eye on the livestock as the mules and horses drank their fill at the creek and then grazed on the grass along its bank. Pike didn't want to go to the trouble of picketing all of them, but he decided it was unlikely they would stray. Maybe he ought to double up on the guards, he mused, so that somebody would be watching the stock all night.

The biggest danger where the horses and mules were concerned was that outlaws might try to stampede them as a distraction, then attack the camp in an attempt to wipe out Pike and his family and friends. Doubling the guards certainly wouldn't hurt anything.

By the time shadows began to gather, the campfire's flames were leaping brightly and the smell of coffee, ham, and beans filled the air. Everyone congregated around the fire to enjoy the twilight supper.

Pike wasn't going to ask Belle or Nessa to stand guard, although he suspected they would argue with him about that. He announced, "Torrance, Grandpappy, you'll stand the first watch, then Sam and Will, then Tom and I will finish up the night."

"I don't mind being a sentry," Fiddler offered.

"I'll take my turn, too," Nessa declared.

"So will I," Belle put in.

"Before it's over, all of you probably will," Pike told them, "but the way I just said is the way it'll be tonight."

"Fine by me," Torrance said.

Dougal nodded. "You'll hear no complaints from me."

"All right. When we've finished eating and gotten any chores taken care of, the rest of you go ahead and turn in. You'll need your rest. You probably don't feel too worn out now, but you will by the time this trip is over, I promise you that."

By the time full darkness had fallen, the group was settling down for the night. The two girls spread their bedrolls underneath one of the wagons. Since it was a nice night, the men would sleep out in the open, using their saddles as pillows.

Pike had taken off his hat, boots, and gunbelt and was sitting on the ground, just about ready to stretch out, when Belle came over to him and said, "This is fine for tonight, but tomorrow night Nessa and I want to take our turns at standing guard. We did a good job handling the remuda today, didn't we?"

"You did," Pike told her honestly. "From what I saw, you did a fine job."

"All right, then. That proves you can trust us to be responsible."

Pike didn't point out that they had been on the trail for only a day. That wasn't really long enough to prove anything. But he just nodded and said, "We'll see about it, tomorrow night."

"Good." Belle started to turn away, then paused and went on, "I don't believe I ever thanked you for letting me come along."

"You weren't taking no for an answer," Pike said with a smile, although he didn't know if she could see his expression in the shadows.

"You could've made it stick if you'd tried hard enough. I'm just happy to be away from Warbonnet and doing something different. The past couple of years . . . dealing with Doak and the rest of my family . . . it's been hard."

"I'm imagine so," Pike said softly. He'd had his clashes with Torrance and even with his mother, but when you came right down to it, the Shannons were family and always stuck together.

"Good night, Pike."

"Good night," he told her, and as she walked away, he thought about how nice it would have been to have Belle curl up next to him, to put his arms around her and sleep with her so close . . .

With a growl deep in his throat, Pike shoved those thoughts out of his head and stretched out on the blanket he had spread on the ground. Within minutes, he had fallen into a dreamless sleep.

There were bunks built into the wagons in which Lavon Branson's followers traveled, and after supper that evening, Elizabeth Meadows told Sophie that she could either use one of them or spread a bedroll on the ground underneath the wagon, whichever she preferred.

"The weather has been so nice that some of us have taken to sleeping outside," Elizabeth explained. "That's what I've been doing."

Sophie thought the other woman was acting a bit more friendly now, so she wanted to stay on Elizabeth's good side. Because of that, she would have said that she would join Elizabeth underneath the wagon—except for the fact that Sophie had never slept on the ground in her life, and she wasn't sure she wanted to start now.

"Aren't there . . . I don't know . . . bugs? And snakes?"

Elizabeth laughed and said, "Maybe it would be better if you slept in the wagon, at least starting out."

"I'm sure I'd get used to it—"

"No, it's all right. The bunks are there for a reason, after all."

Later, as she lay down on one of the bunks with its thin mattress, Sophie still wasn't sure she had made the right decision. But she could stay in the wagon for a night or two, she told herself, until she got used to traveling across the countryside like this.

Even though she was very tired, sleep didn't come easily. She thought about Pike and wondered if he was all right tonight. Sternly, she told herself that Pike Shannon's well-being was no real concern of hers, other than the fact that she was a good person and liked to believe that she cared about everybody, no matter who they were.

She thought about Lavon Branson, too, and how her life had changed when he walked into her café in War-bonnet. At that moment, she never would have predicted where she would find herself at this moment.

Her mind was so busy with those thoughts that she almost didn't hear the stealthy sounds coming from under-neath the wagon. When she noticed them, she told her-self that Elizabeth was just restless and moving around in her sleep.

But then she heard footsteps, and when she rolled over and lifted herself enough to peer over the tailgate, she saw a figure that appeared to be wrapped in a blanket moving away from the wagon. Starlight shining on blond hair that hung loose around the figure's shoulders told her it was Elizabeth. That had been the other woman crawling out from under the wagon she had heard, Sophie realized.

Where was she going? She wasn't headed toward the woods, as she might have been if she'd needed to take care of any personal business. No, she moved quietly along-side the wagons, which had been pulled into a loose circle when the group made camp. She paused beside one of the vehicles and reached up to put a hand on the front wheel.

As she pulled herself up, another figure appeared, this one from inside the wagon. The man stepped over the back of the seat onto the driver's box and leaned down to extend a hand to Elizabeth. She grasped it, and the man helped her climb up onto the box as well.

He pushed the flap in the canvas covering aside, and both of them disappeared into the wagon.

As Sophie watched, she gradually realized that she was holding her breath. Her heart thudded in her chest. She counted the wagons, and as she did, the knowledge broke on her brain that Elizabeth had just climbed into the wagon that had been last in line during the day.

The wagon that Lavon Branson had said was his . . .

Sophie sank back down onto the bunk, but her eyes were wide open and sleep seemed further away than ever. Although she wasn't very . . . experienced . . . in the ways of the world, neither was she a complete babe in the woods. If she was right about what she had just witnessed . . . if Elizabeth Meadows truly had slipped surreptitiously into Branson's wagon . . . there was a perfectly obvious explanation of why. Sophie wished she could believe it was something else, but she just couldn't make her brain accept that.

And it would certainly explain why, more than once today, she had felt like Elizabeth was jealous of her, just because of the way Branson had looked at her.

What the two of them did was none of her business, she told herself. And even the most devout crusader for what was right and moral might have occasional moments of weakness. Such moments weren't enough to just damn someone out of hand.

Yet Sophie couldn't help but feel a pang of disappointment. Would she look at Brother Lavon Branson differently in the morning? Even though she didn't want that to be the case, she knew it might be.

But maybe Elizabeth would be friendlier to her, if she was convinced she didn't have to worry about losing

Branson's affections. That would be something good to come out of this.

Sophie was sure of one thing as she lay there on the bunk, staring up at the arching canvas cover over the wagon bed.

It was probably going to be a long time before she dozed off tonight.

Pike came awake instantly, fully alert, as someone softly laid a hand on his shoulder. It was a skill that a man in his line of work needed to develop, if he wanted to survive for very long.

He sat up, and with his keen vision, the starlight was enough to reveal Sam Crow hunkered on his heels next to him.

"All quiet," Sam reported. "Time for you and Tom to take over. Will's waking him."

"Thanks," Pike said. He reached for his boots and turned each of them over to give it a good hard shake, just in case any snakes or scorpions had crawled in there during the hours since he'd turned in.

He pulled on the boots, shook his hat and put it on, and then stood up to buckle his gunbelt around his hips. He arched his back to stretch the muscles and rolled his shoulders to loosen them. Sleeping on the ground was nothing new for Pike, but a man never got used to it enough that he didn't stiffen up a mite.

Sam had already headed for his blanket. Pike picked up his Winchester, which he had left lying on the seat of a nearby wagon, and walked around the camp, moving all but silently. He spotted a familiar stocky shape and said, "It's just me, Tom."

Tom McGreevey had a rifle in his hands, too. He had

told Pike before they left that he wasn't any great shakes with a handgun and in fact didn't even own one. He turned sharply toward Pike, caught his breath, and said, "Oh. You spooked me a little."

"Sorry."

"No, I'm the one who should be sorry. I'm standing guard, after all. I ought to be more alert."

The same thought had gone through Pike's mind, but he didn't say it to his cousin-by-marriage. Or step-cousin, or whatever you'd call Tom McGreevey.

"Drift on over closer to the horses and keep an eye on them," Pike told him. "I'm going to check out those trees."

McGreevey chuckled. "Need to see a man about a dog, eh?"

"No," Pike said patiently, "I just want to make sure nobody's skulking around. If they are, I'd just as soon flush them out."

"Oh. Oh, yeah, sure, that makes sense. Be careful."

Pike didn't figure that needed a response. He walked toward the trees, paying close attention to his instincts as he did so.

No alarm bells were going off in his brain, but something uneasy stirred inside him, making the skin on the back of his neck prickle and the muscles in his midsection tighten. This wasn't the first time he had walked into darkness where somebody might be waiting to kill him. It wouldn't take much of a warning to make him dive forward before muzzle flame erupted from the gloom and threw lead at him.

Nothing of the sort happened. He moved into the trees, his steps almost soundless on the thick carpet laid down by many years of leaves falling and gradually turning to dust.

Pike stopped several feet into the shadows and stood there, stock-still, as he listened intently. He didn't hear anything except the typical night sounds of small animals and insects. A mosquito whined past his ear.

He drew in slow, deep breaths, searching for any scent that didn't belong there. Tobacco smoke, leather, gun oil, unwashed human flesh . . . nothing. Just rich earth and vegetation.

He stood there debating whether to explore deeper in the grove of trees and finally decided that it wasn't necessary. He didn't want to stay in here too long and cause Tom McGreevey to get nervous. He didn't know the man well enough to be sure what he would do in that case.

Pike turned to walk back out from under the oaks.

As he did, he heard the faintest whisper behind him. He didn't know if it was boot leather on the ground or just the sound of someone's clothes shifting as the wearer moved, but it didn't belong here.

And in that shaved fraction of a second, he knew that whoever had slipped up on him was mighty good, or else he would have realized they were there before now.

He twisted sharply to the side, whirling to bring up the Winchester.

CHAPTER 16

As Pike spun around, a lean shape, barely discernible as a deeper patch of darkness, lunged toward him. Something hit the rifle barrel and knocked it aside. An instant later, a man's shoulder crashed into Pike's chest and knocked him back a step because he hadn't been able to get his boots planted firmly on the ground as he turned.

Even then, he could have caught his balance if his left foot hadn't come down on a broken branch. It rolled as he stepped on it, and Pike's leg shot out from under him. With a grunt, he went down hard, landing on his rear end.

Something exploded against his jaw and drove him on over backward.

The small part of his brain that wasn't too stunned to keep working told him that his attacker had just kicked him. Landing a blow like that in the dark was mostly a matter of luck, but bad luck could kill a man just as dead as anything else.

Pike didn't figure the varmint would be satisfied with knocking him down and then kicking him. Even though his muscles didn't want to respond to his mental commands, he forced them to work and rolled awkwardly to the side. His attacker sprawled beside him with a grunt of surprise.

The man had tried to jump on top of him, Pike realized. Pin him to the ground and maybe choke him or knock him out.

He thrust the rifle butt to the side and felt it strike something. The man cursed this time. Pike didn't recognize the voice, but these weren't ideal circumstances for that.

Pike rolled again to put some distance between himself and his opponent and came up onto his knees. His finger curled inside the Winchester's trigger guard. When he saw the shadowy figure loom up again, he squeezed the trigger. The rifle cracked as flame gouted from the muzzle.

Pike was shooting to kill. His aching jaw was all the proof he needed that the man meant him harm, in fact probably intended to kill him.

In the split second that the muzzle flash lit up the thick shadows under the trees, he caught a glimpse of his attacker spinning away from the shot. Pike couldn't tell if he was hit or trying to keep from getting ventilated.

The next instant, feet slapped on the ground. The varmint was up and running away. So Pike's shot had either missed or not wounded the man badly enough to put him down.

Pike worked the Winchester's lever, brought the rifle to his shoulder, and fired again, aiming at the sound of the running footsteps.

Whoever it was never slowed down but kept crashing through the underbrush instead. Pike fired two more shots after him, but the sounds faded and he knew his bullets had missed. He grated a disgusted curse.

By now the shooting had roused the camp. Shouts came from that direction, as well as hurrying footsteps. Pike was on his feet by the time he heard Torrance call, "Pike! Pike, where are you?"

"Here under the trees," he shouted back. "Hold your fire, I'm coming out."

He walked into the open and found the entire group waiting there, ready for trouble, including Nessa and Belle, who both clutched rifles. Except for Tom McGreevey, who had also been on guard duty, none of them were wearing boots. They had all run out here in their sock feet after hearing the shots.

Torrance stepped forward and asked, "Are you all right? What happened?"

"Sounded like you was fixin' to fight a war in there, boy," Dougal added.

Before Pike answered, he worked his jaw back and forth to see how much damage the kick had done. He could tell now that the impact must have been a glancing one, or else the kick would have broken his jaw, more than likely.

As things stood, it ached pretty bad, but he didn't believe he'd have any more than a bruise come morning.

"I had a little hunch somebody might've been hiding in the trees, waiting to cause trouble. I'd about decided I was wrong, but then somebody jumped me."

"One man?" Torrance asked.

"I only tangled with one, and when I started shooting and he lit a shuck out of here, it sounded like just one man." Pike shrugged. "Of course, there could have been more and I just didn't see or hear them." He sounded pretty disgusted with himself as he added, "I sure didn't hear or see the varmint who jumped me until it was almost too late."

"We should take a better look around," Torrance suggested. "See if we can find anything that might tell us who he was, or if he had any friends with him."

Fiddler said, "I'll go back to camp and stir the fire up, so we can fashion a torch."

"No, all of you go back and turn in again," Pike said. "Morning will come early. We'll have a look under the trees then. That'll be soon enough. In the meantime, Tom and I will continue standing guard."

McGreevey said, "I'd better get back to watching the livestock. Our enemies might try to take advantage of our attention being elsewhere."

"Good thinking," Pike told him.

The others were a little reluctant to go back to their bedrolls, especially the two girls. Pike couldn't tell if they were spooked, worried about him, or some of both.

Torrance lingered and said quietly to Pike, "This proves you were right to be worried. Somebody must have bird-dogged us from the ranch." He shook his head. "I reckon it was too much to hope that we could keep what we're doing a secret. Somebody was bound to find out . . . and once word got around, that much moonshine is just too tempting a target."

"We've come too far to turn back," Pike said. "We'd done that as soon as we left the ranch. I'm not going to let a little trouble stop me from keeping my word."

Torrance clapped a hand on Pike's shoulder in a show of brotherly affection that wasn't very common between them.

"Neither am I," he said. "They'll see that taking on the Shannon family isn't a good idea."

* * *

A gray glow had barely started to seep into the eastern sky, a harbinger of the dawn that would arrive in a couple of hours, when one of the guards nudged Malachi Bouchard's shoulder with his booted toe and said, "Somebody comin', boss."

Bouchard uncoiled from the ground with blinding speed, coming up with a pistol in his hand that wound up cocked and ready to fire with the muzzle only a few inches in front of the guard's shocked and terrified face.

"Don't shoot, boss!" he bleated. "It's just me, Chuck Brent!"

Bouchard's lean figure was taut. Gradually he relaxed as the camp slowly came awake around him. One of the other men said, "Yeah, it's just Chuck, Buzzard. Don't kill him."

Finally, with a snarl on his lips, Bouchard tilted the gun barrel up, away from the guard's face, and eased the hammer back down.

"That was a damn fool thing to do, Brent," he said. He wasn't wearing his gunbelt, having taken it off before he lay down to sleep, so he stuck the Colt in the waistband of his trousers. "I came mighty close to blowing your brains out."

"I know, boss. Believe me, I know!"

"You haven't been riding with us for all that long," Bouchard went on, "so I'll let it go this time. Next time you need to wake me up, though, you be a lot more careful about it."

"I will, I swear it."

"So, what's so important that you nearly got yourself shot over it?"

"Oh!" the outlaw exclaimed. "I almost plumb forgot. I heard a horse coming."

"You forgot?" Bouchard felt like putting a bullet through the man's head, but this time firing such a shot would have been deliberate, not instinctive. "You can't afford to forget something like that when you're standing guard."

"Sorry—"

"Shut up." Bouchard listened. He heard the horse approaching, too. The rider wasn't getting in any hurry. Bouchard didn't think that meant trouble, but you couldn't be sure about that. He said, "Is Coyle back?"

"No, I haven't seen him—"

Bouchard pulled the gun out of his waistband and stalked away from the campfire, which by this time of the early morning was just a circle of faintly glowing embers.

"Henry, is that you?" he called as he held the gun ready.

"Yeah," came the reply. "I was about to sing out, hello, the camp."

"Come on in," Bouchard told the man who was unofficially his second-in-command.

Henry Coyle rode up a moment later and swung down from his saddle. Although the light was bad, Bouchard could tell that Coyle was moving a little stiffly.

"What happened?" Bouchard asked. "I expected you back before now. Are you hurt?"

"Just banged up a little." Coyle rubbed his side. "Might have a cracked rib where Pike Shannon rammed a rifle butt against it."

"What?" Bouchard exclaimed. "Why were you tangling with Shannon? Is he dead?"

"That was the general idea," Coyle said with a note of

bitterness in his voice. "I found their camp without any trouble, and I thought maybe if I hung around, Shannon might take a turn at guard duty and I'd get a chance to jump him. Let's face it, Malachi, without him around, the rest of that bunch would be a lot easier to dispose of."

Bouchard couldn't argue with that. "So you jumped him . . . but you didn't kill him?" he guessed.

"That's right. I was hiding in some woods close to their camp, and he waltzed right in there. It was the perfect chance to get rid of him." Coyle shook his head. "He's a handful in a fight, though. I was about to plant my knife right in the middle of his back, but he got out of the way somehow and turned the tables on me." Coyle pressed a hand to his side again. "I had to get out of there. I got in a good lick or two first, though."

Bouchard snorted. "A good lick isn't going to help us. What you've done is warn Shannon that somebody was snooping around. He's liable to be even more alert now."

"That's not likely," Coyle said. "If he's as smart as you seem to think he is, he would've figured out before he ever left Warbonnet County that that much moonshine is going to attract some unwelcome attention."

Bouchard glared at him in the gray light for a moment, then shrugged.

"What's done is done," he said. "I reckon you got a good look at the precautions they were taking?"

"They had two guards posted all the time, one keeping an eye mostly on the livestock and the other moving around the camp."

"That's probably what Shannon will do tomorrow night, too," Bouchard mused. "We'll figure out some way to distract them."

"We're going to hit them then?"

"That's right. After tonight, Shannon may not expect us to make our move so soon." Bouchard closed his right hand into a fist. "That moonshine's going to make us rich, and the sooner we get it, the better."

CHAPTER 17

The others were up before dawn the next morning. Pike and Tom McGreevey had stood watch the rest of the night, but nothing had happened, which was about what Pike expected. After the fight in the woods, he didn't think whoever was stalking the caravan would make another move quite so soon.

Fiddler and Nessa prepared breakfast. Pike ate some bacon and flapjacks, gulped down a cup of coffee, and then, as soon as it was light enough to see, took his rifle and walked out to the grove of oaks where somebody had jumped him.

Sam Crow joined him. Most folks around Warbonnet County assumed Sam was an Indian, or at least a half-breed. Pike didn't know or care, one way or the other. All he knew was that the stocky man was a formidable fighter and a strong ally.

Sam was also a good tracker, which in most people's mind was another point in favor of him being an Indian. Pike knew that wasn't necessarily true. He had been ac-quainted with plenty of white men who could track a single snowflake through a blizzard, as well as some Indians who couldn't find their own rear ends with a map.

It wasn't hard for Pike to locate the spot where he had clashed with the shadowy figure. Sam immediately pointed out something lying on the ground. Pike bent down and picked up a bone-handled hunting knife.

"Reckon this is what he was trying to stick in my back when I heard him coming," Pike said. "It's a good thing I got out of his way."

Sam nodded and said, "I don't see anything else around here that he might have dropped. He took off that way." He pointed to the north.

They followed the sign until they came out of the trees. That was where the lurker had tied his horse. The fairly fresh droppings they found were proof of that.

Pike and Sam both hunkered on their heels and studied the hoofprints, looking for anything distinctive about them. Such knowledge might not ever come in handy, but it wouldn't hurt anything to do that, either.

"He was alone, no doubt about that," Sam said. "A scout for a larger bunch? Or a lone man, maybe just a simple thief?"

"A simple thief would have tried to sneak on into camp to steal something," Pike pointed out. "And when I came into the woods, he would have gone to ground and hoped that I wouldn't stumble over him. He wouldn't have jumped me like that."

"But a scout would have?"

"Maybe. If he knew who I was and believed he'd been handed an opportunity to get rid of me."

Sam grunted and said, "It would be easier for him and his friends to steal that moonshine if they didn't have you to deal with. Nobody's going to argue with that." He rubbed his chin in thought. "It seems to me like the rest of the way to Pecan County, you might just have a target painted on your back, Pike."

"Won't be the first time," Pike said. "And probably not the last."

Sophie wasn't sure when she went to sleep the night before, but she hadn't ever heard Elizabeth come back to the wagon, she knew that. And that meant the other woman must have spent the night in Lavon Branson's wagon.

Now that she knew that, it didn't change anything, Sophie told herself. She still wanted to stop Pike Shannon from delivering that big load of moonshine to Pecan County—no matter what Branson did, or who he did it with.

In order to prevent embarrassment, she was going to pretend what she'd learned last night had never happened. She smiled and said good morning to Elizabeth in as friendly a fashion as she could manage. Thankfully, Elizabeth seemed to be in a better mood this morning, too.

"Did you sleep well?" she asked Sophie as they prepared breakfast.

"Like a log," Sophie replied without hesitation. "I guess I was tired after yesterday."

"Have you ever driven a wagon before?"

"As a matter of fact, I have. A little."

"Maybe you'd like to handle the team some of the time today. I'm not sure driving wears a person out quite as much as just riding all day."

"Thanks." Sophie smiled. "I'd like that."

The sound of a footstep made her look around. Lavon Branson was approaching them.

He had a flat-crowned black hat on his long dark hair

today. He smiled, nodded, and pinched the brim of it as he said, "Good morning, ladies. I trust you slept well?"

A small part of Sophie wanted to call him a hypocrite and tell him that he should know perfectly well how Elizabeth slept. But she wasn't going to make a scene like that, especially on only her second day with the group, so she summoned up a smile and said, "Just fine, thank you, Brother Lavon." She couldn't resist adding, "What about you?"

"Wonderful," he replied.

Sophie managed not to glance knowingly at Elizabeth when Branson said that.

He went on, "We're going to have a good day today. I can feel it in my bones."

"I asked Sophie if she wanted to try doing some driving today," Elizabeth said. "She agreed."

"I'm sure you'll do an excellent job, Sister Sophie," Branson said. "You should probably wait until after we've gotten rolling, though. It takes some experience to get the wagons lined up properly."

"Of course. I'll do whatever Sister Elizabeth advises."

Branson ticked a finger against his hat brim and moved on. Sophie supposed he didn't want to pay any extra attention to Elizabeth so none of the others might start to suspect something was going on between them.

Sophie had gotten dressed in a regular shirt and long skirt today, instead of the traveling outfit she had worn the previous day, so she didn't have as much trouble climbing onto the wagon. She might not ever be as good at it as Elizabeth, but at least she didn't have to have any help.

A short time later, Branson, now mounted on a saddle horse, rode past and called for the rest of the group to roll out. Elizabeth took the lead, guiding the wagon into position perfectly, as far as Sophie could tell. She looked back as the others formed up and saw that the young man called Curtis was handling the reins of Branson's personal wagon.

From what Sophie had seen of Curtis, she liked him. He seemed like a shy, unassuming young man. Probably innocent, as well, which meant he'd have no idea what had gone on the night before, inside the wagon bed right behind him.

Sophie wasn't going to let herself think about that.

As the wagons followed the trail down the slope, she was glad that Elizabeth was handling the reins. Although it didn't seem all that hazardous, Sophie wouldn't have wanted control of the team to get away from her. She would be better suited, at least at first, to driving when they were traveling a straight route over level ground.

She noticed one thing as she looked around that struck her as odd.

"I haven't seen Brother Ferrell or Brother Hoyt this morning," she said. "And most of the other men who were riding horseback are gone, too."

She didn't add that all the missing men, including Ferrell and Hoyt, had seemed like pretty hard-bitten characters to her.

"Oh, they come and go," Elizabeth replied, apparently unconcerned about their absence. "Lavon's either sent them out on a scouting mission, or else they're hunting for fresh meat or something like that. Don't worry about them."

"I'm not worried," Sophie said. "I was just curious, that's all."

Elizabeth looked over at her for a second and said, "It's probably not wise to get too curious about what goes on in this group. We trust Lavon to lead us on the right path."

"I trust him," Sophie said quickly. "I never would have left Warbonnet and come with you if I didn't."

Elizabeth just said, "Hmm," and concentrated on her driving.

Sophie thought about what the other woman had said about not getting too curious. Maybe she was getting carried away, she told herself . . .

But Elizabeth's words had sounded like a warning to her.

The group of a dozen riders came up to the Brazos River and reined in. The river was fairly low, no more than a foot deep right here as it flowed over a sandy bottom.

"You ever been through here?" Titus Ferrell asked Carter Hoyt as they sat their saddles slightly ahead of the other men and studied the stream.

"No, but I can tell by looking that we need to be careful of quicksand out there." Hoyt took a coil of rope off his saddle, shook out one end of it, and tied it securely around the saddle horn. He handed the rope to Ferrell. "Tie some more ropes on there so they'll reach across the river. Can I trust you to hang on, Titus?"

Ferrell grinned and said, "You've trusted me in a lot of tighter spots than this, haven't you?"

Hoyt didn't respond to that. He just clucked his tongue at his horse and nudged the animal into motion. Slowly, he rode out into the river.

Hoyt let the mount pick its own way. The horse took its time, testing the footing with each step. The riverbed was almost a hundred yards wide. Ferrell had tied four ropes together, and they had just about run out when Hoyt reached the far bank and rode up onto it without any trouble.

Ferrell looped the other end around his own saddle horn and waved the rest of the men forward.

"Follow the rope and you'll be all right," he told them.

They made the crossing without any problems. Ferrell brought up the rear, coiling the now untied rope as his horse headed for the stream's western bank. Hoyt was waiting for him when he rode up the shallow slope on the other side.

Ferrell handed the rope back to Hoyt, glanced up at the mid-morning sky, and said, "Let's give the horses a rest for a spell."

Hoyt nodded in agreement. At Ferrell's command, all the men swung down from their saddles.

"Branson won't be able to bring the wagons across here," Hoyt said with a nod toward the river.

"According to the map he has, there's a ford a few miles downstream. That's the route he'll take." Ferrell took out the makin's and built a quirley. "Wagons can't just cut across country and take the shortest route like we can." He grinned. "That's the reason we can get ahead of that moonshine caravan."

Hoyt grunted. Ferrell wasn't telling him anything he didn't already know, but Ferrell liked to talk about how smart they were. It didn't hurt anything, so Hoyt let him continue.

Ferrell licked the paper and rolled the ends of his smoke closed, then grinned and went on, "All we've got to do is find the right place to spring our trap and then wait for Lavon to lead them into it."

Something was different about this job than the ones they had pulled in the past, though, and it worried Hoyt. He said, "I don't like the way he brought that girl along."

"The blonde?" Ferrell shrugged thick shoulders. "You

know Lavon. He may be hell on drinkin', but he's always had pretty healthy appetites in other areas."

"Maybe so, but she just joined up with us. We don't know if we can fully trust her yet. Most of those other sheep'll do what he tells 'em and swallow whatever load of bull he feeds them. We can't count on the Truesdale girl to do that."

"You forget," Ferrell said, "once they've done been with Lavon a few times, they won't do anything to cross him."

"That's just it. He's still got Liz Meadows sneaking into his wagon at night. He won't have time to get rid of her and bring the Truesdale girl fully into the fold by the time we have to make our move."

"Maybe not, but I don't see how she can do anything to really hurt our plans."

Ferrell had been holding the cigarette he had rolled. He stuck it in his mouth, dug a lucifer from his shirt pocket, and snapped it to life with his thumbnail. He held the flame to the quirley and puffed until the end glowed red. Then he dropped the match, ground it under his boot heel, and blew out a small cloud of smoke.

"Don't worry, Carter," he said. "When the time comes, we'll kill Pike Shannon and all those folks with him, and then that moonshine will be ours."

CHAPTER 18

As far as Pike knew, there was only one bridge over the Brazos River, and that was in Waco, a long ways east of where they were. Anybody else crossing the Brazos in wagons had to find a good ford where the bed was mostly limestone instead of sand—and sometimes quicksand—as was common farther upstream.

He knew of one such ford to the southwest, in the right direction toward Pecan County. The caravan reached it late in the afternoon of their second day on the trail. The river bank was worn down on both sides from the frequent passage of wagons through here.

On the western side the route climbed a couple of miles up a slope to a tree-covered tableland. That would be a hard pull for the teams, so Pike figured it was best to wait until the next morning to make the crossing, when the animals would be rested.

He waved his arm for the wagons to stop a short distance away from the river and called, "We'll make camp here and cross first thing in the morning."

"Good thinkin'," Dougal agreed from the driver's seat of the lead wagon as he brought the vehicle to a stop. He took hold of the brake lever, pulled it back, and set it. "We've come far enough for today."

Pike looked back along the line of wagons at the remuda and saw the way Belle and Nessa were riding slumped in their saddles behind the extra stock.

"I think some of us agree with you," he said to Dougal with a grin.

"Now don't go makin' light of those gals. They're tryin' hard. Nessa's more used to bein' in the saddle all day than Belle is, and even she's wore out, I'll bet you."

Pike nodded and said, "I think you're right."

He heeled his horse into motion again and rode past the wagons to the spot where the animals in the remuda were milling around some while the two girls watched them.

"You two go ahead and get down," Pike said. "I'll keep an eye on these critters."

Nessa gave a defiant toss of her head as she sat up straighter in the saddle. She said, "Don't worry about us. We can do our jobs."

"I know that," Pike assured her.

Belle snorted and said, "He probably just wants us to get started fixing supper."

"I'm sure you're right."

"Fiddler and Torrance can take care of supper," Pike said. "Can't a fella just try to be nice every once in a while?"

"Sure, but I've never known you to act like that," Nessa said. Then, like the little sister she would always be, she stuck her tongue out at him. Pike couldn't help but laugh, which seemed to annoy her even more.

"Do what you want," he told them, "but I'm going to watch these horses and mules."

Nessa and Belle glanced at each other. Belle shrugged. They swung down from their saddles and led the horses off toward the river to let them drink. Pike rode around the remuda and nudged the stock toward the stream, as well. The others were already unhitching the teams so they could drink, too.

Within an hour, the animals had all been watered. Fiddler, with a little help from Torrance, had rustled them a good supper, and they lingered in the gathering twilight over cups of coffee.

"We've made good progress," Pike mused. "We should reach Prescott in another five days. Maybe four."

"If whoever was skulking around last night doesn't come back with some friends," Torrance said.

"If he does, we'll be ready for him."

"Speaking of that," Belle said, "Nessa and I intend to take our turns at guard duty tonight."

"Not at the same time," Pike said without hesitating. "Belle, you'll take the first shift with me. Nessa, you can take the second with Torrance."

"What about me?" Fiddler asked.

Pike looked over at Sam Crow and said, "I was thinking about getting you to take the third shift, Sam. All right if Fiddler joins you?"

"Of course," Sam said. "I'll be glad to have your company, Fiddler."

"And I'll be happy to share the responsibility with you, my friend," Fiddler said. "With that settled, would anyone care to hear a few tunes before we turn in for the night?"

Dougal slapped his knee and said, "Hot dang! You brung your fiddle along?"

"I certainly did."

"Well, get it out and let's have some music!" Dougal grinned at Belle and Nessa. "If you gals ain't careful, I might even get up and dance a few jigs with you!"

* * *

They were all a little too tired for dancing, even with Fiddler's sprightly tunes to inspire them, so Dougal settled for sitting on a wagon tongue and clapping enthusiastically in time with the melodies. So did Torrance and the girls. They even sang along on some of the old folk songs.

It was the sort of peaceful, wholesome evening that had been almost completely missing from Pike's life for many years. Sitting there with family and friends as the sky turned from blue to black and the stars winked to life was a far cry from spending time in the smoky, stinking bar-rooms that had been his usual haunts.

Everything was so nice that he almost forgot how trouble could be lurking close behind them. Almost . . .

Everyone else rolled in their blankets to sleep. Pike picked up his rifle and said quietly to Belle, "Come on, let's walk down by the river."

As they ambled toward the Brazos, where the stream's gently rippling surface reflected the rising moon, Belle said, "On a night like this, if I didn't know better, I'd say you had romance on your mind."

"No, I just figured we'd go over how we'll split up the responsibility on this first guard shift," he said.

Belle laughed softly and said, "Ah, there's the Pike Shannon I know. Strictly business."

"Blast it, Belle, don't twist things around. After a while, it seemed like any courting we might do wasn't ever going anywhere."

"Because you were interested in Sophie Truesdale."

"A fella has trouble, sometimes, getting everything sorted out in his head." He didn't like the way her words made him feel defensive. "Before we left Warbonnet,

Sophie made it pretty plain she doesn't want anything more to do with me."

"So you can turn your attention back to the Ramsey girl, is that it? Your second choice?" Belle's tone was quiet, but the words were scathing. "I know you're not used to hearing this, Pike, but you took your shot . . . and you missed."

His jaw tightened. "All right, Belle. I don't reckon you can put it any plainer than that."

"That doesn't mean I'm not a friend to your family anymore, though. You've got to believe that."

"I believe it," Pike said. "But I also noticed you said you were a friend to my family . . . not to me."

She looked at him for a moment before saying, "I'll always be your friend, Pike, whether you believe it or not."

"Let's just keep an eye on the camp," he suggested.

"Fine. You think your *friend* from last night will show up again?"

"The one who tried to stick a knife in my back?" Pike laughed, but there wasn't much humor in the sound. "He'll have a harder time of it tonight. There's not nearly as much cover around this spot." He nodded toward the carbine in Belle's hand. "Keep that repeater close, though. Never can tell when you might need it."

They split up then, Belle to keep an eye on the remuda and the wagons while Pike circled the camp. He couldn't go completely around it because they had the Brazos on one side, so when he reached the river bank he stopped, listened intently for a few minutes, then turned around and retraced his steps when he didn't hear anything out of the ordinary.

He was on his third trip around the sleeping camp like

that, walking quietly toward the river, when something caught his attention. A light flared on the other side of the Brazos. At first Pike thought it was just a trick of the eye, or maybe the moonlight reflecting off an old air-tight or something that some pilgrim had thrown down over there in the past.

But no, he realized, what he was seeing wasn't a reflection. It moved, and the red and yellow quality of the glow wasn't from a glint of moonlight.

Somebody over there had struck a match and was waving it back and forth. That could only be a signal of some sort.

And that couldn't mean anything good.

He stiffened and was about to let out a yell that would rouse the camp, when he heard a faint splash off to his left. He looked in that direction and saw a dark shape moving out into the water, wading across the river. Anger welled up inside him.

Somebody in the group was double-crossing them, Pike realized, and as far as he was concerned, the traitor could only be one person. He didn't like to think that a member of the family, even one who wasn't a blood relation, would do such a thing, but he was certain enough that he lifted his voice in a shout as he broke into a run toward the river.

"Tom!" he bellowed. "Tom McGreevey! Stop right where you are, you no-good skunk!"

Twenty yards into the shallow river, with the water flowing around his calves, Tom McGreevey halted abruptly and twisted around toward the camp. His arm came up. Colt flame bloomed in the darkness as McGreevey fired.

Pike didn't know where the bullet went. It didn't come close enough for him to hear it. There was no doubt that

McGreevey had just shot at him, though, and anybody who threw lead at Pike Shannon could expect to have some bullets coming back in his direction.

Pike brought the Winchester to his shoulder, working the lever in the same move, and squeezed the trigger. The rifle cracked, the report echoing along the river.

McGreevey went down hard, falling into the water with a big splash that threw droplets high in the air around him.

At the same time, Pike saw muzzle flashes from the other side of the river and heard a bullet whine past his head, too close for comfort. He knew the bushwhackers over there were aiming at the flash from his rifle.

The shooting would have everybody else in camp awake by now. As he levered his Winchester, he raised his voice and yelled, "Everybody stay down! Hunt cover!"

He snapped a shot in the general direction of the bush-whackers, then threw himself into a roll that carried him along the river bank. Bullets thudded into the ground near him, spraying him with small clumps of dirt.

He came to a stop on his belly, fired twice more at the gunmen hidden in shadows across the river, then powered to his feet and sprinted toward the wagons. Ahead of him he saw spurts of flame from behind the vehicles as the other members of the group realized what was going on and opened fire, as well.

"It's me, Pike!" he shouted over the racket. He didn't want any of his allies spinning around and ventilating him as he ran up.

He glanced toward the remuda. Everybody else had been close to the wagons when the attack started and should have been able to make it to cover pretty quickly.

He wasn't sure about Belle, though, and wished he knew where she was.

He couldn't dwell on that, because more lead was zipping through the air around him. He concentrated on running, and a few frenzied heartbeats later, he reached the nearest wagon and ducked behind it alongside a figure who straightened up long enough to fire a rifle toward the bushwhackers, then ducked back down.

"Pike, is that you?"

Pike recognized Nessa's voice, even though he couldn't see her very well. He hunkered down and leaned against the front wheel on this side of the wagon as he said, "Yeah, it's me. Are you all right?"

"I'm not hit. How about you?"

"I'm fine," Pike said. "Everybody else?"

"I don't know. From the amount of shooting going on, I think they're all okay."

"Have you seen—"

He started to ask about Belle, but at that instant, a slug smacked into the wagon wheel only inches from him, chewing splinters from the wood and stinging his face. That was bad, mighty bad.

Because that shot had come from the other direction, and as Pike twisted around he spotted half a dozen riders charging toward the camp, the guns in their hands spouting fire and lead.

CHAPTER 19

"Get under the wagon!" Pike told Nessa. "Stay as low as you can!"

With them caught in a crossfire, here on the river bank, there was no good place to go. By getting under the wagons, the wheels would provide some cover, and some was better than none, Pike supposed.

He covered his sister's move by cranking off three swift shots at the attackers on horseback while Nessa scrambled underneath the wagon. Pike was surprised to see one of the men fling his arms in the air and topple off his running horse. He'd just been trying to blunt their charge. But any damage he could do, he'd take it and be grateful.

By now, the others in the group had realized they were under attack from two directions at once. Some continued firing at the riflemen across the river while the rest twisted around and got busy with their guns. Muzzle flashes lit up the night like a terrific electrical storm. Gun thunder crashed almost continuously.

Nessa opened fire from under the wagon. Between shots, she called, "Pike, get under here!"

He dropped to the ground and wriggled backward, then

rolled behind the wheel against which he had been leaning a few moments earlier. As he lay on his belly, he braced himself on his elbows and raked the attackers with several more shots. None of the riders fell this time, but they veered apart and peeled away from the assault.

"We've got them on the run!" Nessa enthused.

"Don't be so sure," Pike warned her. His Winchester had run dry. He always carried spare cartridges in his pocket, so he dug them out and began thumbing them through the rifle's loading gate as he went on, "They could regroup and double back."

That didn't appear to be the case. The attackers looked like they were trying to light a shuck out of here, heading back toward the line of trees in the distance from which they had emerged. With his rifle reloaded now, Pike sent a few shots after them to hurry them on their way.

He lowered the Winchester and twisted his head to look back over his shoulder at the river and the dark slope on the far side. He realized he didn't hear any shots coming from across the Brazos or see any more muzzle flashes. The men hidden over there must have realized that their partners on this side of the river had broken off the attack and fled. He hoped they were giving up, too.

From underneath one of the other wagons, Torrance called, "Pike, are you all right?"

"Yeah! How about the rest of you?"

"Fine as frog hair!" Dougal replied. Fiddler, Sam Crow, and Will Fisher chimed in, as well, letting Pike know they weren't hurt. A lot of bullets had been flying around, but in the darkness, none of them had found their targets.

But he hadn't heard Belle respond, Pike thought, and

that realization made a cold ball form in the pit of his stomach.

"Belle!" he called. "Belle, can you hear me?"

There was no reply.

"Torrance, where's Belle?" Pike asked.

"I haven't seen her," Torrance said, sounding worried now, too. "She's not with you?"

"She was watching the remuda," Pike said. "Belle!"

Still nothing. Pike twisted around more so he could look along the river toward the area where the livestock had been gathered. He didn't spot any human figures moving out there, but the animals, undoubtedly spooked by all the gunfire, were milling around so it was hard to be sure.

"Everybody stay under the wagons where you'll have some cover in case the varmints come back," he called, then started crawling out from under the one where he had taken shelter with Nessa.

She reached over and caught hold of his sleeve. "Where are you going?"

"To see if I can find Belle," he said as he pulled loose from her grip. He could hear the urgent worry in his own voice and knew the others could, too.

"Be careful," Nessa said.

Pike didn't take the time to reassure her. As soon as he was clear of the wagon, he stood up and ran toward the remuda.

No shots rang out, either from the distant trees or the other side of the river.

"Belle!" he called as he approached the horses and mules. "Belle, where are you?"

He couldn't afford to spook the animals. Belle might have been struck by a stray bullet and fallen to the ground, and if the remuda stampeded, she could be trampled. So he moved among them carefully, at a slow, deliberate pace, his eyes searching the river bank.

His heart slugged hard in his chest as he spotted a dark shape lying on the ground. A human shape, sprawled and motionless. Pike resisted the urge to run toward the fallen figure, but he got there as quickly as he could without startling the horses and mules.

He reached the shape and dropped to a knee beside it. He was close enough now to recognize Belle. Her hat had come off, and her dark red hair flowed out around her head, looking black in the moonlight. She lay on her left side, with that arm stretched out beside her and the other lying limp against her body.

Pike set his Winchester aside and took hold of Belle's shoulders. Gingerly, he turned her onto her back and slid his left arm underneath her back so he could lift her and prop her against his leg. With his other hand, he probed around her head, working his fingers into her thick hair.

He didn't find any blood, although there was a small lump on the left side of her head, above the ear. He didn't worry about propriety as he quickly explored the rest of her body, searching for bullet wounds and not finding any.

He had already determined that she was breathing. When she moaned and stirred a little, an even stronger sense of relief went through him. Other than the bump on the head, she seemed to be unharmed, so he wasn't surprised when her eyelids fluttered open a moment later and she said, "Wha . . . what . . ."

"Take it easy," Pike told her. "The fight's over. Just lean against me and rest."

"P-Pike . . .?"

"Yeah, I'm here. I've got you. You're all right."

"Wha . . . what happened?"

"We got jumped," he said. "I'm sure the varmints were after the moonshine. But we drove them off."

"Are you . . . all right?"

"I'm fine, and none of the others are hurt, as far as I know. You were the only one unaccounted for . . . until I found you." He smoothed her hair, and as he did, his fingers brushed the lump on her head. He felt her wince. "Yeah, you got a good wallop. Do you remember how?"

"Somebody started shooting . . . a couple of the horses spooked . . . I tried to . . . calm them down . . . but one of them . . . rammed me with his shoulder . . . I remember being knocked down and falling . . . then . . . then nothing . . ."

Pike understood. When that horse had knocked her down, Belle had hit her head hard enough to lose consciousness for a few minutes, maybe striking it on a rock or just on the ground. What was important was that she didn't seem to be seriously hurt.

She tried to get up, but he tightened his grip on her shoulders.

"Just rest," he told her. "If you try to stand up now, you're liable to fall down again."

"You just . . . can't pass up a chance . . . to boss me around . . . can you, Pike?"

"No, that's not it," he said. "I can't pass up a chance to hug you like this."

"That's a bunch of . . . bull . . ."

But she sighed a little and let more of her weight rest against him. Her head lowered onto his shoulder. Her deep, regular breathing told him that she was asleep, rather than having slipped back into unconsciousness.

From the wagons, Torrance called, "Pike! Did you find her?"

"Yeah, she's here," he replied. "She's all right, but come give me a hand."

A minute later, Torrance circled the remuda and found them in the moonlight. He knelt on Belle's other side and asked, "What happened?"

"She got a bump on the head that knocked her out for a little while."

"Has she passed out again?"

"No, I think she's just sleeping now. Let's get her over there to the camp and onto a bedroll."

With Torrance's help, Pike got to his feet and cradled Belle against his chest. He could have managed by himself, but Belle was a solidly built girl, and it was easier with Torrance giving him a hand. He carried her toward the wagons.

"Sam, Will, Dougal, and Fiddler are keeping their eyes open in case those bushwhackers make another try," Torrance said as he walked alongside Pike. His voice held worry again as he added, "But I can't find Tom."

"He's in the river," Pike said grimly.

"They shot him?"

"No, I did. The son of a buck double-crossed us. He was working with them, Torrance."

"But that can't be," Torrance exclaimed. "He's kin."

"Shirttail kin, at best," Pike said. "Just before the ball opened up, I spotted a signal from the other side of the river. Somebody lit a match over there and waved it back and forth. Then I spotted McGreevey trying to wade across the river. The signal told him the shooting was about to start, and he was trying to get out before it did."

"Are you sure?"

"Positive. When I called his name, he turned around and took a shot at me."

"So you shot back."

"Yeah," Pike said. "I did. Seemed like the thing to do at the time."

Torrance sighed. "He couldn't have expected anything else. But damn, it's hard to think that a member of the Shannon family, even as distant a relation as Tom, would betray us like that."

They had reached the wagons. Nessa had piled up several bedrolls to make a more comfortable place for Belle. She told Pike, "Put her down here."

Pike lowered Belle onto the blankets. She stirred again and muttered something, but he couldn't make it out.

"How bad is she hurt?" Nessa asked as she knelt beside Belle.

"A bump on the head, bad enough to knock her out. That's all I could find."

"I'll check her over and make sure you didn't miss anything." She started unfastening the buttons on Belle's shirt. "Back off and give us some room. And some privacy."

"Sure thing," Pike said. "I need to find my hat, anyway." It had flown off his head when he first dived to the ground.

Torrance went with him as he walked toward the spot where he'd been when he noticed the signal from the other side of the river. Dougal joined them, and Pike quickly told his grandfather about Tom McGreevey's treachery.

"Blast it, I hate to hear that," Dougal said. "I've knowed that boy for a good long while. Never would have figured he was sorry enough to turn on kinfolks." The old-timer sighed. "Reckon he always did like to drink a mite too much and be a little too fond of poker and loose women. I ain't sayin' any of those are necessarily *bad* things, mind you."

Pike found his hat, banged it against his leg a couple of times, and settled it on his head.

Torrance stood on the edge of the bank, peered out over the Brazos, and after a moment said, "Pike, I thought you told me Tom was in the river."

"That's right," Pike said as he adjusted the hat a little.

"Where? I don't see him."

Pike stepped up beside his brother and lifted an arm to point as he said, "Right out . . . Wait. He went down close to one of those sandbars. We ought to be able to see his body."

Pike studied the riverbed intently for several moments, though, and didn't see anything that looked like a human shape. And the Brazos wasn't deep enough along here, and didn't flow fast enough, to wash a body on downstream.

"He's not there," Pike said. "I would have sworn I hit him."

"You probably did, but you must not have killed him," Torrance said. "He got away."

CHAPTER 20

Malachi "Buzzard" Bouchard was furious as he jerked back on the reins and brought his horse to a stop at the top of the wooded hill he had picked for the gang's rendezvous. He looked around as the five men with him reached the crest, as well.

Bouchard didn't see anybody waiting for them. That meant Henry Coyle and the men who had gone with him across the river hadn't gotten back yet.

Forcing himself to bring his anger under control, Bouchard said, "How's that arm of yours, Tyson?"

"Hurts like blazes, boss, but I think the bleeding's stopped," replied a man who had been wounded during the attack on the moonshine caravan. He'd been lucky: the bullet had passed cleanly through his upper left arm without breaking the bone.

A man named Culbertson hadn't been so fortunate. He had been shot out of the saddle, and Bouchard had been able to tell by the limp way he bounced when he hit the ground that he was dead. Probably drilled through the heart.

They had left Culbertson there. Bouchard didn't like it,

but they hadn't had any choice. The barrage of bullets from the wagons' defenders had been too swift and accurate.

"Riders comin', Buzzard," one of the men said.

Bouchard heard the faint hoofbeats from the western side of the hill. They grew louder, and after a moment the newcomers on horseback came into view, tall, dark, bulky shapes in the shadow-honed moonlight.

Bouchard drew his gun, clicked back the hammer, and called, "Sing out or die."

"Hold your fire, Malachi. It's me and the rest of the boys."

Bouchard recognized Coyle's voice. He let down the gun's hammer and pouched the iron.

"Come on up."

"We've got somebody with us," Coyle announced.

Bouchard saw now that a couple of men were riding double on one of the horses. He squinted and said, "Who's that?"

"It's me, Mr. Bouchard," said the member of the pair riding behind. "Tom McGreevey."

"McGreevey! What are you doing here?"

"I'm wounded, Mr. Bouchard. Hurt awful bad."

"Get him down off of there," Bouchard ordered curtly. "All of you dismount. I want to figure out what went wrong, and why that moonshine's not ours right now."

The outlaws swung down from their saddles. Two of them went over to help McGreevey climb down. Bouchard went on, "Somebody get a fire going and start some coffee brewing."

"You figure it's safe to have a fire, Malachi?" Coyle asked.

"I wouldn't have said that if I didn't think so, would I?" Bouchard snapped. "You reckon the Comanches are going to jump us, Henry? Any renegades still raiding these days are a long way west of here."

"I was thinking more of Shannon and his bunch."

Bouchard shook his head and said, "They'll be hunkered down for the night, worrying that we might come back and hit them again. Besides, we don't know how much damage we did to them. We may have killed three or four of them."

Bouchard didn't really believe that. He wasn't sure they had done *any* damage to their intended victims, because for some reason the whole thing had gone off too early, like a short fuse on dynamite.

Bouchard turned his horse to one of the other men to care for it, then said, "Come over here, McGreevey."

The man hobbled closer, keeping his left hand pressed to his side. Bouchard had never met him before. All he knew was McGreevey's name, which the crooked former judge Phineas Conway had given him.

"I'm sorry things didn't work out, Mr. Bouchard—" McGreevey began.

"How bad are you hit?" Bouchard interrupted him.

"Pretty bad. The bullet went in my side. I don't know if it came out or if it's still in there. Maybe . . . maybe once you get that fire going, one of you fellas can take a look at it." McGreevey paused, then added bitterly, "Damn Pike Shannon to hell."

"He's the one who shot you?"

"That's right. I heard him call my name just before he gunned me down."

"Where were you when that happened?" Bouchard asked.

"I . . . I was trying to get across the Brazos. I saw the

signal from the other side of the river . . . and I figured it would be safer if I got out of there—"

"Before the shooting started," Bouchard finished for him.

"Yes, sir. That was the plan, wasn't it? I was to keep an eye out for a signal before any attack was supposed to begin? The judge said you promised you'd let me know."

Bouchard let some of the anger he was feeling creep into his voice as he said, "I figured you'd just keep your head down until we finished off the others. By doing what you did, you tipped Shannon off early. Henry and the fellas on the other side of the river were in position, but the rest of us weren't. That meant we had to cross too much open ground to reach the wagons. It gave Shannon and the others enough time to mount a defense, rather than us being able to overrun them before they knew what was going on."

"I . . . I'm sorry, Mr. Bouchard," McGreevey stammered. "I reckon I just never thought of it like that. I just wanted to—"

"You wanted to make sure you came out of it with a whole skin, instead of running the same risks as the rest of us. Like Brad Culbertson, who we left back there dead on the ground."

"I'm sorry," McGreevey said again, whining this time. "I . . . I never got mixed up in anything like this before. I just got in too deep to some gamblers, and then the judge offered me a good enough payoff to get me out of trouble. I've never been shot, either. I sure wish one of you fellas could take a look at this wound and maybe patch it up."

Bouchard drew in a deep breath, feeling a cold calm settle over him. He said, "I reckon you do need to be taken care of."

"I'm much obliged to you." McGreevey winced and bent to the side more to favor the injury. "It sure does hurt."

"It won't anymore," Bouchard said as he drew his gun. The other men had already started to move back in anticipation of what was about to happen.

McGreevey realized it, too. His eyes widened in the moonlight. He let out a strangled cry of "No! You can't!" and fumbled at the holster on his hip. The holster was empty, though, since he'd dropped his gun in the Brazos earlier.

Bouchard lifted his gun, eared back the hammer, and pulled the trigger. The stocky McGreevey was too scared to even try to run. He stood there staring while Bouchard shot him in the head, jerking a little as a dark hole appeared above his left eye. His knees buckled and he dropped on his face.

Henry Coyle sauntered forward and said, "You want us to bury him, Malachi?"

"No, leave him where he fell. The coyotes can have him . . . if the stink of such a gutless varmint doesn't turn their stomachs."

"Oh, I doubt if the coyotes will care," Coyle said with a little chuckle. "What do we do now?"

"Let's get back across the Brazos and find a good spot to jump them again."

"They know by now that McGreevey was double-crossing them," Coyle said.

"And they'll probably figure he's dead, too. It doesn't change things either way. They've still got that moonshine . . . and I want it."

* * *

The sound of a single shot drifting through the night air made Titus Ferrell lift his head from the saddle that was serving as a pillow.

"You hear that?" he said to Carter Hoyt, who was stretched out a few feet away.

"Yeah," Hoyt replied. "Sounded like it was a mile or more away, like all those shots we heard earlier. You reckon we ought to go check it out?"

Ferrell thought about it and then said, "No, I suppose not. Whatever it was, there's nothing we can do about it in the middle of the night like this. We'll just push on tomorrow, maybe get close enough to those moonshine wagons to make sure nothing happened to them, and then get ahead of them like we planned."

"You know," Hoyt mused, "we might not be the only bunch that's after those barrels full of moonshine. What if somebody else already jumped them, wiped out Shannon and his friends, and grabbed the booze?"

"If we see that's the case, we'll need to let Lavon know right away. That plan he hatched won't work if it's not Shannon's bunch we're going after. He'll have to just hang back and let us go ahead with our part of it."

"You mean killing everybody and taking the moonshine for ourselves?"

"Yep," Ferrell said, and then he settled his head down on the saddle to go back to sleep.

As Elizabeth Meadows had suggested, Sophie got to handle the wagon team a couple of times that day. Sophie had told Elizabeth that she had driven a wagon before, but that was an exaggeration. She had driven a buggy, with one horse in the traces, and an old and placid horse at that. That wasn't like handling a team of big, strong draft horses.

With Elizabeth's help, though, Sophie had gotten the hang of it fairly quickly. Even so, her arms ached quite a bit and she was glad when Elizabeth took the reins back.

Elizabeth's smug smile as she said, "You did all right. Maybe you won't get so tired next time," was annoying, but Sophie forced herself to be tolerant and just thanked the woman for her help.

That evening, after the wagons stopped so the group could make camp, Sophie helped with supper again. As she was carrying some firewood and Elizabeth was busy with the same chore, she said, "I wonder when we'll catch up to Pike's wagons."

"I don't know," Elizabeth said. "We covered a good number of miles today, though."

"I wish I knew what Brother Lavon plans to do."

"You'll be told what you need to know, when you need to know it," Elizabeth said coolly. "Don't worry about that."

Sophie was curious about something else, too, although she didn't mention it.

She wondered if Elizabeth would sneak into Lavon Branson's wagon again tonight.

However, as it turned out, Elizabeth didn't have to do that in order to see Branson. After supper, as she and Sophie were sitting on the wagon tongue and getting ready to turn in soon, the tall, lean figure of the group's leader approached them in the fading light from the campfire.

"Sister Elizabeth, I need to talk to you," Branson announced. He wasn't wearing his hat now. The firelight shone on his long dark hair.

"Of course," Elizabeth said as she stood up.

Sophie got to her feet as well and asked, "Do you need me, too, Brother Lavon?"

"Not this time, Sister Sophie," he replied with a smile. He put a hand lightly on Elizabeth's arm and steered her away from the wagon. Sophie watched them go and took note of the way they were talking earnestly together.

"I reckon Brother Lavon and Sister Elizabeth might get married one of these days."

The sudden, unexpected statement made Sophie jump a little and look around hurriedly to see who had spoken.

"Oh, I'm sorry, Sister Sophie," the young man called Curtis went on. "I didn't mean to startle you."

"That's all right, I wasn't startled," Sophie assured him, even though she had been. "What were you saying?"

"That I think those two might get hitched sometime," Curtis said with a nod toward Branson and Elizabeth, who still stood talking at the edge of the firelight. "They'd be a good match, don't you think?"

"Um, yes, I suppose so."

"Sister Elizabeth's sure pretty, and Brother Lavon's just about the finest fella I ever knew. That's why I decided to join up with him, after I heard him give a talk back in Missouri, where I come from." Curtis frowned suddenly. "Say, I didn't mean any offense when I said that about Sister Elizabeth being pretty, Sister Sophie. I reckon you're mighty pretty, too. That hair of yours . . . well, it's sort of like the sun shining, isn't it?"

Curtis shuffled his feet, cleared his throat, and looked embarrassed. Sophie was annoyed for a second, but then she took pity on him and said, "That's all right, Brother Curtis. Anyone with eyes can see that Sister Elizabeth is nice-looking. That's just a fact."

"Yes, ma'am, I reckon so." He bobbed his head. "I, uh,

I better be going. Be a good idea to check on the stock one more time before everybody turns in. 'Night, ma'am."

"Good night," Sophie said. She started to tell him that he didn't have to call her ma'am—they were about the same age, after all—but that could wait for another time, she decided.

A few minutes later, Elizabeth came back from her conversation with Branson but didn't volunteer any details of what it was about. Sophie didn't think it was her place to ask, so she didn't.

But she said, "I think I'll spread my bedroll on the ground under the wagon tonight, with you."

"Fine," Elizabeth said. She must not be planning to sneak off to Branson's wagon, Sophie thought.

They got the bedrolls ready and crawled under the wagon. Sophie stretched out, and tonight her weariness caught up with her. She fell asleep sooner than she thought she would.

Just as she was dozing off, she thought she heard some faint sounds in the distance like . . . gunshots? Was that possible?

But she went to sleep before she could figure it out for sure, and she didn't think about it again.

CHAPTER 21

Pike took stock of things the next morning. None of the horses and mules had been wounded other than a few nicks and bullet burns, despite all the lead flying around the night before. The wagons had a few bullet holes in them but hadn't suffered any major damage.

And only one of the barrels had been hit, and that was high up so very little of the moonshine had leaked out. Fiddler volunteered to carve a plug for it so they wouldn't lose any more as the contents sloshed around.

Considering that the attack had taken place in darkness, that was pure luck—but Pike would take it, gratefully.

Belle and McGreevey were the only casualties. Belle had a slight headache but otherwise showed no ill effects from being knocked out. Pike planned to keep an eye on her, though, since he had known men who'd suffered head injuries but didn't show any signs of serious problems until several days later.

He didn't know what to make of Tom McGreevey's disappearance. The way McGreevey had gone down, Pike had been certain his shot struck the man, but he supposed it was possible McGreevey might have just slipped on the riverbed and fallen. Or, as Torrance had suggested, Pike had wounded McGreevey but not fatally. In either case, the man could have slipped away to join his partners in would-be crime.

Whatever the details, McGreevey was gone, which meant he wouldn't be driving one of the wagons anymore.

After breakfast that morning, Pike announced, "Belle, you'll ride with Dougal today instead of wrangling that remuda."

"I can do my job," Belle protested.

"A wallop on the head like that is nothing to mess around with," Pike told her. "For today, at least, you'll ride on the wagon."

Dougal said, "Don't argue with him, darlin'. Have pity on a decrepit old man who'll enjoy havin' a good-lookin' young woman beside him."

"I've heard stories about you, Mr. Shannon," Belle said with a smile. "I'm not sure you act all that decrepit, or that I should be feeling any pity for you."

Dougal chuckled. "Don't worry. I promise to behave myself."

Pike went on, "Fiddler, you can take over driving one of the wagons."

"I'd be pleased to," Fiddler agreed. "I like to feel as if I'm earning my keep."

"Nessa, can you handle the remuda by yourself today?"

She tossed her head a little as she said, "What do you think, Pike?"

"I think you'd say you can whether you really think so or not," he replied with a smile. "But with Tom McGreevey gone and Belle laid up for the day"—he held up a hand to forestall the protest Belle was about to make—"we don't have much choice but to give it a try. I'll keep an eye on things and give you a hand if it looks like you need it."

"I won't," Nessa declared.

With that settled, Pike drank the last of the coffee in his cup and then said, "All right, we'll start getting ready to move out. It may take most of the morning to ford the river and make it up the hill on the other side."

Alton Grenville and his wife Hettie had owned the little greasy-sack ranch a few miles west of the Brazos for a couple of years now, running a small herd of cattle and supplementing the income from the cows with some fields of corn and sorghum. It was a lot of hard work, and Alton couldn't afford to hire any help, so he had to take care of all the chores himself.

One of these days he'd have some fine, strong sons to help him, he thought often. He and Hettie hadn't been blessed with any young'uns yet, but it was only a matter of time.

On this early morning, with gray, predawn light in the sky, Alton yawned as he came out of the shed where they kept the milk cow. He had a bucket of fresh milk in his right hand. He didn't wear a belt gun, and his rifle and shotgun were in the roughly framed house twenty yards away.

Ten years earlier, when the Comanches were still raiding on a regular basis, it would have been worth a man's life to walk around unarmed if he lived beyond the Brazos. These days, there were only a few isolated bands of renegades in the state, and they never ventured this far east.

But there were strangers on horseback in front of the Grenville cabin anyway, and the unexpected sight of them made Alton come to an abrupt halt.

"Morning," he said. "Can I help you?"

They were looking toward the house and didn't seem to notice him until he called out. A couple of them turned sharply toward him. Alton felt a pang of alarm. The men looked like they were about to reach for the guns on their hips.

But then one of the others moved his horse toward Alton and said in a friendly voice, "Good morning. This your spread?"

"That's right," Alton said.

The man nodded and rested his hands on his saddle horn as he leaned forward.

"Nice-looking place. I've often said I'd like to have a little spread like this, one of these days."

Alton didn't say anything, but he didn't think the man looked like a rancher of any sort. Like the others, he was dressed fairly well, at least compared to the patched trousers and homespun shirt Alton wore. All of them wore guns and had rifles sticking up from saddle sheaths.

Men bent on honest business usually didn't go around so heavily armed, Alton thought.

But regardless of what had brought them to these parts, maybe they were just looking to water their horses, maybe get some breakfast. He and Hettie could oblige them on those two things, although their larder was never what anybody would call packed. They could still spare a meal for some visitors. It was the hospitable thing to do.

He circled around them toward the house, still carrying the bucket of milk.

"What can I do for you?" he asked. He didn't say anything about Hettie being inside. It never hurt to be a mite cautious with strangers.

"We were riding past and I saw that wagon," the spokesman said as he pointed toward the wagon parked at the end of the house. It was a fine, sturdy vehicle, probably the best piece of equipment the Grenvilles owned. "You wouldn't be looking to sell it, would you?"

The question took Alton by surprise. He blurted out the honest answer.

"No, not at all. I need it here on the place. I use it to take crops to market."

The spokesman leaned forward even more and pursed his lips. He reminded Alton of something, and suddenly the young rancher realized what it was.

The man looked like a buzzard.

"I'd give you a good price for it," he said. "Say . . . thirty dollars."

Alton grunted and shook his head. He said, "It's worth five or six times that much, and anyway, I told you, mister, it's not for sale. I need it."

The friendly smile went away, making the man's face look even more like a carrion bird.

"So do I," he said. "So if you won't sell it, I reckon we'll just have to take it."

He half-turned in the saddle, jerked his head, and a couple of the other men moved their horses toward the wagon.

"Now hold on a minute," Alton said as he hurried to intercept them. "You can't just come onto a man's place and tell him you're taking his wagon—"

"That's exactly what we're doing, son," the man said. He closed his hand around the butt of his gun and drew it from the holster.

Scared now, thinking only of reaching his rifle so he could protect Hettie, Alton dropped the bucket and lunged toward the house. The fresh milk splashed out on the ground. He saw Hettie appear in the doorway, terror on her face, and he opened his mouth to yell at her to get back inside.

Before any words could come out, a gun crashed, and what felt like a sledgehammer slammed into his back, between his shoulder blades. He wasn't even aware that he fell, but suddenly, somehow, he was on the ground and his face was in the dirt and his toes pushed feebly at the earth, still making a futile attempt to reach the house.

Somewhere far away, a woman screamed. Hettie? Had to be.

"Get the wagon, Henry. Must be a team around here somewhere. Find them and get 'em hitched up. We don't have any more time to waste."

Somebody took hold of Alton's shoulders and turned him over. Pain exploded inside him until it filled every fiber of his being. He looked up into Hettie's red, tear-streaked face as she clutched at him.

"Sorry, ma'am." That was the buzzard-faced killer again. "If we had more time, I'm sure the boys would like to stay for a while and sympathize with you, maybe offer you their condolences, but we have a pressing engagement this morning."

Another boom, and Hettie's face disappeared in a smear of red as she toppled to the side. Alton cried out in shock, but a terrible coldness had begun to creep over him, making it more and more difficult to feel anything, even grief at the brutal murder of his wife. Everything was slipping away, and he was too weak to hold on to any of it.

" . . . ready to go . . . few minutes, Malachi."

The voice rose and fell so that Alton only made out

those few words. Then there was a great roaring sound, as if a train were bearing down on him.

That train carried Alton Grenville away to oblivion.

While the others got the wagons ready to roll, Pike saddled up and rode across the river. He had two reasons for doing this: he wanted to check the ford and make sure this was a good place to cross, and he figured it would be a good idea to ride up the trail on the other side and check their route.

The water was a little muddy, but he could tell from the riffles and eddies where the sandbars and the limestone shelves were located. With experienced teamsters like Dougal, Sam Crow, and Will Fisher at the reins, Pike didn't think they would have much trouble. The wagon driven by Fiddler could follow the lead vehicle with Dougal driving. That way all Fiddler would have to do was make sure he stayed in line.

The sun hadn't come up when Pike reached the far side of the Brazos, but sunrise wasn't far off. As he started up the trail, his eyes probed the trees and brush on both sides, but he didn't see any signs of lurking trouble.

The trail followed a straight path up the hill, fairly steep but not enough so to force it to zigzag. Pike knew the draft horses and mules could make it, but they would be tired by the time they reached the top. It might be a good idea to call another halt when they did, not all day but for several hours so the animals could rest before resuming the trek to Pecan County.

Pike reined in at the crest and sat there studying the county to the west and southwest. It was a gently rolling, sparsely wooded tableland that stretched for miles to another line of hills that were a dark, ragged line at the moment. But then, while he watched, the sun poked its head over the eastern horizon and light flowed like molten gold across the landscape.

That gave him a better look at the hills in the distance. The woods were thicker there, and the terrain more rugged. He knew the trail angled down through those hills, though, and the wagons would be able to follow it. There was a settlement down in there, he recalled, Morton's Mill or something like that. With luck, he and the others might reach it today.

Without seeing anything to concern him, he turned his horse and rode back down the hill toward the river.

The men were on the wagon seats, Dougal with Belle beside him. Nessa was with the remuda at the back of the line.

"Everybody ready?" Pike called.

"Ready to roll," Dougal replied, and Pike got waves of assent from Fiddler, Sam, Will, and Torrance, who had taken over the reins on the last wagon, replacing Tom McGreevey.

Pike turned his horse back toward the river and said, "Follow me, then."

He moved out into the water at a deliberate pace. Behind him, he heard thudding hoofbeats and creaking wagon wheels as the caravan got underway. Dougal's team splashed into the water after hesitating for a second at the edge. Pike hipped around in the saddle and watched his grandfather steer the animals with a firm but deft touch on the reins.

If the river had been deeper, they would have taken the wagons across one at a time, just to make sure they weren't all at risk, but here at this ford, that wasn't necessary. A vehicle might bog down, but there was no danger of them washing away. The water barely came up to the wheel hubs.

Pike reached the other bank, pulled his horse to the side, and turned again so he could watch the wagons. He kept a close eye on all of them, ready to call out a warning if he spotted any signs of potential trouble, but they all seemed to be coming along without any problems.

Dougal drove the lead wagon up the gently sloping bank and continued far enough away from the river before stopping that the others would have room to get out of the water, too.

As the second wagon emerged from the Brazos, Pike called, "Good job, Fiddler!"

The little man waved and grinned in appreciation of the compliment.

One by one, the wagons reached the river's western bank. Pike rode along the line to check with all the drivers, who reported no problems. He watched from his saddle as Nessa hazed the extra stock out of the water.

"Good job," he told her, too. "Think you can get them up the hill?"

"Of course," she said. "They'll follow the wagons. All I have to do is make sure they keep moving."

Pike nodded. "All right, but if you need help, give a yell." He rode back to the head of the line. As he passed the lead wagon, he called to Dougal, "Take it on up!"

Pike held his horse to a walk as the caravan started up the hill. It would take a while for the wagons to make the climb, and he didn't want to get too far in front. From time to time he stopped to watch their slow progress.

The sun was completely up by now, flooding the Texas landscape with light. All five wagons were on the slope, with Nessa and the remuda bringing up the rear. Dougal, the most experienced teamster in the bunch, had gone over the plan with the other drivers. They couldn't stop once they were rolling up the hill, otherwise the teams might not be able to get the heavy loads started again. Not to mention the danger of the brakes failing to hold, which could be catastrophic if any of the wagons began to roll back down the slope. Pike knew all that, and as a result, his nerves were taut as he watched them climbing.

He caught a sudden whiff of smoke, and that caused him to turn in the saddle and peer up toward the hilltop. As he did, he stiffened in alarm. A column of black smoke climbed into the sky just beyond the crest. He had no idea what could be causing it, but he didn't have to wonder about that for long.

The front end of a wagon, with its tongue tied up to the driver's box and no team hitched to it, came into view, rolling slowly forward. The wagon bed was piled high with brush, and that brush was on fire. Bright flames leaped high.

Horror welled up inside Pike as the wagon trundled forward, tipped over the crest, and rolled toward the moonshine caravan, picking up speed with every foot that it hurtled toward them.

CHAPTER 22

Pike knew without having to think about it that men had piled up that brush, set it on fire, and pushed the wagon over the top. It hadn't launched itself at them.

There was no doubt in his mind who was responsible, either. It had to be the gang that had attacked the night before, the outlaws Tom McGreevey had been working with.

He remained motionless on horseback for only a split second, then he dug his heels into his mount's flanks and sent the animal lunging up the trail toward the blazing, careening wagon.

Through the smoke and flames, he caught a glimpse of men on horseback boiling over the crest. That would be the varmints intent on hijacking this caravan, following their fiery projectile down the hill.

Pike threw a glance over his shoulder, saw Dougal hauling back on the reins to bring the lead wagon to a halt. Stopping wasn't good, but the wagons couldn't just keep rolling right into the face of disaster.

A disaster that it was up to Pike to avert—if he could.

The fire hadn't spread to the driver's box on the wagon.

In fact, the wind of its passage down the hill forced the flames back away from the box, and the smoke trailed out behind the wagon, as well.

Pike called on his horse for all the speed it could muster and rode hard up the hill. The gap between them and the burning wagon closed in a hurry. Pike veered to the side, turned his horse sharply, and fell in alongside the wagon, headed *down* the trail now.

The heat from the flames washed over Pike and his horse and made the animal want to shy away. He kept a firm hand in the reins and used them and his knees to force the horse closer to the wagon.

Timing the move as best he could, he kicked his feet out of the stirrups and leaped from the saddle to throw himself at the driver's box. The seat slammed against him and almost knocked him forward, putting him in danger of falling under the rapidly turning wheels.

Pike saved himself with a desperate grab that left him clinging to the seat. He groaned with the effort as he pulled himself up and sprawled half on the seat and half on the floorboards.

This close to the flames, the heat was ferocious. It pounded at him almost like fiery fists. At least the wind kept the smoke out of his nose and throat.

Knowing that he had no time to waste, he pushed himself up and dug in his pocket for his clasp knife. He opened it and sawed at the rope that held the wagon tongue tied up tight against the front of the box, so it stuck straight up in the air.

While he did that, he glanced down the slope. The lead wagon, with Dougal still at the reins, was only about fifty yards away now. He didn't see Belle and was glad that his grandfather had made her get off the wagon in case Pike couldn't prevent a collision.

Dougal needed to get off of there, too. Pike would have waved for him to do so, but he was too busy trying to free the wagon tongue.

The rope fell away. Pike wrapped both arms around the length of wood and heaved to the right as hard as he could, in the hope that he could turn the front wheels and send the wagon angling off the trail to crash in the brush alongside.

The effort failed. Even Pike, as strong as he was, couldn't alter the wagon's course. That left him with just one option.

He pushed the wagon tongue straight forward.

The heavy shaft fell, and the yoke, the short cross-piece at the front end of it, dug into the trail with all the force of the wagon's weight behind it. Pike thought maybe that would slow the vehicle down enough to stop it.

He didn't expect the result he got instead.

Feeling the wagon start to rise suddenly underneath him, Pike let out a startled yell and leaped to the side as hard as he could. The yoke must have hit a rock and lodged solidly against it. Momentum made the wagon's rear wheels come off the ground first, and all the weight still hurtling forward caused the front wheels to follow as the wagon tongue acted as a lever. As Pike sailed through the air, the blazing wagon flipped up and over, throwing burning brush high in the air before it came down with a shattering crash in the middle of the trail.

Pike had gotten off the vehicle barely in time. He landed hard at the edge of the trail and rolled aside as the wagon performed its spectacular somersault.

He might have appreciated the incredible sight more if

bullets hadn't kicked up dirt near him as shots blasted nearby.

Pike reached for his gun, hoping it hadn't fallen out of its holster during all the wild action of the past thirty seconds. His hand closed around the walnut grips and brought the Colt up. A couple of the riders who'd been following the burning wagon downhill reined their horses to the side and charged him. Flame spurted from their gun muzzles.

Pike came up on one knee, lined his gunsights on the first rider, and squeezed the trigger. The man rocked far back in the saddle as the slug punched into his chest. He dropped the reins and his gun and toppled loosely to the side. The horse continued running, dragging the man by one foot caught in a stirrup.

The second outlaw veered around his fallen comrade and fired again at Pike, who felt the hot breath of the bullet on his cheek. He triggered a second shot. The man suddenly hunched his shoulders and bent forward, trying to curl around the agony in his midsection where Pike's bullet had ripped into his guts. He didn't fall off the horse, but he looked like he was out of the fight.

Pike scrambled to his feet but had to throw himself to the side again as several other outlaws twisted in their saddles and threw lead at him. Then the group was past him, splitting up to go around the burning wreckage scattered in the trail.

Pike saw that his family and friends had taken cover behind the wagons and were putting up a fight. There was no telling how long those brakes would hold, though, or if the teams would be able to keep the wagons from rolling back downhill if the brakes gave out. The defenders were in danger in more ways than one.

Pike leaped to his feet and spotted his horse moving

around nervously beside the trail about twenty yards away. He put two fingers in his mouth and blew a piercing whistle that made the horse perk his ears up. He turned and trotted toward Pike, answering his master's summons.

"Good boy," Pike said as he caught hold of the reins, grabbed the horn, and practically vaulted into the saddle. He hauled his Winchester out of its scabbard and kicked the horse into a run.

The hurricane deck of a galloping horse was no place for accuracy, but Pike Shannon was no ordinary marksman. Guiding his mount with his knees, he brought the rifle to his shoulder in a smooth motion and began cranking off rounds as he charged at the outlaws.

The would-be moonshine thieves realized quickly that they were caught in a cross fire. They still had the advantage in numbers, although the odds were narrowing as deadly accurate shooting from the men at the wagons took its toll.

Pike thundered down the trail. He drilled another man and knocked him off his horse. Then he veered his mount to the right to rake the attackers' flank on that side.

Suddenly, Belle Ramsey appeared, also on horseback. She galloped up the other flank, the carbine in her hands spitting fire. The remaining outlaws halted their charge and wheeled around. Pike caught glimpses of frantic surprise and desperation on their faces. Their plan had failed again, and now all they wanted to do was cut their losses and take off for the tall and uncut.

Pike didn't want to let them get away. If those owlhoots escaped, they might just try again for the moonshine. He was tired of it and wanted to put an end to it now.

But he didn't want Belle to get hurt, either, and the outlaws were fighting back fiercely as they tried to battle their way out of the trap into which they had gotten themselves. Pike shouted, "Belle! Get back! Get back!" and waved her away.

At the same time, he whirled his horse to the middle of the trail to block it as the men charged back up the slope. He fired coolly, the rifle butt kicking against his shoulder as bullets whipped around him. Two men went backward out of their saddles as if swatted by giant hands.

That left only two outlaws out of the bunch that had attacked the wagons. They split up to make more difficult targets of themselves. Pike swung the Winchester to the left and stroked the trigger again. The whipcrack of the shot coincided with the sight of the man on that side of the trail flinging his arms wide and sailing off his horse to crash limply on the ground.

Pike worked the rifle's lever and tried to twist back to the other side in time, but he wasn't fast enough. The remaining outlaw was practically on top of him, and the barrel of the gun in the man's fist looked as big around as a cannon as it thrust toward Pike's face.

He jerked away from it just as the gun roared. The outlaw was close enough that Pike felt the stings on his cheek from bits of burning powder that flew from the muzzle. The bullet ripped through the air next to his right ear, missing by no more than an inch.

Then the man was past him, lashing the horse with the reins in his other hand, getting as much speed as he could out of the struggling beast. Pike wheeled his horse and raised the Winchester again, not worrying about the fact that the outlaw's back was to him now.

As far as Pike was concerned, a bullet in the back of a no-account skunk like that was perfectly fitting.

When he squeezed the trigger, the hammer fell on an empty firing chamber.

Pike bit back a curse and rammed the rifle in the saddle boot. By the time he could reload, the man would be over the crest and Pike wouldn't have a shot at him anymore. The range was still close enough that he might be able to make the shot with his Colt, but he wasn't sure he had any unfired rounds left in it, either.

He leaned forward in the saddle and urged his horse into a run after the fleeing outlaw.

Both animals strained. It was a hard run up that hill, the kind that could break the heart of a horse—or the man who rode it. Pike felt his mount struggling valiantly under him to give him what he wanted, the speed to overhaul his enemy. A sudden hesitation went through Pike. Was it worth killing the horse to catch the man?

He was saved from having to make that decision because at that moment they reached the top of the hill and went flying over the crest.

On ground that was mostly level now, the running was easier. The outlaw twisted in his saddle to look back over his left shoulder, a snarl on his buzzard-like face. He turned back the other way and thrust his right arm behind him. The gun he held in that hand boomed and smoke gushed from the barrel. Pike felt as much as heard the flat slap of the slug past his head.

Within moments, Pike knew he had the better horse. He was gaining on the man, slowly but steadily. The outlaw tried another shot at him. Pike bent forward in the saddle. The bullet whined over his head.

The man forgot about trying to shoot him and concentrated instead on getting all the speed he could out of his horse. It wasn't good enough, though. Another few lunging strides, and Pike was almost even with him.

Close enough, Pike thought. Just as he had leaped from his horse to the burning wagon, he brought his mount nearer and threw himself from the saddle, reaching out to wrap his arms around the man as they came together in a bone-jarring collision.

CHAPTER 23

The impact was enough to knock the buzzard-faced hombre out of his saddle. He and Pike fell in a tangle of arms and legs on the far side of the horse. Pike tried to scramble on top and pin the man to the ground, but the outlaw jerked a knee up and rammed it into his belly. Pike grimaced in pain and rolled to the side.

The man writhed around and aimed a kick at Pike's face. Pike caught the boot before it landed and heaved as hard as he could, forcing the man away from him. That gave him enough room to surge to his feet.

The outlaw came to his knees and clawed at the holster on his hip, not realizing it was empty. So was Pike's. Not wanting to take the time to look for the fallen weapons, Pike dived toward his enemy, tackling the man again and driving him over onto his back. They rolled across the ground, slugging and kicking viciously at each other.

Pike was angry enough that he barely noticed the punishing blows the other man landed. He slammed his own fists into the man's narrow face and lean body. The outlaw had plenty of wiry strength, and after a few moments of battling fiercely, he managed to twist away.

He was a second ahead of Pike in getting to his feet, which gave him the chance to launch an attack of his own as Pike came upright. He lowered his bony shoulder and rammed it into Pike's chest. Leanly built or not, he had enough weight behind the charge to knock Pike backward. Pike lost his balance and fell into some brush.

Briars grew all through that brush, twining myriad strands around the branches, and the sharp little stickers clawed maddeningly at Pike as he tried to push free. They left scratches on his hands and face and clung stubbornly to his clothes.

The outlaw tried to take advantage of that and rushed in to stomp at Pike's face. Pike jerked his head aside, but the boot heel struck him heavily on the left shoulder anyway, leaving that arm momentarily numb.

"That moonshine's still gonna be mine," the man snarled as he lifted a foot for another kick.

The sudden crack of a rifle made him pause. Pike tore free from the briars just then and threw himself at the outlaw's knees. With a startled yell, the man went down again.

This time Pike succeeded in getting a knee in the man's belly so he couldn't writhe away. Pike knelt there with his arms rising and falling and the muscles in his back and shoulders bunching under his shirt as he smashed punch after punch into the outlaw's face. Rage boiled up inside him. He couldn't stop, didn't want to stop.

This man was responsible for threatening his family and friends. Some of them might be dead already; Pike didn't know. All he knew was that he wanted to keep hitting this son of a—

"Pike! Pike, stop it! That's enough! You're going to kill him."

That was the general idea, thought the part of Pike's brain that wasn't completely caught up in a frenzy of violence. But he realized that was Belle's voice yelling at him, and that got through to him enough to make him pause.

The outlaw's face was raw, swollen, and bleeding. He was out cold—or maybe dead. As the madness left Pike, he saw the man's chest rising and falling raggedly. He was alive but no longer a threat, at least for the moment.

Pike lifted his head, saw Belle sitting on horseback a few yards away. Breathing hard from his exertions, he said, "Are you all right?"

"I'm fine, but you're about to beat that man to death."

"I reckon he's got it coming, don't you?"

"Maybe," Belle said. "Probably. But even so, he's helpless right now, and I don't think you want to kill a helpless man, Pike."

He heaved himself to his feet and stood over the unconscious outlaw.

"You're right," he admitted. "I'm obliged to you for getting through to me when you did, Belle. Although I don't figure I would've lost *too* much sleep if I'd gone ahead and killed him. I appreciate you firing that shot and distracting him when you did, too."

"Now *I've* got a confession to make. I was trying to shoot the son of a gun. I just missed, that's all." Belle shook her head. "Pike, you look like you tangled with a whole den of wildcats."

He gestured toward the brush and said, "Briar patch. Do you know if any of our bunch is hurt?"

She shook her head. "No, when I saw you chase this

fellow over the hill, I just grabbed a horse and rode after you as fast as I could. Thought you might need a hand."

"Keep your carbine pointed at him while I find my gun and my hat."

Quickly, he located not only his own Colt but the outlaw's fallen revolver as well. He pouched his own iron after checking to make sure it still had bullets in it and dirt hadn't fouled the barrel, then stuck the outlaw's gun behind his belt. He found his hat, knocked it back into shape, and put it on.

He drew his gun and told Belle, "I'll watch him now. See if you can round up his horse. I want to get back down the hill to the wagons."

"So do I," she said as she turned her mount and hurried to do as he asked.

While Pike stood there covering the outlaw, the man groaned and stirred a little. After a moment, his eyelids fluttered open. Both eyes were swollen enough that opening them had to be difficult. He peered up in Pike's general direction but couldn't focus on him right away.

The metallic ratcheting of the Colt's hammer being drawn back got the outlaw's attention. His sight seemed to clear some. His blood-smeared face twisted in a scowl as he glared up at Pike and cursed.

Pike let the obscenities spill out of the man's mouth for a few seconds, then said, "That's enough. If I have to pull this trigger to shut you up, I'll do it."

"Go ahead," the man rasped. "Do it. I would, if I was in your place."

"I know," Pike said. "Not wanting to be the same sort of scum as you is the only reason I haven't killed you already. But don't force my hand." He paused. "How'd you find out we were carrying moonshine?"

The outlaw pushed himself up on one elbow and laughed, an ugly sound that came out through split, swollen lips.

"You didn't really think you could keep a thing like that a secret, did you?" he said thickly. "Hell, I'll bet half of Warbonnet County knew what you were up to."

Unfortunately, he was probably right about that. But Pike wasn't satisfied with the answer.

"How did you rope Tom McGreevey in on the deal? He may not be worth much, but he's kin, in a way."

"Didn't stop you from shooting him, did it?" The man laughed again. "McGreevey's dead."

Pike's jaw tightened. "I killed him last night?"

"No, he didn't die from that. He died because he ruined everything for us!"

Pike frowned at him for a second, then said, "You killed him!"

"I finished him off," the outlaw said. "Maybe he would have died eventually from your bullet, maybe not. We'll never know."

"I still want to know how you got him to betray his own family like that."

"Money, I suppose. I can't really tell you. My partner's the one who brought him on board as the inside man."

"Partner—" Pike began, but at that moment, Belle rode up, leading the outlaw's horse. Pike's mount was tagging along behind her, too.

Pike turned his head to look at her, and as he did, Belle's eyes widened in alarm and she cried, "Pike, look out!"

Pike twisted back toward the outlaw and saw that the man had pushed himself up even more and had pulled a two-shot, over-under derringer that he must have had hidden somewhere on him. The hideout gun went off with a wicked little pop that was swallowed up by the roar when Pike's Colt went off a fraction of a second later.

The bullet made a neat hole in the outlaw's forehead but blew out a good-sized chunk of his skull when it exploded out the back of his head. He fell backward, dead before the gruesome mess ever hit the ground.

Pike knew he wasn't hit, but he jerked toward Belle and asked, "Are you all right?"

She looked startled but appeared to be unhurt.

"I'm fine," she assured him. "That shot didn't come anywhere near me. I'm sorry, Pike. If I hadn't distracted you, he wouldn't have had a chance to get his hands on that little popgun—"

"Don't worry about that. No harm done to us, and he's dead, just like he deserved. He admitted killing Tom McGreevey because McGreevey fouled up last night."

"That's terrible. The whole thing is."

"Yeah." Pike thumbed fresh rounds into his gun to replace the ones he'd fired. "He was saying something about having a partner, too, but I reckon we'll never know about that."

"Unless the partner comes after us, too."

"Could happen," Pike said with a slow nod. "Let's get back down the hill. I want to see what's going on with the wagons."

They left the dead outlaw lying where he had fallen. Later on, they could bury the would-be moonshine robbers—if there was time and it wasn't too much trouble . . .

When they rode over the crest onto the downhill trail, Pike was glad to see that none of the wagons had broken loose and gone rolling back down to the bottom to maybe crash. Each wagon carried four chunks of wood, cut from a square beam, that could be used to block the wheels and keep them from turning. As he and Belle approached, Pike was glad to see that somebody had taken fast action and put all those blocks in place. They weren't foolproof, but they took a lot of weight off the teams and made a runaway less likely.

Torrance and Nessa were standing beside the lead wagon. They saw Pike and Belle coming and walked ahead to meet them.

"I'm mighty glad to see you two," Torrance said. "I wasn't sure who was going to come back over that hill."

"Did that man get away?" Nessa asked.

Pike said, "He did not."

"We heard shots," Torrance said, nodding. "Sort of hoped that was the way it would turn out."

"Just sort of?" Pike's grin took any sting out of the words. Then he grew serious again as he asked, "Was anybody else hurt?"

"No, we were able to take cover before the shooting started, and then when it did, we had better places to aim from than those fellas on horseback."

Torrance nodded grimly toward the bodies of the dead outlaws lying scattered around on the trail.

"As soon as the fireworks were over, Dougal yelled for us to get all the wheels blocked," he went on. "We were lucky that the brakes held long enough for us to do that, but they did."

Pike leaned over in the saddle and watched as Dougal and Sam Crow led some of the extra horses and mules from the remuda forward along the line of wagons.

"What are they going to do?"

"Dougal said we'd tie them on to this lead wagon, so it'll amount to two teams pulling it the rest of the way uphill. He says that's the best way to do it, now that we've had to stop."

"He's right, too," Pike agreed. "I considered hitching two teams to a wagon and taking them up one at a time, but I thought we could make it without having to take that much time." He sighed. "We would have, too, if those varmints hadn't jumped us."

As Dougal came up leading three of the extra horses, he waved a hand at Belle and said, "Sorry she got away from me, Pike. When you chased off over the hill after that hombre, she grabbed a horse and took off hell-for-leather after you."

"And it's a good thing she did," Pike said with a smile. "Otherwise that fella might've gotten the drop on me and I wouldn't be here now."

"Only because I distracted you," Belle said. "He never would have if that hadn't happened."

"Either way, it worked out all right. Let's see if we can get these wagons to the top of the hill."

It was a grueling, time-consuming task for both man and beast, but by late that morning, they had all five wagons on the flats at the top of the hill. Once that was done, the animals needed to rest anyway, so Pike, Sam Crow, and Will Fisher took the horses the outlaws had been riding and loaded the bodies onto them. They brought the corpses to higher ground, too, although Dougal grumbled, "I don't reckon we could get by with just throwin' 'em in the river, could we?"

"No point in fouling the river with dead skunks," Pike said. "We'll plant 'em."

He, Torrance, Sam, and Will worked on digging a couple of mass graves, using the shovels that they had brought along, one for each wagon in case they'd needed to dig the wheels out of sand or mud. Dougal and Fiddler went through the outlaws' clothing and saddlebags, gathering up money, guns, ammunition, and a few personal effects. The horses would be added to the remuda. Belle and Nessa stood watch with their carbines ready in case any other trouble developed.

When the digging was done, Pike leaned on the shovel he'd been using. The day was warm, and his shirt was wet with sweat. More sweat than a bunch of murdering owl-hoots deserved.

Fiddler approached him with a piece of paper he had taken from one of the saddlebags. Pike nodded toward it and asked, "Did you find a letter that'll tell us who one of them was?"

"More than that," Fiddler answered with a serious look on his face. He held out the paper. "I think you should read it."

Pike took it and scanned the words. The letter was addressed to someone named Malachi Bouchard, and it invited Bouchard to a meeting in Bolivar where he would hear a proposal that might prove both interesting and profitable. It was the name signed at the bottom that made Pike's eyebrows climb his forehead, though.

"Conway!" he burst out.

Torrance said, "Phineas Conway, that crooked judge who was part of Doak Ramsey's bunch?"

"He did more than just work for Doak," Belle said. "He was related some way. I'm not sure how."

"Yeah, that's him," Pike said as he thumped a finger against the letter. "And he's the one who set up this whole thing with Bouchard, whichever one of those devils *he* was."

Sam Crow said, "I thought Conway lit out a long time ago."

"He did, but he either came back to this part of the country or else he's been lurking around, lying low, this whole time. Just waiting for a chance to stir up trouble again. He must be the partner that fella mentioned, the one who roped in Tom McGreevey."

Dougal said, "We need to find that no-good Phineas Conway and have us a little palaver with him."

Pike nodded and said, "That's just what I intend to do when we get back. In the meantime . . . let's put these carcasses in the ground and get on down the trail. It's still a long way to Pecan County."

CHAPTER 24

Even though it was past midday by the time they finished with the burying, no one felt like eating lunch next to the mounds of dirt that marked the outlaws' final resting place. So they moved on for another mile or so before stopping long enough to boil a pot of coffee and eat biscuits and bacon left over from breakfast.

They were doing that when Will Fisher announced, "Riders headed this way."

Pike looked where Will was pointing and saw close to a dozen men on horseback coming along the trail toward them.

"Now what in blazes is *this*?" he muttered as he reached for his rifle. Everybody else got their weapons ready and moved around so they could use the wagons for cover if they needed to.

Two men rode a little ahead of the others. One was a burly, barrel-chested older man with white hair and a mustache, the other a younger, lanky hombre in range clothes. The older man wore a dark suit despite the heat of the day, and Pike relaxed slightly when he saw something pinned to the man's vest that glittered in the sunlight.

"Looks like a lawman of some sort," he told the others quietly. "That would make the fellas with him a posse."

"Dadgummit," Dougal said. "I'm glad they ain't more owlhoots, but we didn't need to run into John Law, neither, with this big load of 'shine."

"Take it easy, Grandpappy. I'm not sure what county we're in. It might not be illegal here."

Torrance said, "I'm not getting in a gun battle with the law. I don't mind shooting desperadoes, but peace officers are a different story."

"Don't start borrowing trouble," Pike snapped. "I'll go talk to them."

He kept his rifle in his right hand but let it hang at his side as he walked out to meet the group of riders. He lifted his left hand in a peaceful greeting.

The younger of the two leaders said something over his shoulder, and the rest of the bunch reined in. The two out front kept coming until they brought their mounts to a stop about twenty feet from Pike.

"Howdy," the older man said in a booming voice. "I'm Sheriff Sagamore Wilson. My chief deputy, Prentice Dillard."

The lean man nodded. Neither of them seemed hostile, but they weren't overly friendly, either.

"My name's Shannon," Pike introduced himself. "Are you on the hunt for somebody, Sheriff?"

"We surely are. A pack of murderin' scoundrels so low they'd have to climb on a ladder to lick a snake's belly."

"You wouldn't be them, would you?" Dillard asked in a deceptively soft drawl.

"No, sir, we would not, but I might know where you can find them. What did they do, anyway?"

Sheriff Wilson drew in a deep breath and blew it out, making his drooping white mustache flutter.

"Killed a rancher on a spread not far from here," he said. "Neighbor happened to ride by, saw the bodies, and burned up the trail coming to tell me about it. I put a posse together and rode out right away, hopin' we could pick up the trail of the ones who done it."

"Bodies?" Pike repeated.

Grim trenches appeared in the sheriff's weathered cheeks. "Gunned down the man's wife, too, they did." He glanced toward Belle and Nessa, then added awkwardly, "At least it appeared that they didn't, ah, mistreat the lady first, though that's scant comfort and in no way excuses two cold-blood killin's. And all so's they could steal a wagon." The sheriff's voice shook a little with rage. "What sort of man kills two people just so he can steal a *wagon*?"

"Well, now I'm sure we ran into the same bunch, Sheriff," Pike said. "They filled that wagon full of brush, set it on fire, and used it to try to stop us when they jumped us on the hill trail just this side of the Brazos back there."

He jerked his left thumb over his shoulder in the direction of the river.

"Jumped you, eh?" The sheriff looked shrewdly at Pike. "Why would they do that?"

"I guess they thought we were carrying something worth stealing." Pike shook his head. "I'm not sure what they would have done with all those barrels of molasses, though."

"Molasses," Dillard repeated.

"That's right, Deputy. We're on our way to sell it to a friend of mine who has a store."

"Is that right." It wasn't a question, because Pike could tell that Dillard didn't believe a word of it.

Neither did Sheriff Wilson, more than likely, but he seemed to have something more important on his mind.

"If those owlhoots attacked you, where are they now?" he wanted to know.

"Keep going another mile or so and you'll find them. Just look for the two mounds of freshly turned dirt not far off to the side of the trail."

Dillard stiffened and demanded angrily, "Are you trying to say that you killed them—"

"Take it easy, Prent," Wilson said. "These . . . molasses traders . . . look like a pretty salty bunch themselves."

"We found a letter in one of their saddlebags," Pike went on, figuring it would be a good idea to steer the conversation away from what was in those barrels on the wagons. "It was addressed to a man named Bouchard. Malachi Bouchard."

"Bouchard!" Dillard exclaimed. "Buzzard Bouchard?"

Pike shook his head. "I wouldn't know about that. But come to think of it, one of them *did* bear a certain resemblance to a buzzard. I take it you've heard of the fella?"

"We've got reward dodgers on him and his gang," Wilson said. "Now that I know Bouchard was involved, I'm not quite so surprised that he murdered those poor young folks. Bouchard is plumb evil. Was, I guess I should say, assumin' he's really buried yonder like you said."

"You can dig them up and see for yourself if you want," Pike said. "They haven't been down there very long."

Dillard said, "If you want to claim the rewards on them, you'll have to bring them in—"

"We're not interested in blood money," Pike said, unable to contain his irritation. "We just want to get on about our business."

Dillard edged his horse forward. "Speaking of your business, I'd like to take a closer look at those barrels—"

"Now, Prent, there's no need for that," Wilson said.

"Molasses is, ah, mighty sticky stuff. I'd just as soon not mess with it, myself. And if these folks have done away with Buzzard Bouchard and his gang, why, they've done us a favor. Us and the whole state of Texas, I reckon." The sheriff waved a hand. "So you just go on about your business endeavors, and I wish you good luck with them."

"Thank you, Sheriff," Pike said. "We appreciate that." He turned to nod to his companions. "Let's get rolling again."

While they were climbing onto the wagons, Sheriff Wilson led his posse around them and rode off toward the Brazos River—not without some glares from the deputy, however. As Dougal took up the reins on the lead wagon, he said, "That ol' John Law knew good an' well what we've got in them barrels, Pike. He just decided he didn't want to do nothin' about it."

"I know," Pike nodded. "I guess he really was grateful we got rid of Bouchard."

"Still, I reckon it'd be a good idea if we moved on out of his county pretty quick-like."

"Just as soon as we can," Pike agreed.

Belle came up on horseback and asked, "Are you still going to make me ride on the wagon, or are you convinced that I'm all right now?"

Pike grinned. "After the way you saved my bacon a while ago, I can't very well tell you not to do what you want to, can I?"

"That's right. Back to the remuda?"

"Back to the remuda," he told her.

In truth, he would have rather had her riding up ahead with him, but that wouldn't be fair to Nessa. Sooner or later, Pike thought as he nudged his horse into motion, he and Belle were going to have to work out the question of how they really felt about each other.

That would have to wait, though. They still had a big load of moonshine to deliver.

The trail wound between rugged, flat-topped hills for a few miles. Ten or twenty years ago, Pike knew, roving Comanche war parties had used those heights as lookout spots since they provided a good view of the route used by westbound settlers, just as the Comanches had used Warbonnet Peak back home, in an even earlier era in Texas's bloody history.

Now the Indian threat was mostly over, but the hills could hide other dangers, so Pike kept a close eye on them as he rode ahead of the wagons.

He came to a crossroads. The trail they had been following continued on west, while a north-south route crossed it. They needed to turn south here and follow that road for a couple of days, through several ranges of hills alternating with shallow valleys, until they turned more to the southwest again and came to rolling plains that stretched most of the way to Pecan County. The settlement of Morton's Mill, if that was what it was called, was about halfway through those hills. Pike hoped to reach it before nightfall.

As the wagons came up, he sat his horse at the crossroads and pointed so Dougal would know which trail to follow. The old-timer guided the lead wagon through the turn and the others followed. As the remuda came up, larger now that the outlaw gang's horses had been added to it, Pike called to Belle and Nessa, "Are you girls doing all right?"

"We're fine," Nessa answered him tartly. "You just tend to your own business."

Pike grinned at his sister's sharp tongue and turned his horse to lope back to the head of the caravan.

The ruggedness of the terrain meant that the wagons couldn't move very fast. With its thickly wooded ridges, rocky outcroppings, and creeks flowing through deep gullies, this area wasn't really fit for farming, but it provided enough graze for cattle. Pike saw scattered herds in the valleys and on the slopes. Barbed wire hadn't encroached too much yet on this part of the country, so they traveled through open range for the most part.

There were also plenty of places for bushwhackers to hide, so Pike remained alert. Just because they had dealt with Malachi Bouchard and his gang, that didn't mean there were no more threats waiting for them. Where there was one band of outlaws, there could be another.

However, by late afternoon they hadn't encountered any trouble, and as Pike reined in at the crest of a ridge, he looked out over the small valley in front of him and saw smoke rising from the chimneys of buildings clustered at the base of the next range of hills. Just ahead of him, the hardpacked dirt trail curved down the slope and then crossed the valley to the settlement.

Pike waited for Dougal to catch up and pointed out the buildings to him.

"We'll stop there for the night," he said. "This should be about the halfway point of the trip. Might replenish our supplies while we're here."

"Sounds good," Dougal said. He flapped the reins and urged the team down the slope, which was gentle enough not to cause any problems.

Pike stayed where he was and watched the wagons trundle on down into the valley. Nessa and Belle were still doing a good job keeping the extra livestock bunched together and moving in the right direction, he saw as they came up.

"Are you going to eat dust with the likes of us?" Belle called to him as they went by.

"Not hardly," Pike replied with a grin. He nudged his horse into motion and trotted down the hill to catch up to and then pass the wagons. He rode ahead toward the settlement.

Morton's Mill wasn't a very big place, just a handful of businesses and maybe two dozen houses. Pike saw the grain mill that had given the settlement its name, as well as a cotton gin, a blacksmith shop, a couple of general stores, and a pair of churches—one Baptist and one Methodist— with the town cemetery behind the Baptist church.

There was no saloon, he noted, which was a little unusual unless they'd had one of those blasted local-option elections in this county, too, Pike thought. He wondered what things were coming to in Texas when a man couldn't even get a friendly drink. He was glad he had given up his wandering ways and come home, but he was still a little disappointed in the direction the Lone Star State seemed to be going.

Next to the Methodist Church was a large open area with a lot of towering shade trees around it, a mixture of pecan trees, cottonwoods, and post oaks. It was a perfect spot for travelers to camp, and judging by the wheel ruts that led toward it from the trail, it had been used for that purpose quite a bit in the past. As soon as Pike laid eyes on it, he knew that would be a good place for his group to spend the night.

If they did, though, they would have to share the space, because a couple of wagons were parked there already. One of the vehicles had a wheel off and was blocked up while repairs were made. A hatless, dark-haired man in a white shirt, wet with sweat and with the sleeves rolled up, straightened from the task and wearily wiped his forearm across his face.

A blond woman stood nearby, watching anxiously, and with her were two men, older than the one working on the wagon. All of them looked worried.

Pike rode over there. The man at the wagon heard him coming and turned to give him a rather wary frown. Pike smiled to show that he was friendly, and as he reined in, he said, "Howdy. Looks like you've had some trouble. Can I give you a hand?"

The man relaxed, evidently taking Pike's offer as sincere—which it was. He looked over at the blonde and said, "See, Elizabeth? I told you the Lord would provide any assistance we needed, and now He has, in the form of this gentleman."

"You were right, as always, Lavon," the woman said. She smiled at Pike.

The man called Lavon came closer to Pike and extended his hand.

"Lavon Baxter, Brother," he introduced himself. "The Reverend Lavon Baxter. And you, sir, must be our guardian angel."

Pike leaned down from the saddle and clasped Baxter's hand. He chuckled and said, "Glad to meet you, Reverend. Pike Shannon's the name, and I don't think anybody's ever called me an angel of any kind before. They usually claim I belong in the other place!"

CHAPTER 25

Baxter introduced the blond woman as his sister Elizabeth. The older men were Deacon Matthew Finley and Deacon Frederick O'Leary. Pike nodded to the two deacons, pinched his hat brim to Elizabeth, and said, "It's a pleasure to meet you, ma'am."

"Likewise, Mr. Shannon." She gestured toward the wagon. "Do you think you can help my brother repair that axle? I fear it cracked, back up the trail a ways."

"I hit a rut too hard," Baxter said with a rueful chuckle.

Pike swung down from the saddle and asked, "Do you have a spare axle?"

"I'm afraid that *is* our spare axle. The other one broke a while back, and I haven't had a chance to replace it yet."

Pike nodded and hunkered on his heels to peer underneath the wagon and study the axle. After a moment, he said, "It doesn't appear to be too damaged right now, but if you keep driving on it for a long way, it's liable to crack right in two and then you really *will* be stuck. How far are you going?"

"We're bound for Prescott, a journey of several days to the southwest."

"I know where Prescott is," Pike said. "As it happens, that's where I'm headed myself, along with my family and friends." He gestured toward the wagons that were now approaching. "I think we can fix that axle so it'll hold up that long, especially since there's a blacksmith shop here in the settlement. We'll just take it off and get the smith to fasten a couple of metal bands around it, tight enough to keep that crack from spreading. Could've done the same with some wet rawhide, if we'd had to, but it'll be better to get the smith to repair it."

"That's an excellent idea. I'm not sure I ever would have thought of it myself." Baxter smiled and shrugged. "I'm afraid my mind is better equipped for spiritual matters, rather than the, ah, nuts and bolts of everyday life."

"Well, it takes all kinds in this world, Reverend," Pike said as he straightened. He waved for Dougal to keep coming.

They circled up the five wagons, as usual, and Belle and Nessa drove the extra stock through one of the openings into the circle. While Sam, Will, and Fiddler got busy unhitching the teams, Pike motioned for Torrance and Dougal to join him. Belle and Nessa dismounted and led their horses over, as well.

Lavon Baxter wiped his hands on a rag so he could shake with Torrance and Dougal when Pike introduced them. Since he and Pike had only howdied when they met, not shook, they clasped hands as well. Baxter introduced his sister Elizabeth to the others, Pike introduced Belle and Nessa, and then it was the turn of the two deacons. Getting all that done took a while, but finally it was finished and Torrance was able to comment, "Looks like you've got a problem with that axle, Reverend."

"Indeed, I do. Your brother suggested that we take it off

and have the local blacksmith attach some strips of metal around it."

Torrance nodded and said, "Good idea. That's about the only thing you can do if you don't have a spare. We'll give you a hand with it."

"Thank you, Mr. Shannon," Elizabeth said. "I don't know what we would have done if all of you hadn't come along."

"Things might get confusing with that Mr. Shannon business, seeing as there's three of us," Torrance told her with a smile. "You can just call me Torrance, Miss Baxter."

"Well, if I'm going to do that, you should call me Elizabeth. That's only fair."

"If you say so . . . Elizabeth."

It was all Pike could do not to stare at his brother. Torrance had always been a little awkward and tongue-tied around pretty girls, and yet here he was, flirting with this young woman he had met mere moments earlier. Torrance must find her powerful attractive, Pike mused. Elizabeth *was* nice-looking, he conceded, although he thought both Belle and Sophie were considerably more appealing.

Since one wheel was already off and that side blocked up, they got busy doing the same on the other side so the cracked axle could be removed. Torrance and Dougal had plenty of experience working on wagons, and so did Sam Crow and Will Fisher, who drifted over a short time later with Fiddler and made the acquaintance of the Baxter party, as well.

With that many men who knew what they were doing working on it, they had the axle off in a hurry. Torrance and Sam carried it to the blacksmith shop.

"I can't tell you how much we appreciate your help," Baxter said to Pike.

"Happy to do it," Pike assured the man.

Elizabeth said, "Well, I believe we should demonstrate our appreciation by having all of you to supper tonight. I can rustle up something . . ."

Pike saw the slight frown that appeared on Baxter's face and wondered if they were short of provisions, or at least low enough to make such a generous offer problematical. He didn't want to embarrass Elizabeth, so he said, "We were going to be stocking up on supplies while we're here, so why don't we just all go in together on supper and share a good meal?"

"That sounds like an excellent idea," Baxter said, his worry disappearing.

Elizabeth said to Belle and Nessa, "We can figure out something special to fix."

Belle laughed and told her, "Fiddler's the one you want to talk to. He's probably the best cook in our bunch."

"I won't dispute that," Fiddler said with a grin.

"All right, then, it's settled," Elizabeth said happily. "We'll have ourselves a little feast of thanksgiving for all the assistance you've given us."

"If it's gonna be a party," Dougal said, "then ol' Fiddler there can do more than cook. How do you reckon he got his name? He's the best fiddle player this side of the Cap Rock!"

This was shaping up to be an evening to remember, Pike thought.

It was late enough in the day that the blacksmith didn't want to tackle the job of repairing the axle until the next morning, Torrance reported when he and Sam returned to the wagons. The man had promised to start on it first thing, though, so there was a chance the Baxter wagons wouldn't be held up for too long.

By then, Fiddler, Nessa, and Elizabeth had visited both of the general stores and gathered what they would need for the meal that evening, as well as replenishing the supplies for both parties. They had gotten a good-sized roast that Fiddler was cooking with potatoes and carrots. He had fresh bread baking in a Dutch oven.

Elizabeth was helping him, but Nessa, seeing that she wasn't really needed, had walked over to join the others as they sat around the camp, using crates and wagon tongues as seats. Dusky shadows had started to gather, and a peaceful air hung over the area where the wagons were parked.

Pike sat with his hands clasped together between his knees as he asked, "Why are you headed for Prescott, Mr. Baxter? Or should I say, Reverend Baxter?"

"Either is fine," Branson replied with a smile. "Or simply call me Lavon. I'm just a man like any other, despite my calling. I'm on my way to conduct some services at one of the churches there. I'm an itinerant preacher, you see. A wanderer."

"Nothing wrong with that. I've done a heap of wandering myself."

Dougal chuckled and said, "You wasn't exactly preachin' the gospel, though, son. Six-gun gospel, maybe!" He slapped his thigh and laughed again.

Baxter cocked an inquisitive eyebrow at Pike, who said, "Pay no attention to this old pelican. These days I'm strictly a peaceable man."

Torrance was the one who grunted skeptically at that. Sam and Will just smiled.

"Well, I like to think that regardless of any of our pasts, today is the most important day of our lives, because it's the only one we truly own," Baxter said. "The past is gone, and none of us are guaranteed tomorrow."

"Now, those are true words, Reverend," Torrance said. "Although some of us might have a little harder time putting the past behind us than others."

He looked meaningfully at Pike, who told himself to ignore his brother.

Baxter said, "I believe you mentioned that you were headed for Prescott, too, Pike. What takes you down there, if you don't mind my asking?"

"Business," Pike said. Since the barrels full of moonshine were in plain sight in the back of the wagons, he went ahead and addressed the issue, using the same story he had given the sheriff earlier. "We've got a load of molasses there that we're selling."

"That's a *lot* of molasses," Baxter said.

Dougal laughed again. "You don't know, Preacher, you just don't know. It sure is a lot of molasses!"

Baxter frowned, obviously puzzled by the old-timer's amusement. But then he put that aside and said, "There's something I've been thinking about. I'd like to ask you a question, Pike."

"Sure, go ahead."

"You're going to Prescott, and my sister and the deacons and I are going to Prescott . . . so how would it be if all of us traveled together the rest of the way?"

When Baxter was halfway through speaking, Pike had figured out already where he was headed with the question. He didn't know how to answer it, however.

As he hesitated, Baxter went on, "I admit, it's pretty self-ish of me to invite us along, so to speak. And it's obvious why I would make such a request. If we run into more trouble along the way, as we did today with the wagon, you'd be there to help us. I can't promise anything in return, either, except the pleasure of our company, such as it is."

Torrance looked toward the campfire where Elizabeth and Fiddler were preparing supper and said, "Good company is always welcome, Reverend."

Pike wasn't so sure about that. It wasn't a matter of not trusting the preacher and his companions. Baxter seemed harmless enough.

But there was still a good chance the caravan would be attacked again by outlaws after the moonshine on the way to Pecan County, and if that happened, Baxter, his sister, and the two deacons would be in danger if they came along. Pike didn't want to be responsible for the safety of those innocents.

However, explaining that would make it difficult to maintain the fiction of his molasses story. He was still debating how to respond when Torrance went on, "I think it's fine for you to come with us. What do you say, Dougal?"

"Ain't up to me," the old-timer said. "Pike's ramroddin' this here wagon train."

Torrance frowned and said, "I've got just as much say in things as Pike does. I don't remember making him the boss."

"I never said I was the boss," Pike snapped.

Elizabeth said, "Lavon, look what you're done. You've created friction and hard feelings between brothers."

"I'm sorry, gentlemen," Baxter said quickly. "Please, ignore what I just suggested. We'll make our way on to Prescott by ourselves, and I'm sure we'll be just fine—"

Feeling trapped and not liking it, Pike said, "No, Reverend, that's all right. I reckon you can trail along with us. You've got to agree to do what I say, though, in case we run into trouble."

"Are you expecting trouble?" Baxter asked.

"Not necessarily, but you never know what you might run into."

"Life is uncertain by its very nature. As I said, none of us are guaranteed tomorrow. But of course, in case of any problems, we'll abide by your decisions, Pike. You're a lot more experienced at such things than any of us are."

"More than you know, Reverend," Dougal said. "More'n you know."

Torrance nodded and said, "That's settled, then. We'll all travel together the rest of the way."

Pike gave his brother a hard look. He intended to have a talk with Torrance about the way he'd gotten them into this, all because he was obviously smitten with Elizabeth. Not that it would do any real good, Pike mused. Torrance was too hardheaded to ever admit when he was wrong.

That was when Fiddler called, "Supper's ready, everyone. Come and get it!"

CHAPTER 26

When Sophie got up early that morning, she was surprised to see that Elizabeth was gone. As she looked around the camp, it didn't take her long to realize that two of the wagons were missing, as well, along with a couple of the older men in the group—and Lavon Branson.

Baffled and more upset than she believed she should have been, she sought out the only person she could think of to ask about this, the young man called Curtis.

"Yes'm, Sister Sophie, Brother Lavon and Sister Elizabeth left before sunup this morning with Deacons Finley and O'Leary," he told her. "They took those two wagons."

"But where did they go?" Sophie asked with a puzzled frown.

Curtis shook his head. "I don't know, Sister. Brother Lavon sometimes does things that he doesn't explain, and none of us ask him about it because we figure it's not our place. He's guided by the spirit, so we don't question what he does."

That sort of respect for their leader was all well and good, thought Sophie, but at the same time, it seemed rude of Lavon Branson to just go off like that without any explanation.

"What are the rest of us supposed to do?"

"Head on down to Pecan County, just as we've been doin', I suppose. Nobody's said any different." Curtis smiled. "Don't worry, Sister. I'm sure Brother Lavon will meet us there, or somewhere along the way, and everything will be fine."

Sophie wasn't so sure of that. She looked around and said, "Mr. Ferrell and Mr. Hoyt and the other men who left the group earlier haven't come back, have they?"

She couldn't bring herself to refer to hardcases like Ferrell and Hoyt as "brother," even though she told herself that maybe she wasn't being fair to them.

"No, they're still gone on whatever mission Brother Lavon sent them on," Curtis said. "They'll probably meet up with us in Prescott, too."

Sophie nodded. Curtis seemed to think all these mysterious goings-on were perfectly normal, so perhaps she was just being too suspicious. And maybe, she admitted, she didn't like it that Elizabeth Meadows had gone off somewhere with Branson. That really wasn't any of her business.

So she summoned up a smile and said, "Thank you, Curtis. I suppose we're going to continue our journey just as we would if Brother Lavon was with us?"

"We sure are. That's the way it's always been before."

So this wasn't the first time Branson had disappeared on some enigmatic errand. Sophie tried not to think about that as she got ready to depart with the others, but it continued to lurk in the back of her mind.

Curtis was going to be driving the lead wagon today. He invited Sophie to join him on the driver's seat and helped her climb up. She settled down on the wooden bench as Curtis energetically hauled himself over the wheel on the other side of the wagon and dropped down beside her.

"Here we go," he said as he picked up the reins and reached for the brake lever. "Ought to be a good day."

"Yes, it should," Sophie said, hoping he was right about that.

Titus Ferrell, Carter Hoyt, and the rest of the gunmen were far to the southwest by this time. The terrain was flatter and the soil sandier. A few low mesas were visible in the distance.

The hardcases rode until they reached a spot where the trail went up a hill and ran between two steep banks about twenty feet high. The ridge through which that gap was cut was rugged and covered with brush.

Ferrell reined in, studied the place, and said to Hoyt, "This is a perfect spot for what we need, don't you reckon?"

"Yeah," Hoyt replied. "We've been pushing these horses hard enough that we have a good long lead on those wagons. Shannon and the rest won't get here for a day and a half, more than likely. Maybe more."

"That's all right. You'll have plenty of time to ride back, let Lavon know what we've found, and then get back here in time to join in the ambush."

Hoyt nodded. "Yeah, he can figure out some story to get him and the girl and Finley and O'Leary away from Shannon's bunch before the ball starts, once he's sure they're headed in the right direction."

"Not this time," Ferrell snapped. His usual easygoing grin was nowhere in sight. His craggy features had settled into bleak lines.

Hoyt cocked his head to the side and asked, "What do you mean, Titus? Lavon always breaks off from the bunch before we ambush them. Maybe he has an idea of what's really going on, but that way he can lie to himself that he doesn't."

"Yeah, and I'm sick and tired of it. He acts so blasted pious and holier-than-thou, and all the time he's beddin' those pretty girls who get caught up in his sermons, and he knows good and well we've been takin' over the liquor trade in all the towns we come to, even if it means wiping out the hombres who have been runnin' things. I've had enough of it. He's reaping plenty of benefits from what we've been doin', and it's time he was there for some of the real work." Ferrell turned his head and spat. "The gun work."

Hoyt sat there for a long moment, frowning in thought at what Ferrell had said. Finally, he said, "He's not going to be happy about that."

"You sure? He thinks sinners ought to get what's comin' to him, don't he? Well, that's what's fixin' to happen in a couple of days. Pike Shannon and the rest of his sinnin' bunch will face judgment . . . bullet judgment . . . and the rest of us will wind up richer for it." Ferrell's grin came back. "Who knows? When he sees those sinners dyin', he might just up and shout *hallelujah*."

Despite her misgivings, Sophie found herself enjoying riding on the wagon that day with Curtis. He was a talkative young man and didn't need much prodding to tell her all about growing up on a farm in Missouri in a large family with a lot of siblings.

"I reckon that's why I feel so at home here with Brother

Lavon and his followers," Curtis said. "I've always had lots of brothers and sisters. These folks aren't blood kin, of course, but I'm close enough to them that they might as well be."

Sophie told him about her life, too. He was easy to talk to, and that caused the day to pass quickly.

They made camp that evening at a crossroads where the trail they had been following continued west and another route branched off to north and south. They would be going south in the morning, Curtis explained.

Branson and Elizabeth hadn't rejoined them, and there was still no sign of Ferrell, Hoyt, and the other men who had left earlier. Because of that, a slight unease still lurked in the back of Sophie's mind, but she had enjoyed the day she had just spent with Curtis enough that she told herself to stop worrying and make the most of this journey. She might not ever do anything this adventurous again.

"Since Sister Elizabeth's not here, maybe you'd like to have supper with me," Curtis suggested. He smiled. "I can whip up a right tasty stew."

"I'm sure you can," Sophie said, "but remember, back in Warbonnet I ran a café. I'm a pretty good cook, if I do say so myself."

"Well, I'm sure not gonna turn down an invitation like that. My mama didn't raise any fools."

She hadn't actually invited him, Sophie thought, but if he wanted to take it that way, she wasn't going to argue with him. It had been a pleasant day, and there was no reason for it not to continue into the evening.

But only for a little while. She didn't think Curtis would get any improper ideas, but if he did, she would set him straight quickly enough.

"I need to go help tend to the stock," he told her, "but I can make a fire for you before I do, if you want."

"No, that's all right. You go ahead with your work. I'll get started on supper."

A pot of beans had been soaking all day. She built a fire and got the beans cooking, then put water in another pot and cut up some potatoes in it. Some leftover biscuits warmed up in the Dutch oven and freshly fried salt pork would combine with everything else to make a good meal, washed down by coffee, of course.

Sophie was busy enough that she didn't really notice how long Curtis was gone, but when the food was almost ready, he wasn't back yet. She was wondering if she ought to go look for him when he showed up with a slight frown on his face.

"Is something wrong?" she asked him.

He gave a little shake of his head, as if he'd been lost somewhere off in his thoughts, and said, "What? No, I don't reckon. Why do you ask?"

"You just looked like you were a little worried about something?"

"No, it's nothing," he assured her. "Nothing for you to be concerned about."

"Then it is *something*."

"No, just forget it," he said, his tone a little sharper now.

"All right." Sophie tried not to sound petulant and hurt by his response, but she knew she didn't do a very good job of it.

Curtis must have recognized her feelings, because he said hurriedly, "I'm sorry. I just overheard a couple of the fellas talking about something, and I got confused. But it's nothing to do with you, Sister Sophie, and I don't want it to cause a problem with our supper."

"There's no problem," she told him as she summoned up a smile. "Sit down, and I'll pour you a cup of coffee. The food's just about ready."

His friendly grin reappeared. "It smells mighty good, that's for sure."

They ate, and the brief moment of unpleasantness was forgotten in the enjoyment Sophie felt in sharing the meal with him. Curtis was a nice young man.

Nicer than Pike Shannon, no doubt about that.

Thinking about Pike made uneasiness stir inside Sophie. She wondered where he was tonight. Somewhere ahead of them on the trail to Pecan County, she supposed.

Was Belle Ramsey with him? That was certainly possible. Sophie actually liked Belle and admired her independent nature, but Belle could be brazen at times. Pike was better suited to a girl like her, Sophie told herself.

The two of them never could have had anything serious together. He was just too stubborn and reckless, and he had a wild streak in him that Sophie suspected would never be tamed.

She wouldn't have wanted him if it was, she realized. He just wouldn't have seemed like Pike without it . . .

"Sister Sophie?"

Curtis's voice broke into her reverie and made her turn her head toward him and smile.

"Yes? What is it?"

"Boy howdy, you looked like you were a million miles away just then."

Not that far, thought Sophie. Probably more like thirty or forty miles.

"I was wondering," Curtis went on, "would you, uh . . . would you . . . would it be all right . . ."

"Whatever you have to ask me, just go ahead and ask," she told him gently.

He took a deep breath, obviously working up his courage, and said, "Would it be all right if I held your hand?" He went on hastily, "Just for a minute, you understand. Shoot, it wouldn't be much more than a handshake."

Sophie hesitated as she debated the propriety of what he had just asked. There were people all around them, so it wouldn't go beyond hand-holding, certainly, but even such minor familiarity had its consequences and implications. And she had never been one to give in to impulsive notions.

Maybe that was part of her problem, she told herself. She would never want to be as reckless as Pike Shannon was, but a little impulsiveness might not be a bad thing.

"I believe that would be all right," she said. She held out her right hand, and Curtis took it in his left. His palm was callused and work-roughened, but he made up for that with a deft gentleness of touch that squeezed with just the right amount of pressure.

"I don't have any pretty words," he said without looking at her, "but I sure do like sittin' here with you like this."

"It's very nice," Sophie agreed.

"We'll ride together again tomorrow?"

"Yes," she said. "Yes, I believe we will."

CHAPTER 27

Even though the moonshine caravan had stopped in a settlement, Pike didn't relax much. He still posted guards that night, even though Lavon Baxter and his companions might think it odd that he would have somebody standing watch over barrels of molasses.

Let them think whatever they wanted. Pike wasn't going to take any chances.

He took the third shift, along with Sam Crow. The two of them posted themselves on opposite sides of the camp.

Morton's Mill was a quiet, peaceful settlement. As far as Pike could tell, the whole town was sound asleep most of the night. Along toward morning, when the sky was still black except for an arc of faint gray in the east, he smelled woodsmoke as folks fired up their stoves to prepare breakfast.

He got some wood from the possum belly on one of the wagons and begin building a fire for himself and the others. Usually one of the guards on this third shift got the coffee on to boil as dawn approached.

A short time later, while Pike was busy with that, he heard voices from the wagon belonging to Reverend

Lavon Baxter and his sister. He couldn't make out the words, but he was sure both of them were awake and talking.

The conversation had a bit of an urgent sound to it, as well. That caused Pike's forehead to crease in a frown as he knelt beside the wood he was arranging for the campfire.

He couldn't tell if the Baxters were arguing, but it sounded like they might be. One thing was for sure—he wasn't going to amble over there and eavesdrop. Whatever was happening in that wagon, it was none of his business.

Torrance crawled out from under one of the moonshine wagons where he'd been asleep and came shambling over to Pike. His brown hair was awry from slumber. He raked his fingers through it and asked, "Any sign of trouble during the night?"

"Not a one," Pike replied. He didn't say anything about the Baxter siblings maybe wrangling a few minutes earlier. That wasn't any of Torrance's business, either.

Torrance stroked his chin. His fingertips rasped faintly on the beard stubble they found there.

"Wonder what time that blacksmith is going to get to his forge?"

"I don't know, but it won't be good and light for almost an hour yet. You in a hurry to finish fixing the preacher's wagon and get back on the trail again?"

"No, not really. Just curious, that's all. We've made good progress on this trip, despite the trouble we ran into back there just this side of the Brazos. Your friend Delano probably isn't expecting us quite yet."

"He'll be glad to see us, though, whenever we get there," Pike said. "He needs what's in those barrels."

Torrance grunted. "Yeah. Molasses."

"That was the first thing I thought of," Pike said in a low voice. "I guess we should have figured all that out earlier, in case we needed a story."

"This is the first time we've done anything like this," Torrance mused. "In the past, Shannons always sold their . . . molasses . . . closer to home. What if Delano wants more?"

"You and Dougal and me will have to sit down and talk about that."

"What about Ma and Nessa? They're part of the family, too."

"Yeah, but the menfolks will make any decisions."

Torrance chuckled and said, "You let me know when you're fixing to tell that to Ma. I wouldn't mind watching the show."

Pike started to frame a curt response, but then he laughed softly, too. Mary Shannon had never been shy about expressing her opinions, and she expected them to be taken into consideration. For that matter, Nessa could be counted on to speak up when she thought it was necessary, too.

"We'll work it out," Pike said. "I'm not sure making a trip this long all the time would be a good idea, though. With every mile you add, you're just asking for more trouble."

Torrance nodded. "Yeah. Are you putting the coffee on?"

"Right now," Pike said.

Torrance might have hung around to talk more, but at that moment, Elizabeth Baxter climbed over the tailgate of their wagon, balanced there for a second, and then dropped lithely and gracefully to the ground.

Torrance didn't waste any time going over there to bid her a good morning.

Pike shook his head a little as he watched his brother hurry across the open area. Torrance had fallen hard and fast for Elizabeth, but Pike hadn't seen anything to indicate that she returned his interest. She just seemed politely friendly, that's all.

That's how she struck Pike now as she stood there next to the wagon talking to Torrance. He told her that he would be going to check on how the blacksmith was coming with that cracked axle, just as soon as it was light enough to do so. Pike heard her thank him. He understood only bits and pieces of the rest of the conversation, not enough to know what they were talking about. The conversation looked pleasant enough.

Belle walked up on the other side of the fire as Pike stuck some kindling among the branches. She said, "He's really smitten with her, isn't he?"

"Torrance?" Pike said, even though he knew perfectly well that was who Belle meant. "Yeah, he is. He's never had that much to do with girls, so I guess it was inevitable that when he finally fell, he'd fall hard."

"As opposed to you, who never let your guard down."

"I wouldn't say that."

"Oh, yes, of course. Sophie."

Pike shrugged and said, "Never would have amounted to anything. She's too dead set against drinking. And, well, that's been part of the Shannon family for a long time."

"Things change. So do families. I'm the last of the Ramseys in Warbonnet County, remember."

"I hadn't forgotten," Pike assured her. "Are you saying that you're going to turn temperance, too?"

That brought a laugh from Belle. She said, "Not hardly. In fact, if there was an easy way to tap one of those barrels,

I'd put a little 'shine in my coffee this morning. Might help me wake up."

"The Reverend Mister Baxter might object."

"Reverend Baxter . . ." Belle mused. She was serious now as she went on, "There's something about him, Pike. Something that strikes me as . . . odd."

"What do you mean?"

"Most preachers I've been around, you can tell they're sincere in what they say and believe. I listen to Baxter, and it's like I can't bring myself to believe one hundred percent in what he's saying. It doesn't seem like *he* believes it. He kind of . . . you'll think I've gone loco . . . but he kind of reminds me of Doak."

It was light enough now for Pike to make out the scar on Belle's cheek, the scar that Doak Ramsey had given to her.

"You're not saying you think Baxter's an outlaw, are you?"

Belle shook her head. "No, but I just have a hunch it would be a good idea to keep an eye on him."

"I keep an eye on everybody," Pike said.

But he trusted Belle's judgment, and he vowed that he would be paying more attention to Reverend Lavon Baxter in the future, as the wagons rolled on toward Pecan County.

Baxter did nothing suspicious that day, however. He seemed as mild-mannered, self-deprecating, and friendly as ever. Once the repaired axle had been replaced, he insisted that his pair of wagons would bring up the rear in the caravan.

"If that axle gives more trouble or if we slow you down

in any way, you can feel free to forge ahead without us," he told Pike before they left Morton's Mill.

"I doubt if it'll come to that, Reverend," Pike said. "But we'll bear it in mind."

The two wagons kept up fine, though, and when the caravan stopped for the midday meal, Baxter, Elizabeth, and the two deacons joined in as they had the night before.

Torrance made sure that he was sitting beside Elizabeth while they ate. As far as Pike could tell, she still wasn't really encouraging his attention, but she didn't do anything to *dis*courage it, either.

That low-voiced, intense conversation he had overheard in the Baxter wagon that morning came to mind. For some reason, Pike wished he had been able to make out what they were saying.

While they were stopped, after everyone had eaten, Elizabeth drifted up to Lavon Branson and said quietly, "Torrance asked me if I'd like to ride with him this afternoon."

Branson smiled as if what she had just said was of no real consequence. "Go ahead, if you want to," he told her. "I'm sure it would brighten the young man's day immensely."

"I don't want to lead him on too much," Elizabeth said with a tight little frown.

"I'm not sure if you could even manage that, my dear. If I've ever seen a man practically champing at the bit to be led on, it's Torrance Shannon."

"He's nice," Elizabeth protested. "He doesn't deserve what's going to happen. All that moonshine destroyed . . ."

"It's the devil's brew, Sister," Branson said with an edge

of mockery in his voice. "You know that. It's not fit for anything but destruction."

"I know." She sighed. "And I don't care about the others. They deserve to have the fruits of their sinful labor taken away from them. I suppose Torrance deserves it, too. But I still hate to see it happen."

"Don't worry. Perhaps he and the other Shannons will see the error of their ways and return home to pursue something more worthwhile."

"I hope so," Elizabeth said. "I think I *will* ride with him this afternoon."

"Go right ahead."

That left Branson alone on the seat of his wagon, but he didn't mind. Elizabeth had been good company for quite a while, and she still had her uses as this current situation proved, but Branson's future intentions were set on Sophie Truesdale now. She was as succulent a morsel as he had ever laid eyes on.

He had learned early on that there were certain sins of the flesh he could refrain from—and some he couldn't. He genuinely despised drinking and had ever since he'd watched his mother sink an axe into the head of his drunken father and then wander off in her own besotted stupor to fall into an icy river and drown. That left Lavon to fend for himself, but at twelve years old, he was already big enough and experienced enough to do that.

The preacher in the midwestern town near the Branson farm had taken him in, then regretted it a couple of years later when his daughter turned up with a swollen belly and Lavon was nowhere to be found.

Neither was the bag of gold coins the preacher had saved up.

And neither was one of his Bibles, although he might not have ever noticed it missing.

Lavon had learned a great deal during those two years of listening to the man's sermons. He could deliver the hellfire and brimstone, and Lavon found that he had a knack for that himself. It was odd . . . Sometimes he believed the things he was saying, believed that he could turn away from evil and become a good man.

Then his funds got low, or he saw a pretty girl and wanted her, and he knew that he could never become that man. Not completely.

That hadn't really changed in the years since, as he had amassed more followers, more influence, more money—and more women.

His easy slide into sinfulness tormented him now and then, but most of the time he just didn't think about it anymore.

They had left the ranges of hills behind and were angling almost due southwest now over grassy, gently rolling terrain broken up by clumps of post oaks and irregular sand roughs. A few hills poked up here and there, but the long, rocky ridges were behind them.

Branson knew to watch those hilltops. He had studied a map with Ferrell and Hoyt before they left the group, and Ferrell, who had been through this part of Texas before, had rested a blunt fingertip on the paper and said, "Right along here somewhere, there ought to be a good place to jump them. Watch for a signal, Lavon, and when you see it, you'll know they'll be gettin' to the spot the next day. Sneak away from the wagons if you can. Whoever brings the message will be watching, and he'll meet you and give you the details of the ambush."

"And I should be gone by the time you capture the wagons and destroy the moonshine," Branson had said.

Ferrell had just grunted, and Hoyt's gaunt face was as expressionless as always, so Branson didn't think anything more about it. He just kept track of where they were as the wagons rolled southwestward, and he knew they were far enough along that he needed to keep his eyes open.

That was how he came to be watching closely when a man on horseback edged out from some oaks atop a hill a couple of hundred yards away, lifted his hat from his head for a second, and then clapped it back on and whirled his mount out of sight.

That was Carter Hoyt. Even at this distance, Branson recognized the gunman's lean figure.

Tonight, after the camp had settled down and everyone had gone to sleep, he would slip out and rendezvous with Hoyt.

Of course, not everyone would be asleep, since Pike Shannon was posting guards every night, but Branson was confident that he would be able to get out of the camp and back in without being noticed. Early in his life, he had learned the tricks of going where he wanted without anyone seeing him.

That evening, they made camp next to a giant oak tree with a vast spread of limbs that cast a large area of shade. Dougal slapped the tree's rough trunk and said, "This old fella's positively ancient. Probably been here two hundred years or more. Maybe as many as a thousand."

"Do trees really live to be that old?" Elizabeth asked.

"Some do, these old oaks, especially." Dougal gazed up at the canopy of branches. "Ain't no tellin' what this tree has seen in its time."

"Probably a lot of misery and bloodshed," Torrance

said, "since that's what mankind seems to generate the most of."

"I can't argue with you there, boy," the old-timer agreed.

Branson wondered if the savages who had populated this land in times past had conducted human sacrifices under this tree. He wouldn't be a bit surprised. And no matter how much progress the world made, some things never changed.

Branson wasn't sure if that was a good thing, or a bad one. Some sacrifices still had to be made . . .

"How did you enjoy riding with your beau today?" he asked Elizabeth when they were alone in their wagon. His mocking tone made her face flush in what he thought was a mixture of embarrassment and anger.

"Torrance isn't my beau," she said. "He's a nice young man, that's all. I still hate to cause trouble for him."

Branson cupped her chin in one hand and caressed her with the other. "But you will, though, won't you?" he purred. "You'll do what I tell you and follow where I lead, won't you?"

A shudder ran through her. She said in a husky whisper, "Of course . . . Brother Lavon."

"Very good." He let go of her and his tone became more brisk. "When everyone's asleep, I'll be leaving for a short time. I spotted Carter Hoyt earlier today. He gave me the signal I've been waiting for. He'll be keeping an eye on the camp, so he should see when I slip out and meet him."

"Why are you telling me this?"

"Why, I want to keep you informed of the plan, of course. You're a vital part of this, Sister Elizabeth. You always have been."

"You mean you won't just go ahead and do whatever you want, no matter what I think?"

Branson cocked his head to the side. "I didn't say that," he told her. "But I'd still rather you not be taken by surprise."

"I appreciate that . . . I suppose."

Sophie Truesdale had come along just in time, he told himself behind the bland smile he maintained. He'd had just about all he could stand of Elizabeth Meadows and her resentment and insolence.

They turned in later as usual, Branson spreading his bedroll under the wagon while Elizabeth took the built-in bunk. Ever since they had broken off from the rest of the group, they hadn't been together in the *un*brotherly and sisterly way they were from time to time. They couldn't risk discovery in such scandalous circumstances.

Besides, this way it would be easier for Branson to sneak away from the camp.

Torrance Shannon and the old man called Fiddler were standing the first watch. Branson made sure he knew where each man was before he crawled out from underneath the wagon. The camp was very quiet except for a few horses shifting around. Branson crawled away from the wagon, sticking to the thick shadows under the spreading boughs and angling closer to Fiddler than to Torrance. He didn't believe Fiddler would be as vigilant.

He had to freeze once when Fiddler ambled too close to him, but he lay motionless for several minutes until the man drifted away again. Branson was good at staying absolutely still and silent, another skill he had learned as a youngster when he didn't want to draw the attention of his drunken sots of parents. Having them notice him at the wrong time could easily mean a beating.

Once he was clear, he stood up, pressed his back against the trunk of a smaller tree, and listened intently. Not hearing anything unusual in the camp, he stole even farther away and finally felt confident enough to break into a lope.

Carter Hoyt stepped out from another clump of trees farther on and called softly, "Here, Lavon."

Branson padded up to him and said, "It's good to see you again, Brother Carter, even though I can't make you out very well in this starlight."

"Yeah, you, too," Hoyt said curtly. "Everything going all right with those moonshiners?"

"Strictly according to plan," Branson replied.

"Glad to hear it. We found a good spot to ambush them tomorrow."

Hoyt went on to describe the place where the trail ran between the cutbanks and told Branson how much farther along it was on the way to Pecan County.

"Reckon you should get there late tomorrow morning," he concluded.

"That's good to know," Branson said. "By midmorning tomorrow, one of the horses in my wagon team will have developed a limp and gone lame. That means we can stop to tend to that and allow the Shannon wagons to move on, and by the time we catch up, all that moonshine will have been . . . ah . . . liberated."

"Stolen, you mean."

"I don't need to know the details—" Branson began.

"Oh, yes, you do," Hoyt interrupted him. "Because Titus has made up his mind—and I agreed with him, once we talked about it—that this time is gonna be different."

"Different?" Branson repeated. "What do you mean?"

"What I mean," Hoyt said, "is that this time when the killing starts, you're gonna be right there with us, doing your share."

CHAPTER 28

Hoyt's words rocked Branson, but at the same time, although he didn't want to admit it even to himself, he knew that, deep down, he wasn't really all that shocked.

Even so, he said coldly, "I don't know what you mean."

"The hell you don't," Hoyt snapped. "For a long time, we've been killing moonshiners and whiskey runners and gang bosses for you, Lavon."

"No. You simply threaten them and force them out of business—"

"We *kill* them," Hoyt said, "and then we either steal the moonshine and sell it, or we take over the business and leave a man there to run it and send the profits on to you. How in blazes do you think you can afford to travel all over the country like you do?"

"The people who come to hear me speak . . . they take up offerings . . ."

Branson fell silent when Hoyt snorted contemptuously.

"Those offerings wouldn't pay for half of what you do. But our *guns* pay for it. They've made you a rich man, Lavon." Hoyt shrugged. "Titus and I and the other fellas have done all right for ourselves, too, I reckon. But you've been reaping the benefits without doing any of the work, and you've been turning a blind eye and pretending you don't know what's really going on. Titus got tired of that, and once he pointed it out to me, I decided I've had enough of it, too. So from now on, you can keep the truth from those stupid pilgrims who follow you around if you want to, but you're going to do your share of the real work . . . and I don't mean preaching."

It was a long speech, and Branson had stood still and silent for it, letting Hoyt get out his anger and resentment. When Hoyt finally stopped talking, Branson responded with some fervor of his own, "You forget that I'm a man of—"

"Don't you say it," Hoyt cut him off. "I'm not much of a believer, but I'm not gonna stand here while you spout sacrilege. You're a man who gets those dewy-eyed girls all worked up and then takes them to bed, and more people know about it than you realize. You like having all that money, too. Don't tell me you don't. You've got some people fooled, sure enough, but not me and Titus." Hoyt crossed his arms over his chest. "So it's up to you, Lavon. Either you stay with those moonshine wagons and help us finish off the Shannons and their friends, or we take that load, sell it ourselves, keep the money, and ride on without you. You can make your way without our help from now on."

Branson stood there, his head spinning with shock. These gunmen were disrupting his carefully constructed and comfortable existence.

"What about Sister Elizabeth and Brothers Finley and O'Leary?" he asked at last. "If I do what you want, that means they'll have to be involved as well."

"What do you care about the girl? You're trading her in for that blonde from Warbonnet any day now, aren't you?

As for Finley and O'Leary, if they see something they don't like and want to argue about it . . . well, we can take care of them, too."

"You're talking about cold-blooded murder," Branson said, his voice tinged with horror.

"I'm talking about how what's fair is fair."

"If you and Ferrell want a bigger cut—"

"Believe it or not, not everything's about money, Lavon. We're just tired of taking all the risks in this outfit and you not taking any."

Branson covered his face with his hands for a moment as he tried to take in everything Hoyt had said. No matter how hard he thought or how skilled he was at persuading other people to agree with him, he couldn't come up with anything that would change the gunman's mind.

Besides, he couldn't disagree with anything Hoyt had said. Unpleasant though it might be to admit it, the man had spoken the truth.

"All right," he said. "I suppose you have a right to ask that much of me. I'll stay with the Shannon wagons until they reach the ambush site. Are you going to . . ." He had to swallow hard before he could finish the question. "Are you going to kill all of them?"

"Well, that's generally what it takes." Hoyt shrugged again. "But if it works out so that we can keep those two girls alive, at least for a while, we might do that. You have any objections to that . . . Brother Lavon?"

Anger welled up inside Branson at the gunman's mocking tone. However, he knew that he couldn't really afford to give in to that impulse. Instead he forced himself to nod and said hollowly, "No objections."

"Looks like we're on the same page at last," Hoyt said.

"And when the Shannons get to the right spot tomorrow . . . we'll read 'em from the book good and proper."

Pike was scheduled to stand the last watch of the night with Belle. He was a little uncomfortable about that, but it was her turn, and he wasn't going out of his way to avoid her just because he was unsure what the future held for them.

Anyway, she would have complained if he'd tried to pass her over in the guard rotation.

He woke up when he needed to, a talent he had mastered over the years, but it didn't matter because Sam Crow would have roused him a minute later if he hadn't. When Pike crawled out from under the wagon where he'd been sleeping, Sam was already standing there.

"Anything going on?" Pike asked as he stretched to work out the kinks in his back from sleeping on the ground.

"Not really." Sam hesitated. "When I took over for Fiddler, he told me he thought he had seen somebody sneaking around the edge of camp earlier in the night, but then he never saw anything else and decided he had imagined it."

Pike frowned in the darkness. He figured he already knew the answer, but he asked, "Did you take a look around?"

"Of course, I did. I didn't find anything. As far as I could tell, everybody was right where they were supposed to be, sleeping peacefully, except Dougal, and he'd taken over from Torrance on guard duty."

Pike nodded slowly and said, "Fiddler *could* have imagined it. Or maybe somebody got up and went into the woods to tend to some personal business."

"Or maybe we've got a scout from some other gang checking us out, like back at the Brazos."

"Yeah, that's possible."

Sam headed for his bedroll while Pike walked around the wagons until he found Belle, who had relieved Dougal.

"It's me," he called softly to her as she turned toward him with her Winchester carbine in her hands.

"Something wrong?" she asked. "I haven't seen or heard anything unusual."

"Sam tells me that Fiddler thought he saw somebody moving around earlier. You know anything about that?"

Belle shook her head. "It wasn't me. I was sound asleep until Dougal woke me up just a few minutes ago."

"Well, there's a decent chance it's nothing," Pike said, "but I wanted to let you know anyway."

He started to turn away, but Belle stopped him by saying, "Pike?"

"Yeah?"

"Thanks for standing guard with me tonight. I was a little worried you might try to rearrange things so we wouldn't be on the same shift."

"Why in the world would I do that?" Pike asked, even though in truth he had briefly considered the possibility.

"I don't know, I thought maybe you'd think it would be uncomfortable, the two of us . . ."

"I don't reckon you could ever make me uncomfortable, Belle. Fact of the matter is, you're about the most comfortable girl I've ever met."

She laughed and struck him lightly on the arm with a fist. "That's not the sort of thing you say to a girl, you idiot. I don't want you being *un*comfortable around me, but—"

They had jabbered about this long enough, Pike decided. Acting on his instincts, he leaned closer and kissed Belle. He heard her catch a surprised breath, but she didn't pull away. Instead, she slid an arm around his neck and pressed against him.

Sharing a passionate kiss when both of them were holding Winchesters and wearing Colts was a mite awkward, but they managed all right. After about thirty seconds, Pike lifted his head. Belle sighed and said, "That's not the first time you've kissed me, Pike Shannon . . . but it may have been the best job you've made of it."

He chuckled. "I'm glad to hear it. I reckon I can do even better with practice."

"We'll see. For now, we've got a camp and a big load of moonshine to guard."

"That's right. If you need help, holler."

"I will. Same goes for you."

Pike nodded and moved away into the shadows. He could still taste Belle's lips on his, and it would have been sweet to let that kiss linger in his thoughts . . .

But there was too much potential danger out there in the darkness, and in a matter of heartbeats Pike was fully alert again, primed for trouble if it decided to erupt.

Nothing else happened during the hours between then and the predawn grayness when Pike built a fire and started the coffee. He'd heard nothing except snoring from some of the men, hadn't seen anything out of the ordinary. When Belle came over to the fire to join him, she reported the same.

"You think we'll be on guard duty at the same time again before we get to Prescott?" she asked with a smile.

"I don't know," Pike said. "Could be."

"Well, it would be all right with me if we were. Just thought I'd let you know."

She walked off then, leaving Pike hunkered on his heels next to the fire he was feeding sticks into . . . and smiling.

Everything seemed normal as the group got ready to roll again that morning. They had biscuits and bacon for breakfast, washed down with good strong coffee. Some of the men had hitched up the teams already, so it didn't take long, once they had cleaned up after the meal, to be ready to break camp.

Elizabeth walked toward Torrance's wagon. Before she could get there, Lavon Baxter intercepted her and asked sharply, "Where are you going?"

She stopped and looked at him. "Yesterday was enjoyable enough that I thought I'd ride with Brother Torrance again, if he doesn't mind, that is."

Pike was close enough to hear that and knew that Torrance wouldn't mind having Elizabeth ride with him again today. Not hardly.

But Baxter shook his head and said, "Not today. You're going to ride with me." He added, "And Shannon isn't your brother. I am, remember?"

That put a cool, angry look on Elizabeth's face. She said, "I don't see how I could forget something like that."

"Neither do I," Baxter snapped. He took hold of her arm. "Come along. We're about ready to get rolling."

Elizabeth pulled away from his grip, but with her face now sullen, she retraced her steps and climbed to the seat of her brother's wagon. Baxter followed her the whole way, as if he were ready to stop her if she changed her mind.

Pike went on about his business so they wouldn't notice him watching them, but as he saddled his horse and got ready to take his place at the front of the caravan, he couldn't help but remember Belle's misgivings about

Reverend Lavon Baxter. The way he had just treated his sister certainly hadn't seemed very pious.

Pike recalled as well that Fiddler thought he had seen someone skulking around the camp last night. That might not have anything to do with Baxter. Probably didn't, Pike told himself as he nudged his horse into motion and loped toward the trail, waving for the others to follow him.

All those things taken together, though, made him think it might be wise to keep a closer eye on the good reverend in the future.

CHAPTER 29

Sophie prepared breakfast for two people that morning without knowing for sure that Curtis would be joining her. They hadn't made any such arrangements before parting company the previous night.

But he showed up anyway, smiling in the dawn light as he strode toward her.

"Good morning, Sister Sophie," he greeted her. "It's a blessed day, isn't it?"

"I hope so," she said. She was glad that whatever had been bothering him the night before no longer seemed to be a concern.

"I see you have two coffee cups sitting out. I, uh, I hope one of 'em's for me."

"It certainly is. The coffee should be ready in just a few minutes, and the food will be done soon, too."

They shared a pleasant breakfast, but as they sat there talking idly and the light got better as the sun approached the horizon, Sophie realized that she had been wrong about Curtis no longer being worried. She could tell he was trying to hide it from her, but she saw the shadows lurking in his eyes, and his face seemed drawn with weariness. That probably meant he hadn't slept well.

However, Sophie didn't feel she had any right to press him about it. They had become friends, but that didn't mean she could pry into his affairs.

The wagons rolled fairly early, when the sun was barely peeking into the eastern sky. It hadn't climbed much higher by the time they reached the first range of hills crossing their path. The rugged terrain meant that the wagons wouldn't be able to move very fast.

Curtis kept up a fairly steady conversation, but despite that, Sophie could tell that something was troubling him. Finally, she couldn't stand it any longer, and when he had fallen silent after spinning some long, pointless story about his family's farm in Missouri, she said, "Curtis, why don't you just tell me what it is that's bothering you?"

"Bothering me?" he repeated. "I, uh, don't know what you mean, Sister Sophie. Why would you think anything's bothering me?"

"Because I can see it on your face and hear it in your voice," she told him bluntly. "I realize we haven't known each other for very long, but we spent quite a bit of time together yesterday and I'm a good judge of character, if I do say so myself. You're trying to hide it, but something is eating at you."

He opened his mouth, and she thought he was just going to deny it again, but then he closed his mouth and sat there in silence for a long moment as the wagon rolled along. He was so quiet as the seconds dragged by that Sophie began to worry she had offended him and he wouldn't want them to ride together anymore.

Then he smiled ruefully and said, "I reckon you did get to know me pretty well, pretty fast, Sister."

"I wish you wouldn't call me that," she blurted out without thinking. She hadn't even been aware of feeling that way until now. But since she had already said more than she probably should have, she went on, "It's all right if you just call me Sophie."

"I don't know. Seems a mite disrespectful—"

"It's not," she assured him. "Please, go on with what you were about to say."

He sighed and hesitated. She worried that her quick, unthinking words had made him shut himself away from her again.

Instead, he said, "You're going to think I'm loco."

"I would never think that. You seem to be a very level-headed young man."

"Yeah, I always figured I was. But then, yesterday evening I overheard two of the fellas talking, and I decided I'd lost my mind instead."

He fell silent again, so she prodded, "What were they saying?"

"They said . . . they said Brother Lavon was up to something shady, and that he's too close to Brother Titus and Brother Carter, and they can't be trusted."

From what Sophie had seen of Titus Ferrell and Carter Hoyt, that was probably a fair assessment, she thought. Since Pike Shannon had returned to Warbonnet County, she had been around enough hardcases and gun-wolves that she wouldn't have trusted either man.

They reminded her too much of the sort of men Doak Ramsey had had working for him, as well as that horrible Solomon Henshaw's gang from up in Chaparral County.

Hired killers.

She'd wanted to give these men the benefit of the doubt because they were followers of Lavon Branson, but now that she knew others were suspicious of them as well, she couldn't help but express her feelings.

"From what little I saw of them, I didn't like them, either," she told Curtis. "You think that maybe they're playing some sort of trick on Brother Lavon?"

Curtis grimaced and cocked his head to the side. "The men I heard talking seemed convinced that Brother Lavon is part of whatever they're up to. You see, Sister . . . I mean, Sophie . . ." The young man dragged in a deep breath. "Brother Lavon is a wonderful man, but he has . . . well, weaknesses, I guess you'd call 'em. Nobody's perfect, but when I first heard him speak and then joined up with him for a while, I figured he came about as close as any human man could. But then I saw some things . . . and heard some things . . ."

His face was red with embarrassment now. Sophie knew she might make it worse, but she ventured, "Are you talking about Elizabeth Meadows?"

"Her . . . and others. She, uh . . . she's not the first lady Brother Lavon has been . . . friends with."

That was enough of a surprise to make Sophie pull in a sharp breath. She hadn't expected to hear that Lavon Branson made a habit of getting involved with his female followers.

Her eyes widened as an even more shocking thought occurred to her.

Had he planned for *her* to take the place of Elizabeth? To be the next on his list of conquests?

She couldn't believe that. She didn't *want* to believe

that. But from what she had seen, and what Curtis was telling her, she had to admit that it might be a possibility.

"That's not the worst of it, though," Curtis went on when Sophie was too shocked to say anything.

She couldn't think of anything worse than what he had just hinted at.

"The fellas I overheard, they're good friends with Deacon Finley and Deacon O'Leary. And they were afraid that something might happen to them, that they might get hurt."

"The deacons, you mean?"

"Yeah. They think Brother Titus and Brother Carter and the rest of their bunch might be after that moonshine."

"Well, of course we're going to stop Pike and the others from delivering that horrible brew to Pecan County—"

"No, they think Ferrell and Hoyt are after it for themselves. That they're really outlaws and plan to steal the liquor and . . . and kill everybody in that caravan. And that Brother Lavon is part of it."

The chill that settled over Sophie's blood seemed to freeze her to the very core of her being. She couldn't even find the words to respond to the insane thing Curtis had just said, but she knew she had to.

The ice in her veins got even thicker as she recalled how Lavon Branson had found out about the moonshine caravan in the first place.

She had told him. She had written that letter, and he had showed up in Warbonnet only a short time later. To strike a blow against wickedness, she had assumed—but what if his real goal was to *commit* wickedness?

As shocking as it was, the nebulous theory forcing its way into her brain made sense. She said, "In the past, when your group has confronted moonshiners and tried to stop them, what happened?"

"Well, it wasn't our group, exactly," Curtis said. "We just travel along with Brother Lavon and support him in his crusade. Any time he's stopped a load of whiskey from being delivered or turned a group of moonshiners away from their immoral path, it's always been Ferrell and Hoyt and their friends who helped him. Brother Lavon always says he doesn't want the stain of sin wiping off on the rest of us. So it's up to the others to destroy any moonshine they find and convince the men who have been brewing it to give up their wicked ways."

"But you never actually *saw* any of that happen?"

Curtis shook his head. "No. Ferrell and Hoyt and the others always split off from the group before they confronted the sinners. Brother Lavon may have been there, I don't know. A lot of times, he was gone for a spell, too, and then came back to give us the good news."

"The good news?"

"That the sinners had repented and the liquor was destroyed."

It was a warm, bright, beautiful morning, with fluffy white clouds floating in a brilliant blue sky. And yet Sophie felt as if an enormous thunderclap had just boomed inside her head, and a stroke of lightning had left her blind and numb.

Pike Shannon might not think she was very smart, but actually her brain was rather quick and agile. She pieced everything together in her thoughts and saw that it locked into an undeniable pattern. The picture it formed was an ugly one, too.

"Curtis," she said, "do you know how far in front of us the moonshine wagons are?"

He frowned in apparent surprise at the question.

"I don't have any idea," he said. "But considering how much of a lead they had on us when we left, and how fast we've been traveling, I'd guess . . . half a day."

"But that distance could be covered a lot quicker on horseback, couldn't it? Without the wagons slowing us down, I mean?"

"Well, sure. A rider could catch up by sometime this afternoon, I reckon. Maybe even sooner, depending on how fast Mr. Shannon's wagons are moving."

"I need a saddle horse," Sophie said.

His frown deepened as he asked, "What for?"

She told herself she needed to forge ahead stubbornly with this before she talked herself out of it. She said, "I have to catch up with them."

"With Shannon?" He shook his head. "You can't do that, Sophie. We can't interfere with Brother Lavon's plans."

"Even if he's planning to do something wrong? You said yourself you were worried about that, Curtis."

"Yeah, but . . ." The young man looked utterly miserable as he struggled with trying to figure out what to believe. "Do you really think there's a chance that might be true?"

"Yes, I do, or I wouldn't be saying these things."

Curtis gnawed at his lower lip and sat there silently for a long moment as the mules pulling the wagon plodded on. At last he said, "You think Ferrell and Hoyt and their gang are gonna kill Mr. Shannon and the others?"

He had stopped referring to the two hardcases as Brother Titus and Brother Carter. Sophie had noticed that a short time earlier. Now he was calling the men with them a gang. That had to mean he was coming around to her way of thinking, and Sophie took that to mean there was an even better chance that she was right—even though she didn't really want to be.

"I think they might," she said.

"And you believe Brother Lavon is part of it?"

"I really don't know about that," Sophie replied honestly. "But I have a terrible feeling that my friends are in danger, and I want to help them."

He looked sharply at her. "Your friends? The moonshiners?"

Sophie took a deep breath and nodded, thinking not only of Pike but also Belle, Nessa, Dougal, Torrance, and Fiddler.

"Yes," she said. "Yes, even though I don't agree with everything they do, they're still my friends and I don't want them hurt."

Curtis nodded and hauled back on the reins.

"Well, then, I reckon we've got to warn them," he said. "*If* we can catch up in time. I don't know if we can." He looked more intently at her. "Or if you even ought to."

"But we can try." Sophie didn't even think about how he had included himself in that effort. It just seemed natural to her. "And I have to come along. I'm not sure Pike and the others would believe you, but they would if I told them they were in danger."

He thought for a moment and then nodded in acceptance of her decision.

With the lead wagon stopping, the other vehicles had to come to a halt as well. As Curtis set the brake lever and wrapped the reins around it, one of the other men trotted forward and asked, "What's wrong, son? Why'd you stop?"

"I've got to saddle a couple of horses for Sister Sophie and myself," he replied. "We've got some hard riding to do."

CHAPTER 30

Despite Pike's uneasy feeling about Lavon Baxter, the man did nothing suspicious that morning. At midday, the wagons reached another settlement and stopped to eat lunch in the shade of some trees on the town square. Some of the locals stopped by to greet the travelers and pass the time of day. Baxter was as friendly as could be with them, smiling and laughing.

Pike noticed that Elizabeth still acted coolly toward her brother, however. Evidently relations remained tense between them.

It was such a pleasant respite that the group lingered considerably longer than Pike had intended. When he realized how much time was passing, he told everyone they needed to get ready to roll again.

A short time later, the group moved on, with Dougal leading the way, the two wagons in Baxter's party trailing behind the moonshine wagons, and the remuda bringing up the rear with Belle and Nessa on horseback chousing the extra livestock along.

Pike was out front by a quarter mile or more, checking out the trail. Their route led almost due west now. Pike saw a low line of rugged bluffs several miles ahead of them, running in an irregular line from north to south.

He spotted a gap in the bluffs and figured that was where the trail ran. He hoped the slope leading up to it wasn't too steep. The horses and mules were still carrying on gallantly, but even with the longer midday break than usual, they had to be getting worn out from hauling the heavily loaded wagons day after day.

Two more days to Prescott, Pike mused as he followed the trail toward the gap. Maybe only a day and a half. Then they would deliver the moonshine to Patrick Delano and collect for it, and afterward, they might let the teams rest for a couple of days before starting back to Warbonnet County. They would be in even less of a hurry at that point.

Pike ran his gaze along the top of the bluffs, searching for any signs of potential trouble. He didn't see anything, but that didn't necessarily mean no threat existed. The heights looked rugged enough to provide cover for any number of bushwhackers.

Despite that, Pike knew that he and his companions had to press on. Those bluffs ran for miles north and south, as far as the eye could see, and as Pike looked in those directions, he noted that the terrain was even rougher. That gap up ahead represented the best route through without traveling half a day or more out of their way.

The landscape through which they were passing at the moment rolled westward in shallow rises covered with short grass and dotted with clumps of brush and cactus. Post oaks were still common, but now mesquite trees with their gnarled branches were mixed in.

Ahead, the trail ran almost as straight as an arrow and then climbed to the gap in the bluffs. As Pike came closer, he saw that the slope appeared to be long and gentle instead of steep. That was a relief. At the crest, the gap was fifty yards wide and the trail ran between rocky cut-banks some twenty feet high.

If anybody was going to set a trap, thought Pike, that was where he would have located it . . .

He turned his horse and rode back to the wagons, lifting his hand and waving for Dougal to stop. The old-timer pulled on the reins. The other wagons stopped as well.

"Trouble up ahead, Pike?" Dougal asked.

"Not that I can see. And in a way, that worries me."

"Yeah, I know what you mean. You never want things to get too peaceful-like. That's usually when all Hades breaks loose." Dougal scratched at his beard. "I've been lookin' at that little pass up yonder. That'd be a good place for somebody to jump us. But I don't see no other way to go through."

"There's not," Pike agreed. "At least, not a good one." He nodded toward the Winchester lying on the floorboards of the driver's box. "Get a round in the firing chamber and put that rifle beside you. You don't want to have to waste any time bending over to get it if you need it."

"Good advice."

Pike rode on and shared his concerns and the same warning with Torrance, Fiddler, Sam Crow, and Will Fisher.

"I trust your instincts, Pike," Will said.

"This is one time it'd be fine with me if I was wrong," Pike said fervently.

Pike had conducted his conversation with Will in a low voice, so Lavon Baxter, handling the reins of the next wagon in line, hadn't been able to hear what they were saying. The preacher had a curious look on his face as Pike walked his horse back to pull up alongside.

"Why have we stopped, Brother Shannon?" Baxter wanted to know.

"Little problem with the harness on my grandpa's wagon," Pike lied. He knew Baxter couldn't see what Dougal was doing up there. If he was misjudging the man, which was still entirely possible, he would feel bad about it later—or not. He had no reason to care what Lavon Baxter thought about him. "We'll be on our way in just a few minutes."

"Oh. All right, that's fine. Thanks for letting me know."

Pike ticked a finger against his hat brim and said, "How are you doing, Miss Baxter?"

"Fine," Elizabeth answered. Her tone was sullen and she still didn't look happy.

Baxter smiled and said, "Now, Sister, don't be that way with Brother Shannon. He'll think you're upset."

The smug look on his face made Pike dislike him even more.

"Sorry," Elizabeth muttered.

"No, ma'am, don't you worry," Pike told her. "We'll be on our way soon."

He reined past the other wagon with the two deacons on it, pausing only to tell them the same lie he'd told Baxter. Then he rode around the remuda to where Belle and Nessa had been pushing the extra livestock along.

"Is something wrong, Pike?" Nessa asked.

"No, I'm just a mite worried about that gap we'll be going through up ahead."

Belle leaned over in the saddle to peer toward the bluffs and said, "It looks like a good place for an ambush."

Pike smiled, but the expression didn't reach his eyes.

"Yeah, it does to me, too. That's what I was just saying to Dougal and the other fellas."

"But not Baxter," Belle guessed.

"That's right."

"Good," Nessa said. "I don't think I trust him. There's something about him that seems shifty to me."

"If there *is* any trouble, you two will be in the best position to watch him."

Belle rested her hand on the stock of her carbine for a second. "I reckon you can depend on us for that," she said.

Pike nodded and turned his horse again. As he rode toward the front of the caravan, a part of him wished that he had never allowed the two girls to come along.

But he would have had a hard time stopping them, he knew, and anyway, another part of him was glad that they were back there, guarding the rear.

With a wave as he passed Dougal, he started the wagons rolling again.

Pike kept a close eye on the cutbanks on both sides of the gap as he reached the hill and started climbing toward the crest. The banks didn't rear up and close in until the very top of the slope. Down here lower, Pike could still see out a good distance on both sides. The brush was sparse and didn't really provide enough cover for a good ambush.

Pike took his eyes off the gap only long enough to turn his head and look over his shoulder now and then, to make sure that the wagons had started the long climb behind him. Dougal saw him looking and waved to signal that everything was all right so far. Pike turned again to the trail ahead of him.

He was almost to the top when he heard the swift rata-plan of hoofbeats drumming somewhere behind him. Reining in sharply, he pulled his horse around to see Belle galloping up the trail alongside the wagons, obviously trying to catch up to him.

She wouldn't have left the remuda to do that unless something was wrong, Pike thought. He glanced again at the cutbanks but didn't see anything out of the ordinary. Even so, he grasped his Winchester and pulled it from its scabbard as Belle pounded up to him and reined in her lathered mount.

"What is it?" Pike asked.

"A couple of riders coming up fast behind us," Belle replied, a little out of breath from the hard ride. "If I didn't know better, Pike, I'd swear one of them is Sophie Truesdale!"

"Sophie!" Belle's words startled that exclamation out of Pike. "What in blazes would she be doing all the way down here, so far from home?"

"I don't know, but it sure looks like her. There's a man with her, but I don't know him."

Belle had to be wrong. Sophie was back in Warbonnet, running her café—and nursing her grudge against him.

But even if Sophie *wasn't* one of the riders, who were they and why were they trying so hard to catch up to the moonshine caravan? This couldn't be anything good, Pike told himself, and he wanted to get to the bottom of it as quickly as he could.

"Whoever it is, I'm going back there to meet them," he told Belle. "If they mean us harm, I'll stop them before they ever get to the wagons."

"I'll ride point while you're doing that," Belle said as she pulled out her carbine. "Be careful, Pike."

He nodded grimly and nudged his horse into a run. As he headed back down the slope, he thought that he should have told Dougal to stop and wait for him to return before going up the rest of the way.

He could see the mysterious riders coming up fast, though, so there wasn't time to turn around and give the order if he wanted to head them off before they reached the wagons.

Pike passed the Baxter wagons and saw the startled, confused looks the preacher and his sister gave him, but he didn't slow down to explain.

"Pike!" Nessa called to him as he reached the remuda.

"Keep 'em moving!" he told her, then flashed past and was back on level ground.

The two strangers hadn't turned aside or slowed down. They came on in a hurry, and as the gap dwindled between them and Pike, he saw that Belle had been right. The young woman with blond hair streaming behind her in the wind really *did* look like Sophie. In fact . . . no, it couldn't be . . .

But it was. A shock went through Pike as he realized that actually was Sophie Truesdale leaning forward in the saddle as she galloped toward him. He had never seen the young man with her before.

The crazy thought went through his head that he'd had no idea Sophie could ride like that. They had gone for buggy rides in the past, but he'd never seen her in a saddle.

She wasn't bad.

But the question of what had brought her here remained, and as they came together and Pike hauled his mount to a skidding, dust-whirling stop, he called to her, "Sophie, what in the world are you doing here?"

She and her companion brought their obviously exhausted horses to a stop. Sophie leaned on the saddle horn and panted, "Pike, you . . . you have to turn back. There's a . . . a trap somewhere up ahead!"

"What are you talking about?"

"I'm afraid she's right, mister," said the young man. "We're worried that a gang of hardcases are going to ambush you and try to steal all that moonshine you're carrying. They may be killers!"

Pike couldn't help but glare at Sophie. "You told people about the 'shine?"

With a look of abject misery on her flushed face, she said, "I was just trying to do the right thing!"

A sizable majority of all the trouble in the world, thought Pike, came from folks just trying to do the right thing.

He didn't have time for philosophy, though, because at that moment he heard the sharp crackle and bark of gunfire in the hot Texas air, and as he jerked around toward the bluffs, he knew that Sophie was right—there *was* a trap waiting for them.

And his family and friends had just waltzed right into it.

CHAPTER 31

"Oh, no!" Sophie cried with a look of anguish on her face as she heard the shooting, too.

Pike still had no idea how she had come to be here, warning him of this ambush, but that didn't matter right now. As he whirled his mount, he called, "Stay here where you'll be safe!"

"Pike, I—"

He didn't hear the rest of what she said. His horse's hoofbeats drowned out the words as he charged back up the trail.

If Sophie had something to do with this, he didn't think he wanted to hear anything she had to say, anyway.

He rode hard, waving and calling, "Stay back!" to Nessa as well when he circled the remuda. He didn't know if she would follow the order—with Nessa, it was always safer to assume that she wouldn't do what she was told—but at least he had tried to keep her out of harm's way.

He flashed past the deacons' wagon, but as he reached Baxter's, he spotted the preacher now standing on the driver's box, swinging an arm toward him.

Pike saw the gun in Baxter's fist rising into line. Lines of hate contorted the man's face.

That was no preacher. That was a killer.

Pike's Colt came out with blinding speed. He didn't know if he could beat Baxter's shot, but he would get a shot of his own off, that was certain.

Before Baxter could pull the trigger, he lurched forward, suddenly and unexpectedly. Pike held off on his own trigger as he realized that Elizabeth had tackled her brother from behind. She reached around with one hand, grabbed his gun arm, and jerked it up. They swayed back and forth on the box as they struggled.

Pike held his horse in place and watched for an opening. He didn't want to risk hitting Elizabeth with a bullet.

Then Baxter tore his arm loose and slashed at Elizabeth's face with the gun. She cried out in pain and went down hard as the blow landed. Baxter tried to writhe around toward Pike again.

Pike's Colt boomed as he fired. Baxter had already made it clear enough that he wasn't the sort of man he claimed to be, so Pike didn't see any need to wait.

Nobody with any sense gave a rabid skunk a free bite.

The bullet ripped through Baxter's body and drove him backward. He tripped over Elizabeth's slumped form and toppled off the far side of the box.

"Miss Baxter!" Pike said as he brought his horse closer to the wagon.

One side of her face was smeared with crimson blood from the cut on her head the vicious blow had opened up. But she was able to push herself up and call to Pike, "I'm all right! Go help your family and friends."

Nearby, a man yelled, "He shot Brother Lavon!"

Pike jerked his head in that direction and saw one of

the deacons rushing toward him on foot, brandishing a shotgun. He was about to raise his Colt again and defend himself when Elizabeth half-fell onto the edge of the seat and waved an arm at the man.

"No! Stop, Brother O'Leary, stop! You don't understand, but please . . . please hold your fire!"

The deacon stopped in his tracks, but he still glared at Pike and looked like he wanted to blow him to kingdom come with that scattergun.

Elizabeth turned her head toward Pike again and gasped, "Please go on. Help the others."

"I've got to see about Baxter," Pike snapped. He didn't know how badly he had wounded the man, and it was one of his rules not to leave an injured enemy behind him.

When Pike rode around the front of the wagon, though, he didn't see Baxter lying on the ground—or anywhere else. During the confusion, he must have gotten up and scurried off somewhere.

So he wasn't hurt bad enough to be out of the fight, at least not yet.

Pike figured he ought to remedy that the next time he laid eyes on the varmint.

"Are you sure you're all right?" he asked Elizabeth.

She nodded weakly and waved him on with a limp hand.

Grimly, Pike hauled his horse around and rode hard toward the gap.

Shots continued to roar. Pike heard the gun-thunder over his horse's hoofbeats. He saw clouds of powder smoke hazing the air above the cutbanks on both sides of the gap. Fear for Belle's safety stabbed into him. She had been riding in front of the wagons, which meant she would have been right in the middle of that ambush.

The wagons had come to a stop a little more than halfway up the slope. Pike saw that the drivers had scrambled off the boxes and dived underneath the vehicles when the attack started. Rifle barrels poked out next to wagon wheels and spurted flame and smoke as the men fought back.

Pike knew he'd be in a cross fire, but he galloped past the wagons anyway and looked for Belle deeper in the gap. His heart slugged heavily in his chest as he spotted her horse. The animal was down and not moving, about twenty yards away.

Then a rifle barrel thrust over the horse's body and blasted a shot toward the cutbank on Pike's left. He glanced in that direction and saw a man rise up sharply from behind a rock, then clutch at his midsection as if in pain. He toppled forward, falling off the bank and turning over completely in the air before crashing to the ground.

Belle had gunned down one of the varmints, anyway, thought Pike.

He had holstered his Colt as he raced toward the front of the caravan. Now he reached for his Winchester and pulled it from the saddle boot. He worked the rifle's lever in the same smooth motion with which he brought it to his shoulder.

Belle was still firing toward the cutbank on the left, the south. Pike swung his rifle toward the northern bank. The horse's carcass gave Belle at least a little protection the other way but none at all in that direction.

Aiming at the jets of smoke he saw up there, Pike cranked off five swift rounds, spraying the area with lead to make the bushwhackers up there duck even if he didn't get lucky and hit any of them.

Then he yelled, "Belle!" and angled his horse toward her. He rammed the rifle back in its scabbard so he'd have a free hand.

"Pike!" She raised up slightly with the carbine still at her shoulder and loosed another round at the southern bank. Then she started to stand and reach for the hand he extended toward her.

Before he could reach her, she fell backward with a cry of pain. Pike knew she'd been hit but not how badly. He shouted her name again and started to rein in, but then she rose up, blood on her left sleeve, and lunged toward him with her right arm upraised.

Flesh slapped flesh as they clasped wrists. Pike clamped his fingers around her arm like bands of iron. He had slowed his horse's charge but the animal was still moving, and its momentum jerked Belle off her feet and helped Pike swing her up onto its back behind him.

"Can you hang on?" he called to her.

She didn't answer, but the way she slid her arms around his waist and clung to him was response enough. He felt the wetness from her bloody sleeve soaking through his own shirt, and rage welled up inside him at the knowledge she was hurt.

They couldn't stay where they were without both of them running a considerable risk of getting ventilated worse, so Pike jabbed his boot heels into his horse's flanks and sent the animal lunging forward. They pelted toward the far end of the gap.

As Pike leaned forward in the saddle, he felt Belle rest her head against his back. She shuddered, and as he realized the back of his shirt was getting damp, too, he figured out that she was crying.

"I know you're hurt," he told her over his shoulder. "I'll get you to safety as fast as I can."

"Th-that's not why I'm crying," she choked out. "I've been hurt a lot worse than this scratch on my arm. Those monsters shot Trixie! Shot her right out from under me!"

After a second, Pike understood that she was talking about her horse.

"I'm sorry," he said. "I'll try to settle the score for her—"

"Go back," she practically snarled in his ear. "Give me your Winchester and turn around. Let's go back and kill every mother's son of them!"

"But you're wounded!"

"I swear, Pike Shannon, if you don't give me another crack at those killers, I . . . I'll never speak to you again!"

He slowed his horse. "Are you sure you're not hurt too bad to handle a rifle?"

"I'm fine, blast it!"

Pike drew in a deep breath and looked around. They had emerged from the gap by now and were out on the flats beyond—which meant they could get to the area on top of the cutbanks where the bushwhackers had lurked. He could even see some of them, still concentrating their fire on the wagons trapped below in a cross fire.

This was probably the most loco thing he had ever done in a whole lifetime of recklessness, he thought as he pulled his horse around and slid the Winchester from its scabbard. He had some shells in his shirt pocket, and he paused long enough to work the lever and then thumb six fresh rounds through the loading gate so the rifle was fully loaded again.

"You need to wrap up that arm wound?" he asked Belle.

"It's fine," she grated. "Just give me that blasted repeater."

He passed it back to her and said, "We're going for the men on the right bank."

"You take them. I'll see if I can pick off a few on the other side."

"You sure about this?"

"They've got it coming to them," Belle said grimly.

Pike nodded as he finished refilling the cylinders on his Colt. He heeled the horse into a run again, back the way they had come from.

One of the men kneeling behind a rocky knob at the edge of the bank heard the hoofbeats and swung around to shout an alarm. He lifted his rifle.

The range was still a little long for a handgun, so Pike shouted, "See if you can pick him off!"

"Lean over and give me a shot, then!" Belle replied impatiently.

Pike leaned to his left. Belle leaned the other way and drew a bead, not rushing but not wasting any time, either. The Winchester cracked, and the loud report was close enough to Pike's ear to make him grimace.

If gunshots hadn't made him lose his hearing by this point in his life, they never would, he thought.

The bushwhacker Belle had targeted never got a shot off. Dust puffed out from his shirt where the bullet drilled him. He dropped his rifle and reeled backward, then lost his footing at the edge of the bank and screamed as he went over the edge.

"That's two of them you've ventilated!" Pike told Belle.

"I'm just getting started!"

She jacked another round into the Winchester's chamber and aimed across the gap at the other bank.

The yell and then the scream from the man Belle had shot had drawn plenty of attention. Some of the other outlaws on this side were scrambling to turn around and meet this new and unexpected threat. Pike opened fire on them, aiming as best he could from the back of the galloping horse.

This wasn't the first battle Pike had fought from the back of a running mount. He knew how to compensate for the jolting pace when he aimed, and his nerves were steady and cool when he saw muzzle flashes from the guns the men held and knew they were trying to kill him just as hard as he was trying to kill them.

He never doubted for a second that when it came to killing, he was *better.*

But a certain amount of luck was involved, too, and the fatalistic streak in him accepted that. He just hoped that Belle came through this madness alive.

The gun in his hand roared and bucked and he saw men fall, some spinning off their feet, others with buckling knees, still others in whom the muscles seemed to go limp all at once, like string-cut puppets. But one way or another, they went down, and although Pike heard bullets shriek past his head, he did not.

The Winchester in Belle's hands continued its relentless *crack-crack-crack* of death. Several men on the other side of the gap fell, one of them plummeting off the cutbank like the pair before him as he screamed and futilely windmilled his arms.

Pike and Belle neared the eastern edge of the bluff. Pike swung the horse around for another pass, but he saw that nobody on this side of the gap was interested in keeping up the fight. In fact, it appeared that only a couple of them were unhurt, and they threw down their rifles and shoved their arms in the air.

On the other side of the gap, dust began to rise where

the rest of the bunch over there had abandoned the attack and jumped on their horses. They rode hard to the north, clearly wanting nothing more than to get out of here with their hides intact.

Belle worked the Winchester's lever and aimed the rifle at the men who'd surrendered. Pike got a hand under the barrel and shoved it up before she could squeeze the trigger again.

"What'd you do that for?" she demanded hotly.

"You may feel like it right now, but you wouldn't like it if you shot those fellas down in cold blood," he told her.

"How in blazes do you know that?"

"Take my word for it," Pike said, his voice grim. "You promise you won't shoot them unless they try something funny?"

Belle blew out a frustrated breath but said, "I promise. I suppose."

"Keep 'em covered, then."

Pike rode over to the prisoners and swung down while Belle remained mounted. He gathered up their guns, tossed them well out of reach, then gestured with his own Colt for them to walk over to the edge of the bank.

The men stared at him. One of them burst out, "Mister, you can't make us jump off there! We'll break an arm or a leg—or our necks!"

"You don't have to jump," Pike said. "That bank's pretty steep, but it's rough enough you can climb down it . . . if you take it slow and careful. I figure that'll keep you busy for a little while." He shrugged. "Or I can let the lady shoot you for murdering her horse, if you'd rather."

"Come on," the other outlaw said to his companion. They trudged over to the edge and lowered themselves over it carefully.

Pike stepped to the edge, too, and looked down at the wagons. He saw the men emerging from underneath them now that the shooting was over. Torrance cupped his hands around his mouth and shouted, "Pike, are you all right?"

Pike waved to show that he was, then pointed at the two outlaws and called back, "Watch these two!"

Torrance signaled that they would.

Pike walked back quickly to his horse and looked up at Belle, who was pale and drawn but still frowning angrily.

"You should've let me shoot those two," she snapped.

"Maybe. Or maybe you'll be glad later that I didn't. Reckon we'll have to wait and see." He nodded toward her bloody sleeve. "How's the arm?"

"Hurts like hell," she said. "But like I told you, it's just a scratch."

"All right." Pike put his foot in the stirrup and pulled himself up, a bit of an awkward task with Belle already on the horse's back behind the saddle. As he took up the reins, he went on, "Let's get back down there. Last I saw of him, Lavon Baxter was still on the loose . . . and he's up to his neck in this."

CHAPTER 32

Dougal was waiting in front of the lead wagon when Pike and Belle rode up. Pike's pulse jumped when he saw the streak of red in his grandfather's white beard.

"You're hit," he said.

"Barely," Dougal said with a dismissive wave. "One o' them slugs kissed me on the cheek when it went by. That was as close as any of the no-good varmints came to pluggin' me."

"Anybody else hurt?"

"Don't know. I ain't had a chance to check with ever'-body. I know Torrance is all right. He headed back to the remuda to see how Nessa's doin'."

Pike wanted to make sure his sister was all right, too. He said, "Belle got winged. You think you can take a look at her arm and patch it up?"

"I told you I'm fine—" Belle protested.

"You lost enough blood that you look like you're about halfway ready to pass out," Pike said. "Stop arguing and let Dougal tend to that wound."

"Yeah, get on down from there," Dougal urged. "I got a bottle of 'shine for, uh, medicinal purposes, and I reckon it won't hurt nothin' if a little of it actually gets used for that."

"All right," Belle agreed with obvious reluctance. She started to slide down from the horse's back, but a dizzy spell must have hit her just then, because she had to grab Pike's shirt to keep from falling.

Dougal moved forward to help her. He caught her under the arms, then lowered her to the ground and supported her with an arm around her waist.

"Have you seen Baxter?" Pike asked.

Dougal looked surprised at the question. "The preacher?"

"He's no preacher," Pike replied. "He was part of this ambush. Probably set the whole thing up."

"Really? By grab, I wouldn't have expected that." Dougal shook his head. "But I ain't seen him since the shootin' started. You reckon he's still skulkin' around somewhere close by, or did he take off for the tall and uncut?"

"Don't know, but I intend to find out."

"His sister and those so-called deacons, were they mixed up in it, too?"

"I don't think the deacons were. I don't know about his sister," Pike answered honestly. Elizabeth had prevented Baxter from shooting him, but she could have known what was going to happen and changed her mind about it at the last moment.

That could be hashed out later. For now, he wanted to check on Nessa and the others and have a look around for Baxter.

At some point, he needed to have a talk with Sophie Truesdale and her new friend, too. He was still very curious what Sophie's connection was with this ambush.

He paused when he came to each of the wagons to speak to the man who'd been defending it. Fiddler, Sam

Crow, and Will Fisher hadn't been wounded in the fierce exchange of gunfire. Luck had been with them. As Fiddler put it, "I don't see how they missed me. There were so many bullets flying around me that it sounded a swarm of hornets!"

"I'm glad you came through it all right," Pike said.

"And miracle of miracles, so did the moonshine!" Fiddler reached into the back of the wagon and slapped one of the barrels. "Not a single hole in any of them, as far as I can see. Not a drop of magical elixir spilled."

"That's because they wanted to steal the stuff and were being careful not to waste it. But that was lucky, too, with so much lead flying around."

Pike moved on to the first of the Baxter wagons and was surprised to see that Elizabeth wasn't there. Finley and O'Leary were, though, and they didn't look happy. They still held shotguns, so Pike eyed them warily as he approached.

"Where's Miss Baxter?" he asked.

"Her name's not Baxter," Finley replied. "She's Sister Elizabeth Meadows."

Pike frowned. "She's not actually Baxter's sister?"

"We never did like that deception," O'Leary said. "Lying's a sin, but we took Brother Lavon's word that it was in a good cause. Now, from what Sister Elizabeth has told us, we know it wasn't such a good cause after all."

"Murder and thievery," Finley said. "I never dreamed Brother Lavon would stoop to such things."

"Is his name even Baxter?" Pike asked sharply.

"No, sir. It's Branson. That's another thing we had to lie about." Finley blew out a disgusted breath. "For a so-called good cause."

"Where is he now?"

Both men shook their heads.

"We haven't seen him," O'Leary said.

"What about Elizabeth?"

Finley pointed and said, "She saw your brother ride by, heading back toward the remuda, and followed him. I reckon he didn't see her, because she was inside the wagon, tying a rag around her head to stop the bleeding from that cut."

Even though she had helped him, Pike didn't know how far to trust Elizabeth. Maybe she had followed Torrance toward the remuda, or maybe she just wanted to steal a horse and light a shuck out of here while she had the chance. He still had to check on his brother and sister, so he nodded to the deacons and nudged his horse into a lope again.

He had barely started when a pair of shots blasted on the other side of the nervously milling livestock.

Biting back a curse, Pike urged his mount to greater speed. He didn't know if Elizabeth was responsible for those shots, or if the treacherous Lavon Baxter—Branson, the deacons had said his real name was—had shown up again. Pike wished he could have hunted down Branson earlier, but in the chaos of the ambush, there simply hadn't been an opportunity.

Now as he charged around the remuda, he spotted Nessa's mount—but Nessa wasn't on the horse. She was sprawled on the ground nearby with Torrance kneeling beside her. Elizabeth stood nearby with a bloodstained rag tied around her head.

Lavon Branson had hold of the horse's reins, but it was skittish and he was having trouble bringing it under control. He had a gun in his other hand.

Pike knew instantly that Branson was trying to make a

getaway. He might have shot Nessa in order to steal her horse. Pike wasn't going to let him escape, though, and if he'd hurt Nessa, he would pay.

Branson had to hear the drumming hoofbeats as Pike galloped toward him. He glanced in Pike's direction, then finally got his left foot in the stirrup and swung up into the saddle. As he jerked the horse around, he thrust the gun in his other hand toward Nessa and Torrance, probably figuring that if he shot them, Pike would have to stop to help them, rather than coming after him.

"No!" Elizabeth cried. She threw herself forward as Branson pulled the trigger.

The slug caught her in the chest and knocked her backward off her feet. Pike fired an instant later, but Branson was already whirling his horse to race down the trail, and the shot missed. Pike thundered after him.

Branson twisted in the saddle to throw wild shots back at him. Pike leaned forward and made himself a smaller target. He didn't waste bullets but pouched his iron instead. He knew his horse was faster than the one Branson had stolen from Nessa. He began to close in on the fleeing Branson, slowly but surely.

Branson tried to fire at him again, but Pike could tell from the man's frustrated reaction that the gun in his hand was empty. Branson jerked the trigger several times, then flung the gun behind him in a futile gesture. It didn't come anywhere near Pike.

Pike was close enough now he could have blown Branson out of the saddle without much trouble. Judging by the look of terror contorting Branson's face when he glanced over his shoulder, that was exactly what he expected.

Instead, Pike closed in more, until he was riding almost side by side with Branson. He was about to dive from his saddle and tackle Branson when the man suddenly wrenched his mount to the side, toward Pike.

The two horses collided and went down in a welter of flailing limbs. Pike had already kicked his feet loose from the stirrups, so he sailed out of the saddle and crashed to the ground, his momentum making him roll over several times before he came to a stop.

Instantly, he pushed himself to one knee and drew his gun, just in case Branson tried to attack him. He saw right away that that wasn't going to happen. Something about the awkward, broken way Branson lay on the ground several yards away told Pike that the stolen horse had rolled over him.

Pike stood up and moved closer. He kept the gun trained on Branson just in case the man had any more tricks up his sleeve, as unlikely as that seemed in his obviously badly injured condition.

Branson opened his eyes and coughed a couple of times. Blood trickled from both corners of his mouth as he looked up at Pike.

"That was a damn fool thing to do, Branson," Pike said. "You must have really been desperate." He glanced at the horses. Both of them were back on their feet, shaken but evidently unharmed by the fall. "At least you didn't hurt a couple of innocent horses."

"You . . . you know who . . . I am?" Branson struggled to get the words out.

"I know you're a fake and a killer," Pike said. "You're probably not a real preacher at all."

"Not . . . not true. I am . . . a preacher. A . . . a crusader . . . against the evils . . . of drinking." Branson coughed again and more blood welled from his mouth. "I'm going to . . . die . . . aren't I?"

"You look like you're all busted up inside from that horse falling on you, so I'd say there's a pretty good chance of it."

"E-Elizabeth . . . I didn't mean to . . . shoot her . . . Is she . . . all right?"

"I don't know." The idea of sparing Branson's feelings never even occurred to Pike. "She didn't look like it to me. She's probably not going to make it, either."

Branson closed his eyes and groaned, although whether in pain or regret, Pike couldn't say. He thought the man might just go ahead and die then, but instead Branson managed to open his eyes and gasp, "Tell Sophie . . . tell Sophie . . . I'm truly sorry . . . Ma . . . Pa . . . What are you . . . No! Noooo!"

Branson screeched in pure, mortal terror. His arms and legs twitched. His head pulled back and the cords in his neck stood out distinctly as he grimaced in fear.

Then he slumped and his head fell to the side. His wide-open eyes began to turn glassy.

Pike waited a minute to be sure that Branson was dead, then turned and whistled for his horse. He watched carefully as the animal approached, looking for any sign of injury from the tumble.

Satisfied that the horse was all right, he mounted up and caught Nessa's horse. He led it over to Branson, dismounted, and lifted the corpse to sling it over the saddle. He could tell from the loose-jointed feel of the body that many of the bones were crushed or broken.

Branson's desperate gamble had failed, and he had paid the ultimate price.

After a few minutes of riding and leading the other horse with its grim burden, Pike came in sight of the remuda, the wagons, and the gap at the crest of the trail.

Spotting a number of people gathered at the wagon Branson had been driving, he headed for it. Nobody was watching the remuda at the moment, but the animals didn't seem to be straying.

Dougal, Fiddler, and Sam Crow saw him coming and walked out to meet him. As Pike reined in, Dougal nodded toward the corpse on the other horse and said, "You got the varmint, eh?"

"I reckon you could say he got himself." Pike didn't take the time to explain that as he dismounted. "How's Nessa? Did Branson shoot her?"

Fiddler said, "Don't worry, Pike, she's fine. That man shot at her and spooked her horse. She got thrown, but she wasn't injured."

"Just her dignity," added Dougal. "She didn't like bein' unhorsed that way. Prides herself too much on bein' a good rider for that."

Pike grunted. "It happens to everybody."

"The fella's name was Branson, you said?" Sam asked.

"Yeah. He still insisted he was a real preacher, but he planned on his gang wiping us out so he could steal this moonshine."

"That don't sound much like a preacher to me," Dougal said.

Pike was going to ask Sophie about that when he got a chance to talk to her, but right now he wanted to know, "What about the woman? Elizabeth?"

"Torrance is with her in the wagon," Fiddler said. The little man sighed. "And Nessa is with Torrance. Miss Baxter . . . Miss Branson?"

"Neither of those," Pike said. "She wasn't even really his sister."

"Well, whoever she was, she didn't make it, I'm sad to say."

Dougal said, "Torrance is pretty broke up about it, even though he understands now she was workin' against us. He was still sweet on her. He claims she turned against that fella Branson and died savin' him and Nessa."

"From what I saw, he's right about that. What about Belle?"

"I cleaned up that wound of hers and tied a bandage around it. It was more than the scratch she claimed it was. That slug plowed a pretty good furrow in her arm and she lost considerable blood. I reckon there's a mighty good chance she's gonna be fine, though."

Pike was relieved to hear that.

"What did you do with those prisoners?" he asked.

Dougal jerked a thumb over his shoulder and said, "Got 'em trussed up hand and foot and tied to a wagon wheel, to boot. What do you plan on doin' with 'em, Pike? I was thinkin' maybe we'd take 'em on to the next town and turn 'em over to the law."

"That's not a bad idea." Pike frowned slightly. "Doesn't really sound like you, though, Dougal. You're generally more in favor of taking the law into your own hands."

"Waaalll . . . I sort of figured we could tie 'em to the back of a wagon by their ankles and drag 'em the whole way . . ."

Fiddler looked a little shocked, but Pike and Sam chuckled.

"We'll see," Pike said.

Sam spoke up then, pointing and saying, "Riders coming, Pike."

Pike turned to look back along the trail. He wasn't surprised to see Sophie and her companion riding toward them. The shooting had been over for a while now, so they must have decided it was safe to approach.

Pike stepped away from the others and faced them. His right hand hung near the butt of his Colt. He didn't believe the young man with Sophie represented any threat, but he also believed in being ready for trouble.

As they rode up and reined in, Sophie asked anxiously, "Pike, are you all right?"

"I'm fine," he told her with a curt nod.

"What about Nessa and Torrance and . . . and Belle?"

"Belle's wounded."

Sophie gasped and lifted a hand to her mouth.

"Not seriously, I don't reckon," Pike went on. "Other than being shaken up and upset, Torrance and Nessa are all right."

The young man pointed to the corpse draped facedown over the saddle of Nessa's horse and said in a choked voice, "Is that . . . is that Brother Lavon?"

"It is," Pike said flatly.

"Did you kill him?"

"His horse went down when he was trying to get away from me, and when they fell, it rolled over on him. I didn't do a thing to him."

"Oh." The young man sighed and nodded. "I don't reckon I could blame you if you did kill him, Mr. Shannon. It's pretty clear from what happened here today that Brother Lavon wasn't the man I thought he was."

"He was an outlaw, is what it boils down to," Pike said. "Maybe he pretended to be something else . . . maybe sometimes he actually believed himself to be something else, I wouldn't know about that . . . but he was willing to kill all of us to get his hands on what's in these barrels, and to me that makes him nothing more than a no-good owlhoot."

"He . . . he didn't want to steal it for the profit. He was honestly opposed to folks drinking liquor—"

"Sonny, you tell yourself whatever you want to," Dougal said, "but I know hardcases when I see 'em, and the men who ambushed us were sure enough hardcases."

For a second the young man looked like he was going to argue, but then he sighed again and nodded dully.

Pike said, "You two go ahead and get down off those horses if you want. We're not going to run you off. But right now, I want to go see my brother and sister, and my friend."

"You mean Belle?" Sophie said.

"That's right."

Sophie drew in a breath and lifted her chin. "Tell her I'm sorry she was injured."

"You can tell her yourself, later," Pike said. He turned away and didn't look back.

CHAPTER 33

They laid Lavon Branson and Elizabeth Meadows to rest in separate graves up on the flats, half a mile from the gap where the bloody battle had taken place. Fiddler, who had an exhaustive knowledge of the Scriptures to go along with his other talents, spoke words of comfort and benediction over them.

The ten outlaws who had been killed were buried in two separate mass graves without any ceremony. If it had been up to Pike, he would have dumped Branson in one of those holes, too, but he went along with the separate burial to spare Sophie's feelings. She seemed pretty upset about everything that had happened—and she had reason to be, considering the part she had played in it, albeit inadvertently.

However, she'd had no way of knowing that Branson was a phony and a crook, Pike told himself. Forgiving her for her meddling was the right thing to do.

The young man with her, Curtis Holloway, had identified the dead ambushers, including Titus Ferrell and Carter Hoyt, who had been Branson's right-hand men. After a long talk with Sophie and Curtis, Pike determined it was obvious that the rest of the people in the group coming along the trail were innocent and had had no knowledge of Branson's true plans.

"You're not going to have them arrested, are you?" Curtis asked worriedly.

Dougal said, "We ain't the sort who go runnin' to the law, son. We figure it's better to stomp our own snakes." He nodded toward the mounds of earth marking the fresh graves. "And we've done stomped these."

"There's still the matter of those two prisoners," Will Fisher pointed out.

"We should let them go," Pike said.

The others looked at him in surprise, especially Torrance and Belle.

"Why in the world would we do that?" Belle asked. "They bushwhacked us. Tried to kill us."

"Like Grandpappy said, I don't want to drag the law into this." Pike nodded significantly at the barrels of moonshine in the wagons. "I'd just as soon not have to pull out that lie about molasses again."

"Well, then, just shoot the two of them," Belle snapped.

"They're partially responsible for a woman's death," Torrance added. Pike knew he was talking about Elizabeth Meadows.

"The only one responsible for her death is Lavon Branson, and he's dead," Pike said. "If we put those other two on their horses with no guns or ammunition and only a few supplies, I don't reckon we'll ever see them again. They'll want to shake the dust of this part of the country off their heels pretty quick-like."

"You think so?" Sam Crow asked.

Pike nodded and said, "I do. Especially after I explain to them that if I ever lay eyes on them again, I plan on killing them on sight."

"Well, that might work," Dougal allowed.

Torrance and Belle didn't like it much, but they followed Pike's plan and the two outlaws rode off, heading north as fast as they could after promising that they'd never trouble the Shannons again.

"You really believe them?" Torrance asked with a bitter edge in his voice.

"Yeah, but if they're lying and show up again, I'll just kill them then," Pike said. He turned to Sophie and Curtis. "Now, what are we going to do with you two?"

"I can think of a few things," Belle said ominously.

Sophie gave her a cold stare in return and said, "I didn't mean for anything bad to happen."

"No, all you wanted to do was ruin Pike's plan and maybe get him arrested, if not worse!"

Pike held up a hand and said, "Take it easy. Sophie, I'm willing to give you the benefit of the doubt—"

"Why?" Belle demanded.

"Because everybody deserves a second chance, I reckon. I've had more than my share of them."

Belle glared, but she didn't say anything else.

"As for you, fella," Pike said to Curtis, "I believe you didn't know anything about what sort of skunk Branson really was, so I don't blame you for throwing in with him. When you and Sophie figured out what was really going on, you were quick enough to try to warn us. I have to give you credit for that. You can turn around, go back to the rest of your bunch, and tell them what happened here. I imagine they'll want to scatter and go back to their homes, once they've heard the truth."

Curtis nodded glumly and said, "Yeah, I'll need to get word to them. But right now, I want to go on to Prescott with Sister . . . I mean, with Sophie." He sighed. "I reckon that whole brother and sister business is done with."

"Wait a minute," Belle said. She frowned at Sophie. "You're going to Prescott?"

"I . . . I was hoping you'd let me ride the rest of the way with you," the blonde replied. "And then I could go back to Warbonnet with you."

Belle scoffed and shook her head. "You really *have* gone loco, haven't you? Pike, tell her she can't come with us. She's not welcome here."

"I don't figure that's necessary," Pike said. "She and Curtis can't do us any harm anymore. I don't see any problem in letting them ride with us, as long as they promise not to stir up any trouble."

"But they've done plenty of that already!"

"They'll steer clear of you. You can pretend they're nowhere around." Pike looked at Sophie and Curtis. "Isn't that right?"

"Yes, sir," Curtis responded. "We'll keep our heads down and not bother folks."

"You have my word, Pike," Sophie said with an uncharacteristic meekness. He could tell she was really shaken by everything that had happened.

Belle just looked mad and stalked off.

Pike sighed, looked around at the others, and said, "Let's get those wagons rolling again."

The two deacons came up to him. Finley said, "We're going to wait here for the others in our party to catch up, Mr. Shannon. There's no need for us to continue on with you."

Pike nodded. "That makes sense."

"We hope you don't hold any hard feelings toward us,"

O'Leary added. "Had we known what Brother Lavon was up to, we would have tried to talk him out of it."

"You know, I believe you would have." Pike stuck out his hand and shook with both men. "No hard feelings. And that goes for the rest of your bunch. Might be wise to be a little more careful about who you decide to follow in the future, though."

They sighed, and Finley said, "You're right about that. Sometimes it's hard to know what's the right thing to do."

"I reckon we all struggle with that," Pike said.

Everyone else had spread out to get the wagons ready to move, except for Dougal. He lingered, and when Pike had finished talking to the deacons, he said quietly to his grandson, "I know you're just tryin' to be fair, boy, but if you ain't careful, you're gonna wind up with both of those gals hatin' your guts."

"Belle will either come around to seeing that I'm right or she won't."

"What about Sophie?"

"That's over," Pike said. "Anyway, that young fella Curtis has his eye on her. She probably hasn't noticed yet, but he does."

"Yeah, you're right about that." Dougal turned away, scratching at his beard where a faint streak of pink still showed from the blood that had leaked out of the bullet graze on his cheek. He chuckled and said as much to himself as to Pike, "A woman comin' around to seein' that she's wrong and a man's right . . . By grab, what sort o' locoweed has that boy been chewin!"

They reached Pecan County by afternoon of the next day. The terrain was low, rolling hills broken by occasional buttes and ridges. A number of creeks flowed through the county, but with the exception of its namesake, Pecan Creek, they were all shallow and easily forded.

Late in the afternoon, they came in sight of Prescott, the largest town and county seat. It was located on Pecan Creek and sprawled at the base of another of the rough ridges that ran through this part of Texas.

Prescott was a good-sized town and even had a Baptist college, the leaders of which had been behind the local-option election that had turned Pecan County dry, Pike figured. Knowing Baptists, the next thing they'd do was try to make dancing illegal.

Pike didn't want to parade down Main Street with those wagons full of moonshine, so when the caravan was still a mile or so out of town, he signaled a halt.

"The rest of you wait here," he said. "I'll ride on in and find Delano. We can figure out how he wants us to deliver that 'shine so we won't attract a lot of attention."

"Somebody ought to go with you," Torrance said.

"I think I'll be all right. From what I've heard about it, Prescott's a pretty peaceful town."

"That's not what I meant. We all have a stake in this load. You don't need to be deciding things by yourself."

Torrance had been sullen ever since Elizabeth Meadows' death. Pike understood that his brother had had feelings for the woman, or at least had convinced himself that he did, but while that might lead him to cut Torrance a little slack, his patience still had its limits.

"The price has already been agreed on," he pointed out. "The only question is where and how Patrick wants to take delivery. That shouldn't take much negotiating."

Dougal said, "Pike ain't steered us wrong so far, Torrance. I trust him to handle this."

"So do I," said Nessa. "Although I wouldn't mind going into town, myself."

"You'll get a chance to," Pike promised her. "I figure we'll stay here for a day or two and let the teams rest before we start back to Warbonnet."

Since the other two Shannons had supported Pike's decision, Torrance gave a surly nod and said, "All right. Shouldn't we get these wagons off the trail, though, so people won't come by and wonder who we are and what we're doing here?"

"Good idea," Pike said. "Take them over into those trees. The growth is thick enough most folks won't notice the wagons."

The others got busy with that, and he headed on toward town.

A short time later, Pike crossed Pecan Creek on a wooden bridge. The trail split, one leg going on west, the other angling off to the left to become the town's main street. Hamling Avenue, by name, Pike saw from a street sign as he rode through a prosperous-looking business district that stretched for several blocks. Up ahead, off to the right, he saw the big, red-brick buildings of the college.

Pike turned his horse toward the boardwalk on the left-hand side of the street and hailed one of the men walking along there.

"Excuse me, friend, could you tell me where to find the Big Boss Saloon?"

The man wore a gray tweed suit, white shirt, and string tie, but no hat. He was fairly young, but spectacles perched on his nose and his sandy hair was already thinning. Pike took him for a bank teller or a store clerk.

With a frown of disapproval, the man said, "We don't

have saloons in Prescott anymore, or anywhere else in Pecan County. They've been outlawed."

Pike hung on to his patience and kept a pleasant look on his face. He said, "How about the place that used to be the Big Boss Saloon, then?"

"It's a restaurant now." The local sniffed. "Although I believe that gambling goes on there, too. The respectable element in town needs to do something about that, too."

"Gambling!" Pike exclaimed. "I should've known. I reckon I was wrong."

"Wrong about what?"

"Oh, nothing, friend. I just had a little bet with myself that dancing would be the next thing folks around here would try to get shut down." Pike chuckled. "A bet with myself. I reckon that makes *me* guilty of gambling, doesn't it?"

The man didn't look amused by Pike's sense of humor. He turned and pointed along the street.

"The Big Boss—what a crude name—is three blocks along, on the other side of the street. The corner of Hamling and Kemp."

Pike nodded and said, "I'm much obliged to you." He heeled his horse into motion again.

He found the Big Boss where the man had told him it was. The former saloon's entrance was on the corner. The traditional batwing doors had been removed, Pike saw as he dismounted and looped his horse's reins around a hitch rail. There was a sign on both sides of the corner, one facing Hamling Avenue, the other Kemp Street. Each sign read simply THE BIG BOSS, but they appeared out of balance because it was obvious where the word SALOON had been painted over.

The gilt lettering spelling out the same word had been

scraped off the big front windows on both sides of the entrance. It was a real shame, thought Pike. The establishment looked like it had been a fine one. He could see why Patrick Delano had decided to settle down and run the place after winning it in that poker game.

Now it had a dusty, sort of run-down atmosphere to it. Clearly it wasn't doing the same sort of business it had been before the local-option election.

Pike untied a canteen from his saddle and slung its leather strap over his shoulder. He stepped up onto the boardwalk and went to the double doors on the corner. When he opened them and stepped inside, none of the usual hustle and bustle of a busy saloon washed over him. The smells of smoke, sawdust, whiskey, and beer were missing, too.

A long hardwood bar was to his left, but stools had been placed in front of it so customers could sit there and eat, like a counter in a hash house. Tables were scattered around the room. They had red-checked cloths on them, covering the wood or, in some cases, the green baize on the tables that had been used for card games.

Pike's sadness grew as he looked around and took all that in.

The Big Boss wasn't empty. It was a little early yet for supper, but half a dozen men were already there, sitting at the tables and eating. Pike didn't see a woman in the place, and the customers were all gents in late middle age or older, the sort who sat on benches and whittled or congregated in an empty storefront to play dominoes.

Downright pathetic, that's what it was.

Then a familiar voice exclaimed, "Pike! You made it!"

He looked around and saw Patrick Delano coming

through an open door, beyond which was what appeared to be a small office. Delano crossed the room quickly with his hand outstretched. He clasped Pike's hand and pumped it, then used his other arm to embrace him roughly and slap him on the back.

"You're certainly a sight for sore eyes," Delano went on as he let go of Pike's hand and stepped back. "You're actually a day or two earlier than I expected you, but you won't hear me complain about that!"

"I'm just glad to be here at all," Pike said.

Delano suddenly looked worried. "You had trouble on the way?" He started to become agitated. "You were able to bring the . . . the—"

"Don't worry," Pike told him. "I've got it." He tapped the canteen that hung from his shoulder. "Even brought a little sample into town with me."

Delano's eyes widened. He lowered his voice to not much more than a whisper and said, "That's the famous Shannon moonshine?"

"Try it for yourself and see."

"Oh, I intend to! Come on into the office." Delano inclined his head toward the tables and added sarcastically, "I apologize for all the crowd and commotion. That's the way it's been here recently. But I have a feeling all that is about to change."

CHAPTER 34

Once they were in the office and Delano had closed the door, he went behind the desk and said, "Give me that canteen. I have glasses back here, and I'll pour us proper drinks."

Pike handed him the canteen and sat down in the leather chair in front of the desk. Delano sat behind the desk, opened a drawer, and took out a couple of small glasses. He uncapped the canteen and splashed colorless liquid in each glass, then pushed one of them across to Pike.

"Here's to the conclusion of a profitable deal for both of us, and a new beginning for the Big Boss," Delano said as he raised his glass.

Pike lifted his glass to join in the toast. They threw back the drinks.

Delano's eyes widened slightly. He licked his lips, breathed a little harder, and said, "That really is potent, isn't it?"

"Mighty smooth, though," Pike said.

"It certainly is. Some of the best I've ever tasted." Delano reached for the canteen. "Let me refill these drinks."

"Not just yet," Pike said. "This stuff doesn't muddle me

any, but don't you think we ought to get everything settled first?"

"Indeed we should. Where is the load right now?"

"I left the wagons about a mile out of town," Pike explained. "Didn't figure it would be a good idea to drive up to your front door with them. After talking to one of the locals and asking where to find your place, I'm more convinced than ever that was a good idea."

Delano laughed. "Yes, they are pretty judgmental, aren't they? I don't expect that to change any time soon. Reformers are just like everybody else. Once they get a taste of power, they don't want to give it up. Only in their case, they're worse because they're convinced that their tyranny is just and moral and for your own good."

"Lord save us from people who want to tell us what to do for our own good," Pike said.

He went on to describe the location where the wagons and his companions were waiting. Delano nodded and said, "I know exactly where you're talking about. My men and I won't have any trouble finding it."

"How do you plan on getting the 'shine here?"

"We'll wait until after dark, when the town's asleep. These days, they roll up the boardwalks around here as soon as the sun goes down. We'll get the wagons one at a time, unload them out back and bring the barrels in, then go get the next one."

"That'll take most of the night," Pike commented.

"Yes, but that won't be a problem. My storeroom is big enough to hold all the barrels, and once they're in there, I'll be set for quite a while. I'll only dole out the moonshine to my trusted customers, and they'll be willing to pay a pretty penny for it, too, mark my words." Delano nodded in satisfaction. "Now, how about that second drink?"

"There's still the matter of the payment."

"Of course."

Delano stood up and went to a small safe standing in the corner. He knelt in front of it, worked the combination knob, and opened the safe to take out a canvas money bag of the sort banks used. He placed it on the desk in front of Pike with a satisfying *clink*.

"You mind gold double eagles?"

"Not at all," Pike assured him. He reached for the bag.

"Now for that drink," Delano said, refilling Pike's glass and sliding it into his grasp before Pike could draw the canvas bag toward him.

Pike didn't argue. He raised the glass, Delano raised his, and the gambler said, "To our future endeavors."

"To the future," Pike agreed. He drank down the moonshine, feeling the warmth it kindled all the way into his gut.

Then he thumped the empty glass onto the desk a little harder than he intended to, which made him frown. He reached for the bag again but had to make two tries before he closed his fingers around the top of it. He drew it toward him, saying, "I figured that much gold would be a little heavier."

Delano didn't say anything, just stood on the other side of the desk watching him.

Alarm bells went off in Pike's brain. He yanked the bag open and upended it, spilling a pile of metal washers onto the desk. As he started to his feet, he exclaimed, "What the hell?"

Suddenly, his head spun wildly, as if the earth had

started turning the wrong way. His balance deserted him, and he fell back into the chair. He clawed at the gun on his hip, knowing he had been betrayed somehow.

When Delano poured the drinks, he had slipped something into them, Pike realized. Somebody as deft with his hands as the gambler wouldn't have had any trouble doing that.

Pike's muscles refused to cooperate. His fingers slipped off the Colt's walnut grips before he could pull the gun from its holster. His head lolled back. His vision was swimming, so he saw multiple versions of Patrick Delano as the man stepped around the desk.

"I'm sorry, Pike, I truly am," Delano said. A part of Pike's brain was still working well enough to comprehend the words. "I'm not going to waste the rest of my life here in this backwater town. I was wrong to ever think that I could. But if I'm going to start over somewhere else, I need money, and that load of moonshine is worth a small fortune, especially to someone who has contacts among the Indians and can sell that much firewater to them." He smiled. "Which I do—and can."

"You . . . you . . ."

"Yes, yes, force all the curses out that you can. It won't make any difference. Our deal is concluded. To my benefit alone, unfortunately."

"I never . . . never should have believed . . ."

"But you *did* believe me," Delano said, "because we were old friends, after all. And after I helped you in that shoot-out with Ed Keyhoe and Purgatory Peters and Van-Hook, you felt grateful to me, didn't you?"

Understanding seeped into Pike's foggy brain. "You . . . set that up," he said. "Told Keyhoe . . . where to find me . . .

That's why . . . he was so surprised . . . to see you. Just so . . . I'd feel obligated . . . to you . . ."

"I was confident you'd go along with the idea anyway, but you know me." Delano shrugged. "Why not hedge my bet? It didn't cost anything except a little risk . . . and what is life without risk?"

"I won't let you . . . get away with—"

"There's nothing you can do about it," Delano snapped, his voice hardening. "You're helpless, Pike, and I intend to see to it that you remain that way. Permanently."

Pike felt his consciousness slipping away entirely now. He was aware of it when Delano raised a foot, rested it against the chair, and shoved. The chair went over, dumping Pike onto the floor of the office.

Pike didn't feel that. He was already out cold when he sprawled on the boards.

He woke with his head pounding and his stomach roiled with sickness. His first impulse was to retch. He fought it down. His brain wasn't working very well, but his instincts told him it would be better if he didn't do anything to indicate that he'd regained consciousness.

This wasn't the first time in Pike's perilous life that he'd been knocked cold. The thing to do was to pretend to still be down for the count while he tried to figure out where he was and what was happening.

Besides, his head hurt so bad that if he moved, his skull might explode into a million pieces.

Gradually, he became aware that he *was* moving. The dizziness he felt and the hard, sickening pressure on his guts weren't just because Patrick Delano had slipped him knockout drops in those drinks.

No, he was draped belly-down over a saddle, Pike realized. His head, shoulders, and arms dangled on one side of the horse, his legs and feet on the other. A rope had been looped around his wrists and tied to his ankles. He was helpless.

But not completely, because he was awake again and starting to recover his wits. He had to force his thoughts into ordered channels. He remembered being in Patrick Delano's office in the Big Boss. He remembered his former friend drugging him and admitting that he had set up the confrontation with the three gunmen in Sophie's café back in Warbonnet.

That had been well-played, Pike grudgingly admitted to himself. Delano had known that he could count on Pike's sense of honor to make him feel indebted. Because of that, he would be more likely to go along with the scheme Delano suggested.

Pike heard the hoofbeats of the horse carrying him, but he heard other animals moving along a trail, too. He tried to ignore the pounding pain in his head and the queasiness in his stomach as he listened intently.

Two more horses, he decided. Either Delano and a confederate, or two men who worked for the gambler. Either way, Pike would need to be patient and wait for a better chance to make a move against them.

Luckily, he had an iron constitution. Already, he was throwing off the effects of whatever drug Delano had given him. His brain was clearer. He risked wiggling his fingers. They all seemed to work.

His eyes were closed and had remained so since he

regained consciousness. He didn't see any play of sunlight against the lids, so he finally opened them a narrow slit.

Darkness met his gaze. Not full dark. Off to the right, a narrow band of reddish-gold light lingered along a black horizon. That was west, thought Pike, and his upper body hung on the horse's right side as it plodded along, being led by one of the other men. That meant they were going south.

Even though he was still a prisoner, just being oriented made Pike feel a little better about the situation.

Now he would know which way to go to get back to Prescott, he told himself, once he was free of these men who were taking him to kill him and bury him in a lonely grave.

Pike had no doubt that was the fate they intended for him. Or rather, that Patrick Delano intended for him, because he was sure the men were acting on Delano's orders.

That hunch was confirmed a minute later when one of them said, "Don't you reckon we're far enough from town by now, Pierce?"

"The boss wants this fella planted where nobody's liable to stumble over him," the second man replied.

"Yeah, and this is as good a place for that as any."

"I suppose you're right," Pierce said.

The horses came to a stop.

"You want to shoot him now, Richardson, or dig the hole first?" Pierce asked.

"I think we ought to wake him up and make *him* dig it. That'd save us some work."

Pierce cursed. "Didn't you listen to a word the boss said? That's Pike Shannon. He's been through range wars all the way from here to the Milk River. Shootin' wars that plenty of hombres never lived through. That ain't the sort of man you take a chance with, and turning him loose to dig a grave would be a *big* chance."

"All right, all right," Richardson muttered. "We won't wake him. Hell, I ain't sure he's even alive. As far as I can see, he hasn't budged since we loaded him up to bring him out here. I'm wonderin' if Delano gave him too much of that knockout stuff and knocked him out so much he plumb forgot to breathe."

"Let's leave him on the horse while we dig the hole. I think we're far enough away from anywhere that nobody'll hear the shot, but I'd just as soon get out of here as quick as we can once we've done the job. Just in case."

Richardson was in agreement on that. Pike heard both men dismount, and then a moment later, a shovel blade bit into the dirt with a crunch. The killers had only one shovel, so they took turns with it as they dug the grave meant for Pike.

While they were doing that, he worked at the bonds on his wrists. He wasn't sure what he was going to do, but he knew he'd have a better chance if his hands were free.

At first they weren't paying much attention to him. He chanced lifting his head and spotted the two men about ten feet away. They had stopped the horses under some trees so it was pretty dark already, despite the faint, quickly fading glow in the western sky that silhouetted their figures. They looked like typical drifters and hardcases to Pike, but that didn't mean they weren't dangerous.

As long as they stood there talking and digging and not looking toward him, he twisted his wrists and pulled hard at the rope around them. But after a few minutes, one of them—Pierce, Pike thought—said, "One of us ought to be keeping an eye on Shannon, just in case he comes to."

"I tell you, he's probably already dead," Richardson said as he handed the shovel to his companion, "but I'll go check on him if it'll make you feel better."

The fact that he'd been unconscious when they tied him up must have made them assume he wasn't much of a threat. Maybe they hadn't intended it, but they hadn't pulled the knots as tight as they might have.

Because of that, and because this wasn't the first time Pike had worked his way out of such bonds, he suddenly felt the rope slip as Richardson turned toward him. He let his head drop limply but continued twisting his hands slowly and carefully. In the poor light, Richardson might not see that.

The would-be killer came closer. Pike's right hand was loose now, the rope dangling around it. The loop around his left wrist was still attached to his ankles, though, holding him in the saddle.

He moved his right hand just enough to pinch the horse's belly, causing the animal to move around skittishly. Richardson said, "Hey, settle down, you idiot, it's just me." He reached out to take hold of the horse's bridle.

Pike used the horse's movements to distract from his own as he got his right hand on the rope and tugged it loose from his left wrist. Now both hands were free.

They shot out and grabbed the black-and-white cowhide vest Richardson wore. The man yelped in surprise and jumped back, which was just what Pike hoped he'd do. He clung to Richardson's vest. Richardson's violent leap pulled Pike out of the saddle and off the horse.

His feet were still tied, but he drove them against the ground and rammed himself against Richardson. The impact knocked the man over backward. Pike toppled to the ground with him.

As they fell, Pike reached to Richardson's right hip with his left hand and snagged the butt of the gun holstered there. Operating purely on nerves, guts, and instinct now, Pike deftly flipped the gun around. He thumbed back the hammer as he lifted it.

A few yards away, Pierce had dropped the shovel and whirled around at Richardson's shout. He clawed at his gun and yelled, "You damn fool! You let him loose!"

Pierce managed to get the iron out of leather before Pike fired. Flame belched from the muzzle of the gun in his hand. Pike was just as deadly with his left hand as with his right. Pierce grunted and took a sharp step back as he bent at the waist. Pike knew his slug had taken the man in the belly.

Richardson was still yelling and thrashing around. Pike didn't know if he had a second gun or a knife, so he didn't take any chances. He struck out with the revolver and smashed it against Richardson's head. The man went limp.

Pike rolled away and sat up, switching the gun to his right hand as he did so. Pierce had collapsed and wasn't moving. Neither was Richardson.

After a tense minute or so of watching the two men, Pike felt in his pocket, hoping to find the folding knife he kept there. No such luck. It must have fallen out when they were loading him on the horse, he thought.

Carefully, he moved over to Richardson's side and used his free hand to search the man. He had just found the handle of a sheathed knife at Richardson's waist when the killer suddenly lurched up. He grabbed Pike's throat with one hand and hammered at his head with the other.

Pike had had enough. He remembered how callously these men had spoken of killing him and disposing of his body.

He rammed the gun's muzzle under Richardson's chin and pulled the trigger.

Being shoved against the man's throat muffled the boom a little. Richardson jerked and his hands fell away. Pike grabbed the knife from the sheath, scooted back, and went to work sawing through the rope around his ankles.

The pain in his skull had subsided to a dull ache. The desperate action had driven the sickness from his belly. He got to his feet and was unsteady for a few moments before his head settled down. Hanging upside down would do that to a man.

So would being slipped knockout drops.

The thought of that made Pike's jaw tighten with anger. He had a big score to settle with Patrick Delano.

Before he could get started on that, however, he wanted to make sure he wasn't leaving any threats behind him. He went over to Pierce, hooked a boot toe under the man's shoulder, and rolled him onto his back. The way Pierce's arms flopped loosely to the sides told Pike that he was dead.

Pike didn't have his own gun, but he took both of those belonging to the two dead men, holstering one and sticking the other behind his belt. He took all the cartridges from the loops on their shell belts and dropped them in his shirt pocket.

One of them had been riding his horse, obviously planning to keep it once he was safely dead and buried. He swung up into the familiar saddle, leaving the bodies where they had fallen and leaving the other two horses there as well.

Then he rode north toward Prescott, steering by the stars that had started to come out in the sable sky above. Something even more important than vengeance was on his mind.

Delano intended to steal that moonshine and sell it to the Indians. Dougal, Torrance, Nessa, Belle, and the others were in mortal danger, if Delano hadn't attacked them already.

Pike heeled the horse into a run, knowing that there was no time to waste.

CHAPTER 35

Pike didn't know this area, especially after dark, so all he could do was ride in what he hoped was the right general direction. After a while, though, he spotted a cluster of lights up ahead and knew that had to be Prescott he was seeing.

With that to go by, he was able to steer to the east and circle around the settlement toward the place where he had left the wagons. He hit the main trail and turned right.

A few minutes later, he came in sight of a dark mass off to the right of the trail. That was the clump of trees he had pointed out earlier to Dougal and Torrance when he told them to take the wagons there.

Pike's Winchester was still in the saddle boot. He pulled it and levered a round into the chamber as he approached.

Everything was quiet. No lights were visible. He couldn't even be sure the wagons were still there. The shadows were too thick underneath the trees for that. He reined in, listened intently, and then called, "Hello, the camp!"

"Pike!" That was Torrance's voice, and he sounded upset as well as surprised. "Pike, is that really you?"

"It's me," he replied as he nudged his horse closer.

"Come on in! Hurry!"

Pike would have heard the urgency in his brother's tone even if Torrance hadn't added that. He rode into the trees, and as he did, somebody struck a match. The sudden flare made Pike's hand tighten on the Winchester.

"Over here," Torrance said as yellow light welled up from the lantern he had just lit.

Pike dismounted and let his horse's reins hang free as he hurried toward his brother. Torrance knelt next to Fiddler, who sat on the ground with his back propped against a tree trunk.

"I'm all right, I tell you," Fiddler said as he pressed a hand to his midsection. Pike saw blood under the little man's splayed fingers. "The wound isn't serious."

"You're not any judge of that," Torrance told him.

Pike dropped to a knee on Fiddler's other side and said, "Let me take a look at it."

"There's no reason to make all this fusssss . . ."

Fiddler's voice trailed off and his head sagged back against the tree trunk. His hand fell away from the bloody wound.

For one horrible second, Pike thought Fiddler was dead, then realized that his chest was still rising and falling in a fairly regular rhythm. Fiddler had just passed out, probably from the shock of being shot.

"I reckon Delano and his men have already been here?" Pike asked grimly as he leaned forward to get a better look at the wound. Torrance pulled Fiddler's shirt back to expose the bullet hole.

"That's right," Torrance answered. "We figured we could trust him, but since you weren't with him and we hadn't heard anything from you since you rode off hours ago, I told him he couldn't take the moonshine until we'd talked to you. That's when they opened fire on us."

Pike saw that Fiddler's wound was well over on his right side and low down. It was more than a graze, but given the location, it was possible the slug hadn't hit anything too vital. Fiddler might recover if he hadn't lost too much blood and if the wound didn't fester.

What he needed was some actual medical attention, from somebody who knew what he was doing.

"Where's everybody else?" Pike asked while Torrance tore a piece off of his shirt, folded it into a rough square, and pressed it against the hole in Fiddler's side.

"Will was hit, too," Torrance replied without looking up from what he was doing. "Dougal's tending to him. Sam and that boy Curtis are trying to round up our saddle horses. Delano's men stampeded them before they drove off with the wagons. They had us pinned down and we couldn't stop them."

With a shock, Pike realized that his brother hadn't said anything about Nessa, Belle, or Sophie. In a low, taut voice, he said, "Torrance . . . where are the girls?"

"Gone," Torrance answered hollowly. "Delano took them with him."

The news was a gut punch to Pike. Not only had he been too late to keep Delano from stealing the moonshine and to prevent Fiddler and Will Fisher from being wounded, but now he had to swallow the bitter pill that the three young women had been kidnapped as well.

"Why?" Pike asked through clenched teeth. "To keep me from coming after him?"

Torrance shook his head. He continued to hold the cloth pad on Fiddler's wound as he said, "Delano believed you were dead. He boasted about it, in fact. That's why I was so surprised to hear your voice when you hailed us a few minutes ago. He took the girls as hostages, all right. He warned us not to follow him and not to go to the law. He said that once he was sure no one was coming after him, he'd let them go with enough supplies to get back to Prescott."

"He was lying," Pike said with certainty. "He plans to sell that 'shine to a bunch of renegade Comanches. He bragged about *that* to me. Chances are that he'll try to sell the girls to them, as well."

Torrance started to look a little wild-eyed when he heard that. "We have to stop him—"

"I know that, blast it. Delano made a big mistake. He didn't make sure that I was dead."

"Seems to me that *you're* the reason we're in this mess and the girls are in danger."

Anger bubbled up inside Pike. He couldn't dispute what Torrance said. He already had a bitter, sour taste under his tongue from the guilt he felt. But that wouldn't change anything, and it sure as blazes wouldn't get the girls out of the trouble they were in.

"You just take care of Fiddler," Pike snapped. "Ma will beat us both black and blue with a hickory stick if we don't bring him back safe and sound. I'll go after Delano and get the girls back. *And* teach him not to double-cross me."

"Big words," said Torrance with a scowl.

"Hold on, hold on, boys."

Dougal came through the trees toward them and into the lanternlight. He had an arm around Will Fisher's waist from one side, helping Will limp along. Will's normally dour face was even more drawn and pale than usual. A bloody bandage was tied around his left thigh.

"How bad is it, Will?" Pike asked as he looked up.

"Aw, I've been winged worse than this," Will insisted.

"The bone's not broken. Let me rest for a few minutes, and I'll be ready to go after that no-good Delano with you."

Dougal said, "You ain't goin' anywhere except into town to have a sawbones look at that leg, once Sam and the Holloway boy get back with the horses. It ain't but about a mile into Prescott, ain't that right, Pike?"

"Yeah." He understood what Dougal was getting at. "You can ride that far, even with a bad leg, Will. And you can hold Fiddler on the horse with you and find a doctor for the both of you. The rest of us can go after Delano." Pike looked at his grandfather. "That is, if you're not hurt, too, Dougal."

"You see any fresh blood on me?" Dougal roared. "Just try'n stop me from goin' after that—"

A flood of profanity-laced Gaelic poured from the old-timer's mouth as his fury took him back to his Irish roots.

Torrance lifted the pad from Fiddler's wound and eyed the bullet hole.

"Looks like the bleeding's just about stopped," he said.

Fiddler's eyelids fluttered. He turned his head a little from side to side and moaned. When his eyes opened and stayed open, he said, "Am I . . . alive?"

"You sure are, pard," Dougal told him. He reached in the pocket of his overalls and took out a small silver flask. "You want a little snort to help you buck up a mite?"

Fiddler smiled weakly. "N-no, I . . . I had a difficult enough time . . . giving up the stuff before . . . I don't want to start again . . . Although . . . if it was strictly for medic-inal purposes . . ."

The sound of hoofbeats nearby interrupted him. Sam Crow and Curtis Holloway rode up, both of them bare-back, as they choused several more horses in front of them.

Pike stood up and said, "Get saddles on those mounts.

Fiddler, you and Will are going on into Prescott to find a doctor and let him tend to you, while the rest of us go after those moonshine bandits!"

Curtis asked, "You're going to let me come along, Mr. Shannon?"

"You want to help Sophie, don't you?"

The young man nodded. "I surely do."

"We have a couple of extra rifles. Can you shoot?"

"Back home, I could knock a squirrel off a tree limb at a hundred yards or more."

"An owlhoot's a lot bigger than a squirrel." Pike frowned. "You've been traveling with a preacher. You have any religious qualms about shooting some no-good son of a buck who needs it?"

"If any of those men have hurt Sophie or one of the other ladies, I won't hesitate to shoot them, Mr. Shannon. I give you my word on that."

"All right, then," Pike said. "Let's get ready to hit the trail."

While they were saddling the horses, Torrance told Pike more about how Patrick Delano and the men with him had attacked the camp and stolen the wagons loaded with barrels full of moonshine.

"How many hardcases did he have with him?" Pike asked.

"It was dark, so I can't say for sure. Ten or twelve, certainly. Enough of them to drive off with those wagons while some of them were still on horseback throwing lead at us."

"How did they manage to steal the girls?"

"Rode in and grabbed them, bold as brass."

"I'll bet they put up a fight."

"They did, even Sophie. The men who rode off with Nessa and Belle had their hands full, that's for sure." Torrance hesitated. "I think I saw the skunk who had Belle hit her with his gun, but I'm not certain about that."

Pike pulled a cinch tight on the saddle he was putting on one of the horses and said, "I'm not surprised. She's so feisty you'd need to knock her out before you could carry her off. He'd better not have hurt her too bad."

He expected Torrance to say something else about how this was all his fault, but for once, his brother chose not to snipe at him. That was good, because Pike was in no mood to put up with it.

"How are we going to trail them in the dark?" Torrance asked instead.

"I'm counting on the moon and Sam Crow for that. But if we have to, we'll stop and wait for morning rather than risk losing the trail. We can move faster than those wagons, so we can cut into their lead once it gets light. We ought to be able to catch up to them sometime tomorrow, even if we have to wait."

"Yeah, but where is Delano going to meet those Indians he plans to sell the 'shine to?"

Pike shook his head. "I don't know. There haven't been any Comanches around these parts for ten years. Most of them have gone to the reservations. Which means these are renegades, so they'll probably be willing to run more risks to get what they want."

Dougal had walked up in time to hear the last part of the conversation. He said, "Used to be, anywhere west of the Brazos was Comanche country. They've been pushed back beyond the Colorado River, though. It'd take Delano several days to get that far. If the Injuns are crossin' the river to meet him, that means they're firebrands lookin' for trouble."

"That's what I just said."

"I'm agreein' with you, boy, I'm agreein' with you. *I'm* just sayin' it'd be a good idea to catch up to Delano before he meets up with them Comanch', if we can."

The way to do that was to get started. Pike called out for everyone to mount up. Will Fisher and Fiddler had already left to ride into Prescott, each of them with bandages tied in place to stem the bleeding from their wounds until they located a doctor.

That meant there were five of them to go after Delano: the three Shannons plus Sam Crow and Curtis Holloway. That was a pretty formidable bunch, with Curtis being the only unknown quantity.

But they would be facing better than two-to-one odds, more than likely, and the men with Delano would be seasoned fighters. Delano himself was deadly with a gun and clearly more ruthless than Pike had believed him to be.

He wouldn't make the mistake of underestimating Delano again, Pike vowed. All he wanted right now was a chance to get the gambler in his gunsights, and that thought was uppermost in his mind as he rode out, leading the others as they took up the trail of their quarry.

CHAPTER 36

By late the next day, they had left the greener terrain of central Texas behind and entered a more arid region. Grass still grew in the sandy soil, but it was shorter and coarser, the landscape was painted more in tones of brown and gray, and short but rugged mesas were scattered all around.

Even though the five wagons and the horses of the out-riders left a pretty good trail in places, the frequent rocky stretches made tracking difficult at times, even for Sam Crow. The group had lost the trail more than once and been forced to backtrack until they were able to pick it up again.

That had cost them precious time, and every delay gnawed at Pike's guts. He figured that Nessa, Belle, and Sophie were relatively safe for the moment, until Delano met up with the Indians and possibly sold them to the rene-gades, but even so, the thought of them being prisoners was hard to swallow.

"How far is it to the Colorado River?" he asked Dougal.

"Can't be much farther," the old-timer replied. "We've been anglin' northwest some, or else we would've come to it before now."

Sam was riding a short distance ahead of the others.

He turned and rode back toward them, and Pike's pulse quickened as he wondered if his friend had spotted something.

That turned out to be the case. Sam reined in, turned halfway around in the saddle to point to the northwest, and said, "Dust rising there in the distance. Maybe a mile ahead of us."

"Is that them?" Torrance asked eagerly.

"Can't say for sure," Sam replied with a shrug, "but it's just about the right amount of dust for five wagons and some horses to be raising."

"Then we've caught up with them!"

"Here's the problem," Sam went on. He pointed again. "There's more dust over yonder. If I had to guess, I'd say it's coming from a good-sized bunch of horses."

"The Comanche renegades who are meeting Delano to buy that moonshine," Pike said grimly.

"Could be. We won't know for sure until we get closer."

Pike nudged his horse into motion. "Then let's go."

Even as he led off, though, he knew that if Delano succeeded in rendezvousing with the Indians, it would make the job of rescuing Nessa, Belle, and Sophie that much harder.

He didn't even care that much about the moonshine anymore. Recovering it would be nice, but the lives of the three girls were much more important.

Even though Pike wanted to gallop full-speed toward the dust, he knew he and his companions needed to proceed at a more deliberate pace—otherwise *they* would raise enough dust to give away their presence. Holding back was difficult, but they managed. Pike had to bite back a curse, though, when the two dust clouds ahead of them merged.

Once again he was too late. The rendezvous had taken place.

The sun lowered in the western sky until it was touching the horizon. In that vast wash of reddish-gold light, Pike saw the rays reflecting off the river that wandered through the landscape in front of them, about half a mile away. Pike reined in atop a ridge and motioned for the others to do likewise. They sat and studied the scene before them.

The ground dropped steadily to the river. A couple of hundred yards ahead of Pike and his companions, four of the five moonshine wagons were parked on a small bench. Saddle horses were tied nearby, and men moved around the vehicles.

The fifth wagon trundled down the slope toward the river. In the back of it, along with the five barrels of moonshine, were the three prisoners: Nessa Shannon, Belle Ramsey, and Sophie Truesdale.

Pike's breath caught in his throat when he saw them. They appeared to be unhurt, although it was hard to be sure at this distance.

He motioned the others back. Up here on the ridge, they might be seen if any of the men with the wagons happened to glance in this direction.

At the moment, however, those men had all their attention focused on the area just this side of the river, and with good reason.

Fifty or more Comanche warriors sat there on their ponies, war paint on their faces and long, sharp lances in the hands of most of them. They were a fierce-looking bunch. Warriors just like them had struck terror in the hearts of countless settlers on the Texas frontier. Such painted faces were the last things many of those settlers saw before dying agonizing deaths.

Pike's hand twitched with the urge to pull his Winchester from its scabbard and blow some of those savages to the hell they deserved. That wouldn't do anything to help rescue the girls, though. In fact, acting so rashly probably would make such a rescue impossible.

Instead, he watched as Patrick Delano drove the wagon down the hill to meet with the Comanches. Delano had a man on the seat beside him, holding a shotgun, and four men on horses flanked the wagon, two on each side.

"What's he doing?" Torrance asked in a quiet voice.

"He's taking one wagon down to the Comanches as a show of good faith," Pike said. "He won't turn the rest of the moonshine over to them until they've paid whatever price was agreed on."

"But the wagons are right there. The Indians could just come up and take them."

"Not without losing quite a few men, and they don't have enough warriors to waste," Pike explained. "Remember, the frontier isn't like it was a few years ago. Most of the Comanches have given up the fight and decided to live in peace with the white men. There are only a limited number of firebrands who still want to fight."

"But they're willing to risk coming this close to civilization to get their hands on some moonshine?"

Dougal responded to Torrance's question by saying, "Once they've got a taste for it, those fellas will do 'most anything for firewater. Could be the leaders of that bunch mean to recruit some more members by usin' the 'shine as bait. Get 'em all worked up with the stuff so they'll be willin' to fight a war they're bound to lose in the end."

"I'm afraid I don't care about any of that," Torrance said. "I just want to get those girls back safe and sound."

"Can't argue with that," Pike said. "Look!"

A few of the warriors had broken away from the larger party. They raced their ponies forward and rode in circles around the moonshine wagon Delano was driving. They whooped and waved their lances in the air. Delano and the other men remained coolheaded and pretended to ignore the Comanches, but Pike knew they would be watching the Indians closely.

Nessa and Belle gazed at the Comanches defiantly, which came as no surprise to Pike. They were bound to be afraid, but they weren't going to give in to that fear and certainly weren't going to show it.

Sophie was more visibly frightened as she cowered between the other two girls. She had been around plenty of trouble in recent months, since Pike had returned to Warbonnet County, but nothing to compare with this.

Delano drove the wagon to within twenty yards of the war party before hauling back on the reins and bringing the team to a stop. He sat there waiting as one of the warriors slowly rode toward him, followed by two more men. The one in front had to be the chief, thought Pike.

The Comanche stopped and addressed Delano. Pike couldn't make out the words, and since the setting sun was behind the man, he couldn't see the chief's face very well, either. But he recognized the man's solemn, dignified air.

"They're negotiating," he said.

Delano waved a hand at the girls and motioned for them to stand up. They did so with obvious reluctance.

"Now he's telling the chief that he brought along a bonus and wants an extra price for them."

The chief gestured emphatically. Dougal said, "He don't want to pay."

Delano reached under his coat and brought something out. The dying sunlight reflected off it.

"That's a flask," Dougal said. "He's gonna try to get the redskins drunk, figurin' that'll make 'em easier to deal with."

Pike said, "He wants to give them a taste of what they'll be getting, at least."

"As long as he doesn't tell them they can sample one of the girls," Torrance snapped.

"He's not going to do that. Not even Delano could stoop that low."

Even as Pike said the words, though, he hoped he was right about that. After everything that had happened, he couldn't be sure anymore.

The chief took the flask from Delano, tilted it to his mouth, and took a long swallow. Then he handed it to one of his subordinates, who also took a drink and then passed it along to the other Indian. That man turned his pony and carried the flask back to the war party, whooping excitedly.

"That 'shine won't last very long," Sam Crow observed.

Delano said something else to the chief, then turned the wagon and drove it back up to the flat where the other vehicles were parked. The chief rejoined the other Comanches. A lot of excitement was in the air among the war party. They wanted that moonshine, and Pike was pretty sure they wanted the three girls, too.

"Now what in blazes do we do?" Dougal asked. "With

it gettin' late, it looks to me like everybody's fixin' to make camp down there."

"They're going to wait until morning to finalize the deal," Pike said. "That'll give the chief and his lieutenants time to talk about whatever Delano's asking for Nessa, Belle, and Sophie. That's good."

"How is it good?" Torrance wanted to know.

"Because it gives us a chance to figure out how we're going to rescue them . . . and blow all of Delano's plans to kingdom come."

CHAPTER 37

The Comanches built a big campfire beside the river. Two hundred yards up the slope, Delano's gun-wolves had a good-sized fire going, too. The light from it washed over Nessa, Belle, and Sophie as they sat on the lowered tailgate of one of the wagons. The girls' hands were tied together in front of them, and once they had climbed onto the tailgate, their feet were bound, as well, so they couldn't run off.

They had been able to eat supper, though. Pike had watched them do so from behind a scrubby mesquite bush fifty yards away. Sam Crow was with him. They had crawled down here from the ridge as soon as it got dark enough, staying in the shadows and moving slowly and carefully so they wouldn't be spotted. Delano had posted a few guards around the camp, but Pike and Sam had successfully avoided them so far.

Torrance, Dougal, and Curtis were up on the ridge with their rifles aimed down here, ready to shoot if they needed to. Pike hoped that wouldn't happen for a while yet. He hadn't had a chance to put the plan he'd come up with into action.

Once he did, there would be shooting, though—and plenty of it.

Sam nudged an elbow into Pike's side and whispered, "Comanches coming up the hill."

Pike had seen the same thing. The chief and his lieutenants, backed up by four more warriors, approached Delano's camp on foot. Delano stood up to greet them.

"Welcome, Thunder Horse," the gambler said.

Without any small talk, the chief said in English, "We will pay your price for the firewater and the women, white man."

Sophie whimpered a little. The prospect of her fate must have been beginning to sink in on her. Belle and Nessa still looked angry and defiant.

"I'm very pleased," Delano said. "When will you pay?"

"You will get the gold in the morning, and we will take the wagons."

Delano nodded. "That's acceptable."

"You can get more firewater?"

"Of course," Delano answered without hesitation. He wouldn't want to admit that he'd burned his bridges with the source of this load. If the Comanches believed he could get more moonshine, they had a good reason to keep him alive.

Otherwise they could just kill these white men and take the 'shine and the girls.

"This is good," Thunder Horse said with a grave nod. He turned and went back down the hill.

Delano smiled in the firelight as he faced his men. He rubbed his hands together in satisfaction.

"I promised you this deal would make us rich, didn't I, boys?" he said.

"How much gold you reckon those redskins really have, boss?" asked one of the gunmen.

"Enough."

"Maybe we should've struck a real bargain with the Shannons and kept on supplyin' the Indians."

Delano shook his head and said, "They never would have gone along with that. Pike and his family may not exactly be law-abiding, but they wouldn't agree to take part in running whiskey to the savages on a permanent basis. Besides, those renegades probably won't even be alive in another month or two. I've heard rumors that the cavalry is planning to deal with them."

"Gettin' wiped out couldn't happen to a more deservin' bunch!"

That comment brought a round of laughter from the gunmen.

Pike could have said the same thing about *them*.

He and Sam continued their surveillance for the next hour or so as activity died down in the camp. Sophie began to cry. Nessa put her arm around the blonde's shoulders and drew her closer, trying to comfort her. Things had to look pretty bleak to all three of the girls right now. Pike wished he could have let them know he was close by and planning to help them, but he couldn't risk giving away his presence.

Delano came over to the wagon where they sat and said, "I'm sorry about this, ladies, I truly am."

"You promised you'd let us go when you were far enough away from Prescott," Belle said with a scowl.

"I considered it . . ." Delano shrugged. "But my friend Thunder Horse is willing to pay a good price for you. It won't be so bad. You'll have fine, strapping husbands—"

"You said a few minutes ago that they'll all be dead in a month. Then what?"

Delano shrugged. "I'm sure any survivors will go to the reservation, and you can get back to civilization that way. Of course, by then most people wouldn't consider you fit to return to white civilization—"

Belle leaned forward and spat in his face.

Delano jerked back. His hand flashed up and cracked across Belle's face. The blow knocked her against Sophie, who fell harder against Nessa. All three girls slipped off the tailgate and fell awkwardly to the sandy ground.

"You can sleep there tonight," Delano snapped at them. He walked off as he wiped away the spittle with a handkerchief.

Every muscle in Pike's body was taut with rage, but he controlled himself. Too much was riding on what happened next to give in to anger.

The three girls crawled under the wagon and huddled together. Except for the guards, the rest of the men turned in, Delano included.

More time dragged by as the fire burned down. That meant it wasn't as bright, so Pike and Sam weren't as visible when they finally emerged from their cover and snaked across the ground toward the camp.

Pike would have liked to free the girls himself, but that was Sam's job. He would cut them free and start them crawling toward safety. Pike went toward one of the wagons instead, the one parked closest to the edge of the slope.

He worked his way around the vehicle so that when he stood up, the wagon itself blocked him from the view of most of the men. He drew the knife he had brought with him and, working by feel, wedged the blade into the crack along the lid of the closest barrel. Slowly, carefully, so as not to make any noise that would alert Delano's men, he pried the lid up slightly.

He had brought a long strip of cloth cut from a blanket with him, and when he had created a big enough gap between the barrel and the lid, he fed one end of the strip into it. He lowered it until he could tell that the cloth was hanging in the moonshine inside the barrel.

The next part of the plan was even riskier. He took a match from his pocket, held it down inside the wagon where it wouldn't be seen easily, and snapped the lucifer to life with his thumbnail. All he could do was hope that none of the guards noticed the brief flare.

He held the tiny flame against the other end of the cloth until it caught fire. The coal began crawling slowly up the strip.

By now, Sam was supposed to have cut the girls loose. Pike had no way of knowing if his friend had been successful. But the plan was underway and there was no turning back now.

He hurried to the front of the wagon, grasped the brake lever with both hands, and moved it to where it wasn't set. The wagon was parked facing away from the slope, so he didn't have to go around it again.

He just put his shoulder against it and started pushing.

Pike Shannon was a good-sized man and packed a lot of strength in his body. It took every bit of his strength to make that wagon budge. It rolled back a little, then a little bit more, and then moving it was easier. Pike grunted with the effort and dug his feet against the ground. He was making more noise now, but it didn't really matter.

Before long, if everything went according to plan, there was going to be a *lot* of noise.

The wagon's rear wheels reached the edge and rolled over it. The vehicle's weight shifted. Pike gave it another hard shove as it picked up speed and pulled away from him.

The wagon headed straight downhill toward the Comanche camp beside the river.

The creak and rattle of its wheels sounded as loud as a thunderstorm in the night. Somewhere not far away, one of the guards yelled, "Hey!" Several of the men started up out of their blankets, shouting questions.

Counting on the poor light to conceal his actions for the next few moments, Pike leaped to the closest wagon and disengaged its brake, as well. He put his shoulder against it and shoved.

A rifle cracked and a bullet chewed splinters from the wagon a couple of feet from Pike. The guard probably would have the range with his next shot, but Pike kept shoving.

More gunfire erupted, but these reports came from farther away. Torrance, Dougal, and Curtis had opened fire from the top of the ridge. Pike heard a man howl in pain and figured one of the guards had just been ventilated. The three men on the ridge continued spraying lead through the camp, as planned.

Pike hoped Sam Crow had gotten the three girls out of the line of fire.

This wagon was farther from the edge and took longer for Pike to roll it there. He looked past the sideboards and saw that the first wagon was more than halfway down the hill now, still rolling toward the river. The Comanches had heard it coming and were running around down there, shouting in confusion and alarm.

Pike had the second wagon almost at the edge when

he felt its weight shift, but not because it had reached the slope. He looked up and saw that Patrick Delano had leaped onto the back of it and stood next to one of the moonshine barrels.

"You!" Delano cried as he raised the gun in his hand. "You're supposed to be dead!"

Before he could fire, someone else scrambled onto the wagon from the other side, distracting him. He twisted toward the newcomer, who grabbed his gun arm and forced it up.

The next instant, several things happened at the same time. The first wagon Pike had sent rolling down the hill trundled to a stop among the Comanches, who clustered around it. The coal creeping up the strip of cloth reached the gap under the lid and dropped into the moonshine. At the top of the slope, the second wagon's rear wheels went over the edge and it lurched away from Pike, who looked at the desperate struggle going on in the vehicle's bed and recognized the auburn flash of Belle Ramsey's hair as she fought with Delano. As the boards slanted suddenly under their feet, they both fell among the barrels.

The barrel Pike had rigged as a bomb in the first wagon exploded, and that set off the other barrels, turning the wagon into a huge ball of flame that engulfed many of the Comanches and threw most of the others back off their feet. The wagon immediately turned into an inferno.

And the second wagon full of moonshine, with Belle and Delano in the back of it, bounced and careened down the hill toward the conflagration.

Eyes wide with surprise and horror, Pike bellowed, "Belle!" and charged after the wagon, going down the slope in huge leaps and bounds. Behind him, the pitched battle between Delano's gunmen and the trio on the ridge continued, but Pike wasn't paying attention to that anymore. He had to catch that runaway wagon and save Belle somehow.

He couldn't see the two of them anymore, but then they rose up, still fighting over Delano's gun. His superior strength won out. He jerked the weapon away and slashed at her with it. She cried out and fell back.

At the same time, Pike had closed in enough to leap and grab the tailgate. The jerk he experienced felt like it was going to pull his arms out of their sockets, but he hung on and pulled himself up enough to throw a leg over the back. Delano turned toward him as he hauled himself into the wagon.

"Belle!" Pike exclaimed. He gathered her up into his arms.

Delano stood among the barrels, bracing himself on one of them with his left hand while his right pointed the gun at Pike and Belle.

"I don't know how you got here, damn you," the gambler grated, "but I'm going to make sure you die, here and now!"

Pike pushed himself to his feet. Belle was in his arms, cradled against his chest. She was only half-conscious from the blow Delano had struck.

"You never should have double-crossed me, Patrick," he said, "and you sure as hell shouldn't have left me alive."

Delano snarled and thrust the gun at Pike as his finger whitened on the trigger.

Holding on tightly to Belle, Pike dived over the side of the wagon as Delano fired. The bullet sizzled harmlessly through the space where Pike and Belle had been half a second earlier.

Pike twisted in the air so that he took the impact on his shoulder as he and Belle crashed to the ground. Momentum jolted them apart and rolled them over. They came to a stop side by side, on their bellies, and Pike lifted his head in time to see Delano trying futilely to pull back on the brake lever hard enough to stop the wagon and save the moonshine.

The gambler was too late. Pike thought he heard Delano scream as the vehicle smashed into the blazing wreckage of the first wagon. The earth trembled under Pike and Belle as those barrels exploded, too, and spread the devastation even farther in the Comanche camp. Pike caught just a glimpse of Delano as the flames swallowed him whole.

Then he pushed himself up and helped the groggy Belle to her feet. With his arm around her, they started up the hill. The shooting had stopped above, and down below was nothing but the crackling of the flames.

CHAPTER 38

They never knew how many of the Comanche renegades survived the explosions. Any warriors left alive beat a hasty retreat, after it must have seemed to them that the fiery vengeance of the spirits had descended on them from the heavens.

A couple of Delano's hired guns had taken off, too, but the rest lay dead, cut down by the withering rifle fire from Torrance, Dougal, and Curtis Holloway, who had thrown his arms around Sophie when she came up with Sam Crow and Nessa and hadn't strayed far from her side ever since.

That boy was devoted to her, Pike thought, and he was already talking about going back to Warbonnet with them. Pike hoped the two of them would find happiness together, if that was the way things were supposed to work out.

Belle had a cut on her forehead where Delano had pistol-whipped her, but otherwise she was all right.

"The scar won't be very big," she said with a shrug the next morning, as they prepared to leave. "And anyway, what's one more scar?"

"Life *does* tend to leave folks marked up a little," Pike agreed. "But it doesn't change who they are inside."

The three remaining wagons would be a lot lighter going back. All but two of the barrels of moonshine had bullet holes in them, and most of the 'shine had leaked out. If they combined all that was left, it might add up to another barrel.

"I'm plumb sorry about that, Pike," Dougal had said earlier. "But you told us not to worry about the moonshine if Delano's men took cover behind the wagons, so we didn't."

"And you did the right thing, Grandpappy," Pike had assured him. "I'm taking everything that's happened on this trip as a sign. Maybe it really *is* time to give up moonshining and just raise horses. That'd make Ma mighty happy."

Dougal looked a little horrified by the idea, but he nodded slowly.

"What'll we do with the 'shine we got left?"

"Well," Pike had said with a smile, "if we put it in jugs and just break it out for special occasions—like, say, if Ma and Fiddler get married—it ought to last us a long time."

Dougal had slapped him on the back and grinned. "That sounds like a good plan to me, boy."

Now, as they were hitching up the teams to the remaining wagons, Sam Crow came over to Pike and said quietly, "I'm sorry Belle got away from me last night while I was trying to herd those girls up the hill."

Pike chuckled. "Might as well try to herd a bobcat as to herd Belle Ramsey," he said. "We were lucky. It worked out all right."

"She's a mighty high-spirited gal." Sam smiled. "I expect it'd be a big job for a fella to try to keep up with her. But he'd never be bored, I'll say that much."

"I've always hated boredom."

Sam's smile widened into a grin as he slapped Pike on the back and then walked away.

A short time later, Pike mounted up to lead the now smaller caravan back toward Warbonnet County. Belle came up alongside him on her horse.

"Curtis and Sophie volunteered to take care of the remuda," she said. "I reckon they want to be back there by themselves, even if it means eating some dust. So I figured I'd ride up here with you . . . if you don't have any objections."

"No objections," Pike said. He turned in the saddle to wave the wagons forward.

As they walked their horses side by side, Belle said, "You know, Phineas Conway is still lurking around Warbonnet County, and it's clear he's got a grudge against you. What are you going to do about him?"

"I haven't decided yet," Pike said, "but I'll take that as it comes."

They rode in companionable silence for a few moments, then Belle said, "You know, you and your family did all that work cooking the 'shine, and then we went through all the dangers of bringing it out here, but you wound up not getting any kind of payoff out of the whole deal."

"Oh, I wouldn't say that. I was able to figure out a few things."

"You were?"

"Yep."

"And that was worth all the trouble?"

Pike looked over at her and said, "I think so."

Belle gazed straight ahead, but a smile slowly curved her lips.

Pike didn't say anything about it, but he had gotten something else out of this trip, as well. Earlier that morning, he and Torrance had gone down to the Comanche camp to look through what was left. It was an ugly scene, full of burned corpses, but Pike had found something else.

A big lump of melted gold that he knew had been the coins Thunder Horse planned to use to pay Delano for the moonshine and the girls.

Pike had no idea what the gold was worth, but he had it wrapped up in canvas and stowed away safely in one of the wagons. Nobody knew about it except him, Torrance, and Dougal. Once they got home and he had a chance to deal with it, he would make sure that Sam and Will got their share of whatever it amounted to, and Belle, as well, although she'd probably argue about taking it.

As for the rest, well, it cost money for an honest man to run a ranch. And that was what he was going to be from now on, he told himself as he heeled his horse into a lope and Belle rode alongside him, her hair flashing in the morning sun.

Yep, an honest man.

It would be interesting to see how long *that* lasted.

TURN THE PAGE FOR AN EXCITING PREVIEW!

Johnstone Country.
Where Two Guns Kill Better Than One.

Once upon a time in the Old West, Slash and Pecos were two of the wiliest robbers this side of the Rio Grande. Now they're fighting on the side of the angels—against three of the nastiest killers this side of Hell . . .

SLASH AND PECOS . . . IN THE SOUP AGAIN
Not many men get a second chance at life.
But thanks to a chief U.S. marshal who needs their help, the bank-robbing duo of Jimmy "Slash" Braddock and Melvin "Pecos Kid" Baker are on the right side of the law. As unofficial marshals, they've agreed to pick up three prisoners from a Milestown jail and escort them to Denver. Sounds easy enough—until they learn who the prisoners are: an unholy trio of sadistic cutthroat killers known as Talon, "Hellraisin' " Frank, and the Sioux called Black Pot. And they've managed to escape before Slash and Pecos even show up . . .

It gets worse. The three convicts have turned Milestown into their own savage slayground. Drinking, killing, ravaging—and worse—they're painting the town red with blood and burning it to the ground. Slash and Pecos manage to stop them in the nick of time. But getting these three to Denver is another story—because the trio's leader has offered a thousand-dollar bounty to anyone who can kill Slash and Pecos . . . This is going to be one wicked ride that Slash and Pecos will never forget—if they live to tell about it . . .

THE WICKED DIE TWICE
A SLASH AND PECOS WESTERN

On sale now wherever Pinnacle Books are sold.

Chapter 1

When Town Marshal Glenn Larsen reined up in front of the jailhouse on Dry Fork's main street very early on a Sunday morning in early July, a cold stone dropped in his belly. He could tell by the look on the dark, craggy face of his deputy, Henry Two Whistles, that trouble was afoot.

As the older man, clad in a three-piece suit that hung a little loosely on his lean frame, stepped out through the jailhouse door, a fateful cast to his molasses-dark eyes was undeniable. Not that Two Whistles was ever all that given to merriment. He was three-quarters Ute from southern Colorado Territory, and he was true to the stoic nature of his people.

As he closed the jailhouse door and turned to face Larsen reining up before him on the marshal's sweat-lathered coyote dun gelding, the old man rested his double-barreled Parker twelve-gauge on his right shoulder.

"Anyone hurt . . . killed?" Larsen asked before Two Whistles could say anything, the marshal's voice pitched with dread.

Two Whistles frowned curiously, deep lines wrinkling

the dark-cherry tone of his forehead and spoking around his eyes.

Larsen canted his head toward his back trail. "I was on my way back to town last night when I met three Milliron Ranch hands. I thought it was a mite odd to see Mill-iron hands heading back out to their headquarters so early on a Saturday night, and said as much. They told me that Talon Chaney and 'HellRaisin'' Frank Beecher had come to town, an' were sort of makin' all the stock hands home-sick. They decided to cut out early and avoid gettin' caught in a lead storm."

Two Whistles gave a grim, stony-faced nod. "That damn Cut-Head Sioux is with 'em, too—Black Pot."

"Gabriel Black Pot," Larsen said as he swung down from his saddle. "Yeah, they mentioned him, too. He's an aptly named son of the devil, ain't he? There ain't one thing that ain't black about him, especially his heart."

Henry pursed his lips. "How bad, Henry?"

The old deputy lifted and lowered his left shoulder. "Not bad. This time. They came in late yesterday afternoon. Been holed up at Carlisle's place. All the ranch hands and everyone else in town know 'em well enough by now that they cleared out of Carlisle's as soon as Beecher's bunch bellied up to the bar."

"Not great for business, are they?"

"At least no one's dead. Not yet. They slapped around a couple girls, made 'em dance with 'em while Carlisle played the piano, but they was drunk when they rode into town, so by ten, eleven o'clock, they went upstairs an' passed out with a couple of Carlisle's doxies."

"That was nice of them." Larsen sighed. "When I heard they were here, I expected the worst."

Two Whistles's thick-lipped mouth rose in a grim smile.

"That would likely happen today, when they get goin' again. As Carlisle tells it, they're flush. An' it don't look like they're gonna let any of that stagecoach money burn holes in their pockets."

The three killers, along with the rest of their twenty-man bunch, recently ran down a stagecoach hauling treasure from Deadwood to Sundance. They raped the women aboard the stage, killed the men, including the jehu and the shotgun messenger, stole the gold and the ranch payroll in the strongbox, and ran the stage off a cliff.

The gang split up the gold and separated.

Larsen had been surprised that Chaney, Beecher, and Black Pot had had the gall to show their faces in any town so soon after a holdup, but in a town so close to the scene of their crime most of all. On the other hand, he wasn't all that surprised. Those three killers in particular had reputations for being spit-in-your-face brazen about their wicked ways.

Maybe they felt they'd earned the privilege. They were known to have killed three deputy U.S. marshals and a couple of sheriffs who'd tried to run them to ground over the years, and double that many bounty hunters who'd hounded the gang for the bounties on their heads.

They probably hadn't hesitated to head to Dry Fork because they knew an unproven town marshal and his just as unproven, old-man, half-breed deputy were manning the jailhouse these days. Glenn Larsen and Henry Two Whistles had both been working out at the Crosshatch Ranch up until only seven months ago, when the rancher they'd worked for, Melvin Wheelwright, died suddenly from a heart stroke. His family had sold the ranch to an eastern syndicate, and that company's head honcho decided to hire an entire new bunkhouse of hands, despite every one being as seasoned as any other thirty-a-month-and-found cowpuncher anywhere in the territory.

Funny folks, those tailor-dressed syndicate men, most of whom were foreigners, of course. Maybe that was the explanation right there. . . .

Two of those hands given their time, a sack of grub, and one horse each to ride away on were Larsen and Two Whistles. Henry had been the Crosshatch cook since his bronco-busting days had gone the way of the buffalo, leaving him with a rickety left hip and a pronounced limp in cold weather. Larsen and Two Whistles had gotten to be good friends over the four years they'd worked together at the Crosshatch, even though Larsen now being only twenty-seven and Two Whistles somewhere in his fifties (though he'd never said where exactly) were separated by nearly thirty years in age. It just seemed natural that, when the two lone wolves left the headquarters and neither had anyone else in their lives, and nowhere else to go, that they'd ride nowhere together.

The nearest town was Dry Fork, so they'd headed there for a drink or two to drown their sorrows. It just so happened the town had been in need of a new marshal and a deputy and, since no one else had seemed to want the dangerous jobs, here the two former Crosshatch men were now, sporting five-point town marshal's stars.

Not only had a job been awaiting Glenn Larsen, but a pretty girl, as well. The first moment he'd lain eyes on the mercantiler's comely daughter, Tiffanie Bright, he'd tumbled head over heels. To his astonishment, it had turned out that she'd felt the same way about him, so against Tiffanie's family's wishes, they'd been hitched inside of two months. Now they had a neat little frame house, which her father had staked them to, on the corner of Main Street and Third.

Larsen was eager to head home to his pretty wife now, as he'd been away for the past three days, looking for the two men who'd stolen stock from a local feed barn, and he knew Tiffanie was worried about him.

First things first.

"All right," he said now, sliding his Winchester carbine from his saddle sheath. "They're over at Carlisle's, you say?"

"That's where they are, all right. Carlisle's swamper has been keepin' me updated. I wasn't gonna make a move on 'em till you showed up. Not unless they started shootin' up the place anyways. I didn't even show myself, knowin' that would only provoke 'em."

"No, no, I'm glad you didn't. Hell, Bill Tilghman wouldn't make a play on that bunch solo. An' there's no point in provokin' 'em and risking other folks' lives."

"So you're sayin' I ain't just a coward?" Henry gave a rare smile.

"No more than me, anyway." Larsen gave a droll chuckle and slowly, quietly jacked a round into his Winchester's action, as though the three brigands might hear the metallic rasp from all the way over at Carlisle's Saloon, two blocks away. "I wouldn't go it alone against them three. I sure will be happy to have them under lock and key— I'll tell you that much, Henry. When I took this job, I didn't think I'd be facing the likes of Talon Chaney!"

Again, Larsen chuckled. It was a nervous chuckle. He had the jitters, all right, and no mistake. His knees felt a little spongy, and his hands were sweating inside his buckskin gloves. He hadn't felt this nervy since the night before his wedding.

Tiffanie.

He sure hoped he made it through this morning in one piece, so he could see his lovely bride again. Thinking of her, of walking over to their little house on the corner of Main and Third, and sitting down to breakfast with her, after he had the three killers under lock and key, calmed his nerves a bit.

He kept her image in the back of his mind, and the image of their peaceful, cheerful, sunlit morning kitchen, as well, as he said, "All right, Henry. Let's do this. Me, I'm ready for breakfast."

"Really?" Henry said as they walked east along the main street, keeping to the boardwalks on the north side. "I couldn't eat a thing. In fact, I feel a little off my feed." He winced and pressed a hand to the middle-aged bulge of his belly.

"Truth be told, I was just jawin'." Larsen glanced at the older man walking beside him. "Right now, just the thought of food makes me a little ill."

"Yeah," Henry said.

As the two men walked along, spurs clanging softly, boot heels scuffing the worn boards of the sidewalk, Larsen saw that the street was deserted. That was strange. It was almost eight o'clock.

Normally, there would be some wagon traffic at this hour. Housewives would be strolling toward Mergen's Grocery Store for fresh eggs and cream. Children would be tramping in small groups toward the schoolhouse on the town's west end, bouncing lunch sacks off their thighs, the little boys triggering tree branch guns at each other or at imaginary Indians, the little girls whispering delicious secrets and giggling.

At the very least, a shopkeeper or two would be out sweeping the boardwalks fronting their stores, or arranging displays of their goods.

There was nothing but soft morning sunshine, a few

small birds darting here and there, the light morning breeze kicking up little swirls of dust. Otherwise, the street was deserted.

Larsen didn't even see one of the town's mongrels heading home after a night in the countryside or hunting along the creek, a dead rabbit in its jaws. Occasionally, he saw a face in one of the store windows as he passed—a shopkeeper stealing a cautious glance into the street before letting a curtain drop back into place and scuttling back into the shadows, wary of catching a stray bullet.

Word had gotten around, of course.

Three of the nastiest killers ever to haunt the North Platte country were in town. Folks had learned that the three killers were at Carlisle's, and that the town's two unlikely lawmen, Glenn Larsen and Henry Two Whistles, were going to make a play on them. . . .

Larsen and Two Whistles stopped on the corner of Main Street and Wyoming Avenue, and turned to face Carlisle's standing on the adjacent corner, on the other side of the main drag. It was a sprawling, white-painted, clapboard, three-story affair with a broad front porch. Larsen had never thought the place had looked particularly menacing. Just another saloon—one of three in the little settlement of Dry Fork, though the largest and the one with the prettiest doxies, as well as the best cook. Magnus Carlisle wasn't known to water down his whiskey, either, so his saloon and "dance hall," which was mostly just a euphemism for "whorehouse," was favored by men who could afford his slightly higher prices.

Now, however, Larsen would be damned if Carlisle's didn't look like a giant powder keg sporting a lit fuse.

He turned to his deputy. "You ready, Henry?"

"No," Two Whistles said, staring without expression at the saloon across the street.

"Yeah," Larsen said. "Me neither."

Squeezing the rifle in his hands, Larsen stepped into the street.

Larsen and Henry approached Carlisle's, whose porch and front door faced the street corner, the front of the building forming a pie-shaped wedge. A large sign over the porch announced simply CARLISLE'S in ornate green letters outlined in red and gold. Larsen felt his heart picking up its pace. The young man who had been sitting tipped back in a chair near the saloon's louvred front doors dropped the chair's front legs to the floor with a quiet thump and rose slowly.

That was Eddie Black, the curly-haired young swamper who had been relaying information about the cutthroats to Two Whistles at the jailhouse.

Eddie moved forward, and as the two lawmen stepped up onto the boardwalk fronting the porch, he came quickly down the broad wooden steps, eyes blazing anxiously. He was of medium height and skinny, and he wore a black wool vest over a white shirt adorned with a red cravat stained with beer and the tobacco juice he emptied from the saloon's brass spittoons.

He was "a little soft in his thinker box," as the saying went, and he sported a bushy thatch of curly red hair. He wasn't really as young as he seemed; Larsen had heard he was somewhere in his thirties. But his simplemindedness made him seem much younger.

Breathless, he stopped before the two lawmen and said, "You gonna take 'em down, Marshal?" He grinned delightedly but also a little fearfully. He was fairly shaking with excitement.

Larsen and Two Whistles shared a glance, then the marshal said, "Well, we're gonna give it a try, Eddie. You'd best wait out here, all right?"

"Oh, don't you worry! I know who them fellas are!" Eddie scampered off to the left along the boardwalk and crouched down behind a rain barrel at the big building's far front corner. He looked cautiously over the top, as if he were expecting hell to pop at any second.

The young man's anxiety increased Larsen's. He shared another look with Two Whistles, and saw that the swamper's demeanor had had a similar effect on the normally stone-faced Ute. Henry's eyes were a little darker than usual. He was also a little pale, and sweat beaded his forehead, just beneath the brim of his black bullet-crowned hat.

Larsen adjusted the set of his own tan Stetson, then, opening and closing his hands around his rifle, he and Henry started up the porch steps. There were around a dozen steps, but it felt like a long climb. Finally, the lawmen pushed through the batwings and stepped into the saloon's cool shadows.

CHAPTER 2

"*Damn!*" a voice exclaimed.

Jerking his rifle up suddenly, Larsen turned to see Magnus Carlisle standing behind the bar just ahead and on the marshal's left. The man had been rolling a quirley, but apparently the two lawmen's sudden appearance in the front entrance had spooked him. He'd dropped his rolling paper and tobacco onto the polished mahogany bar top.

Larsen gave a soft sigh of relief and lowered the rifle.

Glaring at Larsen and Two Whistles, the portly, bespectacled saloon owner said, "You scared the hell out of me!"

Keeping his voice down, Larsen said, "Didn't you hear us comin' up the steps?"

"No!"

Larsen hadn't realized that he and Henry had been walking almost as quietly as two full-blood Indian braves on the warpath, but apparently they had. He glanced at Henry, who shrugged and gave a wry quirk of his upper lip.

Turning back to the saloon owner, Larsen said, "They still upstairs?"

"Yep," Carlisle said darkly, looking over the tops of his

round, steel-rimmed spectacles. "Been there all damn night. You sure took your own sweet time getting here."

Larsen felt his face warm with anger. "I got back to town as quickly as I could, Mr. Carlisle," he crisply replied. And he nearly killed his horse doing it, he did not add. "Which room are they in?"

"Third floor. The big room all the way down on the end, right side of the hall. It overlooks the street. You better hope like hell they didn't see you walking over here." Carlisle narrowed an anxious eye and said, "They could be layin' in there waitin' for you."

"We'll handle it," Larsen said as he and Two Whistles walked along the bar, heading for the broad staircase at the room's rear. The young marshal hoped he'd sounded more confident than he felt.

Carlisle followed them, running a hand along the bar. "Take no chances, Glenn. If they get past you, they'll come down here and tear into *me*. There won't be enough of me left to bury!"

"Keep your voice down, Mr. Carlisle," Larsen said levelly, keeping his own voice just above a whisper.

"Shoot 'em through the door! Just shoot 'em through the door!"

As both lawmen stopped at the bottom of the stairs, Two Whistles turned to the saloon owner and said, "Don't they have a couple girls up there?"

Carlisle stared at him thoughtfully and blinked. He looked a little sheepish. "Yeah, I reckon they do. Claudine and Sally Jane. Still, though, fellas, shoot 'em through the door. Please! Don't take no chances. Claudine an' Sally Jane would understand!"

Larsen and Two Whistles shared a cynical glance and then started up the stairs.

Behind them, leaning forward and pushing his pudgy right hand against the bar top, Carlisle rasped, "Shoot 'em through the door! Don't take no chances! Hell, they'll burn the whole town down! You know how they are!"

Larsen whipped his head back to the frightened man and pressed two fingers to his lips. Carlisle just stared up at him, looking anguished. Turning forward again, Larsen and Two Whistles kept moving slowly up the stairs, keeping their eyes forward. At one point, Larsen's right spur jingled. He stopped, glanced at Henry, and then the two men wordlessly, quietly removed the spurs from their boots and left both pairs on that very step.

Spurless, they resumed their climb, crossing the second-floor landing, then continuing to the third floor.

Slowly, quietly, almost holding their breaths, they made their way down the third-floor hall, which was dingy and sour-smelling and lit by only the one dirty window at the far end. As they walked side by side, Larsen holding his Winchester up high across his chest, Two Whistles holding his Parker the same way, the marshal kept his eyes glued to the last door on the hall's right side.

He pricked his ears, listening.

The building was as silent as a tomb. There were still no sounds on the street. It was as quiet as Sunday morning when the whole town was in either of the two churches—the Lutheran or the Catholic.

A door clicked on the hall's right side. The lawmen stopped suddenly.

Larsen's heart quickened as he turned to see a near door open. A girl, dressed in a thin cotton wrap, stepped into the hall; then seeing the two gun-wielding men before her, she stopped and gasped, her eyes widening.

"What in holy blazes is goin' on?" she said way too loudly. Her words echoed around the previously silent hall.

"*Shhh!*" both Larsen and Two Whistles said at the same time, pressing fingers to their lips.

The girl looked as though she'd been slapped.

Larsen dipped his chin to indicate the door at the end of the hall. The girl turned her head to stare in that direction, then, appearing suddenly horrified, apparently remembering the three killers on the premises, stepped quickly back into her room and quietly closed her door.

Larsen stared at the last door on the hall's right side. He prayed it didn't open. Somehow, he had to get those three killers out of the room without getting the doxies killed. If the killers learned that the law was on the way, they might use the girls as human shields. Or they might just start shooting, and the girls would die in the cross fire.

Larsen couldn't wait for a better time. There might not be a better time. He had to arrest the cutthroats as soon as possible. No citizen was safe as long as the three cold-blooded killers were running free. Now was the best time to take them down, when they were either still asleep or groggy.

The two lawmen shared another fateful look, then resumed their slow, deliberative journey.

Finally, they found themselves standing in front of the door at the end of the hall.

Larsen tipped an ear to the panel. The only sounds issuing from inside the room were deep, sawing snores.

He looked at Henry and arched a brow, silently asking, *Too good to be true?*

The deputy gave a noncommittal shrug.

Holding his rifle in his right hand, aiming it just above the knob, Larsen placed his other hand on the knob and turned it very slowly. He winced when the latching bolt retreated into the door with a click.

A loud click. At least, to Larsen's nervous ears it was loud.

One of the three snoring men inside the room abruptly stopped snoring and groaned.

Larsen's heart thumped.

He shoved the door open and stepped quickly inside and to the left. Henry stepped in behind him to pull up on his right side, aiming the shotgun straight out from his right shoulder. Inadvertently, Two Whistles kicked a bottle that had been lying on the floor in front of the door. The bottle went rolling loudly across the wooden floor to bounce off a leg of one of the four beds before the two lawmen.

The bottle spun, making a whirring sound.

Henry looked down at it, stone-faced.

Larsen sucked a silent breath through his teeth, aiming his Winchester out from his right side.

One of the three men, each occupying three of the four beds in the room, lifted his head from his pillow. He was a shaggy-headed man lying back down on a bed ahead and against the right wall. The man sat partway up, but he didn't open his eyes. He merely groaned, then rolled onto this side, lay his head back down on his pillow, groaned once more, yawned, then resumed snoring softly.

Henry glanced sheepishly at Larsen, who gave him a look of silent scolding.

Returning his gaze to the three killers, Larsen looked them over.

A vacant bed lay to his hard right. The other three beds were filled. The two girls lay in each of the two beds on Larsen's left, each with one of the other two killers. The near girl appeared to be asleep, lying belly down beside a man with long coal-black braids and clad in a pair of threadbare long-handles. He also lay belly down. He and the girl were only partly covered by a twisted sheet.

The man with the black braids would be the Cut-Head Sioux, Black Pot.

The man beyond him, in the bed abutting the wall overlooking the street, was Talon Chaney himself. The second girl lay with Chaney, sort of wrapped in his thick arms. No sheet covered them. They were both naked. The girl was not asleep. Her blue eyes peered out through her tangled, tawny hair. They were bright and wide open, cast with terror and desperation. Silently, she begged Larsen and Two Whistles for help.

Something told Larsen she hadn't slept a wink all night.

He couldn't blame her. Not one bit.

Chaney, who had close-cropped hair and a patchy beard on his blunt-nosed face, lay sort of spooned against the girl from behind, his thick, tattooed arms wrapped around her. His face was snugged up tight to the back of her head, his nose buried in her neck. With each resounding exhalation, the outlaw made the girl's hair billow up around his nose and mouth.

Larsen shifted his eyes to the right, to the third killer lying alone in the bed beside Chaney and the girl's bed. That would be Hell-Raisin' Frank Beecher—shaggy-headed, tall, hawk-nosed, crazy-eyed, and with a silver hoop ring dangling from his right ear.

All three were sleeping like baby lambs.

However, these three lambs had guns close to hand. In fact, the room resembled a small arsenal. At least two pistols apiece were buckled to each of the brass bed frames, within an easy reach of each killer. Sheathed bowie knives also hung from bed frames. Rifles—two Winchesters and a Henry—leaned against the walls, also close to each bed. Boxes of shells littered the room's single dresser cluttered with women's underfrillies.

Three piles of tack were carelessly mounded here and there, including saddlebags likely stuffed with the money these three had taken off the Sundance stage.

The room might have looked like an arsenal, but it reeked of a whore's crib in which three drunken men who hadn't bathed in a month of Sundays had been well entertained.

Larsen chewed his lower lip. How were he and Two Whistles going to get the two girls out of here without arousing the three killers? Maybe he should try to get all of the weapons out of the room first. . . .

He nixed that idea. With so many guns and knives littering the room, it would take too long. Doubtless, one or more of the killers would wake up and begin the foofaraw. Larsen would try to get the girls out first. If the killers woke up in the process—well, then there would be trouble.

One thing at a time.

The marshal leaned close to Two Whistles and whispered very softly into the older man's right ear, "Cover me. If one or more of them wakes up, blast 'em."

The old Ute gave a slow, single nod, keeping his eyes on the room.

Larsen started forward, stopped, and turned back to Two Whistles to whisper in the man's ear again: "But wait till I'm out of the way. And the girls, too."

Two Whistles gave a grim half smile.

Larsen stepped forward. He walked past the girl asleep belly down on the bed with Black Pot. He crouched over the girl lying fully awake, eyes glazed with terror, beside

Talon Chaney. He aimed his rifle at Chaney with his right hand and extended his left hand to the girl.

"Come on," he mouthed.

The girl glanced at Chaney curled against her from behind.

She looked at Larsen, beetling her brows, terrified to move.

Larsen crouched lower and said into her left ear, his breath making her blond hair flutter a little, "If he grabs you, I'll shoot 'im." He rose slightly and waggled his fingers at her again.

The girl drew a breath, steeling herself, then, sitting up, slowly lifted her left hand.

Chaney groaned, muttered incoherently.

The girl stopped and whipped her horrified eyes at the man beside her.

"Keep comin'," Larsen whispered.

She turned to the lawman again. She continued to stretch her hand toward him, sitting up. Larsen closed his hand around hers and gently pulled her out of the bed. As she rose away from Chaney, the killer's right arm slid down her side to the bed. He turned his face into his pillow and muttered, "Wh . . . where you . . . goin' . . . sugar . . . ?"

The words were badly garbled. The killer was likely still drunk.

Good.

The girl rose, the long tendrils of her blond hair dancing across her slender, bare shoulders. Larsen stepped aside to let her pass behind him. As she padded on tiptoes out of the room, Larsen looked around at the three killers surrounding him.

All three were still sawing logs.

He glanced at Two Whistles aiming the shotgun into the

room, gave an expression of "So far, so good," then moved to the cot on which the other girl slept beside Black Pot.

Larsen dropped to a knee beside the girl. The chubby brunette was snoring softly into her pillow.

Larsen placed his hand on her right arm, which hung down over the side of the bed.

Instantly, she lifted her head and opened her eyes, which were cast with the same terror as the other girl's eyes, and said much too loudly, "Oh, God—please don't hurt—"

Gritting his teeth, Larsen clamped his right hand over her mouth.

She stared over his hand at him, wide-eyed, the light of understanding gradually filling her gaze. Larsen looked over her at Black Pot. The man shifted a little but only grumbled into his pillow, then resumed snoring.

He didn't wake.

Neither did the two other killers. Snores continued rising so loudly that they almost made the marshal's ears ache. The stench in the room nearly made his ears water.

To the brunette before him, Larsen whispered, "Very slowly, get up and leave the room."

She nodded quickly.

Larsen pulled his hand away from her mouth.

Glancing behind her at Black Pot, the girl slid her body, clad in a thin, torn gown, out of the bed. The bed squawked and jounced. Still, Black Pot snored deeply into his pillow.

The girl placed her bare feet on the floor beside Larsen, glanced up at him with a look of extreme gratitude, then shook her hair back from her face and tiptoed past Two Whistles and out of the room.

Larsen looked around at the three killers. He couldn't believe his luck. They were still asleep.

He still couldn't believe his luck when, ten minutes later,

he had placed his and his deputy's handcuffs on all three killers, cuffing their hands behind their backs. None so much as stirred through the entire process.

Still, they slept like baby lambs.

Trussed-up baby lambs. Only, baby lambs didn't snore nearly as loudly as these three unconscious killers.

Now all the two lawmen had to do was get them over to the jailhouse and turn the key on them. That shouldn't be hard at all. All three men were defenseless. Chaney and Beecher were naked. Black Pot was clad in only threadbare longhandles.

Larsen stepped back over to Two Whistles, who had been covering him with his Parker, and looked over his handiwork.

The two lawmen smiled at each other in deep relief.

Connect with Us

Visit us online at
KensingtonBooks.com
to read more from your favorite authors, see books
by series, view reading group guides, and more.

Join us on social media

for sneak peeks, chances to win books and prize packs,
and to share your thoughts with other readers.

facebook.com/kensingtonpublishing
twitter.com/kensingtonbooks

Tell us what you think!

To share your thoughts, submit a review,
or sign up for our eNewsletters, please visit:
KensingtonBooks.com/TellUs.